'*A Christmas Calling* is a wonder
Christmas Carol, it is insightful, at
human condition and full of hoµ
teacher and he uses these gifts
this book.
Mike Pilavachi, author and senior paɔᴛᴏ́ ᴏ̣ _ _

'I was absorbed by this book and thoroughly enjoyed it. It
moved me in many ways. A slow burner to begin with, this
profound and very human tale bursts into flame and will
consume the reader all the way to its final unexpected flicker
right at the end.'
Baroness Dorothy Thornhill MBE, Elected Mayor of Watford

A CHRISTMAS CALLING

Many voices sounding –
But in them all,
Comes one offer
Of a soul.

Chris Cottee

instant
apostle

First published in Great Britain in 2017

Instant Apostle

The Barn
1 Watford House Lane
Watford
Herts
WD17 1BJ

British Library Cataloguing-in-Publication Data

A catalogue record for this book is available from the British Library

This book and all other Instant Apostle books are available from Instant Apostle:

Website: www.instantapostle.com
E-mail: info@instantapostle.com

ISBN 978 1 909728 70 7

Printed in Great Britain

For my sons, Tom and James.
Very many words, crafted with the utmost care,
could not express how dear you are to me.
(I suppose this means I now have to give you both a copy.)

Acknowledgements

I gladly acknowledge my indebtedness to Charles Dickens for the extraordinary fruitfulness of his story, *A Christmas Carol.* It was not his only Christmas story, but it is certainly his best known, and though not straightforward in Christian terms, it strikes sparks and festive flickerings in so many ways. Perhaps even God Himself might use it to speak in His multifarious and multifaceted ways to those whose search for a genuine Christmas is part of a wider seeking after the true call that comes, like a ghost of a voice, one way or another.

PART ONE

CHAPTER ONE

It was a week to Christmas. Friday, December the 18th.

Not often, something happens, so bizarre that you wonder if it's you that's at fault, or an unnamed reality in the world 'out there'. This was the kind of thing that assaulted an ordinary man on that afternoon, and set his world all a-tumble like stones in a downward slide. Days of fraught and disorientating perplexity beckoned.

David Sourbook was sixty-one, retired, and watching a festive film at home. He felt a pleasant glow, a definite swell of seasonal satisfaction. As the film came to an end, there was a distinct hint of festive joy, even in this solitary house, this so-called home. On the Christmas channel, the sugar-sweet films ran one after another, and many were cheesy and pointless, but this one had been rather good. A couple whose marriage was in difficulties, and who were not looking forward to their Christmas together, were then asked to take their nephew, his sister's boy, for the holidays; they knew he was troubled and seriously badly behaved. His sister simply couldn't cope any more. That seemed the final nail in the coffin of Christmas that year, and probably their whole marriage. But they took him, out of the kindness of their hearts, wanting to help. And the challenge of dealing with him had brought them back together. Their re-lighted love then affected him so much that they finally returned a reformed boy to his mother. A real redemption story. It was titled, A Christmas Angel Calls, which David thought was clever, because it seemed at first that the young couple were the angels – indeed it was said, 'you're such angels for doing this'. But the lovely irony was that the boy referred to as 'no angel' in the beginning was really the angel who brought the troubled couple back together.

It was American, as they mostly were, so with plenty of white ground and snowmen, light-bedecked houses and festooned rooms, beautifully wrapped presents and a ham for the fabulously spread dinner on Christmas Day. It also had a candle-glowing church, references to God, and people praying and giving thanks at meals, all things David regarded as the American veneer of religious hypocrisy. But, it had been well-scripted, and acted with skill by the unknowns who seemed to populate these films, as if it was a specific career. It was robust and had a message of hopefulness rather than just the tinkling of a Christmas bell. He was pleased he'd watched it.

He wondered if anything else worth watching might be on later, so he picked up the Christmas edition of the *Radio Times* to have a look. He flicked to the day and the channel, but his eye was drawn to the time of the film he'd just watched. At that appointed time it said, *A Doggy Christmas*. That wasn't right. He checked the channel, day and time. Those were correct, but not the name of the film. How odd. Something deeply disturbing jabbed at him. He picked up the remote control and pressed for the programme guide but when he got to the channel it wouldn't let him scroll backwards in time. Then he recalled that he'd tried that once before, and it wasn't possible.

Concerned, he picked up the newspaper and flicked to the TV pages, found the channel and once again it said, *A Doggy Christmas*. Now he was really unsettled. For a moment he felt the threat of having shifted to a parallel universe. He'd watched the film from before the actual start, and was sure there hadn't been an announcement of the sort, 'now in a change to the published programme'. And at the breaks, it had said, *A Christmas Angel Calls* before and after, each time, so he wasn't going crazy. He stared at the words, disconcerted, as if some fiendish trick was being played on him. His thoughts started to tumble in a hot swirl inside his head. Was he coming unravelled? Was there something wrong in his head? Had he been visited by some vision?

Then his shrug mechanism clicked in. His chest calmed and his head cooled. Why worry over something so trivial? Or apparently trivial? Yet an elusive feeling remained, like a faint, cold touch on his neck. The merest hot flutter in his chest.

Perhaps he'd been asleep all afternoon, and dreamed it. He did tend to doze after lunch these days. Yet such a perfect muse, and for so long, where might that have come from? It was a puzzle. Best to leave it be. He had long feared that slide into anxiety over the precipice of irrational terrors; the worry that became racing thoughts and escalated into breathless escape. He'd been there once or twice and knew its power. He stayed well away from that place. He wouldn't go back there now. He held on to the Christmas glow he'd just been enjoying instead.

He looked out of his front windows past the big television. Dusk was coming. Perhaps it was the waning day that made his tree lights seem to glow a little brighter, and his tinsel reflect them with more of a jolly sparkle. He decided to have another cup of tea and savour the festive 'lift' while it lasted. He levered himself from his brown armchair and went out of his living room and turned right, down the hallway to the kitchen at the back of his cottage. He put water in the kettle and switched it on. While it heated, he put two spoons of loose-leaf tea in his pot and milk into his 'Eeyore' mug, with the appropriately sad donkey in large, raised relief on the front.

Nothing in here lifted him particularly. The three Christmas cards held by magnets on the fridge door were more of a slap in the face than a reason to be happy – one from his aunt, Mary, in Cheltenham, one from an old workmate who seemed to have had pity on him, and one from the local church, St Mark's, with their services inside. He poured the water and decided to go and look at the dusking sun for a few minutes. Outside in his small and neat front garden he sat on the bench, strategically placed to give the view.

He loved dusk. So much, in fact, that his cottage was called *Le Dusque*. He was, in fact, far too well-educated to think that the French for dusk was *'dusque'*. But he loved things French, and enjoyed the joke of people thinking that's what it was. Such fools they were who passed the front of his cottage down the little lane.

Over the gentle fields across the road and through the stark trees near the rising horizon, the white orb hung, a few degrees of the day's course and of its poor heat remaining. A gentle haze of high cloud made a glowing backdrop to it, such that he could hardly discern that sun from its holy halo, and firmer strips of greyish cloud gave staccato lines of perspective across its front. It was beautiful. The trees against the pale, striped, glowing sky, the way it softened to lightest blue as it rose higher over his head, the land so peaceful and still. Cobalt sparkles of reflection from the lake down there, to the right, catching the last, falling stars of the sky, flashed in glints more intense than any Christmas lights. He started to cry. Great sobs at the sheer, heart-straining beauty of it. Tears rolled down his cheeks and he just sat and saw.

Before it was time to fetch the tea (giving it the required full five minutes) he realised it was jolly cold outside and he wasn't dressed for it. He got up and went inside. Tea poured, he decided to stay in and get warm. He put on the third bar of the electric fire and sat on the front of his armchair, cradling his hot mug and drawing on the welcome warmth. The television still poured forth drivel. He needed it for the company.

He looked at his tree, the usual false one, adorned with the same old bells and baubles, but the festive feeling had fled. A new movie had begun, and a rabbit wearing a Santa hat bounced across some snow, but it had all gone flat. He picked up the remote and switched to the news because that made him feel connected to the world, to other people. Connected, not alone, but also not having to actually deal with them. Connected on his own and on his terms. He knew it.

Ah, there was the tin of Christmas biscuits, all joyfully bedecked in red with pictures of bows and snow around images of the various chocolate delights. Was it time to open them? Yes, it was. He put his tea on the fireplace edge and picked up the tin from under the tree. He struggled with the tape holding the top on, until it finally gave. He balled it and threw it in the bin to his left, under the corner shelf with the lamp on it. Lid off, paper removed, there they lay, at his mercy. Shortbreads, oaty ones, cream ones, nutty ones, all smothered in milk or white chocolate. Expensive, but worth it, for a special Christmas treat. He selected a shortbread one and bit into it. Lovely. He followed that with a slurp of tea. All good. But was it festive? He wasn't sure.

On the sideboard, by the old picture of his mum and dad when young, was the traditional box of chocolates. Beside them, the nuts. Piled on the end, various DVD versions of *A Christmas Carol* – the George C. Scott one, Bill Murray in *Scrooged*, the Disney one with Jim Carrey, two old black and white ones on one disk, from the 1920s, a cartoon one from 2002, even the *Dr Who* version. And *Black Adder*. There was just something about the story that always gave him an injection of festive fizz. In the kitchen were some stollen, panettone, and iced Christmas fruit cake. In the fridge, a special selection cheese-board with some particularly nice bries, dolcelatte, Stilton and cranberry, and such. His mouth watered at the thought. Also two bottles of Bucks Fizz.

Behind the glass door of the drinks cabinet stood three bottles of his favourite Merlot beside his Christmas half-bottle of Famous Grouse whisky. He'd get the satsumas and dates in the supermarket on Monday.

All seemed to be in hand. Most of it would get gradually opened over the next week. But did it make him feel in the Christmas mood?

He selected a chocolate orange cream and unwrapped its foil protection. It saw him through the last of his tea quite nicely, and he put the tin away, not wanting to spoil his dinner. That would be in – he checked the clock on the wall over the mantelpiece – an hour and forty-seven minutes. It being a regular Friday, that would be cod, chips and mushy peas from Batter Fish and Sausages down the lane.

So, bath-time. He left the television on the news and headed upstairs for the weekly ritual. Taps on to run, wet shave, hair wash in the bath, then a nice long soak. Warm and comfy on such a wintry day. That, at least, was reliably nice.

An hour later, after dressing and cleaning out the bath and basin, he made another cup of tea, as there was time before heading down the lane for his dinner. Then a terrible thought struck him. He'd forgotten to get any tartare sauce and, last week, Batter Fish hadn't had any sachets. Disaster! He woke his laptop and found their phone number.

'Hello, Batter Fish and Sausages, Jim speaking.'

'James. This is Mr Sourbook. I'll be down shortly for my usual. But have you got tartare sauce in? You hadn't got any last week, if you remember.'

'I do remember. Most embarrassing. No tartare sauce for our best customer. Now we have a fresh box overflowing with sachets. I'll give you half a dozen for nothing. How's that?'

'Super. Great. See you shortly.'

Relief. What is fish and chips without tartare sauce? Why, it's fish and chips. Ah, no, you see, it isn't. That's exactly it. It isn't.

Time to go. He put on his thick, brown overcoat, his Newcastle University scarf (surprisingly smart after all these years), his Russian army fur hat (traded for a pair of jeans in Moscow back in 1979) and set off out of his front door. He stopped at the path and checked how his tree looked through the net curtains. It shone merrily. He turned right and checked the other houses as he passed them. Next door the Jacksons had lights hanging in icicle strips from the gutters, the regularly descending lightshow supposedly resembling falling snow. Next to them the Stevenses had nothing up, and beyond them the screaming Bleaks had a lit snowman and Rudolph in their paved front garden and net-lights in the bay window. A lit present also stood by the front door.

David stopped and looked back up Lower Lane. The lack of street lighting accentuated the row of (mostly) cheerily lit cottages, and the effect was certainly colourful and Christmassy. Even Mrs James with the miserable dog had somehow got bright icicles hanging from her guttering. But it all left him as the air – cold.

The Batter Fish was on the small parade along with the betting shop, the Chinese takeaway and the offy. He always felt it had its own 'peculiar' clientele. Which made him peculiar, he supposed.

It was warm inside and a white, artificial tree with purple lights assaulted him by the door. He wondered if 'Jim', busy behind the glass warming cabinets, had been having a side-swipe at him about being so concerned for the tartare sauce. Jim looked up, and said loudly, 'Boss is in! Stand by your beds!'

'Hello, James. Merry Christmas and all. A medium cod, small fries and mushy peas, please.'

'Like any tartare sauce with that?'

'Half a dozen, for free, please.'

Mr Edmonds, being served, turned and looked at him quizzically from underneath his battered trilby, as if he was holding the place up at gunpoint. David didn't bother to explain. Too many potential complications. Anyway, since Edmonds lost his wife he wasn't very friendly. Was it Edmunds or Edmonds? It mattered little.

The man scuttled out with his order in a carrier bag, and David stepped up to the warm glass. He looked down at the battered sausages, the pies, the huge 'medium' cod. He waited as Jim wrapped his order up in white paper, not even asking about salt and vinegar, so regular was this Friday dinner tryst, put it all in a brown paper bag and said, 'Five pounds twenty, please, but you know that.' Then he added six tartare sauce sachets, one at a time, and said, 'Sauce is in.'

'Thank you.' David handed over the exact amount as always, and said, 'Merry Christmas and all,' again, and walked out.

He hurried home. The food was always nice and hot and he wanted to keep it that way. The security light enabled him to find the key on his fob with a dozen or so bits and pieces on it, and he let himself in. He put the bag on the ivory-coloured worktop in the kitchen and went back into the hall to take off his coat. Then he pulled a plate from the drainer cupboard – that he'd brought back from France before they were available in the UK – above the sink, and carefully opened the packages. Chips first, fish next, peas from the Styrofoam cup last. He squeezed four of the tartare sauces onto the fish, and dropped the last two onto his tray, then put the plate on, and a glass of water from the purifier jug on the draining board. He added a knife and fork from the drawer and the salt grinder from where it lived at the back of the worktop, under the lights from the upper cupboards. He put water in the kettle and set it going, then carried his tray into the front room where the television was still on. He sat and looked at it.

He carved an end off the fish and stuffed it into his mouth. Succulent, white, creamy, lifted by the sauce, it dissolved as he chewed and filled him with fishy pleasure. The batter was tasty, and crunched nicely between his teeth. He followed it with a fork-load of chips, before adding salt, to test how much he needed. They were crisp, light, fluffy inside, and had some flavour of their own, so he only added a brief twist.

The peas never varied, he just liked them. They gave some extra juiciness to the meal and colour to the plate. Sometimes they also got some tartare sauce mixed in their liquid and that was a treat. There were Fridays when he was extra hungry and he made a slice of bread and butter as well, and used it to wipe up the last of the juice, but not today.

As he mashed four last chips in the remains of the peas, he was satisfied. Not festive, but satisfied. He took the tray out to the kitchen, and poured the tea he'd made halfway through the meal. What to open for his dessert? The stollen? The panettone?

The iced Christmas fruit cake? He decided on the stollen, and carried the box to the worktop under the lights. He opened it, snipped away the plastic wrapping inside, and used a kitchen knife from the block to slice off a decent piece which he put on a small plate from the strainer.

Back in the living room, he settled the tea on his little table with the *Radio Times* and today's newspaper on it, under the remote control, and took a bite out of the stollen. Sweet and fruity it was. Lovely.

So, what to watch? Soon he must pull the curtains almost shut so the tree lights could still be seen outside, but he had proper privacy from prying eyes. There was no knowing who prowled down their dark, unlit lane at night.

These, he reminded himself, were the little treats and indulgences that made living alone bearable. It had always been so.

Soon it was time to go up to The Old Gate for his Friday evening snifter. His naughty nip. He put on coat, scarf, hat and shoes again and opened the front door to see if an umbrella would also be necessary. A clear, moonlit night winked at him. No umbrella. But always the torch. It was a hefty one in case of lurking danger. Very powerful also, with a focusing function so you could widen or concentrate the beam. Last November's birthday present to himself, and very well received, as he recalled.

It swung from a strap round his wrist as he set off.

Mr Banes was walking his German shepherd in the opposite direction, and they acknowledged each other minimally as they passed. He quite liked Mr Banes. A solid fellow, he always felt. Never spoke, though.

He looked at the lights as he went, and caught himself whistling 'O Holy Night'. Lovely tune. Very festive. It actually lifted him, as did the thought of the alcoholic warmth of the single malt. Yes, he felt festive. Perhaps this was it.

At the top of the lane he turned left towards the town square, but well before reaching that he turned right, down Old Pond

Road, then left again into the rather quaint Cottage End, with its row of old cottages all bedizened with lights in white and blue, multicolours, or warm white, or in some cases, the more modern brilliant white. Streams and hangers flashed and flickered in a veritable competition of delight. Whole multipaned windows glowed with red or green or dancing yellow. Bushes blazed and trees rippled. Brightly lit Rudolphs bowed their benign heads and climbing Santas hauled red-lit sacks up low walls. It was a fantasy. A festive fantasy.

The Old Gate had a string of brightly descending icicles around its roof and white-wintered windows. Inside, the low ceilings were snowed-in with bright twinkles and the bar icicled like the gutters. All white, with silver, white and black garlands, and tinsel. Tasteful yet full of celebration.

Mr Edmonds was propping up the bar with his solitary glass of Napoleon's finest. He'd become a bit too fond of it since Mrs Edmonds passed away. David ignored him and went to the other end of the bar. Dale saw him and said, 'Mr S. Must be Friday. Triple of the Auchentoshan '65?'

He thought he was being clever because that was a moderately expensive one. But there were others far more eye-wateringly dear.

Usually David ignored it, but tonight he said, 'No, the Macallan '46, I think.'

'Not got that one. Could get some in.'

'I rather doubt it. No, I'll have a double of the Glenfiddich, thanks.'

Dale poured it and put it on the bar. David paid and sat on the stool. He looked around. Twelve people were in, not counting himself, Dale and Sandra. A group of four having a meal, another of three with snacks and drinks, two pairs and Mr Edmonds. Not overflowing.

'Dale,' he said, 'how can you find out if a programme's been changed if it doesn't show it in the listings?'

'I'm sorry?' Dale said, halting in mid glass-wipe. 'What sort of programme?'

'Television. You know, if they've swapped one film for another.'

'Sorry, Mr S, I haven't a clue. Probably there's a site online. There is for everything, these days. Why do you ask?'

'Well, this afternoon, I watched a rather good Christmas movie, one of those American ones showing all the time on a Christmas channel, and when I looked in the paper it said another film had been on. But I'm pretty sure there was no mention of it being changed. It was disturbingly bizarre, truth be told.'

David heard, 'God wants to talk in your ear.'

He said, 'What?'

'I said, how good was the walk up to here?'

'Oh. Sounded like something else,' David said.

'Like what?'

'Never mind.'

He sipped the whisky. It grated in his throat and burned his chest but then flowed out in creamy smokiness. Vanilla and toffee. He sipped again, and the aftertastes came at less expense.

Straight away a warm haze lifted him. 'In Dulce Jubilo' was playing, and he let it take him. Ah, Christmas!

CHAPTER TWO

By the time he got home it was, disappointingly, only half-past nine, but he had decided what to do. Make his mulled wine. A fine Christmas tradition.

Having shed his coat and still savouring some Scotch glow, he retrieved his enormous pan from its hook at the back of the larder. Into it he poured a whole five-litre plastic barrel of the cheapest red wine, from his latest channel-hop. Cheap wine made the best mulled wine. To that, as it began to heat on the stove, he added water, sugar, cinnamon sticks, cloves and lemon, to his very specific and secret recipe. He watched and stirred as it came to the boil, filling the house with the most fabulous, festive smell. Once it started to simmer, he turned it off, put on its lid, and left it. Tomorrow morning he'd strain it and re-bottle it for heating by the glass right over Christmas. It was famously good.

That hadn't actually taken very long, and as he sat down in his chair and reached for the remote control, he felt flat. The thought of more TV disturbed him, bloating, like too many chocolates. The sight of his tree and its twinkling lights on setting five made him want to tear it all down and scatter it across the lane, in the field. The whisky had worn off. He knew better than to add more. Now what?

A strange compulsion came over him. He must go out again. It settled upon him with an odd certainty. Like something calling. This is what he would do, because it simply must be so. He would go up into the town, to the pond. Take a walk. Try to enjoy the lights. Get some exercise. Not submit to moroseness.

Or morosity. Or morosma. Or whatever it was. Moroseness, strange though it sounded on the ear. Yes, that was the thing.

He shifted himself out of his chair, refusing to entertain any counter arguments, heaved on his coat, then scarf, hat, and this time, gloves, and sailed out of the door without another thought.

It had got yet colder, and without the whisky-warmth, he felt it. He pulled the coat and scarf tight to his neck. His breath was a plume of vapour in front of him as he stared across the fields at the enormous orb of a silver moon. It made the grass shine, and the trees almost look like Christmas snow had blessed them. Stunned into immobility, he stared at it. What were Christmas lights, compared to that? Fading festivity had nothing to compare. He drank it in. It calmed and settled him, but also set off that yearning, that strange pull towards itself. Towards something unnamed and unnameable. Something more. So much deeper and better and … older and wiser, perhaps. Something.

He shifted himself. No time for that familiar feeling. Move on.

The pond, and the grassed area around it, were held by houses on three sides, making a rectangle about 100 yards by eighty. The houses were part of a small, select enclave, and the inhabitants mostly regarded outside lights as garish and cheap, so only a few internal illuminations crept out through gaps in grudging curtains. A few spindly trees were dotted around the pond, and an old wooden stocks guarded history in the direction of the open end of the rectangle. The church, St Mark's, an ancient pile with a forever-crumbling wooden lychgate, stood by the road further down that way, surrounded by lichen-marked graves of endless generations. Their ruffs of grass were testimony to the fact that 'near enough' was 'good enough' for Mr Thomas, often to be seen on summer days mowing round and round with a vacant look on his face as if he couldn't quite remember where he'd already been. The main shops on the left and the Red Lion Inn on the right lined the road, towards the church, which was further down, on the right. The road actually angled away from the grassed area, which was why the pond wasn't completely surrounded by buildings.

Nobody was about. Why was he here? He stood on the opposite side of the pond from the moon, so that it reflected its image from the still water. Reeds studded the nearer shore. The ducks would be around somewhere.

Unsure of what he was doing, he stood, hands in pockets, and stared at the inky water, in no apparent hurry.

'It isn't deep enough,' a female voice said from close beside him, to his left.

He turned his head to see a figure, wearing a parka with the furred hood right up, obscuring most of her face. A couple of long wisps of gently curling, lightish hair protruded, as if by some unguarded error. She also had her hands in her pockets.

'Deep enough for what?'

'To drown yourself in. A dog might drown in there, but not a man like you.'

'No, but at this temperature the shock might well stop my heart. Anyway, I was only looking at the reflection of the moon.'

'My name's Angela.'

'David.'

'You seem very alone, David.'

'Don't you?'

'I came over and made human contact.'

'So?'

'So I initiate contacts and am therefore less likely to be so alone.'

'I didn't even see you.'

'Would you have come over if you had?'

He said nothing. What was this encounter?

After an uncomfortable pause, he said, 'So, what brings you here at this hour?'

'I think I must have come to meet you.'

'Do I know you?'

'You've probably seen me about. Or not.'

'But we don't know each other?'

'Not yet, I suppose. A certain saggedness drew me to you.'

'Is that even a word?'

'No, but it's quite expressive, isn't it? Saggedness. You look a little saggy. A certain slumpyness about you. Like you've lost something, internally.'

He turned his head to get a better view of her, but she was staring straight ahead and down, at the black-mirrored water.

'Maybe I never had it in the first place.'

'Oh, that's sad,' she said, with the sound of real concern. Now she turned, and he saw a pleasant, middle-aged face, roundish, probably a decade younger than he, with eyes that immediately fixed him and held him. She had a strong nose and full but unpainted lips. No make-up. Always a plus. He hated make-up.

'But what is it to you?' he riposted. 'I don't know you. Nor you, me.'

'Just a couple of strangers in the night, then,' she said.

He turned back to the water, discomforted by her steady gaze.

Silence took them. Discomfort abated, then she said, 'You're a bit lost. Is it Christmas?'

'It is indeed Christmas. In a week.'

'Saggy David, you know right well what I meant. Is it Christmas that's made you so slumpy?'

'Who's to say I am so slumpy? Appearances may be deceiving.'

She turned again, this time full-on towards him, and held out an ungloved hand. 'I offer you the hand of friendship,' she said. 'But to receive it, you'll have to take off your glove. It's a sign.'

'You're strange,' he returned. The eyes fixed him again, and a smile played on her mouth, like a cheeky child.

'Oh, all right,' he said, and started to pull off the fingers of his right glove. He gripped her cold hand and shook it.

'You're cold,' he commented.

'Only on the outside,' she returned, realigning herself with the pond. 'And I'm about to get colder. You should join me. It'll warm you up.'

'What are you about to do? Jump in for a midnight swim? Maybe I'll just watch.'

'I'm about to go and take a couple of hours to do something helpful and meaningful. Then I shall go home to bed satisfied and tired, to sleep like the justified. You should help me. You'll feel less slumpy.'

He was intrigued. 'What is it you intend to do? Deliver presents down the chimneys of poor people?'

'Ha ha. Clever. No, I think you should trust me a bit. Come with me and see.'

He was staring at the ribbing moon, some duck in the reeds creating waves, he imagined.

'Nothing illegal or dangerous, then?'

'It's only a little trust I ask.'

'Is that an answer?'

'Yes.'

He sighed. This was, at least, interesting, and had delivered him from the festive fug he'd been in. It occurred to him in some strange place of knowing inside him, that this was why he'd had to come here. Though that made no sense whatever. And that the strange happening with the film that afternoon must then, surely, be connected somehow as well. He'd entered Neverland.

'All right. Lead on, Angela the angel, enemy of slumpedness.'

She took hold of his gloved hand!

'Hoi, hoi!' he said. 'I didn't know this was a date.'

'Nor is it, Mr Slumpy. I'll let go in a minute. I'm intrigued by the level of your discomfort.'

'What if I put an arm around you?'

'By that you'd mean too much. This is small. You're even wearing a glove.'

'Am I being tested?'

'Aren't we all?'

'I mean by you.'

'Yes, I know. Am I not being tested by you?'

He thought. 'Yes, OK, accepted. But I'm not being so … aggressive about it.'

'Oh, this is aggressive?' They were walking and she swung the arm, then let go of his hand.

'Well, no, not exactly.'

'Ah, but, the use of the word indicates the level of discomfort and even invasion and maybe even violation you feel.'

'You're really … unusual.'

'Am I? I'll take that as a compliment. I'm direct. I hope I'm honest. Some people might find me a little too "in yer face, dude!". But I'm not aggressive.'

'Are you actually from this planet?' he asked.

'Inside this parka there's scaly flesh, four more heads and a viciously tipped tail. I like parkas.'

'Are you taking me to your ship? Am I to be abducted?'

'Interplanetary laws say it isn't abduction if you come willingly.'

'Great. Tricked into internal probings and alien zombification.'

'A lamb to the slaughter. Come quietly. It isn't far now.'

They stopped at the lychgate of St Mark's.

'In *here*?' he asked.

'It's parked round the back, out of sight. The rector is one of us.'

'Why is that not a surprise?'

They walked through the gate, up the gravelly path, and into the outer lobby of the church, where a shelf all round divided the lower part of the stone walls and the upper, where there were various notices on cork boards. Mothers' Union, giving figures, meet the bishop's wife, service details, Christian Aid, and more. Angela stood by some piles of something at the end of the shelf nearest the heavy, old, wooden church doors.

'These,' she said, placing a hand on a pile, 'are the church Christmas newsletters.'

Each of three was an A4 pile about one to two inches thick, held in a paper band with a road name on.

'The first service they advertise is this coming Sunday. They also contain seasonal greetings and a message from the rector and invitations to events and groups. These three roads remain, despite repeated requests over recent weeks to take some and deliver them. If they don't go out before Sunday, much of that will be wasted. We're going to deliver them tonight. Quietly. Like Santa.'

'Oh. Right.' He felt a little deflated that it wasn't something more exciting.

'They are on three roads that link up together, which saves time and energy, but maybe you can guess where those roads are.'

'The Royal Estate.'

'The Royal Estate.' She lifted them one after the other. 'King George Road, Queen Mary Avenue and Prince Edward Walk. No one wanted to go up there for fear of being eaten.'

'And not necessarily by the many ravenous wolf-dogs, either.'

'So, that's what we're about to do. Still with me?'

'Hmm. OK, yes.' What intrigued him was her, not the dreary task. In fact, he hadn't been so fascinated by anyone in a very long time. At least, not so innocently when it was an attractive female.

She had the three bundles of newsletters in a bag which she'd slung over her shoulder. 'Which way do you favour?' she asked him.

He considered. The options were to head into the centre of the town, then turn half-left and out from the centre to the estate, or take the road that went round the edge of the town and reach the outer side of the estate and turn right, into it. The former was shorter, the latter more woody and nicer. He realised she was looking at him, waiting.

'It'll be very dark round Lower Field Road, let's go through the town and look at the lights.'

'Good answer!' she said. She turned, and set off. He hurried to be alongside her, not trailing behind.

'If you don't mind me asking, how old are you?' she asked.

'Have a guess,' he answered.

'About sixty.'

'I'm sixty-one. Good guess.'

'How old do you think I am?'

'About fifty.'

'Good enough. I'm fifty-two. So,' she continued, 'tell me about yourself.'

'Not much to tell,' he replied.

'Were you born, or fashioned in a factory?'

'Huh?'

'Well, if you were born then that must have led to a family, home, life, school, education, friends, college maybe, work, three marriages, running an international drug cartel – you know, that kind of thing.'

'Ha ha. OK. Well, I was born.' He left it at that, to tease her.

'Very good,' she said. 'And? Are you still working?'

'Retired.'

'This is like drawing teeth. Retired from what, if you don't mind me asking?'

'I was a physics and maths teacher. And why do you want to know?'

'I don't "want to know"! It's called "making conversation". Finding out about someone. It's what the people who live in this world do. Normally. I'm interested in you because I've just met you and I know nothing about you so I'm trying to get some context. Build an accurate picture. Know what you like and don't like. Maybe try to pin down the planet you come from and whether certain earth foods are poisonous to you. Can you eat carrots? Does custard make you asphyxiate in some horrible way? Do you come in peace? Why are you making this so hard?'

'Are you intending to feed me, then?'

She gave a big sigh. 'Maybe. Who knows? Friends eat together.'

By now they'd come away from the pond and round to the green, with four roads all around its great rectangle and the cricket square still marked out in the middle. Most of the houses weren't actually lit now, but they travelled up End Barn Street which had a few festive lights glowing, and held the pub, The Lord Nelson, a bank, a butcher's, a small supermarket, and other odd places of business.

David looked with appreciation at a large fir tree growing in a front garden, taller than the house, that had been lovingly (and festively) adorned with multicoloured lights and great, rainbow-rich baubles that danced in a nascent breeze, giving a cheerful life to the whole thing. It even had a lit star at the top, which made him wonder how on earth they got that up there.

He had also been chewing over what he felt comfortable saying next.

'We're not friends,' came out. 'I don't mean that insultingly. Just that, friends have to be selected and chosen. You can't be a friend to someone you just met and don't even know. I hate that poster that says, "A stranger is just a friend you haven't met yet". It degrades friendship to nothing more than mere encounter. And that's not right.'

She heard him out then stopped, so he stopped, and something fearsome churned in his stomach. She turned towards him and said, 'I have no particular objection to any of that. But, David, do you actually have any friends?'

He just looked at her. She was quite pretty under that furry hood. He didn't want to alienate her. He struggled to know how to answer.

'Well, it kind of depends what you mean by a friend. I mean ... I have people I see and we're friendly, and we chat.'

'Do you know,' she said, looking him in the eye, 'I even doubt that.'

That hit him somewhere square in the middle like a brick. Or a hammer. 'Oh,' he managed. 'Well, that's not very nice. I mean, I do talk to people. Some people. Around.'

'Like a dog barking at the postman. Just because he happens to have come within range. But they're not friends.'

'Anyway, how do you know?'

'Because here I am offering you a friendship on a plate, and you have absolutely no idea what to do with it! And it's not because you're not intrigued by me, because, admit it, I'm being amazingly intriguing.'

'Yes, you are that,' he said, glad to be able to agree with her.

They were walking again.

'So, David, potential new friend. Tell me about your parents, family and childhood. First off, where were you born and where did you grow up?'

'OK. I was born in Bedford, my dad worked in a big national transport company's head offices there. Apparently there was an older sister, Michaela, but she'd died before I was born, of meningitis. So I was glass, if you catch my drift. Too precious to be let out of their sight.

'I've sometimes wondered if they had no more after me because they felt I had to be the sole focus of their protective attention, or perhaps because I was a mistake in the first place because they couldn't really face losing another child so they didn't want to have any more. Anyway, I grew up as an only child, and though I was provided with everything, I was imprisoned in a protective shield and made to feel vulnerable and overly dependent on them. The funny thing was, I was never close to my mum and resented her before I was even ten, and I enjoyed my dad's sense of humour but I feared his temper.

'There were some nice holidays at the seaside, and kick-abouts with my dad in the garden of our large house with huge hedges and iron gates, but I was conveyed to and from school in Mum's big Rover – she never worked – and though I could have friends over to our house, getting permission to go to theirs was a lengthy process involving my mum speaking to their mum and so on. There, now I'm rabbiting on like some kind of Neanderthal.'

'Did they speak?'

He laughed. 'No, but you know what I mean.'

'Some sort of knuckle-dragging ape.'

'They didn't speak either.'

She made a small amused noise. 'Are your mum and dad still alive?'

'No. My dad died of lung cancer and secondaries in 1992 and my mum died of a chest infection and pneumonia in 2008. All alone in the world.'

'Never married? A confirmed virgin.'

'Bachelor. Not confirmed, though. Hardly even dedicated. Just the variegated path of life in its infinite mystery.'

'Yes, very poetic,' she said, 'but the truth is, you're stuck in-between people making you feel unsafe and needing people to make you feel safe.'

'Is that so?' He felt a little analysed.

'And now you feel a little analysed.'

'Do I?'

'And that's just a defensive reaction to me being right.'

'Are you a psychotherapist or something?'

'Not in fact, no. But tell me it isn't true.'

He cogitated. He looked at the moon casting silvery skeins over the cricket pitch and the roofs of the houses. He saw by that light a man walking his dog on the green, and stooping to scrape up its disgusting doings into a tiny bag – neither of which he could actually see, but the movements of the man made it obvious, while the dog just sniffed at something else it had found.

'Well,' he said, 'you're presenting me with ideas I've not fully addressed before. So I'd have to reserve any sort of judgement as to their validity.'

'Interesting use of language,' she said, digging him in the arm with her elbow.

'You know, this is a bit unfair,' he complained. 'You seem to have slotted into the automatic role of having the upper hand. I should think if you have any friends they're too terrified to tell you the truth about yourself and how small you make them feel.'

'*Touché!*' she said. 'I probably deserved that. Though I might add in my defence that I'm only making observations, not judgements, and I'm doing it to get to know you because I like you, and for no other reason.'

'You *like* me? How is that even possible?'

'Don't you like me?'

'How could I possibly know?' David said, with a touch of frustration. 'I met you half an hour ago. I haven't even seen you properly. You might shove old women into the road and eat small children. You could be about to scam me out of all my money or kill me because you hate men. You could believe all the things I hate and hate all the things I believe. You could be a bad-tempered, bigoted, blathering bull. No offence.'

'None taken. I could indeed "b". Except I'm not and you have no right or reason to assume I could be any of those things. I'm assuming you're a nice, normal man who has difficulty forming relationships. Maybe I do start from the default assumption that a stranger will be a friend, without evidence to the contrary.'

He stopped. His insides told him this was all about to go south and he would, within minutes, be heading home feeling inadequate and angry, leaving her staring at him with disappointed disgust. He saw images of it happening.

CHAPTER THREE

She stopped, a pace or two ahead of him. She sighed as she turned right round and faced him. 'What if I gave you a big hug?' she said. 'We are, after all, very fully clothed.'

'Er, I'm not sure,' he said, feeling not sure.

Without further permission, she threw her arms round him and held him close to her, looking over his shoulder. He responded with his arms tentatively round her coat. He felt hot and embarrassed, then warm and comforted.

She let go. He let go.

'I did that because I want you to know I do like you and I do want to get to know you,' she said, a small smile brightening her shadowed face. Some intensely sweet sadness made him want to cry, but that was one mistake he was *not* going to make.

'And I haven't completely blown it already, then?'

'No. Come on. I still need help with these newsletters.' She jabbed him softly in the belly.

They started up Eden Hill, so named, he always imagined, because its first residents felt they'd found the perfect spot to live. It rose gently and gave great views from its fine houses, all set back from the path by softly sloping front lawns, many with driveways imitating those of some baronial country estate. They boasted small statues, climbing vines draped over columned portals, great bay windows and even jutting balconies. One or two had terraced their frontage, using the levels for water-featured lawns or even table-bedecked patios. Their security lights often came on as they passed, giving a flash of their magnificence to the humble passer-by. Some had Christmas lights strung along guttering or swirled around trees, and every bit along the whole street was in blue and white, as if some edict, merely for notice by the rich and famous, had been issued from on high.

David said, 'If you live here, these are not houses, they're "hises" – rhymes with "sizes". And if you heard me say that, you wouldn't say "yes", you'd say "ears". Ears m'dears. Have another fine sherry and a macadamia nut.'

She laughed. 'You're funny,' she said. 'I like that.'

He went all warm inside. 'I've been told that before,' he responded.

'Then maybe you should start believing it. You have a gift.'

'Ah,' he said.

At the top of the hill was the school, Eden Hill Comprehensive, which meant the slope on the far side, towards the estates, was, from about 3.30pm onwards, Monday to Friday, 'Watch Out Race Track', and woe betide you if you were driving or even walking there without extreme wariness concerning oncoming cycles, or just hordes of rampaging teens.

From the brow they descended past a small and much-contested park, then some large warehouses, surrounded by empty parking lots and iron-railing fences, their security lights and warning signs giving the area an unwelcoming sense of trespassing, even on the pavement. And past there, into the edge of the Royal Estate.

Prince Edward Walk began the other side of the crossroads over Bening Street. There were traffic lights with pedestrian phases. They waited and crossed at the 'green man' and stopped the other side, looking at the wide road stretching away ahead of them, with grass lining the roadway either side, then the footpaths further out to left and right, then the fences in various states of leaning and toothless grins, then the front 'gardens'. Some had been concreted over to make vehicle run-ins; others were filled with old sofas and bits of toys and bikes; yet others had half-repaired and rusting cars. One or two had small and well-cared for grass patches surrounded by plant borders, but even those looked empty and bedraggled at this season of the year.

She slipped the bag from her shoulder and took out the Prince Edward Walk batch. Half she gave to him in the bag, the other half she took in her hand.

'OK, so, you do the left, I'll do the right. You get the bag to keep them in because it's easier, I'll just hold my half. But that means you have to keep the other two roads for the moment as well, in the bag, because I can't hold them and deliver my half here at the same time. You can fold them gently lengthways, or roll them up, which is better. Try not to destroy them in posting them, especially where they've got those spring-loaded plates at the back of the letterbox or those bristle thingys. Keep it quiet, try not to let the spring things make a bang when you release the plate. Don't get your fingers caught and if you think a dog is about to have a go at you, back off and leave it. If somebody asks you what you're doing, these are the church Christmas newsletters, from St Mark's. I'll be over the other side of the road anyway, so let's try and keep together. Anything else?'

'I didn't know it was such a precise operation.'

'It has its moments. Let's get going.'

They set off. At the first house he walked straight over the front grass, which had two heavy tyre tracks on it, and rolled up the newsletter as he went. He lifted the face-plate of the letterbox, which had a strong spring, and slid the roll through. It caught on something, so he put his fingers in and lifted the rear plate so it could pass. The bristles brushed firmly against his fingers. He pushed the newsletter in, withdrew his hand slowly, allowed the face-plate to slide back quietly, and left. He was pleased.

At the third house he was in mid-operation when a loud thump shook the door and a dog's bark added to the surprise. Shock, indeed. He left the newsletter hanging half in and half out. Had it been a larger dog it would probably have had his fingers for a snack.

He looked over at Angela from time to time, working away industriously, and twice she looked over at the same time and gave him a little wave. That warmed him.

Halfway along Prince Edward Walk there was a sort of community area with some walls sporting plants in a thin planting trench at the top, a semicircle of grass and some benches for the weary. David could see from well back that this area was occupied, which worried him, and approaching it just accentuated the dread in the pit of his stomach. It was a gathering of the local 'youth' – half a dozen of them, one with a ferocious-looking dog. The dog was on a long, iron-link chain which ended as a choking-loop round its neck, and the other end as a leather loop round the wrist of a very beefy young man who looked around twenty. He wore jeans and a T-shirt and his head was completely shaved. He was sucking on a cigarette, held in his other hand, and eyeing David suspiciously as he drew nearer. The other five were all younger than he, and smaller, but similarly dressed. They were talking, but this larger and older guy, who was at the back, leaning against a wall, seemed silent. The others were all variously draped over the benches or on the ground. One was toying with a knife that had large serrations on its shiny blade. A street lamp irradiated them in a pool of sallow light.

When David was right up to them, keeping as much distance as he could manage, by the fences, which was only a few metres, one of them spat hard on the pavement, and three of them at once started to hurl abuse at him and question him, peppered throughout with swearing and curses. This resolved to one, a skinny lad with a hard face, who stood up and said, 'What do you think you're doing here? You don't live here, get out!'

David struggled to find a voice. He was terrified. His heart pounded and he felt rather like bursting into tears and pleading with them not to hurt him. 'I'm just delivering Christmas newsletters,' he said, his voice wavering slightly.

'Yeah? Who from?' said another, still seated, puffing heartily on a rolled-up cigarette that was probably the source of the distinct musty aroma.

'From the church. St Mark's. They're just a Christmas greeting.'

'You shouldn't be here, especially this time of day. We're gonna mess you up,' another one, still seated, perhaps the youngest, said.

The one with the dog stepped forward, came right up to David, towering over him by five centimetres or more, and snatched the newsletter from his hand. The others quietened, in deference, it seemed. The dog sniffed at David's leg then gave a nasty, throaty growl.

The big guy took the newsletter back to his previous place, looked it over dismissively, and tore it in half, releasing the pieces to fall and flutter to his feet. Still he said nothing. David felt about the size of a Brussels sprout.

Angela appeared from nowhere. She walked over to the big guy, bent down, and picked up the two pieces of paper from his feet.

'Who are you?' the skinny one said.

'You two doing each other at church, then?' yet another asked, and they all laughed with scorn and derision.

'I only met him an hour ago,' Angela said, retreating with the litter.

'Shame,' the big one now spoke. 'Somebody not going to get their "Christmas greetings"?'

'It's OK,' Angela answered, putting the shredded newsletter in her parka pocket. 'I'll manage. We have a few church people who live over here, they don't really need one, they get one at church.'

David was instantly impressed. She didn't say, 'I've got spares', which might have challenged the guy and caused him to grab the lot, but instead she made a connection between the estate and the church, and thus potentially between this group and the church.

'Shove off, both of you,' the one with the knife said, tipping it backwards and forwards in his fingers, trying to look impressive. 'You don't belong over here. You're not welcome.'

'Donkeys,' Angela said.

'You what?' the big one asked, angrily.

'Donkeys. A bunch of braying fools. How old are you, twelve?' she said to the youngest one. 'You know, when you're younger than that, you can make all kinds of mistakes, and it doesn't have much effect. But once you reach your age – all of you – those mistakes start to affect your lives and your futures. I can only hope something makes you stop and think about it before you're set on the path of violence, criminal habits and prison.'

They were angry, but didn't yet move. David wondered if he was going to wet himself.

'What gives you the right to judge us, you stupid cow?' Skinny said.

'The fact that I have a right to live in this society, because I show some compassion for my fellow human beings, some respect for other people, and some willingness to get along with them for the sake of a better society. You haven't earned that right yet, and if you don't, probably quite soon, then prison is the place where society sends those who refuse to play their part in it. Donkeys. Braying fools. You lot need to wise up.'

'Set Charger on them,' Skinny said to the big guy.

Charger barked as if he'd understood, and pulled against his chain. The big guy hauled it back in and said, 'Shove off, now. If we see you again, you're in for it. Both of you, don't be seen over here again. Crawl away.'

Angela started to advance up the road, so David followed, and caught up with her about five houses along. They were watched for only about the first thirty seconds, then heard lots of rude comments and hilarious, weed-fuelled laughter.

Angela stopped, so did David.

'We should miss out these few houses and maybe do them later,' she said.

'We're not going home?'

'No, we're not going home. Don't let people bully you. If you don't actually attack them, it's hard for guys like them to take the initiative of attacking you. It takes courage, even though they have the advantage. And especially when you stand up to them, because that sets them wondering who you might be. They're mostly bluster, though in the wrong place at the wrong time they will use the dog, and the knife. But this near Christmas, they probably don't want to spend it in trouble. So, come on.'

He was beginning to feel he really needed a pee, but he didn't want to say so. 'Maybe we should come back in daylight, tomorrow,' he said.

'No, let's finish what we started. There are other things to do tomorrow.'

He relented. 'OK, then, but if I get killed I shall blame you.'

'And I will be very sorry.'

They parted again, and as he set off for the kerb she said, 'Anyway, if you want the festive fizz, you have to do the weary work.'

He nearly stopped but told his legs to keep moving. How did she know about the search for the festive feeling? And was that right? He mulled over it as he set back to the dull task of manipulating letterboxes and avoiding traps of many kinds in front 'gardens'. He looked back surreptitiously a couple of times but the gang of youths didn't seem to be following them. His guts were still in a knot. But he was no longer in danger of soiling himself.

The road narrowed and as he looked across at Angela, he saw she was muttering. Strange. Perhaps she was a mad woman after all.

They reached the end of Prince Edward Walk where it turned left and continued as King George Road. He gave her half of the appropriate bundle. A bicycle wheel was in the first tree on the left. Along with a couple of trainers, hanging by their laces. The grass along the roadside was scarred with tyre tracks. The row of council houses faced them with identical indifference. A few had

Christmas lights outside – struggling Santas and roof-Rudolphs. The whole place seemed deserted.

As they worked their way down, now slightly closer to each other, as it was narrower than before, they passed Queen Mary Avenue on the right, which would be the last part of their task. David began to feel very tired and fed up with this.

Who on earth was this woman and why was he helping her?

The first cloud-edges of resentment began to creep in. Why didn't the church members deliver their own newsletters? Why was he doing it for them? Why leave it till the last minute like this? Why wasn't the rector out here doing it?

Grudgingly, he thrust a rolled copy though a letterbox, bending and creasing it as it went. He stepped back and looked at the twisted and ruined half still sticking out. Then he felt bad. He withdrew it carefully, rolled another one and slid it in with care. The now-useless one he stuffed in his coat pocket. So now they both had a spoilt one in their pocket. She for honourable reasons, he for shameful ones. Guilt assailed him. Somehow the bruised paper spoke of crushed hopes and unrecoverable dreams.

It was like a sacrament of himself. Oh, yes, he knew what a sacrament was. Probably better than she.

His last house was thoroughly boarded up, door and windows, so he crossed the road and waited for Angela to finish her last house.

'One road to go,' she said. 'Thank you for helping me with this. I would be doing it all on my own without your help.'

'That's OK,' he said, lying.

She patted him on the shoulder, and they started back towards Queen Mary Avenue. She gave him a little shove up his side of the road before setting off up hers. She was quite tactile, he reflected. He didn't really know if he liked that or not.

This road had more houses that had been bought, and you could tell. Most of the front fences had been removed and the lawns paved over to run in their Fords, Renaults and Cinquecentos. The overall effect of the lights was white –

reindeer, presents, snowmen and trees twirled, all in bright white rather than warm whites. Interesting.

He had encountered not a few of the canine residents in various states of protective fury, but here there were none. The only real issue here was that on some forecourts it wasn't easy to squeeze between two cars pulled up side by side, but on the one or two occasions it was simply impossible, he just left it and passed by. How hard it is for a rich man ... the eye of a needle ... or something.

At the end Angela was waiting ahead of him, as her side had less houses. She was smiling, with her hood down, probably needing a bit more air after the exercise. Light brown hair fell in untamed tresses, with two curly tails either side of her face, playing with the icy breeze. Her eyes looked engagingly deep and her aura cheekily happy. It was enchanting.

'OK, Santa,' he said. 'Elves all finished.'

'You're not an elf,' she said. They started walking back. 'Elves have no names, and you're David. Should I walk you home to make sure you get there safely?'

'You don't know where I live.'

'True. Where is it?'

'Right on the frontier edge of civilisation – Lower Lane. Number 27. Before you get down to the chippy, the Chinese and the offy.'

'I think we should avoid going back via the youth group.'

'Definitely.'

'So, tell me, what time do you get up in the morning?'

Puzzled but feeling affable, he said, 'Ah, well, depends what day. I realised when I retired that if I just lay in bed half the day I'd get depressed, so I've kept some of the old structure to the week. Monday to Friday I get up at 7.30; Saturday and Sunday, 8.30 or even later.'

'That seems to fit,' she said. 'You need structure. You fear depression. So, what do you have for breakfast?'

'Why, do you want to join me?' He felt it was his turn to give her an elbow-dig, so he did.

44

'Hoi!' she said, either to the words or the elbow. 'No, thank you.'

'Well, I have toast. Two slices, with butter and marmalade. Or, on occasion, porridge. It depends how I feel.'

'You adventurous fellow!' she said. 'A choice of two, different breakfasts! My, my!'

Before he could reply, a bark reached them, littered with expletives. 'We told you!' it began. 'Now you're still here. You're dead!'

Beating and approaching footsteps accentuated the shock, and in seconds they were surrounded by seven angry young men. One pushed David hard in the chest so that he tipped onto the pavement with a thump. One took hold of Angela's coat and started to shake her violently. The one with the knife put a knee on David's chest and pressed the sharp tip into his neck.

Angela was thrown to the ground beside him.

'What? Did you think because it was Christmas we wouldn't do you?' Skinny said.

David realised the big, older boy wasn't there, and Skinny had the dog. 'Charger needs his fun, too,' Skinny said, preparing to release the straining and snarling, slavering dog.

David was speechless with presentiments of serious harm. He doubted they'd be killed, at least not intentionally, but a good kicking and Christmas in hospital and a forever-scarred face seemed likely.

The dog was off the lead but Skinny was holding it by the scruff of its neck. A hard-booted kick landed against David's side and blew the wind out of him. He gasped. Someone hit Angela across the side of her head with a solid thud. She let out a small groan.

The knife was pressed in harder, and a trickle of warm blood flowed down his neck to his hairline at the back. Skinny guided Charger over to his arm and pushed him forward for a bite, which he gladly took. The coat ripped but David didn't feel teeth in his arm.

Now one of the boys knelt in front of Angela and used his hands on her thighs to spread her legs. Oh, no, not that!

A voice, seemingly that of the big lad, barked, 'Get off! That's enough!'

Suddenly the boy stood, the dog was pulled away, and the knife withdrawn.

'If you see that as a warning, just think what'll happen if we catch you again!' Skinny said, and like a wind had taken them, they blew away down the street. The big lad was, indeed, with them now, at the back, like he was chasing them away.

Angela was looking at him, a handkerchief in her hand, and she pressed it against the cut in his neck. 'Keep still till I can see how bad this is,' she said, concern engraved on her lovely features.

He put his hand up to the same place, and without thinking, laid it over hers.

She didn't flinch or move.

'I think the big lad saved us,' she said.

'He's a vicious thug like the rest of them.'

'You don't think there's levels of vicious thuggery?'

CHAPTER FOUR

'Are *you* all right?' he said.

'I think so. My ear is ringing and I'll have some bruises but I'm in one piece. This neck cut concerns me, though. Let's have a look.'

'If it spurts, put it back on, tight,' David insisted.

She peeled the handkerchief away. 'Well?' he said.

'No spurting. Might need a stitch, I'm not sure. Or maybe just a decent dressing.'

'Do you do a decent dressing?'

'I have been known to. I'd suggest a small non-adhesive dressing held in place by a large sticking plaster. Have you got those?'

'Yes. Are you not going to take me home and patch me up, then?'

She started to stand. 'No. It's a cut, is all. Not on a major artery and not in danger of letting you bleed to death as you sleep. Be brave, my little soldier.'

She helped him to his feet. They set off again.

'Police station isn't far,' he said.

'I wouldn't,' she countered. 'They'll discourage you from making charges because of the small likelihood of getting a decent sentence even if the whole process led to court. And it'll just inflame them against you. You don't want them coming over and finding your house. Everything's weighted in their favour. Anyway, you might want to just forgive them.'

He stopped and stared at her. 'Forgive them? Why on earth would I want to do that?'

'Do you have any idea how much more your life is than theirs? And do you want to be eaten up inside by the cancer of holding a grievance?'

They walked on. 'More in what sense?'

'Not more important, but more possibilities, more chances, more good stuff, more satisfaction, more achievement. They live in a dip in the gravity of human-time. Like light in space-time, you and they are both travelling life in a straight line, but they live in such a gravitational dip caused by the irresistible pull of parentage, genetics, politics, educational aspirations and assumed norms, that they forever circle the black hole of criminal ambition, violence, worthlessness and tragedy. You sail on by, heading for more planets and suns, dawns and dusks. A bit of compassion might be allowed them. That's all.'

'All?' he coughed. 'Sounds like you're on their side.'

'Someone needs to be.'

'You're not a social worker, are you?'

She gave a little laugh. 'No. Anyway, better to be a school teacher or a youth worker if you really want to help them.'

He was silent, feeling his way between guilty ignorance and guffawing disbelief.

'Let's have another look at that neck,' she said, stopping and reaching for him. He let her inspect the wound.

'It's fine. Clotting nicely. Just don't scrape or bash it. This is where we part company.' She held out a hand to shake his. He took it and responded.

'Thanks again for helping me. This turned into quite a first date. Do you like croissants?'

'Yes. Why?'

'Oh, nothing,' she said, and started to cross the road to go up Carter Lane. 'Bye, David.'

'Bye,' he said, somewhat flustered. 'Angela.'

Halfway home he realised he didn't even know her surname.

Back in his house, he got out of his coat, took off his brown knitted jumper, glad to see it had no stains on it, and threw the blood-soiled white shirt into the laundry basket. He examined himself in the bathroom mirror and took down the first-aid box. His side was bruised but breathing didn't hurt, so no ribs were broken anyway.

He washed his neck carefully round to his hair at the back, and patted it dry by the wound.

He found the antiseptic lotion bottle, put some on his thumb and applied it. Then he opened a two-by-one non-adherent dressing and stuck it to his neck just by the wetness. He dried daintily around it. A slightly larger sticking plaster came next, which he carefully unwrapped and applied over all the edges of the dressing. Then he pressed it all in place for about a minute to ensure a good seal, and looked at himself in the mirror. Not bad.

He changed into his pyjamas and went downstairs for a hot chocolate and two digestive biscuits. He didn't feel like the festive ones he'd opened earlier. He took them all upstairs and got into bed by the light of his night-table lamp. It gave a yellow glow, good for getting sleepy.

Sitting up in bed but well-covered by the duvet, he listened to the news on the bedside radio, tuned to BBC Radio 4. Nothing particularly notable. He lay down, turned off the light, and snuggled on his side. What a day. A spook film, a new friend (also possibly a spook), a fight with yobs, and delivering newsletters for the local church.

His mind went back to the film. How they did something difficult and challenging to help, and it turned out all Christmassy and festive. Like he did. Helping the mysterious and alluring Angela. He had done something good to help at Christmas. A Christmas thing, in fact. A delightful festive warmth came over him, joyful and special, and he drifted off to sleep.

He stood and saw himself, watching the film. He became aware of some bright and flickering, golden-white presence always just out of sight, behind his right side. The film was playing through in edited highlights, and the light intensified and trembled, urging him to see the significance. This was a Christmas Past he was watching. Then he had his laptop open, and was on the website of the TV company, and saw there that a change *had* been made to the published programme, but still the significance lingered of the Christmas Past. 'See it and note it', the flickering flame seemed to be saying.

This was not a nightmare. There was no fear. The presence faded and he slumbered on.

Knock, knock, knock.

'What?'

It was day. Grey-white light insinuated itself by and through his smart, yellow and white curtains.

He squinted at the alarm clock. Five to nine.

Knock, knock, knock.

Did they think the bell was somehow just for decoration? These people. What was it? Another delivery for the Stevenses, 'to be taken in at number 27'? Drat and darn.

He pushed back the burnt-orange duvet and felt for his slippers. Picking up his dressing gown from the chair, he put it on as he descended the stairs. He ached all over. His back ached, his legs ached, his neck ached.

Knock, knock, knock.

'All right!' he shouted, 'I'm coming!'

A green and red apparition stood outside, visible through the frosted glass. He quite expected it to be the Ghost of Christmas Present, but was unsure why.

'I'm here, just wait,' he said, unlocking the door. He opened it.

And there she stood. In bright green trousers and festive red jacket. Smiling. With a green bobble hat sporting a white, fluffy bobble like a snowball. Ridiculous. He tried not to sigh. Yet as his spirits sank his heart lightened, and he found himself saying, 'Oh! Hi! What a surprise! Come in!'

'You were in bed,' she said.

Was that an apology or an accusation?

'My whole body aches,' he replied.

'Oh, poor baby! I must check that neck for you. Look what I brought! Croissants!'

She held up a bag from the bakery in town beside her face, which now shone with a cheeky grin, like she'd stolen them. 'You put the kettle on, then go and get yourself more demurely dressed for a lady's company. I'll make the tea.'

'Yes, OK,' he said, feeling distinctly overrun in his own house.

When he returned, sensibly dressed, she had tea and four croissants out on the kitchen table, and she'd found the butter and two jams – a strawberry and a wild blueberry. She was standing by the worktop waiting for him. With the red coat off he could see the more sensible fawn jumper underneath and the collar of the white blouse.

'Come and have breakfast!' she said, like he'd never done such a thing before in his life. Was she always this chirpy in the morning? He'd have to avoid her before at least ten in future.

He sat, and so did she, opposite. She poured both of them a mug of tea and set to a croissant. He took one, and a knob of butter, and a spoonful of the wild blueberry. He didn't really like strawberry jam. It had been an impulse buy at a market. It was supposed to have some spirit in it, but tasted of none.

She spoke with food in her mouth. 'How do you feel this morning? Pretty beaten-up?'

He swallowed, and answered. 'Yes, you could say that. You said they wouldn't attack us. We were lucky to escape with our lives.'

'Then we should be thankful.'

'Ah, no, that won't do. You got me to trust you, then you got me beaten up.'

'Yes, I'm sorry about that. You're right to be angry. I let you down. I suppose the croissants are a kind of apology. But in general you could expect them to behave like I said. And we don't know that standing up to them made it any worse.'

He ate in silence for a minute, then stood to turn on the radio. 'I like to listen in to Radio 4 in the morning,' he said.

'You don't normally have a guest in the morning,' she replied, looking up at him.

He froze. 'Don't you want to know what's going on in the world?' he said, leaving it off and starting to sit down again.

'I'd rather know what's going on with you.'

'What do you mean? What is going on with me?'

'I just mean in general, though if pushed, I'd have to admit I think you're basically not very happy.'

'Saggedness,' he said.

'And some slumpyness,' she added.

They ate.

'Is it worse in the morning?' she asked.

'Is what worse in the morning? The itching?'

'I wasn't aware of itching. Do you have itching?'

'No, why were you asking me about itching?'

'I wasn't! You said itching. Aww, you're just messing with me.'

'Perhaps. So, is what worse in the morning? The incontinence?'

'The depression.'

'What depression? I don't have depression.'

'Good. If you had real, clinical depression, one sign is that it tends to be worse in the morning.'

'I'm not depressed. I just feel a little flat sometimes. That's all. That's normal enough.'

'Of course it is. Hedgehog syndrome – a little flat in the morning. Do you know why the hedgehog crossed the road?'

'No. Surprise me.'

'To see his flatmates.'

'Oh, gross. But anyway, no, I don't believe I am suffering from depression. What are you suffering from?'

Registering surprise, she was quiet for a moment, then said, 'Jumping on people. Jockey syndrome.'

'Meaning what?'

'I only met you yesterday and I've half-psychoanalysed you, got you into trouble, dragged you round the town, kept you up late, and here I am for breakfast like I'd been invited. And I guess I've kind of taken over your house already. I overengage. I suppose I assume people will like me and want to join me in whatever mad escapade I'm up to at the moment.'

'So I'm just your latest project? Ridden today, forgotten tomorrow?'

'No, no!' she said, reaching for his arm, great sadness in her eyes. 'You can be my friend forever!'

'Now you sound like you're fourteen.'

'Oh. I can be hurt as well, you know.'

'Somehow I doubt that.'

'Just because you don't see me cry doesn't mean I don't cry.'

He felt uncomfortable and confused. Had he just been rude and cruel, or was this still just banter? He was out of his depth. What to do now?

Did he really care?

Funnily enough, yes, he did.

She fixed him with a small smile and said, 'What do you enjoy? You know, in life generally, what do you like doing, or seeing, or listening to, or having done to you, or whatever?'

He liked that question. It was easy enough and seemed to have no undercurrent of subtle agendas. It also gave the impression she cared about him. 'I like dusk. I love sitting out and looking at it, or walking or cycling in it. The terrestrial darkening gives relief to the skies. They brighten to a fabulous variety of subtle blues, with mountain ranges of cloudy peaks on the horizon.'

'That's very poetic!'

'I also love writing poetry.'

'Really? Wow, I'm impressed. I guess I'll never get to hear any?'

'Who knows.'

'What else? Do you like?'

'I like seeing countryside, eating a really nice meal, a glass of wine in the evening with some cheese and crackers, a good film, usually on DVD. Paddling in the sea. Wind. I love lying in bed and listening to wind howling and bashing and sighing outside.'

'The feeling of safety. What about thunder?'

'I *love* thunder and lightning! It's like the biggest, most dramatic light and sound show, all for free. Sometimes I see storms across the fields there,' he indicated the area to the front of the cottage, 'and I just stand under the door lintel and watch in solitary amazement like it's all just for me.'

He saw on her face a conflict brewing. 'What?' he said.

'Well, those last two things make me want to offer an interpretation, but I don't want to sully the sheer dramatic impact of what you've described, or your pleasure in them.'

'Oh,' he said, slightly bemused. 'OK, go on, give your insights.'

'You love stuff that makes you feel safe, and you love solitary pleasures. But, you've admitted, sometimes you feel flat. So those things, though nice, aren't really cutting it for you. And why? Because you don't really feel safe, and to feel safe you'd need people, and you find people threatening. Except me. Of course. And I just inserted myself in your life in five minutes flat and didn't give you an option. And now you feel a little analysed again. But you don't mind so much because you're getting to know me. And I've said I like you. And I brought you croissants. And here we are sitting in your kitchen having breakfast together and the world hasn't caved in.'

'OK,' he said, holding a piece of croissant at bay for a moment, 'and you – you find it necessary to fix people. You insert yourself into the lives of people who seem a bit defenceless, and start to manipulate them into being your next project, to make you feel good. And why? Because you can't manage a real relationship with a man so this makes you feel like you're having one, and doing good, and even being a mother, because that's a bit how you come across. Treating me like a child. It's all for your satisfaction and to mend the hole that's in you by stuffing pretend, manipulated, one-sided, shock-tactic relationships in there.'

She was staring at him, then her head lowered, and she was crying. Tears dripped off the end of her nose onto a piece of croissant on her plate. He felt so sorry for her it seemed he might cry as well. A hot drop ran down his cheek, burning him until it tickled at the side of his nostrils.

'Shall I go?' she managed, quietly, her frame heaving softly.

He wiped the side of his nose as casually as he could manage and said, 'No. *No!* I am so sorry. That was so cruel. Please don't hate me.' He extended his hand and placed it on her sleeved arm. Not her hand.

'I'm not angry at you. And I certainly don't hate you. I'm crying because that might be true. Maybe I'm just a horrible busy-body, an interfering old cow, a nasty piece of work. *I'm* sorry.'

He so wanted to take her up in his arms and hold her. But that was never going to happen. Not with his lack of confidence with the opposite sex. He rubbed her arm gently and said, 'Angela. You're a lovely person. You're only pushy to be kind. You want to help and I reacted that way just because it revealed me in a way I'm not used to. I was just hitting back and it was totally unnecessary and I'm really, really sorry. Please forgive me. Have another cup of tea.' He began to pour.

She sniffed and fished a hanky from up her sleeve. He hadn't seen anybody do that in a long time. It was, of course, a proper cloth one. Linen, even. She dabbed at her eyes but resisted blowing her nose.

'Blow it,' he said.

So she did, noisily, and he laughed. And she laughed.

'Now I'm really disgusting,' she said.

'So you are human after all.'

'Is that the definitive test?'

'It just might be.'

She seemed to be brightening, and he was greatly relieved.

She blotted at her face some more, then returned the hanky to her sleeve. He wanted to mention it but thought better of it.

'Am I an uncaring, stomping, thoughtless pig?' he asked.

'No,' she said, 'you're not stomping.'

They both laughed again. It was a good moment. He recognised somewhere inside that being able to bring laughter and resolution out of such a disaster was a good sign. But a good sign of what?

'I suppose you have plans for today?' he asked.

'I thought we'd do some litter-picking.'

'Surely you thought *you*'d do some litter-picking.'

'Well, I did, and then I thought you'd help me,' she said.

'But I don't do litter-picking.'

'Neither do you have breakfast with a woman you only met yesterday.'

'No.'

'Well, then.'

'Well, then, what?'

'It's a day of new things!'

'It does seem to be,' he agreed, sipping his tea.

'And anyway, if you want the festive fizz, you have to do the weary work.'

'Yes, you said that yesterday. Why?'

'Because it's a basic truth.'

'But what makes you think I want the festive fizz?'

'Because you look slumpy a week from Christmas.'

'Ha. OK. I guess I do.'

'You definitely do.'

'But I can't go litter-picking.'

'Is it against your religion?' she asked, finishing her tea with a slurp. 'Excuse me!'

'I'm not sure I have a religion. No, it's against my self-respect.'

'Oh! Self-respect!' she said, suddenly firing on all cylinders again. 'It's against your self-respect. Because the people of this town, on whose respect and affection you so greatly rely, might see you.'

'Something like that.'

'Oh, good grief! You don't rely on the good people of this town for anything more than necessary supplies and public services. I know, I'm doing it again, but – really!'

'Well, I can do without being regarded as some oddball, some social pariah, "black bag man" – "Do you know, he used to be quite a respected man, had a good job and everything, but then he fell in with the weird witch woman and now he dresses in black bags and picks up muck with his bare hands." "It's a shame." "A shame." Get the picture?'

'I *love* the picture. "Man saved from self-obsessed, self-righteous snobbery by angel woman." Sounds good to me.'

'I'm not doing it,' he said, firmly, feeling that some level of self-protective resilience was going to be necessary.

'OK. OK,' she said. 'But as an apology for making me cry, will you walk with me up into town and buy me a coffee at Kettles and Cups?'

'All right. What's it like outside?'

'Absolutely bitter. But clearing up, I think. Could be one of those lovely, bright, crisp winter days.'

'Hence the hat, I suppose,' he said, with a cheeky half-smile.

'It's festive,' she explained.

'And I'll be wearing gloves just in case you grab my hand again.'

'You should be so lucky,' she returned with a small smile.

He would leave straining the mulled wine till later.

CHAPTER FIVE

She checked his neck before they left. She told him it looked good. 'A scratch is all,' she said.

Crisp it had become. The skies had cleared to a brilliant powder blue, with the merest wisps and suggestions of streaky clouds across it. The white sun was low and blinding. Their breath vapoured out in front of them, and a resilient frost made grass crunch under their shoes. Frosted roofs looked silvered in the bright light, and golden-brown tree branches stood sun-stroked and stately in the sky.

As they approached the centre of town, everyone seemed to be well bundled up and smiling. Families walked glove-in-glove, and Angela's bobble-hat was far from alone. Some folk seemed coatless because they had four or five thick jumpers on, the outermost being of some jolly festive variety. One or two even ventured 'Merry Christmas' as they passed.

Angela walked with a spring in her step and seemed to be filled with a light enjoyment of every moment. She smiled at people and exchanged a greeting with those whom she clearly didn't know, as often as she could.

She caught him looking at her and said, 'You see this?' She looked down at the ground. Her whole demeanour altered in a moment.

Suddenly trapped, he stopped.

He said, 'Well, it's busy. People are coming and going. There's not enough bins. Someone will sweep it up.'

Underfoot was awash with crisp packets, last night's food wrappers, and bottles, and paper coffee cups, and discarded cigarette butts, and bits of newspapers. It was a mess. Actually, it was a disgrace.

'I've been on to the council about all this, a few times. They don't clean it often enough. And there aren't enough bins, not by a long chalk. And now it's Christmas, and look at the place! And it isn't just me – it puts off shoppers, it affects trade, it's got us a reputation as a dirty town, and people go to Bexleigh instead. There should be twice or five times as many people here on the last Saturday before Christmas. It's awful. But a couple of people with gloves and black bags could clear the area round the High Street at least, and make a huge difference.'

They set off again, and soon arrived at Kettles and Cups in the centre of the High Street where it widened around the old cross and the war memorial with its bits of walls and benches and gardens. Looking in through the small-paned front windows of the café they could see it was pretty full, but there was a table for two just inside. They walked in; the old-style doorbell hung from a loopy spring above the door announced them, and they sat down. The table was small, round, and cheerily adorned with a red and green tablecloth bearing 'Merry Christmas' in a scrolling, white script.

'What would you like?' she asked.

'A large latte and a sugar bun, please.'

'Then I'll have the same.'

The waitress came in her smart black uniform with frilly white apron, and the order was placed.

Angela looked out of the window. 'I love this town,' she said, slightly sadly. 'And I think it's going to the pits.'

'Going to the dogs,' he corrected her, 'and it *is* the pits.'

'OK, I think it's going to the dogs and is in danger of being, and becoming known as, the pits. So I can complain to the council and write to the *Clarion*, and harass the MP, all of which I have done, but if I want it to be nice for Christmas, I may have to be willing to do something about it myself.'

'And where's your merry band of helpers?' he asked, offering a cheeky grin.

'Sitting opposite me.'

'You mean, out of all your millions of friends, you haven't managed to find one helper?'

'I expect I could, but here's me and here's you, as it happens, right now.'

The coffees and buns arrived. They sipped, bit and chewed. And made appreciative noises and cradled the warm cups comfortingly in their chilly hands.

'Well,' he said, 'I'm all for it. I agree absolutely. I'd even help you to campaign, maybe. But I'm not coming here to clear it up. Sorry.'

'No, no, I quite understand,' she said, looking across at him but not fixing him. 'It's not your problem. You shouldn't feel responsible.'

'And I don't.'

'Yet I do.'

'Yes. Now, why is that?'

'Maybe I'm just stupid,' she offered.

'You are certainly not that. Odd, perhaps, a tad. But not stupid.'

'There's a relief. I thought I was very odd, perhaps.'

'Moderately quirky, even irritatingly idiosyncratic, but not very odd, no. Feel reassured on that one.'

'Oh, I do. But then I look out of the window, and nothing's changed.' She sipped as she stared.

'It is a shame,' he agreed.

'Shaming, even,' she said. 'For all and each of us, the whole town. But no one's responsible.'

'The council are responsible.'

'That we elected. And they say they haven't the budget for it any more. The recession and the ingrained profligacy of the previous government took it from them. Tut tut. Where *does* the buck finally stop? I know! *God* did it!'

'Then He should clear it up,' he agreed.

'And if we wait long enough I believe He will, in a great final fireball of total clearing up. There, problem solved. Except, I look out of the window, and nothing's changed.'

'Well, you can't fight God. If He says leave it, we should leave it.'

'That's not the way it works. He says, "Do something about it."'

'He says that?'

'Yes, He does.'

'Is it in the Bible or did you hear it personally?'

'Both, kind of,' she affirmed.

'Really? Goodness. Both. Kind of. I'm not sure what to say about that.'

'Nor should you be. Do you believe in God?'

'I did until I realised He didn't believe in me,' David said, sourly.

'Ooh!' she exclaimed. 'That sounds nasty. What did He do? Or not do?'

'Another time, maybe,' he retracted slightly.

'Then at that time I shall also tell you about how He speaks both through the Bible and personally, kind of.'

'Hmm,' he said, not terribly keen. He drank very nice coffee and finished his smooth, sugary bun.

'But you will come with me to the carol service tomorrow evening, won't you?' she said, big eyes engaging him.

'Oh, really?'

'Yes, really! Even people who aren't much religious come to the carol service! The whole church is aglow with a golden, dancing light from 200 candles, and you even get a candle to hold with a circle of card round it to save you from the deadly drips. And the choir in red robes and white ruffs all come in and sing "Once in Royal David's City", starting with the traditional solo from a boy chorister. And we sing nine favourite carols and listen to nine favourite Bible readings about the coming of the Christ, God's own Son, and this year I hear the choir are also attempting "O Holy Night" and the "Carol of the Bells", both of which are just gorgeous. Though I say "attempting" for good reason, bless them. Then there's mince pies and mulled wine in the parish rooms. And you go home feeling all festive and ready for Christmas. Please come.' She grabbed his hands and held them on the table.

He looked down at the clasped hands, felt her warm, soft skin and said, 'Are you supposed to seduce people into church?'

'Yes, as often as possible,' she smiled, and squeezed his hands together. 'Why, do you like it?'

'It's very nice, I'm sure.' He didn't want to go. Not to church. That's not where festive flurries were to be found. Church was a fizz-less place, he knew of old. But after such a nice invitation, it was so hard to say no. Thoughts raced. So, she'd turned on the waterworks earlier. Then the political pressure. Now the hand-holding again. What was she after?

'Oh, go on, please!' she said, and smiled such that her eyes drew him in.

He gave a small laugh. 'Puppy,' he said.

She cocked her head and kept smiling. 'I'll let you be my master,' she said, then turned red and added, 'Oh! No! That's not what I meant at all!'

They laughed so hard people were staring, but with festive forgiveness.

When they'd gathered themselves sufficiently, he said, 'Anyway, so far, you're the dominant one.'

'Yes, well, I'm sorry about that and let's not go there. Look, what if we came up to litter-clear after dark? The street lights here are pretty good and most people will have gone home. After teatime, say.'

He sighed. It was clear she wasn't going to let go of this. Was he willing to be badgered into it for the sake of her? She whom he hardly knew but was still intrigued by? For a friendship so fresh and unplotted? Poetically 'unplotted', both in the sense that he didn't plan it and in the sense that he didn't know where it was going. He must write a poem about her. 'All unexpected and unseen, just lurking on the village green, as silver moon played off the lake, did you attend me for my sake? I didn't ask you to my side, nor beg you with me to abide, but flitting like some angel fair, you soon got caught up in my hair.'

She was studying his face, as he'd been absently watching the progress of a crisp packet across the street. 'What's going on in there?' she asked.

'I'm imagining a poem.'

'Ooh! Is it about me?'

'It's about how annoying you are.'

'Ha!' she said. 'I inspired you. So, if I call for you at about six, will you come up here with me this evening and do a fabulous clean-up job in about an hour, and then we can go for a festive drink and the rest of the evening is ours?'

Put like that, it sounded much more acceptable. 'Oh, all right, I'll come. But I won't be doing any actual cleaning up if the place isn't pretty much deserted by then.'

She smiled such a smile as to make him feel quite fortunate to be sitting with her. Who was she, exactly?

As they walked up to the centre of town that evening, he said, 'I am going to be *so* embarrassed if I see anyone I know.'

'I was *so* embarrassed about letting you be my master.'

'Hmm. Are you not into that kind of thing?'

'Don't even ask. It's not an appropriate conversation for us to have.'

He was a little disappointed. He'd wanted her to say, 'Why, are you?' Just for fun. Never mind.

It was dark and with the exception of a couple of late home-goers, the High Street looked deserted. And it was even colder than before. Both of them had snuggled up nicely and sported scarves, hats and even gardening gloves. He was wearing his Russian army hat, which was incredibly effective for the warmth of his whole body.

They arrived at the start of the High Street, by the bank. She gave him a black bag, one of the good quality, thick ones she kept for such occasions. She had a roll of them in her pocket.

They'd decided to work together, not at opposite sides of the street. At first it seemed as if the amount of litter was too much, but once tackled it swiftly became more 'do-able', especially as large items went in the bag or a collection of smaller ones were grabbed and bagged. There was no wind, so no chasing after fleeing packets, which would have wasted a lot of time. They progressed steadily, and his back held up to the amount of bending without stiffness or pain.

After twenty minutes they'd both filled a bag, which they tied up and left by the window of a hardware shop to be collected later. The second bag sufficed them as far as the central area, where Kettles and Cups was, and they stopped and sat on a bench.

Chatting about their progress, he happened to look to their left, and his insides collapsed into his boots as he saw the big lad with the dog and a group of others, this time including some girls, approaching. He nudged her to make sure she saw. They were too near. There was no escape.

A fresh torrent of vicious abuse was once again seasoned well with curses.

The dog growled in apparent recognition, and they surrounded David and Angela. David thought he saw the flash of a knife blade. He heard Angela say, 'Lord, save us now, please.'

The big lad stood slightly apart, and watched. Angela stood and was immediately pushed back down. David went to stand and was thumped, hard, in the back, so that he lurched forward onto the ground. A kick was coming. He tightened and felt sick. But then everything stopped, and another voice, from outside the circle of hate, said, 'Police. What's going on here?'

Two policemen on an early foot patrol down the High Street had arrived. One stood off a few yards, while the other came right up to the group. He said, 'McConley. Davis. Phelps. Law. Masters, that dog isn't properly restrained. And who are you three?' He took out a notebook. The other one was radioing the incident in.

They gave names, which he wrote down, with addresses and dates of birth. The other policeman was now giving them a light frisk, and found the knife.

'Oh, so, Phelps. This time I think you'll be going away for this. You're nicked. You know the drill, you don't have to say anything. But it may harm your defence if you do not mention, when questioned, something which you later rely on in court. Anything you do say can be given in evidence.'

He tied his wrists behind his back with a plastic restraint, then radioed again, this time for a van.

The first officer was speaking to David and Angela. 'Were you assaulted by anyone here?'

'Yes,' she said, and pointed to two of them. 'That one pushed me down when I tried to get up and that one thumped David, then was about to kick him.'

'Do you need an ambulance?'

'No.'

'Do you want to press charges?'

'No.'

David followed suit, 'No.'

'Very well, then.' The policeman turned to the youths. 'I warn you that this sort of behaviour will land you in a lot of trouble. You cannot go round attacking innocent people just for the sake of it. You can be arrested for threatening behaviour, not just actual assault. The rest of you can go, but if I catch you over this side again tonight, you're in trouble. Get going. And Masters, I've told you before, that's not a proper restraint for the dog. Get another one.'

They slunk away, shooting glances back at David and Angela. A distant siren took on flashing lights and arrived at the kerbside. Officer two guided Phelps into it. But officer one looked hard at Angela and said, 'I need to talk to you two. Sit down on the bench there. You're Angela Adams. You've been warned about this behaviour before. So, sir, what's your name?'

He had his notebook out again, and wrote down David's details.

He flipped it closed. 'Listen, Ms Adams. You've been warned before that you can't just come here cleaning up the streets. That is the proper work of council employees, work that you are illegally denying them. Furthermore, you're not part of an allowed group on an activity with council permission. You aren't wearing appropriate safety gear. You don't have the proper equipment. Do you have insurance cover for harm that might come to yourselves in the course of this activity?'

'No,' she said.

'Do you have public liability insurance for any harm that might come to a member of the public?'

'No.'

'Do you have damage insurance for any damage that you might cause to property or facilities, private or public?'

'No.'

'And I doubt you have a printed copy of a risk assessment to give to me.'

'No.'

'Those bags you're using are not of regulation durability, nor are the gloves you're wearing of regulation protective quality.'

'No.'

'Well, let me make this abundantly clear. Next time you're caught doing this, you will be arrested. Even if that means you spend Christmas in a cell.'

'And won't that make a good picture in the *Clarion*, with you festive fellows who arrested two good Samaritans in a seasonal act of charity and public concern?'

'I'm not interested in the publicity, I'm telling you to stop this. And you, Mr Sourbook. This is your first offence, I think. Take warning. You might do well to avoid this woman. You could find yourself liable to criminal prosecution and civil liability. Goodnight.'

He joined the other in the van and they drove away.

'Well, that was disappointing,' she said.

'Disappointing?' David repeated, in disbelief.

'Yes. If those two coppers had just turned up and frightened them all away, I'd have thought they were angels. The fact that they also gave us a hard time makes me think they were just coppers. Though, actually, still angels in the sense that God sent them.'

'Angels?'

'Yes, you know, emissaries and messengers from God. The word "angel" means messenger.'

'I know that,' he said, a little tetchily.

'A *real* angel has no place here and just returns back to heaven. Someone *acting* as an angel is sent by God but returns to their life and home here on earth.'

'Yes, very interesting. I must be the second sort because I'm going home now.'

She turned and caught his arm. 'No! We're only half-done.'

'Didn't you hear what he said? Be arrested? In a cell for Christmas? I've never, ever, had my name taken by a policeman before!'

'Sometimes,' she said, 'you just have to do what's right, and hang the consequences. I'm going to finish this High Street. You should see it as a badge of honour – persecuted for standing up for what's right. I do.'

'And why does that not surprise me? Is there anything else you're not telling me?'

'Oh, a *huge* amount!' she said, with a cheeky and wide grin. Then, 'Come on, I'm setting you free.'

'Are you? Really?' It felt more like she was sending him to a small cell. The thought entered in that he really needed to take the policeman's advice and cut her loose.

She stood and pulled his hand, saying, 'Come on, Mr Slumpy, let's get it done!'

He pulled back. 'Can you imagine how I'm feeling right now?' he said.

She sat, and looked at him, listening with a concerned expression knitting her features.

'I feel angry. I feel betrayed. Well, let down, anyway. And disappointed. And guilty. And in trouble with the law, which I've never been – ashamed. And all because of you.'

'OK,' she said, releasing his hand, and looking intently into his eyes. 'This is the dark valley. This is part of the cost for standing up for things. For being a doer of right and a righter of wrongs. But Psalm 23 says that in the valley even of the shadow of death, God is with you. Right now, on this bench, with your name in a policeman's book, God is with you. Isn't that more important than anything else? God is here with you. Pleased, in fact, at the stand you're taking. Like Martin Luther, and Martin Luther King. In a very tiny way, you're becoming a holy hero. Isn't that good? Doesn't that make more of your life?'

'I don't want to be any kind of hero. Especially not a holy one. Are you a holy hero?'

'I have holy hero hope,' she said.

'Nice. I feel very much like just walking away, like the cop said. I don't quite know why I haven't, actually.'

'Don't you know God saves people one at a time?'

'What kind of answer is that?'

'One that goes to the real heart of the matter. The kind you're not used to. The kind you desperately need.'

'I don't desperately need anything,' David said, feeling increasingly irritated, and suspecting that she had no idea of that.

'Said the crippled man as the fire engulfed all around him.'

'You're arrogant.'

'Only if I base what I tell you on a proud dependence on my own opinions.'

'And you don't?'

'No. I don't. You do. I'm based on something very different, which leaves me constantly humbled, not proud; dependent, not self-sufficient; and listening, not spouting.'

'I hardly dare ask.'

'I hardly dare tell you.'

'And I have to say spouting is a real issue for you. Actually.'

'Well, it's good to be honest,' she said.

Was she beginning to feel his irritation with her?

His head felt hot, despite the freezing air, and he took off the hat. The cool was a relief. He leaned his elbows forward on his knees and held the hat in both hands, staring at it.

She watched him, and said, 'You're so lovely that even as angry as you are, you're not shouting at me but just taking on your feelings. I really appreciate that,' and she took off her glove and ruffled his hair.

He turned his head to look at her and her face seemed to shine like an angel. Was it the smile? Was it the reflected street light? Was it purely psychological? Or was she about to return to heaven?

'Do you not get it that ruffling my hair is effectively treating me like a child?' he said, softly.

'Oh. No. I just meant it as an affectionate touch. What should I do? It's just the same as putting an arm round you.'

'No, it's not. It's the kind of thing you do to a child, not an adult. It is, in that sense, not appropriate. But you don't seem to get that. There's a level of social demarcation you seem to be missing.'

'Oh!' she said, sounding hurt. 'No, actually, I have to disagree. I think it contains a level of affection and intimacy you're not comfortable with.'

That silenced him. He stared at the hat like it was the bringer of magic answers. She let him be, then he said, 'So, what is this, then?'

'I don't know. Are you going to walk away from me?'

'I'm considering it. Why not? I only just met you. It's hardly a great loss for either of us.'

'You assume more than you should.'

'So, what, you're telling me you're emotionally invested in me already?'

'"Emotionally invested". That is so cold,' she said.

'Oh, come on! What, then? Are you falling in love with me in two days?'

'No.'

'Then that's what I was asking. What is this?'

'Friends. New friends. But friends can be of real significance. I really like being with you and talking with you and doing things with you. That implies nothing further and demands nothing more. It doesn't demand even that. Why is that so hard?'

'Because you have a tendency to dominate me, treat me like a child, and get me into unwarranted and unwanted trouble. And I can do without all of that, none of which I ever asked for. You think you're somehow blessing me, but in fact you're a pain.'

'Oh!' she said, clearly hurt now. 'That's cruel. A pain! When I'm only trying to get to know you and be nice to you. Walk away, then.'

He went to stand. She grabbed his arm. 'Don't!' she said.

He sat down again.

CHAPTER SIX

How long can you stare at a Russian army hat? Quite a long time, as it turned out. And she, so patient beside him as to belie the impression of impatient jockeying, riding him to an early grave.

He began to get cold, and put it back on. This seemed to be a signal to her, and she said, 'So? Are you going to forgive me and be my friend? And finish what we started? Or are you too stuck in the little world you've created for yourself, in which case I'm not interested anyway?'

She was tough, without a doubt. But she clearly believed resolutely in doing good. And feared no one – not the council, not the police, not public opinion and not knife-wielding gangs of youths. All of which was pretty impressive. And no, she wasn't bonkers either, as she had good reason for it all. She *was* dangerous, but maybe she was right. The festive fizz is to be found through the weary work. The chancy chores. The dangerous duties. A festive fizz that didn't all bubble up and go flat as quickly as a shaken can of cola was not to be sneered at.

He stood, reluctantly and wearily. 'All right,' he said, not looking straight at her. 'But if I get arrested …'

'It's because, having been warned, you chose to continue with me and do this. Don't blame me. Take responsibility.'

He deflated internally but continued to pick up the bag. As he straightened, she was staring at him, a questioning look on her face. 'You do understand that, don't you? You're a clever man. Do this because you choose to, not because you somehow had to, or had been manipulated into it. The benefits accompany the choice. Joy is born not of any old suffering, but of suffering freely chosen. Be a hero, not a victim.'

'I'm a hero,' he said, firmly, and that brightened her.

'You're my hero,' she said, and kissed him on the cheek. Her face was soft and nice, her lips warm.

It didn't stop him worrying. All the time he was bending, grabbing and stuffing, he was half-looking for anyone coming – in particular any police-people, either on foot or in a car. Halfway down, he heard a car coming up the High Street and realised to his horror it was the police.

He shouted, 'Angela! Police!'

They both dropped their bags and turned to look in the windows of the big bargain store. As it passed he was so frightened he slipped his arm round her waist and held on.

It didn't stop. It didn't become all flashing lights and sirens and 'step away from the window'. It passed on steadily down the road.

'All right, Amorous Andy,' she said, struggling slightly against his arm. That upset him.

'OK, OK, don't have a fit,' he said. 'You know why I did it. At least I didn't kiss you.'

'I was only joking,' she replied. 'You can put your arm round me – for a good reason, and from time to time!'

They carried on, and he saw the end of the street approaching with great relief. He finished a black bag and leaned it against the front of a furniture store, and she pulled him off another one from the roll. This he set to with a force and scuttled down the last thirty yards like a man possessed of a black bag. He scooped up the last few items, tied the neck, and threw it on the pavement. Relieved beyond measure, he put his hands on his hips and looked up the High Street. Even by street light, it looked clean and tidy. Perfectly presentable to all-comers, trade or casual, local or foreign. A High Street to be proud of, not ashamed of.

'You see?' she said, joining him.

'Yes, I see. Thank you.'

'Now we just have to take the bags to the bins behind the supermarket and we're off the hook.'

'I'm right behind you.'

They set off up the road, collecting the full bags as they went. They ended up with six each, and struggling somewhat with the volume, not the weight. They were most of the way to the top, looking rather as if they were wearing huge, crinkly, shiny trousers over massive hips, when another police patrol car turned the corner and started down towards them.

David felt the blood drain from his head and chest into his bowels and bladder. Caught bag-handed. Nowhere to run. It turned on its emergency lights and David nearly dropped the lot, then it sped up and roared down the road, off to some real incident.

He swore.

'Hoi!' she said. 'No need.'

'Tell that to my underwear.'

'I'll tell it to your dirty mouth, not your dirty drawers,' she answered.

'Sorry,' he said.

'I should think so. You're forgiven, but sin no more.'

'Do you never swear?'

'Only in the car, and *in extremis*, and then I say sorry.'

'Not so pure, then. That was *in extremis*. Now I'm sorry.'

They'd reached the supermarket and made their way round the back to its deliveries and recycling area. They dumped the bags beside a bin and took off their gloves.

The Old Tun was heaving, and noisy, and definitely benefiting from the gravitational pull of the festive great day. It had lights all over the wooden ceiling beams, and strewn across the top and sides of the bar, and the tree was large, full and festooned; they even had Christmas hits playing, somewhere in the background.

At first David and Angela had to stand at the bar, but a small table became free and they went to that. He had a pint of bitter and she a Baileys and ice.

'What did you have for your tea?' she suddenly asked.

'For my dinner I had a fresh baguette filled with roasted chicken, roasted potatoes, freshly made stuffing and some Brussels sprouts. It was delicious.'

'Flip! That does sound good. I had macaroni cheese and broccoli with sweetcorn. Nowhere near as grand.'

'A baguette is hardly grand, I think,' he countered.

'No, well, you know what I mean. I'm impressed! Maybe you can teach me to cook.'

'Maybe.'

'I'd like that,' she said, raising her glass.

He raised his also and they toasted something. Teaching her to cook, maybe. Or life and freedom. Or courage and standing up for what's right. Or being a holy hero.

He drank the last of his pint and said, 'Another one?'

'Yes, please, same again.'

He went to the bar and returned with the drinks, having struggled manfully through the crowd. It was even more full and noisy than it had been when they came in. And very jolly, he decided.

Or was it the 'f' word?

He put her drink in front of her as he sat, and she said, 'Thank you.'

She had a very happy look on her face as she gazed around at the festive revellers and put her hands either side of her glass.

'You look very pleased with yourself,' he said, slightly unkindly, perhaps.

'And so should you! You've done a good thing for Christmas.'

It welled up inside him like a fountain. Pure festive fizz. He looked her directly in her smiling eyes and said, 'Actually, yes I can!' He reached over and squeezed her hand. She squeezed back. Then he let it go. But they kept smiling.

A warm glow enveloped him, as he took in that he'd done something good for Christmas. Taken a real chance. Put it all out there. Served. Done the weary work. And this was his reward.

Christmas. The lights glowed, the noise rang, the sense of everyone here returning to homes of seasonal anticipation, many with children barely able to contain their excitement, hummed around him like an unfamiliar but enticing tune. He caught the throat-ripping strains of Noddy Holder over the hubbub announcing the season from Slade's famous song, 'Merry Xmas Everybody'. A little shiver went through him. He took a drink and let it all wash over him.

'You're happy!' she said.

'I am!' he admitted.

'You have a definite festive glow,' she added.

'I do,' he agreed, happily.

'I told you!'

'I know. You did. And it's true.'

Was it the beer, or the lighting, or was she truly an angel? But her smiling face glowed. Then, so did all the wide and heaving room. And he felt that he did, too. Ah, Christmas. Nothing like it.

They talked of Christmases past, which David soon realised was a very festive thing to do. It filled him with a warm joy to recall some of the childhood ecstasies of school nativities, of wished-for presents received, of waking to the Santa sack on Christmas morning, of walks in the snow. He recalled how, as a grumpy and surly teenager, Christmas had somehow reduced him to the wondering child, happy and carefree, glad with the simplest of things, even watching stupid but very funny TV shows with his parents. He remembered playing with silly toys from his Santa sack, well below his years, with a simple and unaffected joy on Christmas morning, lying on the white lounge carpet by the tree and the fire. He recalled the pleasure of his mum and dad at receiving his modest and badly wrapped gifts, and their hugs that seemed like he'd never been hugged before (though he had). He dwelt on watching the Queen with forced solemnity, then the fun of the Christmas film, watched all together with cups of tea and 'fruit' from the tree, and shortbread biscuits in posh shapes from a big, shallow tin, and orange and lemon jelly slices, and nuts cracked open by his dad's strong hands. And a chocolate bar or two from his selection box. Then tea of ham and cheeses and crackers and butter, with a slab of Christmas cake. Then the 'down time' for much-needed rest before the comedy shows of Christmas evening – *Morecambe & Wise* always came to mind.

Oh! What joys. And oh! How he missed them. But in this moment, nostalgically, not sadly. With that sweet remembering of lost times while catching again their happy hours and special days.

Yet, yet, even in the delight of telling her these wondrous things, something was missing. What was it? He didn't know, and only sensed it mildly, so he let it go. If it mattered, it would arise again. For now, he was happier than he'd been in a while.

Her questions and her unashamed delight in his memories kept the revelations coming, and when they checked their watches it was half-past nine. He was hungry. So was she. They decided to order something before the kitchen closed. She went and fetched menus from the bar and they studied the tall, shiny cards plastered with pictures of the fare. Festive fare, as it turned out – a special Christmas array of cooked bar snacks.

'I think I'll have the Christmas dinner wrap,' he said, reading the contents of turkey, stuffing, roast potatoes, sprouts and gravy inside a floured tortilla with a side jug of cranberry sauce.

'Ooh, yes, me too!' she agreed. 'That'll take away my jealousy at your tea!'

'I'll get them,' he said, and went to the bar. He paid the ten quid and rejoined her.

'Ten minutes,' he announced.

'Another drink, then,' she offered.

'I'll have a Cointreau over ice, please.'

'Wow! We are getting in the festive spirit.'

'Yes, we are. What are you having?'

'I do believe I'll have the same.'

'Isn't it supposed to mean something when two people start mirroring each other?' he asked.

'I believe it means there's an engagement happening, possibly with emotional overtones.'

'So much for that, then,' he said, noting how clinical her reply seemed.

She went and got the drinks. They sipped, and pulled faces at the alcoholic strength of the innocent-looking cloudy liquid.

Then it went warm down inside his chest, and everything brightened again. He didn't want this to just be about alcohol. But, then, it certainly wasn't. The alcohol was just going along with it. This was Christmas. This was the best of Christmas.

The wraps arrived, along with knives and forks and napkins and condiments. He ignored them all and just picked it up and bit the end off. It was delicious. Gravy dribbled down his chin. He closed his eyes and savoured the mouthful of Christmas dinner. It was more than food. It was festive food.

She cut the end off hers and lifted it daintily to her mouth on a fork.

'Mmm, good!' she managed round her chewing.

'Mmm,' he replied, considering that to not count as speaking with food in your mouth.

He lifted his coat off the hook by the pub door, and reached inside the arm for his precious hat. The gloves were in a side pocket.

Ready for the bitter night, they stepped out. He felt warm, and full, and thankful, and just a tad light-headed. The lights of the town seemed to shimmer and glow with a renewed sense of colour and style. The snowflakes in brilliant white were extra snow-flakey, the Santa hats in red were more Santa-hatty, the Rudolphs in brown were unusually Rudolphy, the trees in green were impressively tree-ey. Even the sky was festively frost-laden and Christmassily crisp.

They walked in silence side by side till they came to the point of parting. She stopped, turned to face him and said, 'So, twenty-five past six outside St Mark's?'

'Yes, OK. I'll be there.'

Then it struck him, like his belly had descended into his bowels – he had no idea how they were going to say goodbye. Was this a 'see you, then'? Was it a handshake? (Surely not.) Was this a quick hug? Kiss on the cheek? He was staring at her chest like some forlorn idiot. She looked down to see if she had something attached to her. Satisfied that she didn't, she said, 'So, then …'

'Yes,' he said, suddenly inspired.

'Thank you for this evening. For the help. And for a really nice evening.'

'Yes, thank you,' he said, managing to engage her eyes.

'I think I'd like a little hug,' she said, breaking the spell.

He stepped forward, arms open, and found himself giving her a huge hug. Maybe partly out of relief, certainly in part out of festive affection.

'Oh!' she said, finally stepping back. 'I guess I wanted a big hug.'

'So did I,' he admitted. 'Goodnight, Angela, see you tomorrow.'

'It'll be fabulous, you'll see,' she promised, and walked off towards her road.

He watched her for a few seconds, then set off homewards. The night sparkled as he walked. Christmas was all around him, in lights and colours, figures and chills.

A man walking a small dog said, 'Goodnight. Merry Christmas,' to which David replied, 'Merry Christmas to you.' That was a far more engaging greeting than he usually gave.

Two scantily clad teenage girls staggered past and giggled loudly at the sight of him. 'Go on home and get warm,' he offered, then, 'and Merry Christmas!'

A garden full of Christmas figures and lights wound around trees and threaded across the face of the building caught his eye, and he stopped and stared. It did something to him, inside. The house owner stepped out of his front door for a moment to put something in a bin, and David said, 'That's truly lovely. Merry Christmas!'

'Why, thank you,' the elderly man said. 'That's appreciated. Merry Christmas!'

David moved on, very aware of every icy slant and every red and green, blue, yellow and white. A window aglow with traditional lights frosted out by a net curtain captured him with its simple festivity. He wished them a silent 'Merry Christmas' before he set off again.

Home was not far now, and he was anticipating a warm sit down and the sight of his tree. Maybe a glass of cold milk and a chocolate fruit or two from the tree before bed. Watch a bit of something nice – see if there was a *Christmas Carol* version on. He felt so chuffed he felt he could fly.

The field opposite the row of houses was disarmingly dark and bleakly blank. It looked lightless and lost. He was glad of his front gate and swiftly opened the door, closing it equally quickly and firmly.

Ah! Inside! Warm and safe by the welcoming radiance of the colourful tree. He shed his coat, hat and gloves, taking those last into the kitchen to leave them by the back door. He decided tea would be better with some chocolates, and to rehydrate himself from the alcohol and the salty food. Kettle on, he went into the front room and switched on the TV. He navigated to the search box and put in *A Christmas Carol*. Nothing at the moment. He tried 'Muppet'. No. Then he tried 'Scrooge' and the Bill Murray film *Scrooged* appeared, only fifteen minutes in. He chuckled at the thought.

He made the tea, selected three chocolates and sat down in his armchair. As he watched he laughed merrily, and it made him feel good.

He thought of Angela, and hoped she was home safely and feeling as happy as he. Should he text her? Probably not. Might be invasive. He fished the phone from his pocket and checked it, then put it on the little table.

He sank into the comfort of his chair, sucking the chocolate off a brazil nut, and reflected that this was Christmas as it should be. As he remembered it.

He went to bed happy, and found under his comforting duvet a warmth that wasn't just outside but inside. A self-generating glow of kindness and true, festive gladness. It seeped into his dreams as he slept, and held him all night.

CHAPTER SEVEN

Sunday's dawn came and went with him unstirred and unstirring. He turned over and stretched a couple of times, aware of the delicious soft nest that held him, but drifted off again as if he'd become part of the luxurious cocoon.

He would like croissants for breakfast. That was the first truly intentional thought of the day. And he would like another day like yesterday.

He turned on his side and asked himself the dreaded question. 'Do I still feel festive? Is it still truly Christmas inside me?'

He nearly shot upright as he realised the answer. Yes. Wow. It had lasted the night. He got up.

He had no particular plans for the day but maybe he should go and clean something. We'll see, he thought.

The bakery in town, which sold nice cakes and baked goods and where he had a coffee from time to time, was a good twenty minutes at a fast pace. He put his nose out of the door and assessed that it was darned cold. Any croissants would be almost as cold as him by the time he got them home. So he put the kettle to heat and switched the oven on to 100 degrees. He shrugged into his coat and went round the house to the garage. He opened the up-and-over door and got into his red Hyundai i10. He was justifiably proud of how 'green' he was in the use of it. This was only the second trip this week.

He drove up to the bakery, parked along the street on the single yellow line, walked in and bought two croissants, then headed straight home, garaged the car and put the croissants in the oven. He made tea, got out the butter and jam, and set up the kitchen table just like yesterday.

And that was his mistake. Before he'd even finished the second croissant, he knew it. He remembered. You can't just recreate happy moments. It doesn't work that way.

The festive fizz fled. He looked at the half-eaten croissant with butter and jam in his hand, and he knew something had left him. The gain of yesterday was the loss of today. Christmas had deflated. This, today, was not yesterday, and this was not the breakfast of yesterday leading to all that they'd done. That was gone. Life was back to normal.

He finished the croissant and slurped the last of his tea. Well, actually, so what? As the young people liked to say, 'whatever'. He had a poem to write. That was the task for this morning, at least. Maybe a nice walk this afternoon. Enjoy the cold air. Cold air wasn't just Christmas air. It held all the glories of winter. The frozen grass, the glistening roofs, the brilliant arch of the sky, the lowering, white orb of the sun, the astringent air. All of it, glorious.

But first, as he stood and cleared away the breakfast things, that poem. He went into the front room, ignored the lights on the tree – that is, didn't bother to switch them on – fetched his pads and pens, sat in his chair and stared out of the window. He cast his mind back.

> All unexpected and unseen,
> Just lurking on the village green,
> As silver moon played off the lake,
> Did you attend me for my sake?
>
> I didn't ask you to my side,
> Nor beg you with me to abide,
> But flitting like some angel fair,
> You soon got caught up in my hair.

Did that capture enough of a sense of menace and mystery? Because she was both.

> All peaceful stood I, as you came,
> Without permission, took my name.
> Invisible, the net you cast,
> With mores exalted, held me fast.
>
> You led me off with strings unseen,
> To places I had never been,
> Nor ever hope to see again,
> To be attacked by angry men.
>
> You tangled me up with the law,
> Inside a PC's notebook saw,
> My own sweet name, condemning penned,
> 'This night within a cell will end.'
>
> Who are you then who swoops all low,
> And without warning takes me so?
> An angel, or an eagle here?
> To bless me or consume me

Then he was stuck for a last word on the line. He was pleased how he'd replaced 'asked' with 'took' in the second line of the third verse, suggesting both that she had stolen his name from him and perhaps that this had a much closer future, or that she was designing a much closer future. It also resounded with his name being in the policeman's book – causing it to be somehow sullied and diminished. He liked the 'exalted mores', referring to the way she seemed to set herself superior to him. And the encounter with the cops and the gangs.

An hour and a half had passed, and various dismissed attempts lay on the floor, torn from his spring-bound pad and so attended by the thin strips of paper that annoyingly came off with the pages. Now he twiddled the pen between thumb and forefinger and rehearsed various rhymes with 'here'. None were any good. 'Here' would have to change to something that would give a sensible rhyme in the last line. He stared out of the window and mulled it over. Nothing was coming, so he went and made himself another coffee. He brought it back and sat down.

Consume me … what? Consume me gone. Up. All. 'All' rhymes with 'fall'. But that would be 'an angel or an eagle fall' and it should be 'falls'. What about 'consume my' something. To bless me or consume my … life? Bones? Flesh? How about something more metaphorical – to bless me or consume my name? Then it could be 'An angel or an eagle came?' That wasn't bad, actually. It took up the theme earlier of the name being taken. Good work.

> Who are you then who swoops all low,
> And without warning takes me so?
> An angel, or an eagle came?
> To bless me or consume my name?

He wrote it all out neatly on one page, and set it aside to review later, or tomorrow. Good work. He looked over it. He was pleased. Until he saw that 'came' and 'name' had already been used as a rhyme in verse three. Was that far enough away from verse six? Yes, and anyway that captured the main theme of the poem – she came for his name. To bless it or destroy it. To take it in a good way or a bad way. Yes, all good. Maybe its title should be, 'She Came for my Name'. He penned it at the top then put a smiley face at the bottom of the script.

Who needs Christmas anyway?

Lunchtime. A sandwich would do, while watching the news, then he'd go out.

The phone rang. He ignored it. Then his mobile rang. He ignored that, too. Just nuisance calls, he always imagined.

He went into the kitchen. As he buttered bread, he decided he'd show her the poem. It would be a sort of trap. She would point out the double 'name' and 'came' and that would confirm that all she really wanted to do was criticise and belittle him. She was one of those people who made herself feel good by making others feel bad. Gotcha!

He put the ham, cucumber and pickle sandwich on a plate, along with a few crisps and a single marshmallow chocolate teacake, and with a mug of tea in the other hand, he returned to the lounge and put on the lunchtime news. Settled in his favourite armchair he watched, detached, as mayhem and misfortune unravelled before him. No one, he thought, could become emotionally moved by a whole world's misadventures. Even the eyes of starving refugee children only stirred him for a second as he took another bite of his sandwich. Sure, there were those who would criticise him for being so removed from it (not least her) but everyone was the same, really. In truth, he *was* removed from it. A starving child outside his house would be another matter.

Did she cry over her croissants? Did she weep over her waffles? Did she ... blub over her blinis? He laughed. He laughed because he was insulting her. Getting his own back for how inferior she made him feel. Oh, it was probably incidental and not intended, but still, that's how it felt.

Maybe that was the cost of being 'improved'. But he never asked to be improved. Nor did he need to be improved. He was fine just as he was. A little isolated, perhaps, but who wasn't these days?

The sky promised snow, and that, quite simply, thrilled him. It was white and low and stretched flat like a blanket, not the usual heavenly dome. The air was less cold, which was also a good sign. Cold, but mildly rather than bitterly so.

Still, he had wrapped up well in extra jumper, long coat, university scarf, normal gloves and Russian army hat. And wellington boots with two pairs of socks. He felt stiff and fat inside it all. He turned right out of his front gate, past the driveway gate, and crossed the road to the grass on the other side. This he trod, until he came to the footpath. He turned left onto it and climbed the simple old stile, and began the pathway that led away from the road alongside the bushy, post and wire fence. He could see the horses the far side of the field, over to his right, hanging around where they might be fed.

A family passed him – parents and two girls, one of about ten and the other of about seven. They ignored him completely, taken up with their own games and conversations. Excited.

He looked around and all he could think of was snow. Blessed snow. Exciting snow. Everything covered in a smooth, white blanket of snow. The quietness it brought – a sort of holy stillness. The way it sat in piped lines on tree branches. The fairy-detailing it gave to roofs. The sense of everyone and everything being gripped together in some wonderful moment of blessed joy. And to come at Christmas! Well, that was blessing upon blessing, grace upon grace, joy upon joy.

Two birds squawked and cawed in a tree beside him. There was a fluttering and a flapping as they seemingly fell out, and one swung away in a great arc over the field, while the other sat still and looked down, not even watching. Did they know it would snow?

> Did they know,
> It would snow?
> Are you tense,
> With nature-sense?
> Do you spy,
> The whitened sky?
> Is that the test,
> That guards your nest?

A shiver shook him. Not of cold. Of anticipation. Winter. What fools who only looked for heat and beaches! The pale glories and cool joys of winter were no less beautiful and amazing. Oh, no, you didn't want to lie in them almost naked, but wrapped up well, they were a treat to the eyes and an uplift to the heart. And spring for its bursting freshness and summer for its green shades and autumn for its golden browns and cherry reds. Appreciate all the seasons.

He remembered a piece he wrote on the subject.

> If you love the trees in their stark, sky-pointing,
> filigree finery;
> If you love the trees in the fresh hope of their
> new-life bud and bursting blossom;
> If you love the trees in the full-green shading of
> their verdant canopy;
> If you love the trees in the radiant glory of their
> gold and crimson fire;
> Then you know a deep truth,
> From love, not knowledge,
> And you are blessed indeed.

It was almost religious. Not that Angela would think so. But it moved that there is something almost sacred about being able to appreciate each season, and therefore each stage and part of life, as good in itself and to be enjoyed. It suggested that recognising this truth from simply reacting to the seasons of life is a deeper and better form of knowing than just words, and logical 'truth'. It was almost Druidic. An ancient, archaic mystery, hidden deep in the human consciousness, a connection with nature and 'life' beyond the scientific and rational. Which, for an ex-physics and maths teacher, was quite a step! One he had only taken in the nearly four years since retirement as he'd begun to write.

It connected also with this modern rediscovery of centring, being in the moment, meditating on the now. Now, here, in this place and in this moment he was revelling in the day, the sky, the trees, the feel of it, even the isolation of it. This moment was uniquely precious, and not to be compared to any other but to be fully known and appreciated just as it was, in and for itself and for him to enjoy. Mindfulness. Being-ness. Senses alive. The sight of the empty fields and the stark trees against the soft, cotton-woolly sky. The sound of the birds twittering and tweeting, fluttering and fighting. The feel of the cool air on his face, washing him. The smell of musty wood from the trees beside him. The taste of dry coldness in the air. This moment was supreme.

Then why didn't he apply it to himself and forego this foolish foray for festive felicitations?

He chuckled to himself. How strange that a man given in all his working life to figures and numbers, should, in his retirement, so take to words and sounds. Yet there was a logic even in this. Because to say that in mathematics there is a rare beauty of form and pattern was no mere metaphor. It was truly there, like a poem of numbers, a symphony of exquisite balance.

And as in language there was beauty in simplicity, so in numbers simplicity was important. The multiplication of complexities was (like the appearance of infinities), a sure sign that something was fundamentally wrong.

Another bird plunging carved a perfect curve in the air. So simple. So profound. So delightful. So skilful. Such a delight.

He crossed another stile and was faced with the open field towards the row of threadbare trees at the slightly raised skyline. Distant birds worried at the branches. From somewhere he heard the muffled bark of a dog. A young couple holding gloved hands appeared from the trees and made their lazy way towards him. He looked around rather than at them and they passed with a happy, 'Merry Christmas,' to which he replied, 'Have a good one.' And smiled.

Pleased with himself, he carried on. He decided he would get all the way to the trees before turning back.

Time to get the roast going if he was to be at church for 6.30. He checked the instructions on the lamb joint, unwrapped it and put it in the pre-heated oven. Then he started on peeling the potatoes.

As he worked he listened to a Radio 4 programme he'd recorded about a physicist called Dr Andrew Thomas, and his book called *Hidden in Plain Sight*. It was fascinating stuff. This guy realised that philosophy provided more answers to the mysteries of quantum mechanics and relativity than the endlessly increasing complexity of mathematics – which to David, as a physics teacher all his working life who had emphasised the mathematical nature of all physics, came as a surprise and a strange relief.

David loved the detail, but wondered how anyone without a degree in physics followed it. It was all so familiar to him, in outline if not in this particular expression. Somehow, it made him feel happy.

He began to par-boil the potatoes ready for roasting as he listened to how the dreaded inflation theory of the mysterious ultra-rapid expansion of the earliest universe could be avoided. He smiled as he put carrots out to scrape. It felt like these more philosophical explanations took a weight off him. Removed a necessity he had laboured under his whole career. What a fine afternoon he was having. Would he even go tonight? The programme finished and he put on some classical music instead, from Radio 3. What a refined and clever fellow he was. Also wise, as he'd realised early on in his retirement that living alone it was essential to retain the fixed points that gave structure to your day. Preparing a proper meal at least once a day was an important part of that – for him, anyway.

He drained the potatoes and put them in some goose fat in a pan he'd been heating in the oven, turning them carefully to be fully coated, enjoying the sizzle. He set the carrots and sprouts on to boil. It could be left now, and as dusk was falling he went and sat outside to consider the world.

As the land reduced to darkness the sky became bright and clear in comparison, like a candle when the light of day stops overshining it. Bright, white clouds ruled from heaven over spindly branches, pleading upwards in silhouetted relief. The blanket of snow clouds gave a sense of distance not so much upwards as away, horizontally. Far, far, far it took his eye, and his heart followed. The something beyond. The Yearning. The existential loneliness that, wisdom said, could not be met by anything in this world. The void within himself.

Or was the void out there? Something more was there, pulling at him, stirring him at a level beyond rational understanding or human relationship. The sky normally delivered this nudge to him, and very effectively. Though other inspiring views could do the same. Mountaintop displays. Extended, flat valleys, like the central, low plain of Majorca in blistering, undulating heat. Was it merely a construction of his own mind, a questioning, a searching?

A tear escaped his eye. It held such beauty. This whatever-it-was that pulled at him with such joy, and promises of meaning, and satisfaction. Could it be just his need, his seeking after something he was made and designed for, but which was not entirely here? Was that what we called 'God'?

Or was it God?

Birds flew away, calling him to join them, come with them, to the place they knew he needed. He watched them disappear behind the trees and a great regret overwhelmed him like something he had lost, like a child who had died and left him hollow. Tears flowed.

Stupid question. But it had to be asked. Was the search for the festive feel of Christmas a manifestation of the same thing? A small, specific leaking out of the same existential urge?

And she. Angela. She had opened up a box of tricks. She'd certainly got under his skin, whether as friend or more. She intrigued him. He feared she'd ruined him for his simple isolation. She'd shown him colour out of his black and white. Should she be thanked? Or avoided?

PART TWO

CHAPTER EIGHT

Six o'clock passed and still he watched the news. But now he was irritated. He couldn't settle, and it struck him that the path of least resistance was just to go.

He hurried into his coat, hat and scarf, and swept out, banging the door. Take the car? No, it might snow later and he'd be left unable to get it back up the hill. Walk fast.

It was still mild and he let the scarf hang loose. Walking at pace warmed him and he opened the coat. Mrs James was at her front gate holding Harpie, the yapping Boston terrier with the disapproving mouth and suspicious eyes. It yapped at him, and she gave him the look that always suggested to David that she'd learned it from the wretched dog. He looked away as he commonly did and carried on. It yapped a couple more times then gave up on him.

He looked at his watch. Better hurry up. His step became a half-trot. He felt much too full to be doing this, but he really had no one to blame but himself. Except, her, perhaps.

Up the lane, down the road, over the grass, by the pond, up the road, twenty-seven minutes past and there she was. He panted up to her.

She didn't check her watch but smiled and said, 'You came!'

'Yes,' he replied.

She seemed to want to give him a big hug, but was holding back. She looked lovely. There was no hat, and her strawy-coloured hair hung down in long and ever so slightly twirly tresses. Her face beamed above the high collar of a cream-coloured, turtle-neck jumper, partly obscured by a smart brown coat.

She turned and led him in through the porch where they'd found the cursèd newsletters. Then through the great wooden doors into the font area at the back of the church, before it turned right, along the aisle. And it wasn't all candle-lit, like she'd said. The lights were on and hardly a candle flame anywhere. What sort of subterfuge was this? The sort that Christians play to get you to sign on the dotted line? The horrible thought occurred to him that she wasn't just a casual churchgoer, but an actual Christian. That might explain a lot.

Two men in moderately smart suits stood just inside and were handing out service leaflets, large carol sheets and candles with circles of card. These they accepted, as one of them said, 'Hi, Angela,' and David followed her up the central aisle. There were two other aisles, one either side, before the outer pews and stained-glass windows, now dark. It was all pretty full, but she'd spotted some seats ahead, near the front. They sat on the old, wooden bench-seats with high backs. Quiet organ music played over the muted hubbub. It smelled musty but also slightly aromatic.

'I thought you said there'd be candles everywhere,' he said, looking around for effect.

'So I did. And I didn't lie. Just wait.'

At six-thirty on the button the rector walked in, robed to the nines in black and white, and stood at the huge, golden, eagle-shaped lectern. He looked to be in his fifties, with a pleasant, clean-shaven face and a side-parting in his slightly greying, dark hair.

'A very warm welcome to St Mark's for our Carols by Candlelight!' he said, obviously chuffed with himself. 'Everyone is very welcome,' he added, repeating himself. 'In a moment we will light the candles, and then we can begin. The choir are all excited, robed and waiting, especially Steven Ames who is singing the solo for "Once in Royal David's City". Then we'll all join in after the first verse. From then on, carols will be announced by the reader of the lesson each time, and you'll see from your service sheet that we have readers from all our church organisations, from the crèche to the Tea Club. Now, in case of fire, your exits are back the way you came in, or through the choir door at the opposite side, or with me through the vestry at the front left as you look at it. If you have a mobile phone on, please turn it to silent. If you have small children with you, please remember that it's not easy for our readers to come up here and read in front of you all, and Mrs Staines' choir have practised hard for tonight, so please consider taking your child into the crèche area at the back if they become noisy, where you'll still be able to hear the service. If in doubt, ask the sidespeople at the back of the church.'

'Oh, for goodness' sake,' David muttered.

'Patience!' she whispered back, pressing his hand into his lap. 'It's all necessary with this number of visitors in church.'

He sighed.

Finished at last, the rector left, and people with candle-lighting tapers on short wooden poles began to go about lighting candles around the pillars, windows, amplification desk, altar, rails and anywhere else that seemed safe, where candles had already been put in place. The people lit from one another. The lights went off, and David was in a wonderland of flickering, golden brightness. It was magical. It had a strangely unifying effect which the electric lights hadn't had. It pulled everyone in together by the shared illumination, somehow. The shared epiphany. It was excitingly warm. Festive. Definitely festive. And the great Christmas tree at the front on the right now gave a fabulous, colourful glow all its own.

A rustle at the back announced that the choir had arrived. And a bell-clear boy's voice began to sing the uplifting notes of 'Once in Royal ...' His voice soared and flew, taking all with him. When he finished, David sighed with satisfaction, but everyone was standing and starting into the second verse.

As they sang, the choir, draped in heavy red with white ruffs, processed in stately order down the aisle, followed by two other leaders in white robes with blue scarves, and the robed rector. They all filed into their places at the front.

The carol finished. All sat. The rector spoke again. Everyone prayed silently for a moment. Next an old lady stepped up to read a passage from Genesis, moderately well, after which everyone stood to sing 'Silent Night'. It nearly reduced David to tears.

And so it progressed. The choir sang 'O Holy Night' and it was half-decent. Later they sang the 'Carol of the Bells' and it was pretty good. He loved that carol.

He sang his lungs out in 'Hark the Herald' and helped raise the roof in 'O Come All Ye Faithful'.

Before he knew it, the rector was inviting everyone back to the parish rooms for 'the usual celebrations' and the organ was playing some Mozart to get them all to leave.

Letting others move around them, Angela turned full-on to him and said, 'What did you think?'

'It was beautiful. It was moving. It was – very special. I loved it. Pity you only have it once a year.'

Her face brightened. That was definitely not a good thing to say.

'Will you come on Christmas morning?'

'Er, I doubt it,' he said, merely wanting to circumvent any commitment about it, or even expectation.

'OK. But you'll come to the party, after the refreshments?'

Ooh, clever, he thought. He was being manipulated. Let him say no for the moment to Christmas Day, but use that to propel him to come along now. It's only a party, after all. Clever.

'OK,' he said, 'but I can't stay long,' which was a lie, but it was, surely, up to him how long he stayed.

She sidled herself against him and looked up, puppy-dog-like, into his face. 'Well, stay as long as I stay, please?'

'As long as it isn't life-crushingly boring or embarrassing, all right,' he said, and kissed her on the forehead. Whoops. Not planned. Nice, though.

She smiled that nothing-held-back, winning smile at him and something inside melted. Something he needed.

He gave her a gentle shove. 'Come on, then, everyone's going,' he said.

The parish rooms were heaving with people squeezing and excusing themselves around central trestle tables bearing plates of warmed mince pies, crisps and biscuits. A hatch from the kitchen was serving mulled wine, coffee, tea and squash. The wood-plank floor and noticeboards with tatty posters seemed to be telling him something.

David noticed in particular the brownish-red curtains hanging in funereal folds like Dracula's cape. He wondered how long they'd been suspended there and if they'd ever felt the benefit of a vacuum cleaner's touch.

He was squashed against the dull-green painted plaster wall by a large woman trying to get through with three mince pies on a plate in one hand and a large glass of mulled wine in the other. Undeterred, he pressed towards the tables at the middle, because that was where Angela seemed to be leading. She stopped, and said, 'Tell you what. You get us two mulled wines while I get us some mince pies.'

'OK, good plan.'

He peeled off and headed towards the servery, only to be cut short by the rector trying to make his way to the stage which was over to their left.

'Sorry,' he was saying, 'excuse me. Oops. Hello, Mary.'

He got to the stage, ascended some removable steps and said, 'Hello, everyone. Sorry for the squash. We didn't quite expect so many. Anyway, do be patient, there's plenty to go round. And a big thank you to the ladies in the kitchen. Anyone who can help put some tables away afterwards, that would be much appreciated. And please do sign the card for the Addisons' fiftieth celebrations, which Mr Lewis has. That's all, I think. Thank you for coming.'

David rolled his eyes at the amateurish and largely pointless way of doing things. But he said nothing and kept trying for the kitchen hatch. After a couple of minutes he got there, and waited behind a few others until it was his turn. He took two glasses and carried them away. He was immediately bumped into from behind and nearly lost the lot. Muttering under his breath, he continued, trying to spot Angela near the tables. There she was, talking to an old man with a cap and a threadbare, green scarf over his long, tweedy coat. Farmer Joe, he imagined.

'Hello,' David said brightly as he got within range.

'Hello,' the man replied. 'Is that for me?'

'Of course,' David said, handing him one, and the other to Angela. She winked at him.

'Do you not drink?' the man said.

'Sometimes.'

'You should try this. The vicar makes it himself. It's jolly good, too.'

'Maybe I will,' David said, and set off again.

'Fine young feller,' he heard from behind him. 'You should try and keep hold of that one, Angie.'

'Angela,' he heard her remind him.

When he got to the servery he was nearly the last, and was finally told, 'Sorry, dear, it's all gone.'

He sighed.

'You can buy a bottle, though,' the small and slightly bent, white-haired lady with the thick glasses said, pointing to a round tray with half a dozen bottles proclaiming, 'Rector's Mulled Wine – £3 a bottle for the Roof Appeal'.

'What if I bought a bottle and you heated it all up and gave me just one glass and had some more to serve everyone else?' he asked, as nicely as he could.

'Oh, no, dear, I couldn't do that,' she said. 'That's not for heating. This was for heating,' she held up the large, empty pan for him to see.

'Aha. OK. Thank you,' David said, mystified at the impenetrable ways of the local church. 'I'll buy a bottle, thank you,' he added.

She grabbed one as he put his hand in his jacket pocket to see if he had change. Failing there, he took his wallet from his inner coat pocket, and handed her a fiver. She held it like she'd never seen such a thing before, then looked at him all concerned and said, as if it was the most obvious thing in the world, 'I don't have change, dear!'

He remembered the solitary pound in his trouser pocket, fished it out and added it to the fiver. 'I'll take two bottles,' he said, with an actual smile.

She turned to someone else in the kitchen to her right and out of sight and said, 'Suzy, can we sell two bottles of the rector's mulled wine?'

'Of course we can,' the invisible woman said. 'Unless it's a minor.'

She looked back at him. 'He doesn't look like a minor. Do we need to see identification?'

'No, silly!' the other woman said, stepping into view. She was quite large and buxom, with a silk scarf round her shoulders over a thick, knitted cardigan. Her hair was more grey than white, with a bluish tinge. She wore a lot of very pink lipstick.

'Excuse Mrs Naylor, she has a heart of gold but she's never been quite the same since her Horace passed, isn't that so, Agnes? Here you are. Heat it by the glass in the microwave, or in a pan on the stove, if you like. I don't believe I've seen you before.'

'Angela invited me,' he said, taking a bottle in each hand from her.

'Oh, Angela! Well, well,' she said, and left it hanging in the air like he should know what that meant. Expecting a follow-up but getting none, he gradually moved away. He was sure she was following him with her eyes as he went.

When he got back to Angela, she looked up and said, 'Thirsty?'

'Ha ha. They'd run out of the hot stuff so I negotiated the purchase of two bottles for the roof fund. Where's your friend?'

'Gone off to the loo. Complained he shouldn't have drunk the mulled wine as it always goes right through him.'

'Good grief, what a bunch!' David said, putting the bottles on a piano next to them. 'Are they all like this?'

'Here, have your mince pie. I imagine it's a little cool by now.'

He accepted it on the paper napkin and took a bite from it. 'Mmm, it's good!' he said. 'Home-made.'

'Mrs Tansing. Makes them every year. They've got brandy in, but don't tell the rector.'

The old gentleman returned, saw David and said, 'Goes right through me, you know. Prostate like a rusty sieve. Comes with the years.'

'Oh,' David said, not wanting to continue that conversation. 'Are you going to be at the party?'

'The party? No, I don't go to the party. Young people at the party. I go home. If I want to see young people, I'll go to the cinema.'

Angela could contain herself no longer and burst out laughing. 'Oh, Mr Young, you're so funny!' she said.

'Am I?' he said, sounding like Eeyore on a dull day. 'Glad to know it.'

'You always make me laugh. You're such a character. Where do you get it all from?'

He brightened slightly and said, 'A lifetime of hard work and eye-opening experience, I expect. I'm glad you find me amusing. Most people just find me annoying.'

'I keep telling you to get a dog,' she said. 'Dogs appreciate you all the time and whatever you say.'

'Someone was selling some Labrador retriever pups down my road this week. Maybe I should get one. They did look lovely.'

'A Labrador is an excellent dog,' said Angela. 'Intelligent, friendly, loyal, peaceable, and they tend to settle down as they get older so you won't be chasing it around the garden when you're eighty-five.'

'You're blooming right I won't!' he said. 'Well, anyway, goodnight to you both. I'm tired. Happy Christmas, I hope.'

He searched in his pockets for something until David said, 'It's on your head, sir.'

'Fool!' he returned, and walked out.

'Well done!' Angela said to David. 'He isn't easy. Well, look, it's easing in here so are you still up for the party?'

'Is it the same people?' he asked.

She chuckled. 'No. It's only church members and their guests, really, it's the rector's annual "open house". It's nice. The older people mostly go on home, so it's our age and younger. Anyone *can* come, but they don't tend to.'

'Go on, then,' he agreed.

She led him out of the parish rooms by the door they'd come in, back towards the rear of the church, then right, along a narrow, stepping-stone path towards the Rectory. It was a large, old, brick building with magnificent chimneys and looked surprisingly well maintained in the overshine from the exterior lights of the church. Coloured bulbs in profusion draped down the windows inside, giving the whole building a multicoloured glow. There were none outside. Maybe that would be thought improper. But, reasoned David, what he did inside was his own business.

A few others were going in ahead of them. A middle-aged couple, a young married couple (by the look of them, with a baby in a carrycot) and three young people. Inside the door, a smiling woman, probably in her fifties, was taking coats and hanging them up on hooks, and saying, 'Welcome,' 'Hello,' and, 'Do go in.' She took David's bottles as well and put them on the floor behind some coats.

Down the hall and on the left was a large lounge, bedecked with hanging decorations and lights everywhere. The main lights were off, giving a lovely glow, and the smell of mulled wine drifted on the warm air. Multicoloured sets of lights were twinkling and darting in hanging bows suspended from the top of every available bit of wall. A fat tree sat by some leaded windows in a corner, decorously draped with fine tinsel and delicate lights all in red and white. People milled around happily, while some festive music was playing in the background – it sounded like Celtic versions of the nicest Christmas tunes, currently playing 'Happy Christmas War is Over'. There was a table of drinks and nibbly food against one long wall, with quite a lot on it. A bunch of teenagers were socialising in a friendly fashion on some beanbags and bothering no one. David just stood and stared. It was amazing. It was Christmas in a box.

The rector came by, in his collar, carrying a plate of something hot from the kitchen. He stopped and said, very pleasantly, 'Hi, Angela. You staying out of trouble? Hello, I don't think we've met. I'm Colin Barber, I'm the rector of St Mark's. Are you with Angela?'

He held out a hand, which David shook. 'Hi,' he said. 'David Sourbook. I bought two bottles of your mulled wine.'

'Very wise,' he said. 'It's good stuff. Look, relax, get a drink and something to eat, and stay as long as you like. See them?' he pointed at the young people on the beanbags. 'Chat to them. They're a really nice bunch and they like it when adults bother with them.'

Then he went off.

'What was that about?' David said.

'I'll show you,' she answered. 'Come on.'

She led him over, and stopped right by them. 'Hi, Lucy. Hi, Amber. Hi, Darren. Hi, Josh and Katy. Hi, Kai!'

They all looked up at her and each one responded with, 'Hi, Angela,' and, 'You good?'

'This is my new friend, David. Can we sit with you?'

Hardly were the words out of her mouth than they were shifting over. A very attractive dark girl with beautiful, long black hair said to David, 'Sit here. It's clean. Darren hasn't sat on it.'

They all laughed and David joined in. He sat, and wriggled a bit to get himself comfortable. He had Angela the other side, pressing her left leg against him.

Lucy, with round glasses, mousy hair and a slightly spotty face, looked at him with a lovely intensity and said, 'So, David, do you think we'll find life on other planets?'

'Oh!' he said. 'Straight in! Well, yes. Microbial life, not advanced life-forms.' And so began an interesting conversation with them listening and probing and making their own suggestions. The Drake Equation came up, which was about the number of places in our galaxy that might be trying to send us messages but was often used to estimate the amount of life in the universe, and finally the Fermi paradox: where is everyone? The suggestion that 'they' aren't contacting us because we're the only ones.

Someone said, 'Are you a biology master, then?'

David felt so relaxed with them he replied, 'No, I'm a Ninja master. Only joking. Physics and maths.'

They all laughed, which was surprisingly nice.

CHAPTER NINE

Two foam cups of mulled wine and many cheese nibbles later, they decided to leave the gathering of the young, which had by then grown to ten, and transpose themselves to two spaces on a sofa by some of Angela's friends. Some sat on upright chairs, others on cushions or leant against the sofa. One was on the other end of it.

He said to Angela, 'I was a teacher all those years and never had a conversation like that.'

'Different environment,' she answered. 'In school, it is by nature adversarial. That was altogether equal and friendly.'

'Hmm, I suppose,' David said, not entirely quietened.

'Anyway,' she announced. 'Everyone, this is my friend David Sourbook. David, this is Sue and Ian Staines, Anna Lovren, Bill and Mary Granger and that's Holly Ruben with Greg Davis sitting on the floor next to her. He may look cool down there but he'll never get up again!'

They all laughed, and the man said, 'So true.' He was younger than most, but completely bald, as was the current style for those of receding hairlines.

David said, 'So, excuse me, but if you're all in here, who were those other people in the parish rooms?'

'You mean the ones serving?' asked Mary Granger, a tall woman in a tweedy jacket and dark red trousers. 'They're the social team. Pillars of the church from time immemorial. They just get on with their tasks, and we're just entirely thankful.'

David noticed the lipstick on her thin lips matched her trousers almost exactly. 'Oh, I see,' he said, not seeing.

'They're fairly elderly, most of them,' Ian Staines added. He was bald on top of his head, but had a mess of white, mid-length hairs hanging unrestrained in all directions. 'I'll be glad to be as active when I'm ninety. There's about ten of them in all. They run all sorts of things. But you wouldn't expect them to still be serving on the PCC.'

'That's the church council?' David asked.

'Yes. That's the likes of us. Still shifting furniture and applying for diocesan permission, balancing the books and making sure Greg knows we've got an eye on him!'

'Oi!' Greg said. 'That money was just resting in my account.'

Laughter flowed. Clearly he was the treasurer and that was a reference to *Father Ted*. David wondered how many times that joke had been used in the years since the TV series.

'Well,' he said, 'there seemed to be a lot of other people in there. Like a rather rotund woman who shoved me out of the way as she sallied forth with a plate of mince pies in one hand and a glass of mulled wine in the other.'

'That's Ella. She has some problems and the rector's taken her under his wing,' Angela told him.

'This church certainly attracts its share of people with problems,' Bill Granger said. He was formed and dressed just like a male version of his wife. 'Which is a good thing.'

'Is it?' David asked.

'Of course! If a church isn't attracting people with problems, that doesn't mean there *aren't* people with problems out there, it just means they don't think there's anything in here to help them. And that's not how a church should be.'

'Oh. I see,' David said, fully seeing. 'So you see attracting and sheltering lame ducks as your mission.' It was deliberately provocative.

Sue Staines piped up. 'Not exactly. We see it as our Christ-given calling to recognise that people need help and to try to give it, whether that just comforts them, or actually helps them to change their situation. We do it as a calling because we must, not a hobby because we might. And we do it without any sense that they are the "lame ducks" and we are the good and responsible people of the church. We do it with love and respect. We aim to empower and release people, not trap them further in a downward spiral of dependency. You might gather I'm a social worker, and I do understand the issues.'

David wasn't sure whether to apologise or not. He'd clearly ruffled her, at least a little. Perhaps he should antagonise her a little more, just to see where it went.

'But they're not welcome in here for the party?'

That caused a much bigger, though silent, reaction.

'Of course they are!' Holly Ruben blurted, and Greg reached up and put a hand on her hand. 'And they're also welcome to not come if they don't want to, which not everyone does. There's no first and second class. No inner group and then the rest.'

'Oh,' David said, feeling Angela's hot, but silent, indignation beside him. 'But there must be an inner group. Organisations always have an inner group, if they have any kind of leadership structure. You have staff and office-holders, I imagine?'

'Yes,' Holly retorted, restraining anger, 'but not in the sense that anyone is excluded by that from social gatherings or parish events. Good grief! What do you take us for?'

'David, why are you baiting my friends?' Angela said, quietly, but loudly enough for the whole group to hear.

He felt the animosity and antagonism towards him. They'd gone very quiet.

'I'm going to get some more wine,' Anna Lovren said, and Mary Granger added, 'I'll come with you.' 'Me, too,' Bill agreed.

They stood, and walked away politely.

Sue Staines looked at him hard, and said, 'What is it you're trying to find out, David?'

He felt slightly pinned by her. She was perhaps a bit younger – late forties – dressed in a long, silver dress with a grey woollen jumper over the top, and her nicely turned calf muscles ended in smart, shiny grey shoes. She wore thin-rimmed glasses in the narrow style. She was fairly blonde, and her blue eyes had a fixing stare.

'What am I trying to find out?' he repeated. 'What makes you tick, I suppose. I'm suspicious of religious groups. Wary of undeclared motives and the cloaking effect of corporate thinking, together with the dulling effect of authoritative diktats. Do you really think independently and creatively? Or does what you have invested make that effectively impossible? That kind of thing.'

She softened. 'You know, those are all good questions. When the others come back we should discuss them.'

'Oh,' David said, not expecting the others to come back and taken off guard by such a reasonable response. 'OK.'

'Maybe Angela is more important to you than you realise,' Sue said.

What David realised was that he could bring this whole church thing to an end quite quickly, by just being intransigent and unreasonable. He wondered if that was what he was really doing.

As he waited he looked across the room and his eye caught a picture the other side. It was about two feet high by a foot wide, in a wooden frame, and on a swirling grey and white and purple background were these words:

> It may have been rough,
> Roman fingers,
> That twisted, and knotted, the branch;
> But only Jesus Christ Himself,
> Made out of piercing thorns,
> A crown.

> It may have been rough,
> Roman hands,
> That held the awl, and struck it home;
> But only Jesus Christ Himself,
> Made out of beams and nails,
> A throne.

It may have been rough,
Roman arms,
That grasped the spear, and drove it in,
But only Jesus Christ Himself,
Made out of spurting blood,
A fount of eternal life.

He was strangely moved. It revealed an insightfulness and a subtlety he hadn't imagined of this religious lot.

Then he cast his eye further along the wall and there was another, of the same design but with a different message. He had been unaware, but Angela had her hand on his arm and was gently squeezing it. Maybe she sensed that there was danger here, too. He turned and looked at her. She looked sad.

'These are my friends,' she said, very softly. 'I respect your principles and your questions, but please can you respect them?'

He said nothing. Then he felt sorry for her and said, 'I'll try.'

They came back with a tray of drinks for everyone and another tray with plates of the nibbles. They started handing them round.

'I didn't realise it was a raiding party!' David said.

'It just helps Ruby with getting the food and drinks served out,' Sue said. 'She's the rector's wife.'

'Now, there's an interesting thing, then,' Anna interjected. 'What seemed to you to be self-serving, though it was in literal terms self-serving, was actually done for the motive of helping out, and did in fact give assistance.'

Anna was about fifty-five, and vivacious. She never seemed to be quite still. Her hair had retained a strong copper hue and her skin was white.

'Good observation and analogy!' Bill blurted. 'Is that what you suspect us of – some sort of self-serving dressed-up-as-religious concern?'

'I don't suspect you,' David said. 'I guess I'm just wary of religious people and their true motivations, and whether they've lost the power of really free thought because of the religious dogmas they've had to give assent to.'

'Well, that all sounds eminently reasonable to me,' said Mary, sounding surprisingly friendly for such a stern-looking woman.

'Yes, it's a fair question,' Greg agreed. 'Sorry if we sounded a bit defensive before, but you seemed to be casting aspersions on what is, to us, a genuine and even costly intention to do good.'

'There certainly are people and institutions that come across like you suggest,' Sue put in. 'I see it in my work. Their motives are more to make themselves *feel* good than to actually do good, and policy seems to constantly take precedence over common sense and people's real needs. I can't say that social work is entirely free of the problem.'

'Nor the church!' added Angela from beside him. 'So, yes, it's a fair question, but it did come across as a bit attacking, like assuming it was true of us without actually knowing, David.'

This was the opportunity for him to say 'sorry' as well. Hmm. Oh, for goodness' sake, he didn't have to come to church if he didn't want to! He didn't need to insult these people just as a way out of that. And upset Angela needlessly. Oh! Wait! There was a better way. A way that would reveal more about her.

He said, 'I guess I was maybe reacting to feeling a bit trapped. I only met Angela a couple of days ago and already she's had me out delivering church newsletters, and here I am at church, a thing I'm not the slightest bit used to, and she's wanting me to come on Christmas morning as well. Perhaps I felt you were all closing in!'

'Ha ha!' Bill said. 'I can sympathise with that! Daniel in the den of lions. About to be eaten – in a very proper, Anglican way, of course, but eaten nonetheless. Sorry if we rather surrounded you.'

'That would be my fault, then,' Angela said. 'Pushing you too hard. Sorry, do you want to go?'

So, she could take a fairly obvious and even public rebuke and respond gently and with humility. That was encouraging. He felt a lot better. 'No, it's OK,' he said, putting a hand on her arm. 'And I'm sorry if I was a bit rude.'

'Sometimes we forget we all know each other and know the religious ropes and all,' Mary said, 'and that to someone new it's all very unfamiliar and without context. You stick with us, you'll find we're OK really.'

'Thank you,' he said. 'And I do accept that your philanthropy is well-motivated and rightly directed.'

'Good man!' said Bill, beaming. 'All friends, then. Especially Angela!'

'Hoi!' she said. 'Spare my blushes.'

'I don't think I've ever seen you blush,' Greg said.

'Hoi again!' she said. 'What do you think I am? Some sort of automaton?'

'Just a tad tough, perhaps,' he replied.

'Double hoi!' she called out. 'You like 'em compliant and subservient, do you, Greg?'

'You'd better be careful how you answer that,' Holly cautioned.

'I didn't know you two were an item,' Angela said, clearly sensing an advantage.

'Obviously it isn't just me that gets you fighting,' David was glad to observe.

'No, we all bear the scars!' Bill agreed, and they all set to accusing each other in a very jocular fashion. It was nice.

When they settled, Holly said, 'So, David, have you no "religious" or church background, then?'

'None at all. My parents were confirmed agnostics, and never even sent me to Sunday school.'

'I didn't know you could be confirmed as an agnostic,' Ian piped up.

'Oh, yes,' David replied. 'I think they were ordained agnostics, actually.'

'Surely you've come across Christian faith in some form somewhere?' Holly asked. 'Films? *The Passion of the Christ?* TV series like *The Bible*? Church newsletters? Books? Did you come across *The Shack*?'

'No to all of them. Not that I was looking to. I am untainted by any such influences since RE at school.'

'Ah! RE at school!' Greg said. 'And what did you make of that?'

'Less boring than geography but otherwise nothing to commend it. I didn't take it at O level.'

And so the conversation continued, not just around David, but branching out into other things. He had to admit to himself that he rather liked them, and enjoyed the talk and banter more than he would have thought.

Until it happened. There was a commotion at the front bay window, and a couple of the young people cried, 'It's snowing!' and, 'It's really heavy!'

David shot to his feet, Angela beside him, and they headed straight for the front door, ignoring the log jam at the window. David pulled the door open and they stepped out into a wonderland.

It was a friendly invasion. Bulky snowflakes parachuted in, each clearly determined to link up with its brothers and simply overwhelm any resistance by the ground forces. Many of the first wave died quickly, disappearing from view, but even as David watched, greater battalions descended, slow and silent from the clouds, landing and forming continuous beachheads, subduing all defences. Like an operation planning map, the ground turned from grey to white as allied forces took hill and bunker, field and road. The invasion was swift and decisive. And still they came, settling in drifts of purest white and recasting the landscape according to the new order. Snow ruled.

He was almost breathless in awe. It was Christmas like never before. It was Christmas as Christmas is of its most beautiful nature, still and joyful and perfect. It thrilled him with a childlike chill of pure expectation and happiness. It was as if it recalled some memory of a perfect Christmas from when he was small and the world was young, and such celebration was all of its most awesome essence. Not created, but merely experienced as pure and wonderful, fully of grace, a gift, as to children, he supposed, it really is. He let it wash over him in white wonder and never wanted to leave this moment ever again. Was this, truly, festive? If not, then nothing was, or ever could be. He was happier than he had any right or hope of being.

He felt her hand at his side, and he recognised a moment. This was not just the incidental necessities of the past. This was holding hands. She was holding his hand, and he, hers. He smiled. Had she just overwhelmed him with her soft and lovely invasion?

Content beyond mere stillness, he waited, and rested, and thrilled quietly at Christmas and the snow and the moment and Angela. She was moving her fingers gently against his. He slid his thumb across her palm. The moment was a whole. This was not Angela and Christmas and snow, and even a seasonal party at the church. This was Christmas *with* Angela and snow and party and new friends, even, maybe. This was fully festive. Full Festive Jacket (referring to the very unfestive film about Vietnam, *Full Metal Jacket*).

Inside, he sighed. Mindfulness. Be here now. He certainly was.

She, also, was very still. What if she tried to kiss him? Don't worry. Don't let worry enter in. Be here now. The moment is everything.

Others were around them, David gradually realised, and his head started to feel cold and a little wet. He laughed. 'We're not exactly dressed for this!' he said.

'No,' Angela agreed. 'We should go back in.'

He flicked snow off his head in the hallway, and she helped him. He did the same for her. It meant them standing quite close, but she didn't try to kiss him. He was glad of that. Not that she shouldn't. But he wasn't sure.

Then she put her arms right round him in a big hug and rested her head on his chest. It fitted quite nicely just under his chin, which he laid on her hair. It was surprisingly comfortable. He could feel her breathing. No one seemed to notice or bother.

'That was just amazing,' she said. So, she'd sensed it, too.

'It was utterly breath-taking for me,' he agreed. 'It was like a seminal experience. Like a big lifetime moment. One of those moments I don't think I'll ever forget.'

'And I was part of it,' she said.

'Yes. Only, I hope it doesn't become one of those experiences you're forever trying to recreate.'

She wriggled against him. 'You're such a worrier!'

'Am I?'

'Sometimes. Just accept it. Keep enjoying it! Wasn't it festive enough?'

'Oh, yes! Completely. Full Festive Jacket!'

She gave a little laugh. 'You're funny.'

'I know. Let's have some more mulled wine and rejoin your friends.'

'I'd really like them to be *our* friends.'

'For goodness' sake, you're never satisfied!'

'Sorry.'

They disengaged and walked back into the big living room, where some of them had recongregated at the settee. She sat on an upright chair and he went off to get mulled wine and nibbles, then sat at her feet on the floor. Like her dog.

CHAPTER TEN

The journey home was amazing, wonderful, magical and awesome, in pure, festive, childlike glee. They didn't walk together very far as there was no need, then they separated.

There was no awkwardness, no kiss, no further holding of hands, and no plans for the morrow. All of which both relieved and surprised him somewhat. They parted with a, 'goodnight,' and a, 'thank you so much for coming,' and a, 'I really enjoyed it.'

He didn't look back and he imagined she didn't. But he was happy enough to fly. Christmas lights peeped from under the snowy blanket. A suspenseful and full hush ruled the streets. The denizens of heaven yet fell in a gentle brush of haloes. He whistled 'O Holy Night', enjoying every magical, lifting, epiphonic phrase. He made the word up, and liked it so much he kept it. Epiphonic. An epiphany of sound. A revelation of noise.

Such a contented dream was it that he drifted home in, that only when he stood inside did he realise that his shoes, socks and the bottom six inches of his trousers were drenched with snowy water. So he scooted up the stairs and changed for bed, then, shouldering his dressing gown, he descended into the kitchen. Far too excited to go to bed yet, despite it being gone eleven, he considered his options, and settled on hot chocolate and digestives, that being a staple favourite. Not festive, to be sure, but nothing could presently diminish that. He heaped extra Belgian chocolate powder into his Eeyore mug and put just milk on to boil. Ah, but did he have digestives? A momentary panic, and there they were – an unopened packet from last week's shopping. German digestives – the very best!

He took the hot mug and virgin packet into the living room, sat in his favourite chair, and admired the tree and decorations. Oh, so festive! So very seasonal! He picked up the TV remote and pressed for the programme menu. And there it was. His joy knew no bounds. The Mr Magoo version of *A Christmas Carol*. He snuggled down in the chair and pulled the dressing gown around his pyjama-clad legs. Heaven. Festive heaven.

He watched. He sipped. He chewed. He laughed. He went, 'Aww!' and he nearly cried. He was so glad that this little retreat was just his. No one to come home to. No one to question him about the evening, or nag him about the shopping, or remind him about the loose gutter section, or bore him with endless details of their trip to the doctor. No. Just him. Lovely. In moments such as this, worth it all.

He realised he'd eaten seven biscuits by the time he'd finished the hot chocolate, then decided he didn't care about getting fat, it was Christmas. And there was no one here to squint at him about it. Or judge him. Or belittle or diminish him. No. Perfect peace. Just him. And Mr Magoo, that dear old chap, whose short-sight got him into such scrapes. And his funny old voice, all wavery and croaky.

It was gone two when he woke up. The empty mug was on the floor but the packet of biscuits had stayed on his lap. Some Christmas cartoon was on in front of him. And he was still happy. Deliciously happy. What part Angela played in that, exactly, he didn't know. But that didn't matter. This, this was Christmas. Up half the night just watching TV. Falling asleep in your own precious chair. Clear up in the morning. Off to your warm, safe bed while blessed snow continued to fall, cold and white, outside.

In his bedroom, he draped the dressing gown over his chair and parted the curtains for a peep outside. Yes, good, snow was still falling. Gosh! How deep would it get?

He snuggled down under his duvet and yawned a huge, happy yawn. Had he, in fact, ever, been this happy?

This festive?

Brrd. Brrd. Brrd. Brrd.

The phone was plugged into its charger on his night-table and was buzzing at him. It wasn't the alarm. It was a phone call. He could imagine from whom.

He picked it up and checked the time. Five past ten in the morning. He jiggled the lit green circle with his thumb and said, 'Hmm?'

'Sorry, I thought you'd be up.'

'No. I stayed up very late watching telly. I was too happy to go to bed.'

'Too happy to go to bed! That's not a thing you hear often.'

'Well, it is Christmas.'

'And who's getting all festive, then?' Angela observed.

'It's true. Yesterday evening was truly magical. Magnificent. Mystical. And yes, you were part of it. I will never forget it, as long as I live, and may it be superlatively long.'

'And you enjoyed the service and meeting my friends.'

'I did! There's a thing not to be sniffed at. At which not to be sniffed. They were very nice, if a little stiff at first.'

'Yes, well, we'll let that pass. Anyway, get up, we have work to do.'

'You're kidding! I have no intention of getting up or doing work. It's Christmas!'

'A time of goodwill and sharing, loving and giving, if I recall rightly.'

He groaned. He groaned because she was right, and she knew it.

'Have mercy on me.'

'No. Be up in fifteen minutes, showered, dressed and with tea on the go and I'll bring croissants.'

The line went dead. Darn her. She was riding him. Jockey syndrome indeed. The question was, how much did he mind?

And how did the inconvenience stack up against the fun? And against how she intrigued him? And against how she was maybe taking to him?

Ooh. Hot stuff. Handle with caution. Just get up.

Knockety knock knock. Knock knock.

Why didn't she use the bell?

He opened the door, and there she stood, bakery bag in hand, a big smile on her face, hair all over the place, no hat. Red coat. She tugged herself out of her green wellington boots on the doorstep and left them there. Behind her, the air was free of falling snow.

'You're relentless,' he said.

'And good morning to you!' she replied, entering in her blue socks. 'Come on, these are still warm.'

She hung her coat on one of the empty hooks in the hallway and joined him at the table in the kitchen, already laid out with tea, butter, jam, plates and cups. They sat opposite each other and began to eat.

'Radio 4?' he asked.

'Oh, David, I've come to have breakfast with you, not listen to the radio.'

'OK. Anyway, I do feel a bit jockeyed, you know.'

'You would just be lying in bed,' she said, mollifyingly.

'Yes, but maybe I *want* to just lie in bed. And surely that's up to me.'

'But this will be so much better. And I want you with me, doing it.'

'Yes, yes. OK, enlighten me, what is it?' he asked, slightly resigned now.

'You know the alms cottages opposite the church and a bit further down? Well, the old people in them, they only need to get to the little local shop up there, but they're snowed in now. And the rector has a special responsibility for them, seeing as the alms cottages are part of the church.'

'Then he should get his shovel and brush out and get on with it.'

'And he will. But he likes a bit of help. And you, me and some of the younger people from last night are going to help him. What do you think of that? Shifting snow for elderly folk for Christmas?'

'Oh, don't try to make it sound festive! I'm not so stupid. It's back-breaking work, that is.'

'Not if we all do it together. Then it's just fun.'

'Hmm.'

'Hmm,' she repeated.

He finished his first croissant and took a good slug of tea from Eeyore. 'Maybe I don't have a shovel and a stiff garden brush.'

'I bet you do.'

'Where are yours?'

'Leaning against your front fence.'

'Oh. OK, I do have those items.'

'So, you'll help me?'

'For the sake of the elderly and infirm, I will.'

She beamed at him. She locked his slippered feet in her stockinged feet under the table and said, 'I might as well confess I think I'm warming to you.'

'I noticed,' he replied, 'and I might as well confess I don't quite know what to do about it.'

She looked a little disappointed, and said, 'Well, that's honest, at least.'

'You're a bit of an enigma. A bit overwhelming. A bit dangerous, actually. But also very engaging and warm and fun. So ... you're a riddle hiding in a paradox inside a conundrum.'

'Are you glad we met?'

'Well, did we meet? I mean, it seemed rather as if you cornered me by the pond. I was engaged before I hardly even noticed. I was being ridden round the town before I'd had time to think.'

'Yes, but are you glad I befriended you?'

'I guess I'd have to say yes, provisionally, because knowing you is certainly making me happy, but also it depends where it leads because you also make me a bit wary. I'm just trying to be really honest.'

'You're trying to not get into more hot water with me than you can handle.'

'There is that!' he agreed.

She smiled. 'I think I know what you're trying to say. I'm very glad I make you happy. You make me happy, but also sad. So, if I'm perfectly honest, I'm a bit ambivalent as well.'

To his great surprise, that made him feel disappointed. He thought she was really taking to him. It didn't occur to him that she also found him a bit less than she'd hoped.

Somewhere inside, he determined to do better.

Breakfast finished and dishes dealt with, he put on his wellingtons, coat, scarf, and gloves, but not hat, as that seemed unnecessary. He went down the back garden and fetched a shovel and stout broom from the shed. Then they set off, on foot, up the lane.

Children were sliding on sleds, and throwing snowballs, while some parents joined in and others just watched or worried; the lane was a good place as it had little traffic and a nice, straight slope, with grass along one side. David enjoyed the sight.

The ground was deeply and perfectly covered to about six to eight inches. Roofs were overhanging, cars turned into white bubbles, and trees outlined in correction fluid. It was proper deep snow, a thing not often seen in these days, and he appreciated the specialness of it. He dropped his tools, picked up a large handful, made a very puffy and light snowball, and threw it gently against her front as she stood watching him. It disintegrated into powder down her coat. She just laughed.

'Oh,' she said. 'Was your coat ruined the other night? By the dog?'

'Yes. I binned it. Saved my arm, though.'

'Oh well, sorry about that. But better than your arm, for sure.'

Up through the bottom end of town they walked, enjoying the crisp air, then down towards the pond and the church. The snow was nice and dry, not slippery, and they didn't falter once.

As they walked he said, 'I didn't tell you. Something really strange happened the day I met you. Apart from meeting you. That afternoon, I watched a film on the telly, and when I went to look it up in the TV guide, it didn't exist!'

'That sounds very dramatic,' she replied.

'Yes, well. It was called *A Christmas Angel Calls* or something very like that, about a couple whose marriage is failing and they're asked to take in the nephew, who's a really bad lot, for Christmas, and they can see this will be the end of their plans for Christmas and probably their marriage, but it's a real redemption tale because they take him and he gets changed and their marriage is strengthened and they end up having this most amazing Christmas together.'

'But it doesn't exist?'

'Ha! No, apparently not. Bizarre. But then in a dream it occurred to me I could try to find the TV company's website and look on there for the change from the published programme, but that it wouldn't really make any difference because the point of what I saw remains the same.'

'Are you going to?'

'Ah, no. I think I'd rather leave open the calming possibility that it was all a misunderstanding. Shove it in my shrug drawer.'

'Your what?'

'Shrug drawer. The place where you put stuff that makes no sense to you even though people claim it's really true. Everyone has one, but we agnostics have a really big one.'

'Sounds to me like God wants to talk in your ear.'

'What does that mean?'

'It means He manipulated the situation to set you thinking, maybe even to get you ready to meet me.'

'Oh, come on! I don't believe in any kind of God who does anything like that.'

'No? The God I know is utterly outrageous. He raises the dead, walks on water, sends angels, makes the sun go backwards and recreates a withered hand in front of a crowd of sceptical people. He sends dreams, and puts people and situations in front of you, and calls to people through a mysterious myriad of whispered voices. If He really wants to get through to you, there's no knowing what He might do. You should feel privileged. I think He's after you.'

That left David not knowing how to feel. 'You think He made up a whole film just to get my attention?'

'I think it probably exists anyway and He just got it in front of you then mystified you as to where it came from.'

'No. I can't see that.'

'Apparently, you did! See that!'

She stopped, downed tools and threw a soft snowball against him. It powdered down his front. She was smiling. 'You could be a very special person,' she said.

'Sure,' he said. 'Meeting you proves it.'

That was nicely enigmatic.

Outside the Rectory, the girls were on one side of the road and the boys on the other, furiously pitching snowballs at each other with howls of laughter. David quickly joined the boys and weighed in. Angela just watched from a safe distance.

He missed at the first few attempts but then got Lucy on the chest and Amber on the head. He was swiftly covered with five or six himself in righteous retaliation. Quickly he was hot from the exercise and icy water was going down his neck from the snowball hits, which wasn't a nice combination, and he withdrew. They were stopping anyway.

The Rectory door opened and the rector stood there, dressed for a journey to the North Pole. Everyone drifted in through his front gate and gathered round him. Equipment was handed out and he gave a little speech.

'Thank you all for turning up. It's a while since we've had to do this! But the old folk in the alms cottages need help with their snowy front paths, and after that some other folk besides will benefit from the offer of some assistance. We need to split up such that each young person or group of young people has at least one adult with them. Didn't used to be that way, but now we have these extra rules we have to follow. I'll also need to take the names of everyone here, in fact, Mr Strong, our churchwarden, will do that for me. Just give him your name. If anyone needs a shovel or a brush, ask him about that as well. Then we'll divide up into teams. All good?'

There was a general murmuring of assent. Mr Strong stood beside the Rectory door and started to write in his notebook. He asked the age of all the young people as well as their names, though many he already knew. David saw with pleasure the chumminess between Mr Strong, clearly in or near his eighties, and the youngsters, in their teens. It was good to see.

'All right, we're set,' the rector called out. 'Please remember, don't go in to people's houses if you can avoid it, and then be very careful about your feet. Preferably, accept mugs of tea outside. They know we're coming so you don't have to knock or anything. Don't under any circumstances accept money or gifts. If they tell you the rector's a very fine fellow, just agree. Here are your teams.'

Mr Strong called them out. David and Angela were with Lucy and as-yet-unseen Luke, who stepped forward, a very handsome lad with blondish hair. They all picked up their tools and set off across the road to the cottages.

At the first one they approached, net curtains twitched. They set to work. Lucy and Luke heaved mounds of snow off the front path as Angela and David did the same from the footpath outside the gate, then they all went to it with their brooms until the paths were swept and dry. Conversation was limited; mostly about what they were doing.

They moved on. They had a second cottage five along, and this time they'd only been there a minute when an old man in slippers and two cardigans opened the door and asked if they'd like a cup of tea. Angela thanked him and said yes, as long as they could have it outside. Sure enough, less than ten minutes later he reappeared with four mugs of tea and a plate of biscuits on a tray. He held it for them to take what they wanted, then leaned against the door jamb as they drank and nibbled.

'This is very kind of you,' he said. 'Time was I'd have done it myself, but my back doesn't allow such activities these days. I have spondylitis. Means my vertebrae have glued together. Gives me back pain something chronic. I went to the doctor and he sent me to the hospital and they did all kinds of scans and such, but it turns out I've had it so long the damage is done. I should've gone to the doctor back years ago when my Doris told me to, but I was too busy and I didn't want to make a fuss, so here I am. They sent me to a pain clinic but it doesn't do much. I don't like the exercises, either. Is your tea all right?'

They all said it was, and soon got back to work, as he continued to regale them with anecdotes about his medical history.

'Don't you get cold, Mr Barker,' Angela said, 'standing at your door like that. You might not see Christmas.'

'Not that it'd bother me much,' he said.

'Aww, come on, aren't you coming to the lunch on Christmas Day?'

'Yes, I expect so,' he said. 'This is very kind of you. Anyway, I'd better go in. Just leave the mugs on the tray there by the door. Oh, and happy Christmas.'

They all wished him the same, and he shut the door.

'Poor old chap,' Lucy said. 'It's a shame. So old and stuck and lonely and sad. I mean in the old sense.'

'We do what we can for them,' Angela agreed. 'What with the lunch club and the outings and other things, but they don't all want to take part. Mr Barker is one who's hard to get involved. But he does get on with Mr Smith in number three, and they play cards together and even have a lunch at the pub occasionally, so that's nice.'

'That is nice,' Luke agreed. 'And I expect they pop into each other's houses.'

'Well, funnily enough, I don't think they do,' Angela said. 'They seem to think that would be living in each other's pockets and might become intrusive, so they draw the line at that much contact.'

'Aww!' Lucy said. 'He could come to my house any evening, and watch telly with us.'

'Can you imagine how awkward and difficult he'd find that?' Angela suggested.

'Yeah, especially with what you watch!' Luke added.

'I bet he watches *EastEnders*,' she said. 'Or Corrie. And those series on Universal.'

'Yes, but the point is, he'd feel he was really intruding, and he'd worry he wasn't behaving right, and that he was imposing, and that you weren't able to watch what you wanted or do what you wanted. It sounds nice, but he'd rather sit at home on his own. That's what makes it hard.'

'Yeah, I s'pose,' Lucy agreed, and they all carried on heaving and sweeping until the paths inside and out were perfectly clear.

All the alms cottages were now finished. There was a gathering happening outside the Rectory. 'Come on in, leave tools and snowy boots outside,' the rector's wife was saying.

In the extensive lounge, which had the main lights on, but also all the Christmas lights and some festive music, there was coffee, tea and hot chocolate, and biscuits and warmed mince pies. The rector was standing proudly by the table saying, 'Come on, you workers. Get warm and restored.'

He'd been out as well, and his face shone red. David wondered if he suffered from high blood pressure. Or maybe it was just the cold.

Lucy and Luke came and stood with Angela and David. Lucy said, 'My dad agreed with you that the Drake Equation is a load of guff. I had to ask him what guff was.'

'Tosh,' David informed her.

She looked puzzled. 'What's tosh?'

'Guff,' he said, without a smile. They all laughed. 'Rubbish. Wrong. Nonsense, drivel, garbage, bunkum,' he added.

'Yes, I get it,' she said.

David couldn't help but reflect how good this was. Being part of a group helping the elderly and gathering at the Rectory for festive refreshments, especially with young people as well as the more seasoned like himself. It was truly a Christmas scene, what with the snow outside, worthy of any soppy American film. Even *It's a Wonderful Life*.

After being refreshed, the rector said, 'So, we're off as a group up to Dean Street and Amwell Place, because there's quite a few elderly people up there who will need digging out. Use the loo if you need to, there's another one at the top of the stairs, and we'll set off in five minutes.'

David grabbed Angela's hand, and said, 'Thank you again. This is lovely.'

She leaned in and kissed him lightly on the cheek. 'Isn't it?' she agreed.

He wasn't shocked or embarrassed or anything. It was very soft and warm and nice. Goodness!

She went off towards the toilets. He waited, confused but glowing inwardly.

CHAPTER ELEVEN

They spent the next hour and a bit knocking, sweeping, heaving, politely refusing invitations to come in, but gladly accepting cups of tea and coffee. They got hot and tired while their toes and fingers got cold, and ached.

When the rector gathered up the young people to take them back to the Rectory to go home, Angela and David bade them farewell and headed up into the centre of town instead.

'I need to sit down and to get my fingers warm,' David said. 'I think they're turning to chilblains. They really hurt.'

'How about lunch at the Red Lion?' she replied.

'Brilliant idea.'

The Red Lion was an old, town-centre pub that nowadays catered, as it seemed they all did, with food all day. They provided a decent, cheap lunch menu.

Inside was naturally dark, with low, old beams, plaster walls painted off-white, and tall, round tables with bar stools scattered about. It was fairly quiet, with a couple of dozen people. Bright, warm-white Christmas lights fell from the ceilings and wrapped a bulbous tree by the end of the bar. Silver reflective stars twisted and twirled in the movements of air, flashing the lights everywhere. It was very well done, David decided. They found a free table and perused the menus.

'I'm going to have the avocado and prawn sandwiches with salad and crisps,' David announced. 'And as I'll sleep all afternoon anyway, a glass of Merlot. What about you?'

'I think I'll have the chilli-beef wrap with salad and chips, and a nice glass of Chardonnay. Excellent. We're table fifteen.'

'I'm going up, am I?' he said.

'If you like. I don't mind. I pay my way. I've brought you croissants twice!'

'So you have. OK, wait here.'

He went to the bar and ordered, then came back with cutlery wrapped in paper napkins. He didn't sit, but said, 'My fingers still hurt. I'm going to put them in some warm water.'

'Be careful it's only warm,' she advised.

He found the gents and went inside. It was clean and had stone and tiles in understated browns and creams. He poured water into a handbasin, made sure it was just above body-warm, and plunged both hands in it. The pain was awful; like shards of ice moving deep in his flesh. He comforted himself with the knowledge that this would only last a few minutes. Sure enough, it started to abate. It hadn't been the worst finger-freeze.

He returned to find her checking her mobile phone.

'All OK?' she said.

'Yeah. Was painful, though.'

'I know. Well done for suffering for the poor and elderly, lonely and infirm.'

'Yes, well, I still don't really see why I should.'

She looked both surprised and disappointed. 'Oh! Really? I would have thought it was obvious.'

'It might be obvious that some of those people need some help, but not at all obvious why it should be me doing it. I know it can be fun, but there's plenty of other fun things we could be doing. Things that wouldn't make me ache and sting. To be really honest, that's not my job, is it?' He felt a little bit like he'd been duped into it just because it was Angela. Something of his accustomed reluctance was definitely hovering in the wings. His cold indifference had abated, not gone away.

The food arrived, and they sorted themselves out and tucked in. His sandwich was juicy and full.

'So,' she said, 'you don't think you should be called upon to help old and needy people in our society?'

'No.'

'To show them an act of kindness?'

'No.'

'Then who should do it?'

'The rector, if he has a special responsibility, like you said. Or the council.'

'The council?' she blurted. 'Are you kidding? They're cutting library services and refuse removal and you think they should be able to find funds to sweep snow?'

'Then a charity or some do-gooders, but I don't see why it should be me.'

'Why did you do it, then?'

'Because you asked me to. Because you wanted me to.'

'Well, I should be grateful for that, at least. Why do you think *I* wanted to do it?'

'To help the church, and the rector.'

'Hmm. Partially. But I'm part of the church, so that's not really an answer. Why did *we*, as the church, want to do it?'

'Good for public relations. Good for your community image. Gets people into services, I guess.'

'Are you really that cynical?' she asked him. 'Tell me, what do you think the essential Christian gospel message is? You're well-read, I imagine you know.'

'Yes, we're all sinners because we do stuff that offends a holy God, but He is also a loving God so He sent His Son to die on the cross to take our sins away so we could be forgiven and come to Him and be His friends.'

'OK, yes. And is that not divine kindness?'

'I think it's normally called "grace". Even "mercy". Not usually "kindness",' he pointed out.

'Don't nitpick. It is called kindness as well. So when I accept that kindness, and it gets inside me, and I feel and know the kindness God has for me, then it makes me kind towards others, in all sorts of ways. I can't help it. Kindness leads to kindness. It's infectious. So the acts of kindness are genuine, motivated by kindness received. It isn't some kind of cynical publicity stunt.'

'OK. So why should *I* do it?'

'To help me express kindness, because you like me and we're becoming friends. And anyway, don't you think you'll need people to be kind to you?'

'No. I don't want people to be kind to me. That suggests some kind of weakness or inability: I don't want to be seen as in need of kindness. Lots of people don't want charity.'

'Let me get this straight,' she said, staring at him. 'You don't want anyone to be kind to you?'

'No.'

She went quiet then, and just ate her wrap. After a while, he said, 'You've gone quiet.'

'Have I?'

'Yes. Why?'

'Well, I'm sorry, but I'm going to do the classic female thing now, and say, "If you don't know then I'm not going to tell you." In other words, I should have thought it would be blindingly obvious.'

'Oh,' he said, feeling a bit irritated. 'Well, I'm going to the loo.'

When he returned from the gents, she wasn't there. Her empty glass and plate were still on the table, but there was no sign of her. She must have gone to the loo as well. So he waited. After five minutes he began to get concerned, and after ten he knew something must be wrong. He looked over at the ladies and saw a young woman come out. Before she got far from the door he approached her and said, 'I'm sorry, excuse me, but I think my friend might be in there. Would you mind just asking inside if Angela is in there?'

She eyed him for a few seconds then said, 'OK. Angela?'

'Yes. Please.'

She pushed the door open and let it close behind her. He heard her calling, 'Is there an Angela in here? Anyone? Angela?'

She reappeared and said, 'Sorry, there's no one at all in there. Sorry.'

'Is this the only ladies here?'

'In the pub? Yes, I'm sure it is.'

'OK, thanks very much,' he said.

Disturbed now, he decided to look outside. He went out of the side door into the garden. No one was there. He walked round to the front of the pub and in the front door. No sign. This was beyond odd. Then the thought occurred to him that he should look at his phone. To his great relief there was a text from her. He read it.

'Hi, David. I left. If someone has no desire for others to be kind to them, and no particular wish to be kind to others, why would I bother to invest time and affection in such a person? I'm switching my phone off now. A.'

He read it again. A horrible guilty fear gripped him. She was really angry with him. He had messed up big-time.

He trudged home, not sure if he was angry with himself or with her, alternating between the two. Bright, powder-blue skies didn't help. Nor did children enjoying the snow.

He lifted his phone from his pocket a couple of times. Well, a few times, actually, but there was no further message. He got home, shrugged off his outside gear, threw the broom and shovel in the pantry, and put the kettle on. Tea was always necessary in these kinds of circumstances. And a Christmas biscuit or two. Forget her. She would have to contact him. Or not.

It was Monday, 21st December, four days from Christmas Day, only three from Christmas Eve, the most magical night of the year. He wasn't going to be deflected from the search for the festive fulfilment. She had breezed into his life three days ago and if she breezed out again today he wasn't going to stop living all of a sudden.

Into his tea he put a small measure of Tia Maria, and took it into the front room to view some telly before he would most likely drift off. He got the biscuit tin with its festive red designs and sat it on his lap. Perhaps he should get a cat. A nice, friendly one that would like him and be affectionate and sit on his lap.

Remote in hand, he switched on and selected the Christmas films network. Yes, back to where this all started three days ago.

He flicked and found a nice film about a young woman with no money trying to make her children's Christmas fun, while her parents tried to get her to give up on her useless husband, but she held out hope for him because she loved him. In small-town America, of course. With snow.

He settled down, sipped very appreciatively at his tea, and bit into a chocolate shortbread biscuit in the shape of a sleigh. Very nice, too. He kept the tin on his lap. He had often registered how nice it was, having something on his lap. A newspaper. A tin. A cushion. Sort of comfortable. Comforting might be more like it. So – a cat?

It was dusk when he awoke. He stirred wearily and took in his situation. It had been a deep nap and he felt a bit rough; almost unsure what day it was and what was going on. He managed to rescue the biscuit tin as it started to slide floor-wards. That would have been a crumby mess. The TV was droning on. Snow and American emotions. He put the tin on the floor and stretched. Another cup of tea would see him right. Tea and coffee seemed to be the skeleton of his life.

Weren't they for everybody in civilised society?

He put the kettle on and went for his customary peep outside the front door. Ah, the snow clouds had all moved on, and a fabulous dusken scene was forming over field and forest. He would take his tea out to see that.

Coat and hat on, he sat on his bench, Eeyore mug warming his hands. He breathed it in – the forming glory across the road. Across the very world. Stretching through the universe. As the land darkened, in relief the sky seemed lighter, and thus set free from the brightness of the earth; it took on a beauty and a colour scheme all its own. The trees became mere silhouettes, delicate borders to the wash of light and sky, cloud and trailing mist. Diaphanous, the sun, in delicate cloud-coats, whitening the lower heavens against upward branches, lighting high-floating wisps of grey and silver, cast carelessly across the failing blue of day. It drew him. Drew him with that yearning, that sense of something out there that called to him in some deep place beyond words or description. Pulled the very soul out of him.

Beautiful. Endlessly, eternally, upliftingly, searchingly, beautiful. His deepest spirit ached and cried at the song of it, the necessity. So peacefully yet powerfully fitting, filling, lifting, lilting. It was a song. A song in sight. A haunting melody, a lament of a loss so profound no words yet existed for its character or name. Something in the very sky, the very clouds, the very stars and endless space knew him, and called to him, and pulled a yearning like nostalgia and loss and the sweetest memory of desire.

Tears flowed in free floods down his cheeks. His eyes did not restrain them. There was no burning, no sobbing, no anger. It was like this was what tears were for. Nothing else was their true purpose or calling. This, this distant fullness of emptiness was what they were designed and created for. It linked to them. It sent and they received.

He sighed, a great, deep sigh of unsatisfied satisfaction. Of sweet woe. Of completeness of loss. It was an enchantment of sorrow, a charm of regret, a charisma of incomplete being.

'Is it God?' he asked, into the air, louder than he intended, but when he checked, nobody was there to have heard. 'Is that the incompleteness without my creator? The loneliness of the soul made for its maker and desiring Him yet unable to form the design of the missing part? Is this You?'

No answer came. No twitch, no glow, no sign, no friendly star.

'I think I'm supposed to say, "If You're really there, please show me." But I'm not even sure if I'm really asking. Then again, You're supposed to be unthinkably kind, so …'

The tears departed as easily as they'd started, leaving no shadow of sadness, only a ringing wonder. Something out there connects with something in here. Something very 'out there', be that in distance, or ontology, or purpose, or whatever. Of course, it might be merely a projection of an inner condition of the human soul – if it's reasonable to speak of such a thing. But that really wasn't how it felt. But then, against what measure do you compare such a thing? What reliable measure could there be? It was the quantum mechanics and relativity problem, in fact. There is nothing outside the universe to give any absolute measure, so all is relative and nothing has its own inalienable values. He buried his head in his hands. He realised he'd crossed a line. He'd encountered the knowing of unknowing. Not theoretically, but existentially.

Back in the house, he climbed the stairs and went into the back bedroom. There, in his wicker chair beside the spare bed, was Bart. Bart, the enormous teddy. Bart was his guilty secret. He was big and cuddly and friendly and warm. He liked to give a hug and be cuddled. He had brown fur and a smiley bear-face.

David stared at the old friend. He was about four feet tall, a foot and a half across, with a big, round head. His arms and legs were over a foot long and his arms three inches across, his stumpy legs an inch wider, ending in sweet little feet. David picked him up and cuddled him with a great hug. He felt so warm. His arms went round David's shoulders, his legs round David's middle, and he surely was returning the affection.

David clung on in the great hug, and felt comforted, held, loved. He leaned forward onto the bed and rolled over with Bart in play fighting. He nuzzled the great soft head with its playful snout. Then they lay still and just enjoyed each other.

David felt all tension leaving him. All regret evaporating. All confusion resolving into simple unities. Angela was a distant memory. God a non-interfering possibility. That was the true form of agnosticism.

Bart was on top of him, lying still and happy. This is how David would like to die. Or maybe sitting on the bench with Bart, watching dusken skies.

He couldn't sleep; didn't want to. He'd napped heavily half the afternoon. Or more – he wasn't sure how long. But he did fall into a kind of reverie. Something out there had the frequency of his soul. Was it some alien? What would be the point of that?

He wasn't being inclined to destroy his planet or fly through space. No, it wasn't an alien, it was *the* alien. Patiently, individually, David was being called. And what had been going on for a while was coming to a head.

The reverie passed, quietly and innocently. So, what to do this evening?

Well, he'd need a meal. Maybe sausages, cowboy beans and mashed spuds. And he should make a start on drinking that mulled wine. And there was bound to be something worth watching on telly. Maybe a trip up to the pub, later.

He was fine, after all.

He washed, peeled and cut the potatoes, then put them on to boil. He emptied a whole tin of baked beans into a dish and put them in the microwave to begin warming while he started to heat the oven. He also put a little extra virgin olive oil in a frying pan and set it on a low heat. 'We need extra virgins!' he said to himself for the 100th time, and chuckled.

He took the beans from the microwave and added brown sauce, a little red wine, a little balsamic vinegar and some soy sauce, stirring it all up nicely. He grated a decent cheese hat on it and put it in the oven to heat and melt and brown. He put four sausages in the frying pan and set the heat to a gentle sizzle. He tested the potatoes and found them about half-done.

Fifteen minutes later he had a tray on his lap with the beans in the dish, the spuds and sausages with some instant gravy on a plate, and a big glass of mulled wine. The tree lights were on, and the telly handset in his hand.

With the side of a fork, he cut through the cheese hat and scooped out some beans with the cheese. It was, as ever, utterly delicious. Smoothly buttered, milked and beaten mash followed, and half of a very nice Irish sausage. He drew in cool air over the hot food. He did hate burning his tongue.

A good swig of warmed mulled wine pursued it down. It was sweet, spicy, fruity and full-bodied. And very festive.

So, on the telly… He flicked to a constant Christmas music videos channel. S Club 7 were on, singing 'Never Had a Dream Come True'. It was very melodious, and what amazingly attractive girls, he thought, not for the first time. Amid all the swirling mists of ice and snow. Very seductive, in fact.

He turned the volume up, and let the music surround him and block out everything else. Song after song enticed him with festive promise, childhood memories, lilting and exalting tunes, and just that allowable hint of the birth of Christ. Just a hint, except, of course, for dear old Cliff, who sang it out, bold and clear. A Saviour's Day. But many others, in the guise of celebration, decried it and debased it. Yet with enough subtlety to avoid offence if you didn't really listen to the words; which most people didn't, let's be honest, he thought. Most people had no idea what was being said and sold to them most of the time. Heads down, eyes fixed on the next thing, right in front of them, they didn't really want to know. It annoyed him. Constantly. But then again, it wasn't really his concern.

Meal finished, he fetched tea and Christmas chocolates, and ate more than he really should have. Then he felt gorged with guilt. He who judged others had now condemned himself.

Why so empty?

Was it the familiar lack of festive fuel? Was it Angela? Attractive, intriguing, puzzling, annoying, challenging, and yet promising so much, Angela? Or was it God, ringing in the hollow cavern of some inner place that ached as a yawning chasm of existential emptiness? Hmm! Suited to a poem.

He finished his tea and stared at Eeyore. You and me, you mug. Is it simply this? Was she right at first? I'm a depressive, and the mug is always half-empty.

He looked at the cheery lights on his tree. They might as well have all been grey. He looked at the telly. More festive froth. Probably recorded in a studio in the summer Californian heat. All false. All of it, false. He looked back at Eeyore. The sad, long, drawn face and droopy, pleading eyes. The ears hanging all floppy and helpless.

'Did you ever have a girlfriend, feller? They say nobody can love you if you don't first love yourself. Didn't even Jesus say, "love your neighbour as you love yourself"? Love your Eeyore as you love yourself. Maybe you never did have one because you put them all off with too much self-pity. I guess it makes sense. If you, knowing yourself as you do, can't stand yourself, then why would anyone else? If you, spending all that time with yourself, don't like yourself, then why would anyone else like spending time with you?

'But isn't it only really shallow people who really like themselves? I know, I had "really" twice in that sentence. Anyway, isn't it? Really? Except it does seem to be the confident types who get the girls. They like someone with a bit of something about them. Do they want to be protected? Entertained? Led?

'Yet Angela seems just the opposite. She likes to take the lead, make the decisions, give copious judgements, some of which are highly undermining. Is it a test? If it is, I have completely failed to show any initiative, strength, resilience or character. All I've managed to do is whinge. But, equally, why would I want to spend my time with someone who only seems capable of undermining and criticising me? Who needs it? Isn't that exactly why I've settled to this solitary life? And I am settled. Perfectly content. Well, not perfectly. Who but the freshly in love are perfectly content? And that's a fool's paradise. Underneath the ecstatic emotion is the dread that this could all come undone, and now I've tasted it I'd collapse without it. And it never lasts like that. Maybe the Dalai Lama, bless his eco-socks, is blissfully content in his meditative reverie. But that's a bit of a specific calling. For all his good wishes, most of us can't live at the top of a mountain being feted by reverent admirers. And I bet he gets lonely. I get lonely. Some people don't get lonely, they get the opposite – desperate for a bit of solitude. Nothing's perfect. But I reckon both a contented marriage and a contented singleness are both real and I reckon I have the latter, pretty much. Don't I, old donkey friend? I'm not a sad-faced droopy-ears like you. There's lots of my life I really like. There's dusk, and walks, and routines, and poetry, and reading, especially physics, and good, home-cooked food. There's my favourite DVDs. And Christmas. And spring. And summer evenings. And Merlot.

'And I really don't need to be sweeping the drives of the rich and lazy, and confronting murderous yobs, and braving the wrath of the authorities, to be happy. No, sir. Or ma'am.'

CHAPTER TWELVE

He hadn't kept score of the amount of mulled merriment he'd guzzled, and it became a great, festive infusion. As he sloped up the stairs he chuckled at the thoroughly overindulgent imbibation, as he liked to think of it, playing with words as he did. And when he hit his bed, he slept. He slipped, indeed, into some chasm, and his mind was caught up in contemplations far and wise.

He sits in an armchair, watching. Behind him, always just out of sight, is something enormous. Enormous and alive. Very alive. It might even have its hand on his right shoulder. Without seeing it he knows it is a jolly giant, crowned with shining holly and surrounded by a great feast, and yet it is not just that. It is something much more than the image from Dickens. It shows him and moves him with a wisdom far greater and a voice far deeper, resounding yet unheard. As if the very familiarity of it somehow mediates to him the utterly mysterious voice of God. He watches thus while the children scatter themselves on the red carpet surrounding the sparkling tree and its pile of festively wrapped gifts. Eager anticipation is in their eyes. In their hands, each has a Santa sack, and they are pulling out the contents for the second time to show each other. They are all in dressing gowns over pyjamas, hair all over the place.

Michael and Sarah, the elder two, who look about thirteen and eleven, respectively, don't always get on, David knows. But this is Christmas, and all enmities are forgotten. Emily, the youngest, at about eight, aligns with each of them at different times, but is unconcerned for such matters. She pulls out the small tub of magic gel and shows them, easing off the top and scooping it into her fingers with a terrible sucking sound which makes them all titter. It begins to run from her hand but then she slaps it and it goes solid. They laugh again in amazement. Michael gets out his chocolate Santa, unwraps the top and bites off its head with an exaggerated, violent crunch. Again merriment breaks out and Emily finds hers to do the same.

Sarah shows them the lighted Rudolph snow-globe in her sack. She switches it on and the reindeer begins to pirouette, stirring up the fake snow in stormy swirls, lit by colour-changing LEDs from beneath. Now Michael has the wooden puzzle out. He takes it from the plastic casing inside the cardboard box, saying, 'The secret with these is to get it out all in one piece so you can see how it goes together,' and while he is still speaking it falls into a dozen wooden chunks on his knees. They all roll on the floor in mirth at this great disaster.

Emily has a small, plastic train set in a box, consisting of a wind-up engine, two carriages, and ten pieces of plastic track so designed as to make a variety of layouts. She leans down and begins to assemble it, taking another bite at her chocolate Santa and growling at it like a lion. Sarah lays down right beside her to help. She wouldn't normally give the time of day to such a childish occupation, but this is Christmas, and it is sheer joy.

'I wonder what time Mum and Dad will appear,' Michael says.

Sarah and Emily stop working and grin at him. 'Then it must be time for you to make them a cup of tea!' they say, in the Christmas-honoured fashion. So he sets off to the kitchen to do so. Presents under the tree must await the fully gathered family.

He's back in ten minutes and says, 'Five minutes, they'll be down. They said put the telly on a Christmas music channel.'

He hardly needs to say it, and they do it. Ah, David reflects, Christmas traditions – even the simplest things. 'Fairytale of New York' fills the room.

Michael starts to flick through his Liverpool FC Christmas magazine, while Sarah and Emily have finished with the train layout for now and have put it back in the box to make space for the great and joyous explosion of paper and presents that is to come. They each have a see-through plastic Rudolph full of jelly beans, and one comes out of its rear end each time they push it down. It is a source of much merriment and pretend disgust. When Sarah gets an actual brown one, they are inconsolable with hilarity.

'What's all this, then?' Dad says, coming through the door, mug in hand, closely followed by Mum.

'Happy Christmas!' the children all cry, and leap at them, surrounding them both with hugs. Even Michael, who is not normally so forthcoming with his affection these days.

The time, David sees, is nearly half-past six.

'Well, now,' Mum says, 'let us finish these teas and make some more and then we'll find something more Christmassy to do. I'm sure I don't know what, though.'

'Open presents!' Sarah and Emily cry.

'Oh, yes, presents,' Dad replies. 'So, what did Santa bring you all this year?'

Out come the little, fun, cheap things, and all three of the children surround their dad with their gifts, Emily climbing up onto his knee, Sarah kneeling at his feet, Michael bending, while Mum goes off to set the kettle going again.

Fresh tea arrives. Michael has a mug as well, while Sarah and Emily have juice. Dad puts his on the small table beside him and pretends to fall asleep. He snores. Emily bounces on him. Sarah rubs his chin-growth the wrong way. Michael flicks drops of tea in his face.

'Oh, poor Daddy!' Mum says. 'Don't you know he's very old?'

'Oi!' he says. 'Only a year and a bit older than you, which makes me just right.'

'Yes, Daddy, you're just right,' Emily says, and plants a big wet kiss on his scratchy cheek.

'All right, then!' he announces. He takes a swig of tea. 'I think I'm ready for this. Who's handing out the presents this year?'

'You are!' they all chorus.

'Okey-dokey, then I will,' he says. He kneels beside the tree. 'Oh, there are so many! I don't know if I have the energy!' he complains. 'Maybe I am very old, after all.'

'Daddy, do it!' Emily cries.

He picks one up. 'Well, this one can't be ours to start with. It says "Emily". Does anyone know an Emily?'

'It's mine!' she says, taking it off him. She rips into the paper.

'Paper in a pile in the middle,' Mum says, 'for later checking for missed items. You know the drill.' She is sat on the settee while the children are all on the floor, leaving a space in the middle.

In her present, Emily finds a box with a blonde-haired head, almost full-size, and all kinds of make-up to apply to it. It isn't by any means an expensive gift, but she is utterly thrilled. 'Oh, thank you!' she says. 'Make-up Marcie! Oh wow!' and she starts trying to get into the top without ripping the cardboard.

'Leave it a minute and I'll help you with that,' Dad says, without being asked. She puts it down, and smiles up at him.

Sarah has carefully removed a real make-up set from a whole sheet of golden paper. She intends to keep the paper, so she rolls it up. Once again, the gift is surprisingly modest, and David wonders what year he's arrived in. Where are the mobile phones, tablets, game consoles?

'Ooh! Thank you,' she says, and rises to kiss her mum, then her dad. 'I'm gonna look *so* grown up!'

'Sure you are!' Michael comments, busily extricating a 'Make-your-robot electronics kit' from its box and expanded polystyrene without making a mess.

'Michael,' Mum says, quietly warning.

'Oh, look at this!' he says, not acknowledging the caution. 'It even senses its environment. It is so cool!'

'You're not disappointed about the phone, then?' Dad asks him.

'No, most of my mates lose them half the time anyway and spend all their money getting credit on them. Maybe for my birthday.'

'Such a wise head on such young shoulders,' his mum says, looking at him, full of pride. 'Just remember to be nice to your sister.'

'Which one?' he asks, with typical teenage cheek.

'It's Christmas!' Mum answers. 'Both of them!'

'Aww, both!' he answers, and receives his next present from Dad.

A large box appears with all three children's names on. They know who it's from. Dad opens the box and hands out the three individually wrapped presents inside. Opened, they become a simple board game, a letter-writing set, and a book of puzzles. Michael doesn't look much impressed until he realises he's being watched by his mum, and he brightens. 'These will be a challenge,' he says about the puzzles.

'And how many grandchildren does Nanny Newsome have?' Mum asks.

'Fifteen!' they all chime.

'And how much money does she have?'

'Not a lot!' they continue.

'So what is this?'

'Very kind of her!'

'And what will we do after Christmas?'

'Send her a thank-you letter!'

'Yes, we will,' says Mum. 'It is very kind of her, and it's quite a feat for her getting all these presents and sending them. She's a very kind lady.'

'And very old,' Michael says. 'Very kind and very old. Just like you, Mum.'

'Oi!' she says. 'I take it you want some delicious turkey dinner today?'

'Yes!' they all peal, like untuned bells.

'Can we help?' Sarah and Emily ask.

'Of course you can. You can get behind the turkey and help to push it out of the oven.'

'Aww, Mum!' they call. 'We want to chop carrots and cross-cut sprouts and make cranberry sauce and stuffing.'

'Good, thank you,' she says. 'You're kind too.'

The handing-out is slowing, the pile of paper now quite large. Dad and Mum have made small stacks beside them so as to attend to the children's presents first.

Dad picks up a parcel from Mum, and out slides a new wet razor. 'Aha!' he says. 'It's the one with the swivelly bit and more blades. Thank you, Jane!'

'It's my Christmas pleasure,' she answers, holding a bottle of eau de toilette and taking the cap off for a sniff. 'Ooh, smell this, girls,' she says. They get up and come to her, and she sprays a little onto their wrists.

'Posh!' Emily says.

'You'll smell like the Queen,' Sarah adds.

'Tweedy and musty?' Michael asks.

'Cheeky boy!' she says. 'I'll bet she smells fantastic. Every day.'

The general air of celebration and gladness is present even to David in his insubstantial and inconsequential form. He can't help but smile at them. They are so happy. Together. Genuinely, no-holds-barred happy. Not at all wishing to be back in their own room. Relaxed and at home in their shared life-space. Their shared life. It's odd.

And yet it's not odd at all.

Mum wades into the paper on her knees and begins to inspect it for lost items that mustn't be binned. Finding none, she folds it as neatly as possible for the recycling.

David looks around at the precious piles of goodies. All the presents are very modestly priced. This is not a rich family. Yet they are so happy with the gifts. And with each other. With, he supposes, the kindness behind it all. The loving-kindness, as he vaguely recalls the Bible said.

'Are we dressing for breakfast?' Dad asks.

'Do we ever?' Michael retorts.

'Not on this day, no,' Dad replies. 'So, is it pancakes and chocolate sauce and bananas and squirty cream?'

'Yay!' goes up. David sees how even Mum loosens the chains of her careful eating regime today.

'Can I flip one?' Emily asks.

'After last year?' Dad replies.

'Yes, but I'm a whole year older!'

'A *whole* year!' Michael prods at her.

'Of course you can,' Mum interjects. 'I haven't seen you flip one, my boy,' she says.

'Then I'll take that as a challenge!' he says.

'Better put some toast on as well, I think,' Dad observes as they all head out for the kitchen. There is some good-natured shoving and tickling as they move along the hallway.

David is staring at a laid dinner table in the dining room. In the centre is a small candle arrangement of balls and bells, holly and tinsel, stuck with a hot-glue gun around a holder for a tea light. The flame is alight, and is dancing a little in the warm air.

High above it, from the central room light, hang twirls and drapes of party-popper paper. They are also strewn where the poppers have been fired across the table-top. Each of five places has a place-mat and a glass-mat with a glass on it appropriate for whatever will be drunk. Knives, forks and spoons are laid, and there are mats in the centre of the table for gravy, sauces, condiments and, later, custard and cream. A small bottle of absinthe sits beside a lighter and a dessert spoon at the head of the table, where Father will sit. His wine glass is also there.

A large, shiny, golden and red cracker lies alongside each place.

The TV is on in the front room, and the Christmas *Top of the Pops* can be heard. Mum shouts from the kitchen, 'Lewis, my love, can you get them down?'

'OK,' comes back from somewhere.

They trundle into the room and take familiar seats. Sarah says to Emily, 'Crackle!' and they giggle conspiratorially. Something has set them off.

'Come and get this, Lew,' Mum says, and a moment later Dad appears with the turkey on the huge, old, chipped blue and white serving plate. He puts it in front of his place on the table, and all are agog at its brown and golden glistening skin. The smell promises crackly skin and succulent, butter-basted meat.

'Kids! Come and carry, please!' Mum calls, and they get up again and troop off, returning with a bowl of sprouts, another of carrots, another of stuffing, and sauce boats of gravy and cranberry sauce. Mum appears with five plates delicately balanced, each already supplied with goose-fat roasted potatoes. The smell grows more mouth-watering. David takes it in. Rich turkey skin, sprouts, stuffing, piquant cranberry.

Michael goes and fetches bottles and pours what's needed in each of the glasses. They all sit. The anticipation can be felt on David's skin, like an airborne static electricity.

Dad alone stands, a carving knife and fork in his hands. He slides one against the other.

'Mother?' he says.

'Yes,' she agrees, and all bow their heads. 'Lord, thank you for this special day, and for all the good things we have together, and everyone who's worked hard to provide us with all this food. And we pray a blessing on everyone who has so little. Amen.'

'Mum's annual prayer,' Michael says, and the girls titter.

'Which is one more than you,' she says back.

'Might be more honest to say none, then,' he says.

'Excuse me,' she says. 'Keep it to yourself.'

'May God bless us, each and every one,' Emily says, with that way she has sometimes of diffusing things with a charming simplicity.

They all agree, and Dad begins to carve. The knife slides across the browned skin and in, and a slice of crispy-topped, succulent white meat begins to pare away from the bird's breast. Steam rises from the incision. He uses the fork to lift it onto the first plate, being held by Sarah. She watches with barely contained desire as it falls on the hot plate, alongside the crispy, golden potatoes. Everyone goes, 'Mmm.'

'Let's get the vegetables started,' Mum says, and they begin to serve themselves with spoons already in place.

'Pigs!' she calls out in dismay.

'It's OK,' Dad says. 'Fetch them, we haven't even started.'

Mum dashes into the kitchen and returns with pigs-in-blankets on a serving plate. The porky smell is unbearably fabulous. She passes them to Michael, who takes three, considers for a second, and decides to not be greedy. He passes them on.

'We were all watching,' Sarah says.

They all rumble amusement.

The turkey is going well, the vegetables are on the plates, the gravy and stuffing and sauces are spooned, and everyone is sorted.

Dad holds up his cracker and waves it at Emily, next to him. 'Feeling strong?' he asks.

She grabs the end with both hands and yanks as hard as she may. With a satisfying 'snap' it separates and things come flying out. She picks them up as other snaps follow. Hats go on, and silly cracker novelties are examined. A wooden spinning top. A little book with tiny pen. A keyring measuring tape. The usual style of stuff. A swap or two is engineered, then jokes are read.

'"In which compartment will you find a snowman on a train?"' Mum asks, looking quite pleased with herself.

They all look blank. 'Frost Class!' she says, and they burst out laughing like it was Morecambe and Wise at their peak.

'OK, OK,' Michael says. 'What about this: "Why was the Christmas saint so cold?"'

'Because he was at the North Pole,' Dad suggests.

'No. Anyone else?'

'Because he was Frosty the Saint,' Emily tries.

'Hardly. Give up? "Because he was knicker-less"!'

That gets a good reaction as well, and David is very pleased.

They begin to eat. After a while of appreciative noises, Dad raises his glass and says, 'Merry Christmas, and to all the pops and grans and cousins.'

They all respond alike, with a chinking of glasses like it makes something good actually happen.

Much festive conversation accompanies the eating. The plates are cleared away, and Dad and Mum process in, bearing the pudding. It steams and gives off a spicy, sweet blessing.

It is placed on the table in front of Dad's seat. He sits. All eyes are on him. He unscrews the cap of the absinthe, takes the spoon and pours in a good few millilitres. He sparks the lighter and holds it underneath until the black liquid starts to trouble. Then he tips it slightly and a blue flame spreads across its surface. Immediately he empties it over the pudding, over which it immediately spreads and sends a brilliant white, blue, orange and yellow flame halfway to the ceiling. A cheer goes up. It blasts upwards for a few seconds, then settles to a low glow.

'Wow!'

'Cool! Did you see that?'

'Good job you didn't want those eyebrows, Dad.'

'That really is the only way to do it,' Mum, who is normally very cautious about flames and fires, agrees.

The treacly black, shiny pudding is spooned into bowls and passed round. Custard and cream are added. Silence descends as jaws are gummed together in a delicious darkness.

Finally, sounds of overstuffed satisfaction follow, and Mum says, 'Who's up for a tea or a coffee?'

They all are, in differing specifics, and the box of chocolate mints reserved for this moment is fetched. Dad extricates it from its shrink-wrap, with his usual comment. 'Tough stuff, till it loses its integrity. One tiny split, and it all falls apart.'

'We know,' Michael says.

'Maybe you above all need to know,' Dad sends back.

Cracker toys are toyed with as hot drinks are drunk and chocolate mints enjoyed.

Perhaps the most intriguing thing of all is that even as David watches it, displaced and disembodied, he knows that it is current, and real. He is watching *this* Christmas, happening a few days from now. It is, in the shade of the thing behind him,

Christmas Present. If he could but seek out the right house, he would find this very scene being lived.

'God bless you all,' she says, royally, and Mum claps as the National Anthem begins.

'Isn't she marvellous?' Mum says.

'She certainly is,' Dad agrees.

'Can I go now?' Michael asks, sullenly, like he's been chained for hours to an uncomfortable seat.

'Yes, son, I think I shall be asleep in fifteen minutes myself,' Dad says with a cheeky grin.

'I'm not going to *sleep*,' Michael objects.

'Of course not. How silly of me,' Dad admits.

Mum flashes him a small smile. She and he settle down against each other on the settee. Michael looks down at them as he walks by and is about to say, 'Get a room,' but Mum says sternly, 'Don't say it, Michael. Ham, cheese, salad, crackers and cakes at six.'

Emily and Sarah put on the Christmas afternoon Disney cartoon film. They also settle down, side by side on the beanbag. They are leaning right against each other, in a flop that could best be described as sisterly.

Mum and Dad both seem to last about the same length of time before sinking into a soft slumber. Emily takes a bite of her chocolate Santa.

'Pig!' Sarah says.

She grunts, and they both laugh.

After an hour, Dad awakens and goes into the kitchen to make a pot of tea. It's a very relaxed part of the day, with the evening still to come, and a good DVD they're going to watch all together (even Michael has agreed to participate) about the funny creatures that make up a young girl's mind. Before that they'll play charades. Then after Emily goes to bed, Sarah will stay up for some, at least, of the latest Bond film. Chocolate liqueurs will be eaten, and nuts cracked, and wine drunk, and

Dad and Mum will see their bed about midnight, with no particular reason to be up on the morrow.

But oh! David is in the bedroom as they lie in bed. Mum is cuddled up behind Dad, and he says, 'It was really good, just like usual.'

'Yes, it was,' she says, sleepily.

'I was worried it wouldn't be.'

'Don't,' she says.

'Yes, but I still feel so guilty.'

She strokes the back of his neck with her free hand. 'It doesn't help that you can't let it go.'

'But it was so wrong.' Tears are in his eyes. A little shudder goes through him, and she gives a moan of tenderest sympathy.

'Listen, my love. I know she seduced you. I know you didn't deliberately go down that path, or betray me or the kids. I know you're a good man and you're really sorry for what happened, so briefly. You can't undo it, but you have to move on from it, whether you feel worthy or not. It does us no good. I don't think about it. I don't hold it against you. I will never tell anyone. Because I love you. Frail as you are. We all are.'

'I don't deserve you.'

'Nor I you,' she answers.

'I'm so glad it was a happy Christmas.'

'So am I,' she answers, squeezing him.

David smiles as he sees it all, receding from him, or he from it. The traditions. The simplicity. The bright, simple, cheap decorations. The air alive with unforced, festive fun. The fact that it actually hasn't cost them a huge amount of money, which they clearly don't have. The kindness. The simple kindness. The heartfelt kindness of belonging.

The great being behind him, so alive, without word or signal, makes him to know that the meaning he has recognised in this Christmas Present is the point. The whole point. And that he will be tested on it. Not in knowledge. But in action. And very soon.

He takes a last blessing by breathing it in, inside himself, as if it is in fact part of the something else that calls to him.

He hopes it is.

CHAPTER THIRTEEN

No knocking. No kindly ringing of his bell. David lay awake in bed, both reviewing the revelations of the night and evaluating the lack of Angela. It was gone nine. Nearer half-past. He could hear a wind. What day was it? Tuesday. December the 22nd.

Is the dream more real than the day?

Was the revelation tailored to the loss of Angela, and the reason for it? Kindness. In its simple goodness, it really must be as essential as she said. And as she clearly felt, very keenly. And as her friends also felt, judging by what he'd seen of them.

And as beautiful. Not that she actually said that. It contained an amazing freedom of forgiveness. A grace. A kindly grace, not a forced or grudging mercy.

Was kindness, then, the true nature of the Divine? What they usually called 'love'? Maybe in this culture, with the one word for 'love' rather than the many words of the Greeks, and this culture so confused about what love was and how to have it and show it, maybe 'kindness' really was a better word, a better image, for the heart of the Divine. If such a Being existed. And it was He Who Called.

He Who Calls. Is Kindness. That's either a great theological insight or a load of words that mean nothing. Such is theology!

He shifted himself and got out of bed. It was cold. It felt like the temperature outside had dropped overnight, precipitately. He moved his curtain aside and looked out on the scene. It appeared much like yesterday, until he stared closer. The snow had frozen. What was a benign dusting of friendly powder had become a rock-hard, icy wasteland. A child was being picked up by a parent the other side of the road, having slipped while

151

sliding, and discovering that it was no longer a safety blanket, but a slicing, jagged, concrete slab.

He let the curtain fall back. The call of his bed reached his ears. He wasn't sure he wanted to be up at all today.

Was it too late to take her some croissants? Possibly not. But where did she live? Strange, she knew where he lived, but he didn't know her address. And why not? Because he'd never thought to ask her. Because every bone in his body was isolated selfishness, that was why. He should be called Ebenezer. She knew all sorts of things about him, but he knew practically nothing about her, because she was too kind to load information on him if he wasn't interested enough to ask. All their conversation had been about him. 'Me, me me.'

Guilt and shame overcame him as he pulled up his trousers. Then a plan hatched, fully formed. He grabbed his phone and disconnected it from its overnight charge. He started a text to her.

'I am so sorry. I had a strange dream last night – more like a vision – all about kindness. I think I get it. Can I come and bring you croissants? David.' He looked it over, then sent it. Nervously, like a teenager.

He put the phone in his pocket and went down the stairs into the kitchen to start on tea. He switched the radio on, and Radio 4 greeted him with items of world significance. As the tea brewed he put his nose out of the front door. Goodness, it was cold! The wind cut him. He put a slippered foot onto the snow. It was as it seemed – a frosty rock of unforgiving hardness. The opposite of kindness. More like what he was. Or had been.

He shivered as he shut the door and headed back to the kitchen.

Brrd. Brrd.

He opened the phone and eagerly read: 'I will meet you in the bakery in twenty minutes, if that's OK. Angela X.'

'Thank you. See you then. I'm buying,' he texted back.

'You bet you are! ;-)'

Ha. He poured himself a mug of Eeyore tea and took it into the front room. He was so happy. She'd sent him a wink. And an X. All was not lost. Kindness overcomes. He'd better get it right this time. He started to think again about the dream-vision. And kindness.

A horrible thought struck him in the guts. Maybe she had no actual home here. Angels don't, because they don't really belong here, she'd said. Once their mission is finished, they go back to heaven. In fact, even if she was living in a house, it might turn out in the end not to have been hers at all. Not just his boorish insensitivity, perhaps. She kept him, somehow, from asking those questions. Mind manipulation. What else do you expect from a creature who is, essentially, an alien?

Be very careful.

He got as far as his front gate and his wellington boot slipped alarmingly from under him. An automatic reaction enabled him to reach out for the gatepost, which steadied him, but the front fence wobbled, which didn't please him at all. Better be cautious.

Left, and up the slight incline. Children were still sliding by, careless, as children will be, of their skin, teeth and bones.

They were, at least, well wrapped-up, with scarves and coats and gloves and boots and bobble-hats. But Mrs James, at her front gate holding Harpie, the yapping Boston Terrier, with the disapproving mouth and suspicious eyes, was in just a dress and jumper and slippers. The air had ice in it and pressed cold knives through any gap. She must have been frozen. He eyed her without seeming to as he approached. She didn't move. The dog didn't move, either. How long had she been standing there? He got close enough to see her colour. Face, ashen; lips, cyanosed. She looked catatonic.

He was about to pass on by as usual, when some half-remembered motive nudged him. Kindness. It will be tested. Soon.

Was this it?

'Mrs James?' he said, rather uncertainly, expecting a spat rebuke. No reply. Not a twitch.

'Hello, Mrs James?' he said, arriving right at her gate. Nothing. Not even her eyes moved.

Reluctantly, he opened the gate and walked in. If she was aware in the slightest, that would fire her up. No.

'In for a penny,' he thought. He reached out and touched her shoulder. There was a very slight movement. The dog looked dead. Had it been outside for a while to do its business as it normally did in her front garden, and she came out and found it thus, picked it up, started to talk to it and was overcome by a bitter wind herself?

He peered closer into her eyes, which were only open a slit, and as if the force of his questing gaze was physical, she began to tip over backwards. He made a grab for her, managed to catch both arms, and held her upper body a couple of feet from the ground as her legs completely gave way. Harpie fell to the ground with a heavy 'plop'.

Was she dead? A wave of something very serious and nasty washed through him. Now he'd done it. Now he was committed. The test indeed, he suspected. He had to get her back inside. He dragged her by the arms, pulling on his back, in through the front door, which was a little ajar, up her short hallway and right, into her lounge. He intended to take her to the settee along the wall behind the door but she was extremely floppy and ended up half-on and half-off it and so she slid in an undainty fashion onto the floor. Her eyes closed. He looked at her crooked, cyan lips surrounded by ancient bristles and really didn't want to do CPR on her. How far did the test of kindness go?

What first? Emergency services? Warmth? Heart compressions? His mind became a blur of fear of doing the wrong thing. Of becoming a poster-boy for the importance of learning First Aid.

Warmth. He dragged an old throw off the back of the settee and put it over her. He turned up the gas fire to full. He decided to assume she was still alive and sit her up, which seemed good. So he rearranged her and propped her back against the settee.

'Mrs James?' he said, right into her flaccid face.

Was that a tiny mumble?

'Mrs James?'

To slap or not to slap? Well, if he had smelling salts he'd use them, so ... no, wait, let's start with a hand. He pulled one hand out from under the throw and pinched the skin on the back, hard.

'Ah!' she said.

He rubbed it better. Still her eyes stayed closed. She was still in danger.

He held her wrist and tried to get a pulse. Thin and thready was the phrase that came back to him, and it certainly was. But present. And colour was returning to her face, just a little.

Tea! The Universal Elixir! The Universal Fixir! He said, 'I'm going to get you a cup of tea. With sugar. Do you take sugar?'

No response. Sugar was good in these circumstances for reviving purposes. Reluctantly, he left her, and went into her kitchen. Kettle, on. Teapot, two spoons of the loose tea leaves he found in her caddy. He should have guessed she'd have proper tea. Milk from the fridge. No fridge. From the larder, in a bowl of water. Sugar? There was a bowl in a cupboard over the kettle area; it held a spoon and looked recently used.

He poured hot water over the tea leaves and left the top open for a bit of cooling. Then he went back into the front room. Oh, no! She'd slumped down and looked much worse.

He knelt, and eased her back up into a sitting position. Spittle was coming out of her mouth. No, no! Had she died while he'd abandoned her to make tea? Another black mark in the local paper's report.

He felt for that pulse again. Nothing. He moved his thumb. Nothing. Desperation was beading his brow, but then he found it. A single pulse. Then nothing. Then another.

Why hadn't he phoned for an ambulance? Wasn't that the first thing you were supposed to do? Not make tea!

He felt for his phone, pressed 999 and was greeted with, 'Which emergency service do you require, police, fire or ambulance?'

'Ambulance.'

'Please hold.'

'County Ambulance Service. What is your emergency?'

'An elderly neighbour has collapsed in the cold, outside, and I've brought her inside but I can't find much pulse.'

'What is the address?'

He gave it.

'Please stay with the person, and stay on the phone with me, an ambulance is on its way. Now, sir, just be calm. What is your name?'

'David Sourbook. From number 27.'

'You found a pulse?'

'Yes, in her wrist.'

'Very good. Can you check that again for me? Just put your thumb lightly on the thumb-side of the inner wrist, just below the big thumb muscle. Don't press hard, just rest your finger there and be patient. Can you feel a pulse?'

'No.'

'Wait, move your thumb a little, keep feeling for it.'

'Yes! One pulse.'

'All right, very good. Now tell me when you feel another one.'

'Now!'

'Good. She's alive, so she must also be breathing. Is there anything obscuring her airway?'

'No. I have her sitting up against her settee.'

'Well done. Can you open her mouth and have a look in there for me?'

'Ok.'

He didn't want to, but hey, so he put the phone down on the settee seat. He pulled down her lower lip but all he got was dentures. So he tried the upper lip but got more of the same. In fact they'd come loose from her gums. He tried to pull them out, but they were all slimy with spit and wouldn't move.

'I can't see because of her dentures.'

'OK, that's fine. Can you wiggle those out of her mouth?'

'I tried.'

'Try again. Get a good hold on them. Ignore the spit. Little old ladies don't usually carry nasty diseases.'

'Like TB and pneumonia,' he said, sourly.

'Just give it a try for me, please, sir.'

'Yugh,' he thought, but tried again.

Angela! How long had he been seeing to Mrs James? He was certainly late already. He imagined her looking at her watch and deciding he really was not worth the effort.

Pushing the thought back, he wiped his fingers on her dress and made a second grab for the teeth. They didn't move. So he forced his hand in between them and pushed her jaws open. The teeth came loose and he pulled them out, dropping them on the floor. He wiped his hand fastidiously on the pale blue dress.

'OK, top teeth out,' he said.

'Good. Now, is there anything obstructing her breathing?'

He looked inside. 'No.'

'Good. The ambulance will only be minutes from you now. How's her pulse?'

'Thready but steady.'

'Oh, very good. Just stay there with her. What's her name?'

'Mrs James.'

'OK. Is anyone else injured?'

'Only her dog. I think it's dead. They were standing outside in the cold for too long.'

'Well, that's a problem we can't fix. Do you hear the ambulance yet?'

'No.'

'OK. Is it nice and warm in the room where you are?'

'Yes, I turned the fire up and put a throw over her.'

'Very good. You're a neighbour, are you?'

'Yes, from three doors up. Or down.'

He heard the distant wailing of the ambulance.

'I can hear the ambulance.'

'That's good. Is there anyone who can stand outside and signal them in?'

'No, I'm all alone here. There are children playing outside on the ice. The road is very icy. Dangerous.'

'OK. Just wait. Is the front door open?'

He had to think. 'Yes. Do you want me to go outside?'

'No, stay with Mrs James. They will find you.'

Sure enough, within two minutes the siren peaked and died, he heard doors opening, and voices. A male and female ambulance crew came into the room with a bag and a stretcher.

'Hello, sir,' the man said. 'Please step aside. That's lovely. Are you or is anyone else hurt or injured at all?'

'No, it's just her. And the dog.'

The woman knelt down beside Mrs James and said, 'Mrs James? Can you hear me?'

'Hmm?' came back.

'Great, she wouldn't speak to me,' David thought.

'Mrs James we are paramedics and have come to help you. We're going to check you're OK, then we're going to take you to hospital. Is that all right?'

'Mmm.'

'Can you open your eyes, please?'

The eyelids fluttered.

'OK, try again.'

Both eyes opened, revealing irises of the palest grey-blue.

'You're not my Lilian!' she said.

'No, Mrs James, we're an ambulance crew.'

'Where's Harpie?'

'Is that your dog?'

'Yes, Harpie.'

'I'm afraid he got very cold. I'm not sure where he is.'

'Can we bring him with us to the vet's?'

The woman cast a wry glance at the man, who smiled.

He said, 'We're not going to the vet's, Mrs James. We're going to take you to the hospital. You're not very well. You got much too cold outside.'

'Thank you, you're very kind,' she said.

David watched as they checked her vital signs and started to get her wrapped and bundled for transportation.

The woman said, 'Now, we're going to lie you on a stretcher, and make sure you're all wrapped up warm, and take you to the hospital just to get you checked out. Is that all right?'

'I suppose so. I don't feel too well, actually. Perhaps I shouldn't go out.'

'We are going to look after you. Mr Sourbook, is it?'

'Hmm? Yes, that's me,' David said, taken by surprise.

'We need you to leave the property so we can make sure it's secure when we go. Thank you so much for looking after her and calling this in. And happy Christmas.'

'Oh, and to you. Happy Christmas,' he said.

He got up, looked around, picked up his phone from the settee and left.

Angela! Blast it! What time was it? Oh, goodness, he was already half an hour late. He opened his phone to call her. As he did so, the thought struck him, I had to choose between kindness to an elderly neighbour or croissants with Angela. I chose right. I bet she even knows this. I bet she set the test. Not that she'd make Mrs James nearly die. Or even Harpie the haughty terrier.

She had powers beyond those of a mere human being.

He rang her and she answered immediately.

'I am so sorry,' he said. 'I got held up. An elderly neighbour nearly died and I had to look after her till the ambulance came.'

'Really?'

'Yes. I'll tell you all about it. Are you still there?'

'I am. And the fact that I've waited half an hour for you tells you something about my intentions towards you.'

'Right.' What did that mean? 'I'll be there in ten minutes. Thank you so much for waiting. Bye.'

'Bye.'

He showed her his torn trousers and bloodied knee. They were sitting on the high stools at the long, raised counter looking out of the window at the front of the shop, over scenes of frozen peril.

'That's what comes of hurrying on treacherous ice,' Angela said, not seeming anything like as warm and sympathetic as she had been. 'And maybe wellies are not the best footwear for it.'

'These are an expensive pair, not some cheap old rubbish. They have decent treads.' He looked down. 'Anyway, you're wearing them.'

'So I am,' she agreed, looking down at her bright green pair.

'And I was hurrying for you.'

'Because you were late for me.'

'Because I helped someone.'

'So you say.'

He took another bite of his warm, buttery croissant and chewed it with pleasure tainted by a profound uncertainty.

'Don't you believe me? I was being *kind* to someone.'

'Convince me.'

He drank coffee.

'I'm not sure what that looks like. All I can do is tell you what happened.'

'Do that then,' she said. She seemed very distant. He didn't like it at all.

'OK, well, first of all, the dream. It wasn't a regular dream. It was more, like, real. Like I was really there, even though a disembodied observer, this Christmas, here in town. I reckon this family actually exist and will have this exact Christmas Day in three days' time. So, as I watched, they were a completely ordinary family, getting up and opening their presents and having Christmas dinner and watching the Queen and so on, right through the day. They didn't have much money. They had stresses in their relationships, especially the three kids. But what came through was the sheer kindness with which they were treating each other. And in the very end it turned out that the dad had cheated with some other woman, this year, I got the impression, and the mum was so nice about it – so forgiving and concerned for *him*. And I recognised this brilliant, gentle, loving-kindness between them, particularly stirred up by Christmas, but not only. I guess it was like seeing the Cratchits in their Christmas Present. It was there all the time, ready, under the surface. And it just made me realise – maybe kindness is the very definition of the love of God. Maybe it's really that important, and my lack of understanding that was serious, and that was why you reacted like you did. Who wants someone without a shred of kindness in them?'

He could see her face softening, and it was lovely. Then she became serious again and said, 'I hope you don't think talking about God will just win me over. Go on.'

'Well, like that film I told you about, and like the other dream, I was sort of being shown it, by this huge thing behind me, and it said but without words that I'd be tested, soon.'

'And that was the Ghost of Christmas Present?' she said, pushing him.

'Well, no, obviously, but you said God can try to get your attention in any number of strange ways. The principle is the same, surely.'

'I suppose so.'

'OK, so, I came out of my house to come and meet you, and Mrs James three doors up was just standing in her front garden holding Harpie – the dog – and I realised she looked frozen stiff. So I asked her if she was OK, and she didn't even flicker, and when I touched her she just collapsed. I caught her, dragged her inside, made her tea, took her pulse, phoned for an ambulance and stayed there till it came. And warmed her up. And took out her dentures. It was all very discomforting. The dog's dead, but I reckon she'll pull through.'

She was admiring him now. She was trying to hide it but he'd just become her hero. Whether holy or not was yet to be decided. Or decoded.

He waited for her to respond. 'So, you kept me waiting for half an hour to look after this old woman?'

Dismayed, he said, 'Yes. Of course. She would have died. Definitely. What could I do?'

'You could have called me.'

'I was overwhelmed. Focused on the task. I had to keep her alive.'

As he talked he was mostly looking out of the big windows at the people passing by. Every so often a car slid and slewed across the road, threatening much mayhem. So far nobody had been mown down. One or two had slipped on the ice. And as he watched, a young woman, maybe thirty, came by with two heavy shopping bags and her feet went right out from under her and she hit the ground with a great and heavy thump. David saw her face – shock and instant pain.

He jumped off his stool and went for the door. He heard Angela saying, 'Did you come for a coffee with me or not?'

Ignoring that, he was out of the door and kneeling beside the woman. He prevented some tins and fruits from rolling away while he said, 'Are you OK?'

'I think I've hurt my back.'

'I'm not surprised. Lie still. You might need an ambulance.'

'Ooh,' she said in pain. 'My husband is just there. He's coming.'

The man rushed up and knelt beside them. He took her gloveless hand and said, 'I told you this was a silly idea. Have you hurt your back?'

'Yes. Sorry.'

'OK, just stay there a minute.'

David was taking off his coat to lay over her but the husband said, 'That's OK. I've got this. Very kind of you to come and help.'

'Anyone would do it,' David said, wondering where that had come from.

'Do you see anyone else doing it?' the man said. Clearly he was a rather hard-faced sort. Ex-military or something. 'Look,' the man continued, 'I've got this. Thanks very much, it's very kind, but you can go on your way now.'

'I was just in the bakery,' he indicated behind him.

'OK. Thanks. Very much. Bye now.'

David took the woman's hand and said, 'I hope you'll be OK.'

'Thank you,' she said, with a pained but very sweet smile right at him.

David stood and went back into the bakery. He climbed onto his stool and looked at Angela. She was beaming at him. 'One thing I know now,' she said, taking his hand. 'You're not doing any of this just to impress me.'

'No,' he said.

'Kindness has to *be* kind because it *is* kind. Let me tell you something interesting. The Greek that the New Testament was written in uses the word *Christos* for Christ, and the word *chrestos* for kind. That happy circumstance wasn't lost on the early Christians and writers of the New Testament. To be Christ is to be kind.'

He smiled at her.

She added, 'But don't let any of that alter the fact that you're in trouble for what you said to me, which isn't overcome by a few wise words from you. It goes a lot deeper than me simply forgiving you, which I do. It's about who you are.'

He looked at her for a few seconds, and said, 'I think I love you.'

As soon as he said it he knew he was in trouble.

CHAPTER FOURTEEN

'If I upset you enough you'll ask me to marry you.'

'What?' David said. They were walking down towards his house, very carefully over treacherous surfaces. Not holding hands.

'You have a very bad habit there. If things get emotionally confusing, you opt to make it right by committing to the next step, rather than acknowledging the problem and resolving that.'

'You've lost me,' he complained.

'You'd better hope not,' she replied, cannily. 'So, a young couple find their initial intimacy has waned, and they want it back, so they say, "Let's get engaged", thinking that will relight the spark. But you should get engaged when things are well, not weak. You don't use engagement to try to put right a relationship that's going wrong. That's madness. And that's what you did back there, telling me you love me.'

'I said I *think* I do.'

'It was the same thing. Recognise it, and don't ever do it again. It's a very dangerous trait.'

'Good grief, you can be hard-faced.'

'Perhaps you're not the only one who's overprotective of their feelings.'

'Wow! Is that an admission of emotional vulnerability?'

'No, it's a declaration of love for pavlova, Dr Freud.'

'"Professor", please. I earned it, so you should use it.'

'*Ja, sicher,*' she said.

She slid off her glove and took his hand, slid his off as well, and held his hand between them as they walked.

'I do know this, though, in your defence.'

'I have a defence?'

'*Ja, sicher.* I'm being very hard to read and giving you very contradictory messages. And I can't help it. You seem to bring it out in me.'

'Well, that sounds more hopeful. But then, asking for a simple explanation of what we are together and where that's heading isn't going to fly?'

'*Nein.* But on the other hand, there's nothing to stop you from telling me how it seems to you.'

'As long as that doesn't just earn me a rebuke for my bad habits and a stern warning never to do it again.'

She laughed and swung their hands between them like a little girl. 'At least our very demure and restrained behaviour together means no lasting damage is likely to be done. No commitments rushed. No feelings unnecessarily confused.'

'I'm so glad!'

'I thought you would be!' she said, swinging and smiling. He wondered how much of this was just 'happy' and how much was joyous affection for him.

'So, what would happen if I gave you a real kiss?' he asked her.

'Depends when, where, why and how.'

'Oh.'

'Well, of course it does! Anyway, you're just terrified, so it's hardly likely to happen.'

'That's Mrs James' house. Oh, no! Harpie!'

He stopped in horror. The dog was still lying in the front garden, on its side, looking a bit flat.

'Oh my goodness! She can't see it that way! She'll be so upset!' he added.

'You can't bury it. And the house will be locked up.'

'I know. This is terrible. I may have to take it home and leave her a note.'

'Oh, nice!' she said.

'I know. But if I bundle it up nicely in some cloth, leave it in the shed so foxes can't get at it, that should do. Surely.'

'Sounds about as much as you can do.'

'OK, well, that's what I'll do. I'll get an old jumper or something, and come back up. I'll do it now, just in case. And leave a note. Maybe later. I suppose nobody saw it lying there.'

'More likely nobody cared very much,' she said.

'Yeah. Shame for her. She loved that dog.'

'You noticed that?'

'Always seemed that way, I suppose. She was always holding it. Come on.'

As they stepped inside his hallway she said, 'You realise that this, too, is being really kind.'

'I know. I don't know what's come over me. I'll get a gardening jumper from upstairs. You put the kettle on.'

'Yes, sir, I will,' she answered, and set off.

David's gardening clothes were at the bottom of his wardrobe, piled up together. He pulled them out onto the floor and selected an old, red, jumper with holes in but not too much paint on. He realised he wanted to show a bit of respect for the dog, for Mrs James' sake. The rest he piled back in, and took the jumper downstairs.

Angela was waiting for him in the hallway, and said, 'I'll come with you.'

He looked at her quizzically. 'You're not going to say prayers over it or something, are you?'

She hit his arm, playfully. 'No. I just don't think you should have to collect a slightly pancaked dead dog on your own. It might leak or anything. It's for company and support.'

'You're being kind,' he said.

'And so are you, my love, so are you.'

She linked arms with him and they set off out of the door, without coats or gloves. When they got to Mrs James' garden they went and stood by the dog, either side of its deflated body, rather like a fat, dog-shaped, brown rug, as if they were actually about to hold some kind of ceremony.

'Do you know elephants, orangutans and even birds mourn their dead?' she said.

'Do you know human beings are so predisposed to meaning, pattern and significance that they read their own emotional and intentional responses into animals?' he replied. He bent down and laid the jumper out next to the carcass. He took hold of all four paws and rolled Harpie onto the jumper, then folded it over and around him. He used the arms to tie round and make a sort of carrying handle.

'Good job,' she said.

He lifted it and Harpie slid out slowly but unceremoniously onto the icy snow.

He was abashed. 'Ah,' he said. 'Not so good. Try again.'

This time she helped him, and they put Harpie inside the jumper and tied it up. That was better, and they took an end each to carry it back to the house.

'Good job I came,' she said.

They manoeuvred it down the lane, up the path, through the house, and into David's back garden. At the bottom of the path he opened the shed door, and they carried Harpie inside and laid him on top of a workbench. They stepped back and looked.

Angela said, 'I'll just say a prayer to send him to dog heaven.'

He turned his head and stared at her. Was she mad?

'Why not?' she said.

'There are no words,' he began, then she let out a burst of inappropriate mirth.

'Excuse me!' David said. 'This is a solemn moment. We're dealing with the dead here.'

'I'm sure he won't mind,' she said. 'Just make sure you don't smile over your next ham sandwich. Meat is murder.'

'No, no, no,' he said, a little irritated. 'This is Mrs James' precious dead dog, Harpie. She's going to be devastated. She might even want him cremated or buried in a cemetery. She might even want words and prayers said over him. She will need to know he was handled with respect.'

'So, you don't want *me* to say prayers over the dead dog, but you want it to be treated with respect in case *she* does. Is that not a little – contradictory?'

'Not from where I'm standing, no, but neither am I willing to get into a fight over it. Maybe we can discuss it later. For now, we've – er, not "laid him to rest" – "left him to sleep" in as decent a manner as possible, for her sake. There.'

'Good enough,' she agreed. 'Must be time for a coffee.'

They exited the shed and as they walked back up the garden path he said, 'Please tell me you haven't already got my day planned.'

'How could I?' she said, entering the house ahead of him. 'I didn't know we'd be back together so soon. Or at all, truth be told. I was very angry with you, and deeply disappointed. And, being honest, I'm not yet sure how much of that is really fixed.'

'You didn't know?'

'No. What do you mean?'

'Sometimes I get the impression you know things before they even happen. Like you allowed Mrs James to freeze and you allowed the nice lady to slip outside the bakery just to test me.'

'Allowed?' she queried.

'Yes, I hesitate to say you would cause such a thing.'

'Well, that's interesting, because that's how we get round saying God causes all the bad things that happen, while maintaining His power and authority. He allows. So you're assigning to me a God-like power. Are you sure you want to do that?'

He switched the kettle on to reboil. 'Don't angels appear with God-like power? Representing Him? Bringing a whiff of the numinous? The unnameable stirring behind the curtain?'

'Ooh, chilly!' she said. 'The numinous. So, I'm an actual angel, am I?'

'I don't know the rules. I imagine you're allowed to deny it.' He reached for some mugs.

'I doubt that! "Angel" means messenger. The messenger straight from Almighty God. How could such a one tell a lie?'

'Like I said, I don't know the rules.'

'So you should ask me outright,' she said, sitting down at the kitchen table.

'Are you an angel?'

'I believe I am some sort of messenger from God to you.'

'Aren't all Christians supposed to be messengers from God to people?'

'Yes, they are. We are. To tell them about Jesus. But that doesn't prohibit some people being sent to a person in a more specific sense. Maybe I'm that. Maybe sometimes an angel is straight from heaven, maybe sometimes an angel is a human being planted in your path for a specific purpose. Maybe sometimes they don't even know it themselves.'

'So much for asking you outright,' he said, sourly. 'In fact, you suggested an angel can't deny the truth because they come direct from God, and then you tell me there are types of angels that don't come direct from God, which would suggest what I said was true – some angels can deny that they are angels. That sounds like evasion, special pleading and disinformation to me.'

'Maybe I'm wrong, then, and I'm not any sort of angel. But I do feel God put me next to you for a purpose. Though His ways are incredibly inscrutable and layered in mystery and "otherness".'

'But He doesn't lie.'

'He cannot lie.'

'I thought He can do anything,' David said, feeling he'd got her.

'Anything that is consistent with His nature and His perfect will. Which lying isn't.'

He brought two coffees to the table and sat down.

'So there are things God cannot do.'

'Yes. He cannot be untrue to Himself. Though in fact He chooses not to be untrue to Himself. His being totally self-consistent is *both* His nature *and* His will. If His nature and His will became divergent, then that would be non-self-consistent, wouldn't it?'

David sipped his hot coffee. 'You've had this conversation before.'

'Many times.'

169

'It's important to you.'

'Yes, it is.'

'You feel the need to defend God.'

'No. Not at all. I feel the need to help people to see the truth about God.'

'Why?'

'Because He made us all for Himself and we are lost without Him.'

'You have an answer for everything.'

'I don't. But I do try to.'

'Isn't that arrogant?'

'Not if its intention is to be helpful, and not just to win arguments. Or seem superior. Or bash non-believers, like some religious fanatics seem to want to.'

'Am I a non-believer?'

'Are you? You tell me, sweetie.' She took his hand on the table. 'As far as I'm concerned, this isn't intended to be confrontational. You're asking me questions and I'm trying to answer them as honestly and helpfully as I can.'

'And this,' he shook their clasped hands on the table, 'isn't some sort of manipulation?'

She withdrew her hand. 'Can you walk and talk at the same time?'

'Yes. Why?'

'Can you start a relationship and discuss about God without the one making the other impossible?'

'But the one can confuse the other. So, tell me, if *you* had to choose, Angela, between loving me, and converting me, which would it be?'

She went quiet, and looked down at her coffee.

When she didn't speak for a while, he said, 'Perhaps we should take this into the front room. Sit in comfortable chairs. Less confrontational.'

She looked up. 'Oh, I'm to be allowed into the actual home. The living room.'

He took that as a rebuke. As it surely was. But he was unsure of the degree of seriousness.

As soon as she walked in she said, 'This is nice!' and she went and touched the tree. He switched its lights on.

'Very festive!' she added, and sat down on the settee. David sat in his armchair.

'The captain's chair,' she said, 'from which all is directed and ruled.'

He sipped his coffee, and looked at her. After a few seconds she realised he was staring at her and said, 'Yes?'

He was unsure about whether to press her for an answer to his question, which had so silenced her. Did he really need it? Was it really fair? What would she answer? Would an answer actually help at all?

Oh well. 'You didn't answer my question.'

'Because I'm puzzled by it. I think it paints a false picture. Can't the liking of friendship grow quite naturally into both feelings of love and the desire to see a person accept the faith they were born for? Why must they be at odds? Why must I choose? And when did I ever claim to love you, particularly in the sense that seems implied by your paradox?'

'For a woman, you seem very analytical.'

'You're analytical,' she said. 'And that's a good thing. You're intelligent, imaginative, well-read, and creative. Though I'm beginning to suspect a tendency to react to closeness by saying something that distances you from me again. And is it possible that you're suggesting that as a woman I should be quiet, submissive and essentially ignorant?'

He was insulted. 'Good grief, no! I'm just referencing the fact that women tend to be more emotionally wired than men, who tend to be more analytically wired, yet you seem to respond to me in a very analytical way, which causes us to strike sparks off each other. Somewhat.'

'So the sparks are my fault?'

'I wasn't suggesting a fault.'

'It felt like a fault.'

171

'It felt like a fault,' he repeated, savouring the assonance.

'That emotional enough for you?'

'And poetic, to boot. I liked that.'

'I did something right,' she said, with a sly look at him.

'I think I'm actually having a bit of a go at you,' he admitted, 'because at first it seemed like you were constantly judging me and finding fault, and I just wasn't going to be continually in that position. Truth be told.'

'Ah!' she said. 'Now, that makes sense. That says a lot. I rode you, like I do, and judged you for not being a good horse, and now you're trying to unseat me because you're not going to be a nice, tame horse that's been broken in. You won't be ridden, and quite right, too. I'm sorry I did that.'

Now David felt safer, and quite warm towards her, and as if they were getting somewhere. And a little sorry for the way he'd upset her, again. 'Can I come over and sit next to you?' he asked.

'It's your settee!' she said.

'I'd prefer something more affirmative than that.'

'Sorry, yes, please join me on the settee.'

He moved over. There was room for them to angle towards each other without actually touching.

'This is nice,' she said.

'This is nice,' he said, at the exact same moment. They laughed.

'It feels like we're navigating and negotiating our way through our differences,' David said.

'We're both too old for all this,' she agreed. 'We're hardly love-struck teenagers any more.'

She smiled at him, and it was a lovely, warm, heart-to-heart and eye-to-eye, attractive, engaging, inviting smile. It deserved a kiss. A proper kiss. He smiled back.

She reached out and took his hand, and held it between both of hers. 'Oh, my goodness,' he said, 'I really want to kiss you.'

He was agitated with anticipation. She looked so lovely and he so wanted to touch her and feel her lips and her face.

'Sorry, David, not going to happen,' she said, gently but firmly. 'I really am very fond of you but I've only known you four days and I have no idea where kissing you might lead to, and I think we have some more work to do and some more "getting to know you" before that's going to happen. Sorry.'

He was so disappointed. 'Then why are you holding my hand?'

'Because *that* seemed appropriate. Fond and friendly but not committed. The kind of kiss you're talking about commits a person. And people have very different assumptions about what goes with it. Look at the films! With even that first kiss goes hungrily undressing each other and having gaudy sex. Fraught, it is, with hidden agendas and assumptions, connections and commitments. Can't you just be happy that we're making some progress today?'

'Well,' he said, 'let the record show, I wanted to kiss you. I want to kiss you. There.'

'And let the record also show, I saved us both by deferring the said request.'

He said nothing. He felt frustrated, hurt and embarrassed.

'Can we just be friends?' she asked. 'Let's go for a walk.'

'In this?'

'Over the fields it'll be safe. The snow will still be crunchy rather than compacted like icy concrete. Come on, it'll do us both good.'

'So, you don't have my day planned for me in service to the community?'

'No, except we've been invited to a party tonight.'

'Oh,' he said, highly uncertain about parties.

'It's basically my friends you met on Sunday. It's a dinner party at the Grangers' – Bill and Mary. You'll be sat next to me. Not milling about to loud music.'

'They don't want me there. They only invited me because of you.'

'They do want you! I was invited weeks ago. They could easily have said nothing about you at this late stage. They felt they roughed you up a bit, actually. They like you.'

'Sure.'

'They do!' she insisted. 'Please come.'

'Will I be your date?'

'Yes, you will. In the most demure and proper fashion. Dress up, too, it'll be smart.'

'Shall I bring a bottle of wine?'

'If you like. So you'll come?'

'I'm considering it. Come on, then, let's go and break a leg.'

The air actually smelled frigid. The frozen top level of the snow crunched noisily with every step as their feet went through it into the softer stuff beneath. Their wellington boots protected them, and their two pairs of socks inside.

He drew in a great breath of the clean, clear, biting air. 'Does you good,' he said.

She did the same, and coughed. 'What doesn't kill you,' she sort of agreed.

Each step required them to lift their foot high out of the snow before replanting it. It was harder work than normal walking, and they took it slowly. A sharp 'crack' like a gunshot set several birds flocking away in a flurry from the heights of the bare trees. Sound did funny things in these conditions.

They continued forward, heading away from the road where his cottage was, to the line of trees at the bottom, where they could have gone on ahead, through the trees, to the next field, or turned right to follow the trees along. This second course was the one they took, taking them towards the lake, hidden just like the grass under snow that had settled on its icy surface.

The trees didn't go at right angles to their previous course, and the path beside them, now invisible, caused David and Angela to head gradually further away from the road. They kept near the trees to guide them away from the lake, which would have been extremely dangerous to stray across, though there were signs at points around it to give warnings.

A wind as chilled as a Siberian night blew at them and made them stop for a moment to take it in. 'Listen,' David said.

They hardly breathed. All around them, and especially from the trees, everything seemed to be entertaining a faint but persistent cracking sound, as if the whole world was creaking apart.

They saw no one until they saw him, then their hearts sank. The big lad with the dog on an insecure lead was sitting on a fallen tree trunk just in the cover of the strip of forest, and they were on him before there was time to change course or direction. He looked cold, in just jeans, a white T-shirt and a black, leather-style jacket, which wasn't even fastened.

He looked up and the dog barked madly, straining at its chain. He jerked it violently and the dog yelped. It sat on its haunches but stared at them as they approached, its mouth pulled into some sort of silent, sneering growl. The only way to avoid the guy would be to retreat the way they'd come, and that dog could outrun them easily. David swallowed hard and they kept going. This, he reckoned, could be nasty. No one around, no witnesses, no police would get there in time. Not good. His guts griped, his pulse thumped. He expected the dog to be released at them. That dog had already had a taste of him. It certainly would want more.

CHAPTER FIFTEEN

As they passed the guy, he stopped looking at them and stared down at the ground, holding the lead firmly. His face was a grim mask of something dark. But it wasn't anger or hatred or violent rage.

Angela stopped. She was looking right at him, from twenty yards away. David thought that was probably quite dangerous. What trouble was she about to get them into now? The guy looked up at her and said, 'What?'

She started towards him, and asked, 'Are you OK?'

'What's it to you?'

'Angela,' David cautioned, but she kept going.

'You look really fed-up,' she said, 'what's happened?'

'What do you care? Shove off,' he said.

She stopped two yards from him. 'I do care. You look really troubled. That upsets me. I want to help.'

'Well, you can't help, so just keep going.'

'No,' she said. David was horrified.

'Talk to me,' she said. 'Let me help you. What's the matter?'

'Like you *really* want to know!' he said.

'Yes, I do.' She continued up to him and brushed snow off the tree, then sat down.

He looked at the ground like it held the answers.

'What's your name?' she said.

David just stood there, completely uncertain what to do, like a gearstick in neutral.

'Ruf. Masters. Rufus. My dad thought it made me sound hard.'

'I'm Angela. Ruf as in roof of a house?'

'Yeah. But not Rufio.'

'OK. Where is your dad?'

'Locked up, where he deserves to be. Where I'll be joining him, sooner or later.'

'That's a very depressing life-expectation!' Angela said.

'Tell me it isn't true,' he challenged her.

'It isn't true. It's a possibility stated as a fact. It's inherently untrue.'

'Thanks, lady,' he said, 'wordy mumbo-jumbo makes me feel so much better.'

'So you do need to feel better. Listen, Ruf, I could just walk away. Leave you and Charger in peace. But I care about the fact that you look so sad.'

'You remembered his name,' he said.

David watched in amazement as the cruel yob seemed to soften. Amazement tinged with dismay. He just wanted to keep going. That wasn't going to happen. So he wandered over as casually as he could manage, and sat on the tree trunk next to Angela. Everything seemed utterly still, as if time itself had ceased. Which, he knew, in a block-universe, was actually the fact of the matter. Time didn't flow. Every moment owned that same property of seeming like the special 'now'. Well, that was just how it seemed, block-fashion, right now. Nothing flowing at all.

Ruf had gone quiet, staring at the snow. The dog sat still at his feet, looking up at him. He reached out a hand and ruffled the hair on its neck. 'Good boy,' he said, very quietly.

'What's happened?' Angela asked.

Ruf took in a long, deep breath and said, 'He attacked the postwoman. Bit her. Took out a chunk, I reckon. She was bleeding from her leg. They were pressing stuff against it to stop the blood. They called an ambulance, and the police. As I was getting away, my mum shouted after me not to come back. She's thrown me out. They'll take Chargy away from me and put him down. No question. He's had it. Second offence, eh, boy? And for me. I'll be banged up this time. Or a huge fine I can't pay which amounts to the same thing. It's over.'

'That's terrible,' Angela said. She reached over and stroked the dog's ear. It pressed its head against her hand.

'You like dogs?' Ruf said.

'Yes. I don't have one at the moment, but I do like them, and they like me. I'm really sorry to hear what's happened.'

'Still nothing you can do about it,' he added.

'Well, maybe. How about we come with you to the police station? And I have friends that could put you up for a while. You're over eighteen, aren't you?'

'I'm eighteen.'

'That counts as over eighteen.'

'And why's *he* being so quiet?' He was referring to David, who was listening, quite fascinated by where this was heading.

'Oh, David, he's my apprentice, my Padawan learner. A mere acolyte. He's fairly new to all this.'

'All what?'

'Helping people. Showing kindness as followers of Jesus.'

'All right, Dave?' Ruf said.

'Yes, fine thanks,' David said. 'But I prefer David.'

'Yes, but you're only a disciple, a stupid assistant, so I guess you'll get what you're given.'

'I guess I will,' he said, not wanting to spoil the pattern Angela was weaving.

'I'm still going to be dumped on from a great height,' Ruf said.

Charger had been sitting at his feet, initially staring up at him, then just looking around. Ruf reached down and unlooped the collar. Charger gave a single bark and headed off at speed, chasing some suspected adversary.

'He may not be safe,' David said. 'There's water under the ice over there.'

'He's not stupid,' Ruf said.

'Really, I wouldn't,' David continued.

They watched Charger's progress. There was a terrible crack. Charger disappeared. A single yelp followed, and the sound of frantic splashing and doggy-crying, then a horrible silence. Charger had gone.

Ruf stood up and leapt after him.

'No, don't!' both Angela and David shouted. It was far too dangerous.

Ruf got five yards before David set off after him, pounding at the deep snow.

'Ruf, stop, you'll drown!' Angela called from behind him. But Ruf was deaf to it.

David closed quickly, but the point where the dog disappeared was less than fifty yards off. He got what he hoped was just near enough and thrust himself forward, throwing himself towards Ruf's pounding feet. He would only get one chance at this. He straightened himself as he lurched and reached out his hand in horizontal slam-dunk style. He caught round Ruf's right foot and gripped it with tendon-straining might. The big boy tipped and sprawled face-first in the snow. David was on his feet in a second and sat down on Ruf's back, pinning him to the ground just with his weight.

Ruf swore a torrent of desperate abuse, but couldn't get up. His hands and feet could get no purchase on the snow. There was no sound from ahead of them. Charger was truly gone.

Angela rushed up, and knelt, and put a hand on Ruf's shoulder, both restraining him further and offering comfort.

'Charger!' he called.

'You must stop,' Angela said. 'People drown every winter trying to rescue dogs from places like this. He's gone. Stop, Ruf, he's gone.'

The boy started to thrash at the ground, pounding it and crying out with deserted rage. 'My dog. That's my dog. That's Charger,' he was shouting and wailing.

David could feel already the damage he'd done to his shoulder, and his back. And his knee. In fact, he recognised that getting up from this position wasn't going to be easy. Anyway, he'd have to decide somehow when Ruf was safe to allow up.

He looked at Angela, who said, 'Are you OK?'

'A bit strained, but I'll live.'

'Rufus,' she said. 'Are you going to be sensible? Charger is dead. He's gone. He was gone as soon as he hit that cold water. I bet he froze more than drowned. He's gone.'

Ruf stopped scrabbling with his arms and legs, and said, 'Let me get up. I'm freezing myself.'

David got off, with a bit of pulling from Angela. He straightened his back and said, 'Aah.'

He was frightened that Ruf would attack them. He stepped away, and his knees nearly gave way under him. Angela reached out to steady him, but he was OK. 'I've done myself a bit of a damage,' he admitted, hoping this would restrain Ruf's need for revenge, should there be such.

Ruf sat up. He looked pale and shocked.

'You need to get warm,' Angela said. 'David only lives ten minutes from here. Come with us.'

'What about Charger?' he said, without any sign of anger. He looked emptied. In shock, actually.

'I guess you can get his body back once the snow all goes,' Angela answered.

He huffed, and pushed himself to his knees then stood. 'OK. I'll come. I don't feel too good.'

'Shock and cold can be dangerous allies,' David said. 'Come on. I'll make you a nice mug of something hot.'

They set off, with Ruf between them. He said nothing as they walked, and David became concerned that he really wasn't too good.

'How do you feel, Ruf?' Angela said.

'A bit sick. A bit faint. A bit spaced. And I just lost my dog. My best and most constant friend in the world.'

'I know,' Angela said. 'Hang in there.'

They reached the road, crossed over, and arrived at David's door. He opened it and ushered Ruf into the warm. They took him into the kitchen and sat him at the kitchen table.

'Coffee? Tea? Mulled wine?' David asked.

'Cold water,' he said.

'OK,' Angela agreed, 'but then you've got to have something hot.'

'Tea, with two sugars,' he said, wearily. 'Thanks.'

Angela got him a glass of water while David started on the tea, for all three of them.

Ruf sat disconsolately with the glass in both hands resting on the table, staring at it. 'That dog was my life,' he said. 'Now my life is going to stink even worse. What's the point?'

'Did you have another dog before?' David asked.

'Yeah, a cocker, when I was little. Skint. Got run over.'

'Well, you survived the loss of that one. Of Skint. You can get another dog again.'

'I'll be banned from owning a dog, at the very least.'

'Maybe it's time to get a girlfriend, instead,' David suggested.

'Had a few of those. Never lasts.'

'Maybe it's time to get one with a bit more commitment,' Angela suggested, sitting next to him.

'You offering?' he said.

David was pleased he felt able to make the joke; it was a good sign in more ways than one.

'You're very kind, but I kinda like older men. Like David, here. You should go for someone more like your age. Someone who doesn't just sleep around, but wants some respect and affection. Do you know someone like that?'

'Nobody that thinks anything of me.'

'Time to get your act together, then. How do you feel?'

'Warmer, less faint and sick. I really cared about Charger.' His eyes had blue rims around and his face seemed sunken. 'Now he's gone. But he was gone anyway, wasn't he? Since he had a slice of postie, that was it for him. Expensive piece of meat. I bet she'll sue.'

'I bet that's ruined her Christmas,' Angela said. David thought that was maybe unwise.

Ruf said, 'Yeah, I guess. Maybe her family, as well.' He swore. 'Why did that have to happen?'

'It didn't have to happen. You let it happen. You failed to properly restrain a dangerous animal. You'd been warned. But we might be able to keep you out of jail. This could be a whole new start for you. Some good might come of it. Don't feel too hopeless.'

He didn't seem to mind her pointing out the error of his ways. He seemed to just accept it. Maybe he felt beholden. But now he knew where David lived. That might turn out not to be so good.

'Are you wet?' David asked.

'No.'

'You must be. You could have a hot shower if you like, and I could dry your shirt and jeans for you. How about it, after your tea?'

'Nah. I'll survive.'

Angela reached over and pressed her hand against his chest.

'Get off!' he said, angrily, pushing her hand away.

'You're soaked and freezing!' she accused. 'Get out of those clothes now and David will lend you a dressing gown or something.'

He released three expletives in a row, then said, 'All right. Where can I change?'

'In the spare bedroom, if you like,' David offered. 'Take everything off and put on the dressing gown I'll put in there. Then come down here for your tea.'

Ruf finished the glass of water and stood. He was still pale and drained-looking, his lips still cyanosed. It was definitely psychological as well as physical.

'Follow me,' David said, and led him up the stairs. He put a spare dressing gown in the back bedroom (not the one with big teddy) and left Ruf to it. He went downstairs and put hot water on teabags in the pot.

'OK?' Angela said.

'Yes.'

Ruf was back down by the time the tea was brewed, and David made him a good strong mug with two spoons of sugar. He and Angela had one as well. She went up and brought his clothes down and arranged them over a couple of radiators. They all went into the front room.

'This is festive,' Ruf said.

'Yes. Thank you,' David responded. 'Biscuits?' He held the tin open for Ruf to take some.

'Yeah,' he said, taking three chocolate ones.

Angela and David took a biscuit each, trying not to be too obvious about how much they were watching him.

'How do you feel?' Angela said.

'If you keep asking me that I'm going to bust you,' he said, then gave her an actual smile.

'Sorry. We're concerned, is all,' she said.

He drank tea and chewed at his biscuits, in silence.

'How do *you* feel?' Angela asked David.

'It was a great tackle, given I gave up playing rugby thirty years ago. But I've definitely pulled my shoulder, back and knee.'

'Oh, I see!' Ruf said. 'That was a proper rugby tackle. No wonder you got me down.'

'At a cost,' David said. 'But I feel rather good, actually. I saved a life today – yours.'

'I guess you could say so. Sort of.'

'Sort of?' Angela said. 'You'd be at the bottom of that lake right now with fire crew risking their lives to find your lifeless, stiff, white corpse.'

'I know it,' he admitted. 'And now you're giving me tea and biscuits and offering to go with me to the plods. What kind of aliens are you?'

'Nice ones,' David said.

'Christian ones,' Angela said.

'Just don't expect me to go to church,' Ruf insisted.

Teas finished, Ruf said, 'OK, I'll have that shower.'

'I'll make sure you've got everything you need,' David said, and led him up to the bathroom. He got out a clean towel, and checked the shower gel and floor mat. Then he put the shower on, adjusted it to a nice temperature, and showed him how to switch it off.

'I'd rather you didn't lock the door,' he said. 'We'll be downstairs anyway.'

Ruf nodded, and David left.

He found Angela worrying over the clothes in the kitchen. 'His jacket is OK. His socks and T-shirt will dry. But these jeans – jeans hold a lot of water, and it's very cold. I guess he kept his underwear.'

'So, is he anything like my size? I could lend him some trousers.'

'Let's see.' She held the jeans up against him. 'He's got a longer leg than you, and a smaller waist, so I wouldn't be hopeful. We need to get these dry. Have you got a fan heater?'

'Yes, in my bedroom. I'll get it.'

She was draping the jeans over the back of a kitchen chair when he got back, so he set the fan heater on full to point at them. 'If I light the rings on the cooker as well and we shut the door, it should become a real steam-bath in here,' he said.

'Good plan. We can but try.'

They were halted by the sound of a terrible cry from upstairs. Rage and great sorrow bellowed out from the bathroom. Another peal followed, shot through with expletives. They looked at each other.

'He's keeping it away from us,' Angela said. 'He won't be that weak-looking in front of us. He'll hide it. But we must remember he's suffered a very great loss, and he's feeling it.'

'I agree,' David agreed, a little frightened by the force of what he'd just heard.

They finished setting up the kitchen and retreated to the lounge.

'I'm really impressed,' he said to her, 'with the way you've handled him. You're both tough and caring. You're amazing.'

'Well, I've been impressed with the compassion and wisdom you've shown. And the rugby tackle was a doozy! And how you sat on him. Let me have a look at your injuries.'

She took hold of his right arm and put her left hand on his shoulder. She manipulated it slowly. He winced.

'You've maybe torn something, or you might be lucky and you've just pulled a muscle. How's the back?'

'It aches.'

'Show me where.'

He turned round and pointed it out.

'Do you usually get back pain there?'

'Yeah.'

She pressed her thumb in. 'Does that hurt?'

'Aah. Yes.'

'Bend forward. How does that feel?'

'It pulls.'

'Hmm. Turn your upper body to the left for me.'

It strained that side of his lower back. 'It pulls,' he said.

'Hmm. I'd say you've just pulled some susceptible muscles, is all. How about the knee?'

'That's stopped hurting.'

'Aww! I was hoping to get my hands on it.'

'Funny. That could lead to all kinds of compromising behaviour. Best not.'

'OK, then.'

They sat down, both on the settee.

'What a morning!' she said.

'This was a double dead-dog day!'

'It surely was!'

Ruf reappeared in the doorway in the dressing gown. Something about the set of his face looked different.

'OK?' David said, standing.

'Yeah, but I'm not going to the plods.'

CHAPTER SIXTEEN

He was drying his hair on the towel, which he then threw onto the armchair and sat on it. 'Nice damp patch!' David thought.

Ruf looked belligerent, and a little angry. 'Why should I go and hand myself in? Especially just before Christmas.'

'Because you don't have much option?' David offered.

'Easy for you to say, you're not the one facing being banged up.'

'Actually we were,' David continued. 'Nearly banged up – for clearing up rubbish from the High Street without a licence.'

Ruf laughed. 'You two? For picking up litter? Sick!'

'It turns out Angela has her mugshot on police bulletin boards across the county,' David added.

'Anyway,' Ruf continued, immediately losing his good humour, 'you said you've got someone who'll put me up.'

'Not if you're on the run!' Angela replied. 'Good grief, one of them is a JP. The other is a GP. They're not going to harbour a wanted criminal. *After* we go to the police station they will put you up.'

'I guess Mary is the JP,' David said. 'She has the face for it.'

'Hoi!' Angela objected. 'That's my friend you're talking about.'

'I just meant stern-looking.'

'Huh. Well, OK, I see what you mean. Maybe it goes with the territory. Though she's a very kind and thoughtful person. They both are. Anyway, Ruf, they will put you up in their very nice house in the country not far from here. I phoned them while you were both upstairs. But it's police first.'

Ruf looked deflated. 'OK,' he said. 'You're not gonna let up on that, are you?'

'I don't think so,' she said. 'We just want to do our best to help you.'

'We're not your enemy,' David added.

'I'll go and check your clothes,' Angela announced, and left the room.

There was an awkward silence. 'She seems to wear the trousers,' Ruf said.

David laughed. 'We've only known each other a few days. We're still negotiating about the trousers.'

'I'd say she's winning.'

'I'm not done yet.'

'Sure.'

She came back. 'I think we need to give them another half hour, probably. Let's watch the telly. What do you like to watch, Ruf?'

'I like to channel skip. Drives my mum mad. Whatever you want.'

David switched it on and said, 'How about a Christmas music channel?'

Ruf shrugged. Angela shrugged. 'Driving Home for Christmas' came on.

'How about some lunch?' Angela suggested, and all agreed that would be a good idea. More because it was something to do than anything else.

David went and made lunch while Angela stayed with Ruf. The kitchen was really hot and only slightly steamy, but not pleasant. He felt the jeans – they still had a way to go.

He made ham sandwiches and crisps with a jug of fruit juice. He loaded them on a tray and carried them into the front room. They all pitched in and the time seemed to pass quite pleasantly, with limited, polite conversation. They tried to find out a bit more about Ruf, but he wasn't giving much away. David thought the strain was telling on him. He still looked a pathetic and deflated version of the boy they'd seen four days ago.

It got to half-past one. Lunch was finished and the clothes were acceptably dry.

'We'll go up in my car,' David announced. He was aware that Ruf's jeans weren't completely dry and that could put him in danger on such a cold day.

They drove to the police station, he parked, and they walked in to the reception area. A non-police person was behind a glass screen above a wooden-looking counter. There was a vertical speaking-slot, and no queue, so David went straight across and waited for her attention. She looked up from her computer screen and said, 'Good afternoon. How can I help you?'

'We're here with this gentleman, Mr Rufus Masters, who believes you are trying to contact him concerning an incident with his dog.'

She looked across at Ruf, and said, 'Would you all take a seat, please. I'll get someone to come out to you.'

She picked up a phone and spoke quietly into it, and almost immediately two uniformed officers came out through a door next to the glass screen.

'Hello, Ruf,' one of them said. 'You'd better come through with us. And who are you, if you don't mind?'

'Friends,' Angela said.

Through the door was a small corridor leading to other doors, and they were led to the one on the left at the end. Inside were a simple table and four chairs. An obscured-glass window let in daylight.

One of the officers dragged in a fifth chair, and they all sat, with Angela and David either side of Ruf, opposite the two policemen. One had a file and plonked it on the table.

'I told you about that dog myself more than once,' the one with the file said. 'So, I am Sergeant Strong and this is Constable Ayers. A complaint has been lodged that your dog, Charger, attacked and injured a member of the postal staff this morning at your address, 55 King George Road. They say that the dog wasn't properly restrained and after the attack you fled the scene with the dog. Where is the dog now?'

'He's dead,' Ruf said.

They both looked unconvinced. 'Do you have anything to corroborate that?'

'We were there when it drowned in the lake at the bottom of the fields opposite Lower Lane, two hours ago,' Angela said.

'I'm sorry, and you are?'

David answered. 'I'm David Sourbook and this is Angela Adams. I live in Lower Lane. Angela and I were taking a walk and came across Ruf. We spoke with him, as he seemed very upset. He let Charger off the lead, and he raced off over the snow, fell through the ice and was gone in a matter of seconds. He *is* dead.'

The one without the file, the silent one, Ayers, leaned forward and whispered something in the sergeant's ear. He turned his head very slightly and whispered about three syllables back, then Ayers stood and left the room. David thought, 'Great, this is where we get nicked for finishing clearing the High Street.'

The sergeant continued. 'Well, if that's true it deals with what needs to happen to the dog, but not the offences you've committed, Rufus. Under the Anti-Social Behaviour, Crime and Policing Act 2014 you face both criminal and civil proceedings.'

'I know,' he said.

'And I gather your mum has thrown you out of the family home, so I'd like to know where we can contact you, or we might have to consider keeping you in custody.'

Angela spoke up. 'He'll be staying at Briars Mead, Stanley Lane, Cuffold, which is the home of Dr William Granger and Mrs Mary Granger, JP. They're friends of mine.'

'I see. So you're going to vouch for his whereabouts.'

'Yes,' both Angela and David said.

He started flipping up the pages of the file to look at them, and it all went very quiet. Ayers came back in, nodded to the sergeant, and just sat down. Maybe they weren't going to be reminded and remanded for their own misdemeanours. David became aware that Angela was giving him some sort of sideways signal. But what? That was the problem with women, he'd discerned. Because what they're thinking is obvious and clear in their own head, they think it is in yours, and if you don't respond then you're being deliberately slow, or obstructive, or obtuse. And for that you get it in the neck. He turned ever so slightly towards her, aiming at a look of questioning. She seemed to be urging something at him. Then inspiration flared. Had she sent it directly into his brain, like some mental projectile?

David said, 'How is the poor postwoman?'

The policeman didn't look up. 'She lost a litre of blood and will need reconstructive surgery but she's in no danger, as long as the dog wasn't rabid. I imagine her union will be filing a civil suit on her behalf. That could be pretty expensive.'

'I suppose we could send her some flowers,' David said to Angela.

The policeman gave out what could have been a stifled guffaw and said, still without looking up, 'She's at St Margaret's.' He flipped the file closed. 'Investigations into this offence will be ongoing. We will be contacting you in the New Year, Mr Masters. There will be some documents for all of you to sign on your way out. But for now, you can go.'

There was no 'Merry Christmas'.

'Do you want us to take you home to get your stuff?' Angela said, as David started the car.

'Yeah, thanks. Maybe my mum won't tear such a big one in me if you're there.'

'OK,' David answered, and set off in that direction.

They pulled up outside the rather ramshackle house with bits of children's bikes and settee springs in the front 'garden'. The door was open. Ruf looked dejected.

'Come on,' Angela said. 'Soonest started, soonest done.'

They all got out and David and Angela walked either side of Ruf up to the door. David knocked loudly.

'Hang on!' a woman shouted from within.

She appeared, dressed in trodden-down slippers, slacks and a T-shirt, her hair tied up in some sort of cloth, giving the impression she'd been doing housework, though the glass of something with floating ice cubes in her left hand suggested otherwise. She said, 'You're not welcome,' to Ruf. 'You social workers?' she added.

'No,' Angela said. 'We're friends of Ruf. He's come to collect some clothes and such, please.'

'Five minutes,' she said, and stepped aside to let him in. 'Where's the dog?' she asked.

'It died. Drowned in the lake in the lower fields this morning,' David answered.

'Good. Horrible nuisance of a dirty thing. It was trouble from the first day he got it. Good riddance, say I.'

'Well, it's gone now. We saw it drown,' Angela confirmed.

'What about the law?'

'We've taken him to the police station and he's going to be staying with some friends of mine, for the moment, a JP and a GP,' Angela said.

'What's a JP? A politician?'

'Justice of the Peace. A magistrate. Just a friend of mine.'

'Well,' she took a sip from her glass, 'he's not welcome back here. He's eighteen now and I've no space for his messing about any more. He'll join his dad soon enough.'

Ruf reappeared with a duffel bag and stopped inside the hallway, seemingly waiting for her to say something nice to him. She said, 'Don't come back.'

He squeezed past and they said, 'Goodbye, Mrs Masters.'

'It's Ms Riley,' she said, smoke accompanying the spat words.

Back at David's house, sitting in the lounge, Angela said, 'Don't unpack here. We're taking you to their house this evening. Now, listen, we're going there for a dinner party, with a few friends. You're invited as well. You might as well come, because we're taking you there and they're offering to feed you. It'll be a nice meal and you can sit between David and me. There'll be about a dozen of us. It'll be a bit posh so they'll lend you a suit and such. What do you think?'

He looked less bemused than David expected. 'S'all right,' he said, then swore. 'Aren't you worried I'll show you up?'

'I'm confident you're quite capable of not showing us up,' Angela said, 'and these aren't snooty people who'll be looking for your faults and slips of grammar. Though they might not be comfortable with bad language. Some people just aren't. And we aren't that easily shown up, either. Actually, David's quite capable of showing me up, truth be told. It'll be fun. And very Christmassy. A sort of Christmas dinner. Just accept it gladly. Eat, drink and be merry.'

'Will there be alcohol?'

'Of course there will! Just don't get yourself totally bladdered! And throw up on the table. But I think we'll all be getting a bit merry.'

'Sounds fine. I think I need a lie down. Is that all right?'

'Sure,' David said. 'On the bed in the spare room I showed you before. Go for it. We'll get you up if necessary.'

'Right. And thanks for helping me today.'

When he was gone, David said, 'I'm amazed your friends would just take him in like that.'

'The Grangers? They've done it before. A few times. They're experienced at watching over troubled teens.'

'Well, what a day!' he said. 'Truly a double dead-dog day.'

'A double dead-dog day. That will become a saying between us. Yes, just be glad of your day off tomorrow,' she said.

'A day off! Why?'

'I have to go and look after my nephew, Andrew. He's ten. My sister, Thelia, has to work and her husband, Martin, is away on business in Dubai right over Christmas, so I'm going there, to the fair town of Lifford.'

'That could take a couple of hours, in bad traffic.'

'I have to be there at half-past eight, so I have to leave at seven. She gets back from work by half-past three, so I should be home by six. You'd like Andrew. He has ASD.'

'Autism Spectrum Disorder! Thanks a lot!'

'No, I don't mean you'd like him because you're autistic – though now you mention it! No, you'd like him because he's really sweet, once you get used to him.'

'You sure it isn't SAD he has?'

'Seasonal Affective Disorder? No, that really is you. I wonder if there's an SDA as well.'

'Hoi! I'm not depressed.'

'Winter blues? I think a bit, maybe.'

'And SDA is Seventh Day Adventists.'

'I know that! Not quite the category I was thinking of.'

To his great surprise, David said, 'Can I come with you, tomorrow?'

'Oh. Why?'

'To meet Andrew. I do have experience with ASD kids, from teaching. And to help out. And because I haven't got anything else on. And I guess I'm getting used to spending time with you.'

'Of course you can come! I'll pick you up at seven in my car. Speaking of which, I'll pick you and his lordship up at seven tonight. You should be dressed. We'll dress him when we get there. Bill has clothes that'll fit him.'

'Do you want a lift home now?'

'No, I'll walk up, thanks.'

She stood, gathered up her things, and went into the hallway. He helped her in a most gentlemanly fashion into her coat. He opened the door for her. She stepped outside into the bitter cold and turned, facing him. He made a move to give her a hug and she did the same, and they fell into each other's arms like long-lost lovers. They hugged and held, and seconds passed. He really didn't want to let go. It was so comfortable and right and warmly exciting.

She said, 'It's a bit like that film you told me about. The one that doesn't actually exist. How the rogue boy brought the two adults together.'

'She seems to have her stuff together, but why are you doing this? You're only the learner.'

Ruf was sitting at the kitchen table looking a bit hungover from his two-hour 'nap'. David wondered how much he slept at night. Ruf was waiting for the offered mug of tea. Even yobbos survived on tea, so it seemed. David was standing by the kettle, waiting for it to boil. Ruf seemed quite relaxed in T-shirt, boxer shorts and bare feet. David wanted to point out to him that's it's not nice to sit on people's furniture in your underwear, but he was fairly sure that wasn't kind, and he really didn't want to set up any sort of enmity between them.

'Y'know, that's exactly the question I'd be asking about now. And the truth is, simply put, she's trying to teach me to be kind.'

'Why?'

'Another good question! Well, so she says, because she is kind because God is kind.'

Ruf groaned. 'Why can't you religious types ever say anything just straight?'

'I'm not really a religious type. Well, not yet.'

'Yeah, but she's got her hooks into you. Tell me she hasn't.'

'Yes, kind of, she has. OK, explanation. The word that best describes what God is like is kindness. It's just who He is. Now, kindness can't be something forced or "programmed in". To be genuine it has to be chosen. If you force someone to be kind it isn't kindness, it's obedience, or submission, or fear, or self-serving for their own ends. No, genuine kindness has to be chosen. It has to be done simply for the desire to be kind, to help, to give, and all that. With me so far?'

'Where's the tea?'

'You really don't want to hear this, do you?'

'No, I don't. And, by the way, you should know I never actually did anything to you and her. That was my mates. I dragged them off you. So don't talk to me about being kind.'

'OK, fair point.'

They sat in an awkward silence with Ruf staring around at the kitchen.

'Tea?' Ruf asked.

'Has to brew for a full five minutes.'

'Why?'

'To get all the goodness out,' David explained.

'There's goodness in tea?'

'Yes, lots. Are you still at school?'

'Nah. You used to be a teacher, didn't you?'

'Yes. Did I teach you?'

Ruf just shrugged. 'This Angela, you're after her. Tell me you're not.'

'I couldn't possibly say either yes or no.'

'Huh.'

CHAPTER SEVENTEEN

The house was a colourfully lit tapestry of seasonal, festive delights. In the grand entrance hallway there was a fine, tall tree, maybe twelve feet, all decked out in red. It glowed and twinkled with many kinds of rosy lights. Bill and Mary both met them all at the door, and made a special point of a friendly welcome to Ruf.

'Come on, my boy,' Bill said, putting a hand lightly on his nearer shoulder, 'let me show you where you're billeted and what we've got for you to wear this evening. I used to be a similar size to you until ten years ago when middle age caused a middle relaxation of my up-till-then middlingly strapping and sturdy frame.'

Ruf shot David a glance (it looked like raised eyebrows but without the raising of eyebrows) and followed on up the stairs which wound forwards and left from the stately hallway. The upper landing was open to the view from the ground floor so they were watched until they disappeared past a wall corner.

'It's nice to see you again!' Mary said to David, taking his arm in a most coquettish fashion and getting him to walk beside her into the dining room.

'Well, of course, and you,' he managed. 'You look very lovely.'

She was wearing a long evening gown in silken coral. It accentuated her slim figure. Her hair was up in a stylish bun-type creation. She still looked severe, but was smiling. He realised the narrow glasses on the neck-string added to her look of sternness. She did tend to peer over them, making her look disapproving.

'You look very smart in your stylish grey suit and matching tie,' she replied. 'You just need a sprig of holly on your lapel. I've got one for all the gentlemen.'

Sure enough she picked up such a sprig from a box she'd prepared, each of three leaves and some berries on a short stalk, pre-attached to a pin, and put it on his lapel. Then she landed a hand on each of his shoulders and kissed him, formally but with intention, on the cheek. Her skin felt dry and a little hairy. It reminded him of an aunt when he'd been little. Aunt Maudy, with the bristly kisses. And of metal tubes that had once contained big pills but then contained one shilling coins, for him. And for Michaela.

'Thank you. Very nice,' he said, careful not to indicate whether he meant the sprig or the peck.

The dining room was laid out with lights, draped from the ceiling in cascading torrents of snow-falling white. There was another tree, smaller than the one in the hallway, also all in white with silver baubles and real, lit candles, their flames dancing merrily in the small, carefree breezes. The overall light level had been carefully set so that the festive lights showed well but it was intimate rather than dingy.

The table was fifteen feet long, clothed in white and set with fourteen place-settings in silver and sparkling crystal. Tree lights reflected in dancing starbursts off the shiny accoutrements. For David, it set the juices flowing with anticipations of fine food and wine.

'Now come into the sitting room,' Mary said. 'This is where we'll gather when the others arrive for a drink and some nibbles and festive chat. What can I get you?'

'I'll have a sherry, please,' David said.

'I guess I'll be OK with a small one of the same this early,' Angela added.

'We can always call you a taxi later and you can fetch the car tomorrow,' Mary suggested.

'Thanks, Mary, but I need it early. I'm OK not to drink, anyway. I imagine you've made some of your famous non-alcoholic festive punch.'

'Indeed I have!'

Mary brought them the drinks and sat down next to them on the large, white settee with her Cinzano and a slice of lemon, over crushed ice. Yet another tree was by the roaring fireplace, fat and full and covered in lights and tinsel braids of all colours. Even the star on top changed colours as you watched. Again, the lighting had been carefully set to give the decorations their full, joyful, vividly colourful and festive effect. Flame-light from the fire danced mercurially around the room.

'This is where we actually live,' she explained to David. 'We moved the TV out but usually it sits over there, in front of the French windows.' She pointed towards the long, heavy, creamy curtains.

'Now, Angela, dear,' she continued. 'Just warn me. You know I don't mind, but is this an unexploded grenade we've just invited to dinner?'

'He might have some undisclosed buttons,' Angela replied. 'You know how it is.'

'Only too well. Now, I suppose you want him to sit between the two of you?'

'Yes, we thought so.'

'Well, belay that thought. I've put you two together, not least for David's sake, poor lamb, and I've put Ruf between you and me. I think he'll be most malleable between two women.'

'And especially two such attractive ladies,' David added.

'You're too kind,' Mary said, then she dropped her voice about a whole octave and said, 'You're *much* too kind.'

'Oh,' he said, abashed, 'I see.'

Angela smiled at him and gave a tiny wink.

'Don't encourage him, dear,' Mary said. '"A flattering mouth causes trouble."'

'Ta-daa!' came from the doorway, where Bill stood, arms wide, ushering Ruf in. He appeared, in a well-fitting, dark blue suit, white shirt and navy tie, with black shoes. He certainly looked the part.

Mary said, 'That's very smart indeed. Very smart. Let me get you some holly. All the men will be wearing it.' She went to fetch some, and brought in the whole box.

David watched her pin the holly on him, and thought she lingered a bit too long as near to him as she could get. But he couldn't be sure. She didn't kiss him on the cheek, so maybe not.

Anyway, what did he care?

'Now, Ruf, dear, come and sit with your friends and get comfortable. All the others will be arriving soon. There will be fourteen of us. Would you like a drink?'

'Have you got a beer?'

'Yes, of course I have beer. Lager? Bitter? Something else?'

'Lager, a cold bottle of Fosters would be good.'

'I'll go and check,' she said, with a smile. She came back immediately with an opened, cold bottle of Fosters, and handed it to him. 'Are you sure you wouldn't like a glass with that?'

'No. This is fine,' he said.

The front doorbell went, and people arrived in a bunch. They started pouring into the sitting room. All the men were wearing suits, except for one old man who was wearing a jacket over a jumper, and trousers that nearly matched. All the women were in evening dresses or blouses and long skirts. Not a knee was to be seen.

They started to perch round the furniture. Mary attached sprigs while Bill became the drinks waiter. Apparently there was just one person they were waiting for, Anna Lovren. Conversation erupted in small huddles, then five minutes later the doorbell rang again and a slightly harassed-looking Anna Lovren came in, Bill still trying to get her coat off her.

'I'm sorry, I'm sorry,' she said to all. 'Flipping car wouldn't start. I guess it was the cold. But it started eventually, so here I am.'

She was settled, and Mary and Bill shared a beanbag, which seemed to David a bit chancy given that they might never get up again. Then Bill said, 'Well, we're such a mixed group this year, I think some introductions would be in order. If you'd rather not, I'll give a brief introduction for any of you, and if you want to add to it, because I've damned you by faint praise or damned you with flattery, you just go right ahead. I'll launch it off. I'm Bill Granger, I'm married to Mary, I'm a retired GP and member of St Mary's, I use my time these days for some painting and volunteering when I'm not off on some medical jolly to treat people in need of extra help abroad. And I'm a thoroughly fine fellow.'

Everyone laughed. Mary took it up. 'I'm Mary, and Bill is indeed married to me.' Pause for more tittering. 'I'm a retired lecturer, and I spend some of my time being a JP, and I volunteer with NewLink, the homeless project in town. And I'm an absolute beast!'

There were murmurs of assent then much laughter.

Holly and Greg from last Sunday were next. 'Hi, I'm Holly, I'm only twenty-nine so I think I'm the second youngest here by … about … three generations! I'm a nurse at the hospital, I've been a member of St Mary's since I was born. Some of you know my parents, Stewart and Irene.' She did look nice in her long, green dress with her dark hair put up, even though she was a little tubby in David's eyes.

'Hi, I'm Greg, Holly loves me but won't admit it in public, but if you keep an eye on her, you'll see. I'm a teacher with special needs kids, I come to St Mary's because Holly drags me, but I have to admit I'm beginning to like it.'

Next were the Staines, also from last Sunday. They both looked very smart, he in a designer slate-grey suit and she in a matching grey evening gown. 'Hello, I'm Ian Staines, this is my dear wife, Sue. We own and run U.R. Beautiful in town, offering all kinds of haircuts, treatments, remedies of the legal variety, and such. We've been members of St Mary's for nearly forty years. My goodness, that's a long time!' David thought he had a rat face, though a kindly one.

'So, I'm Sue, I seem to spend my life snipping, foiling, blowing and generally dyeing. That's with a y.' Everyone responded merrily. 'I recently retired from social work. And I feel like I'm still doing it!'

Next was David. 'I'm David Sourbook, and somehow I've become a friend of Angela's. I'm a retired teacher of physics and maths, and I spend my time doing not very much. And I've been to St Mary's once, with Angela.'

'Who are all these blasted people in our house?' blurted the man in the jacket and jumper. His wife touched his arm and said, 'Brian, this is the Christmas party, these are our friends.'

'They're not my blasted friends! I don't even like half of them. What are they doing in my bedroom?'

'Brian, calm down. Look, there's Bill and Mary. You know them. This is their house. We're here for a lovely dinner, just like we said before. And I'm here.'

He looked at her. 'Jan? There you are,' and he seemed to settle.

Jan said, 'He doesn't always remember things too well these days.'

'Look,' Bill said, 'you go next, seeing as you've started, Jan dear.'

'OK, thank you, Bill. We are Brian and Jan Carstairs. Brian used to be a designer at Boeing until he retired, but then our plans for a sunny retirement were rather cut short by his developing Alzheimer's. We're not members of St Mary's, but Bill used to be our GP and we became friends, years ago.'

'Tell them what you do,' Mary Granger said.

'OK,' she said, looking shy. 'I'm an author. I have eight published books on issues relating to ecology and wildlife. You won't know any of them.'

'I think it's back to Angela,' Bill said.

'Well,' she began. 'I'd like to say I'm just Angela. I teach Comparative Religion and Ethics at the college, I live alone, I help to care for my nephew who has ASD, not SAD –' she looked at David and smiled, 'and I've been a member of St

Mary's and on the mission team for ten years or so. David is my new friend.'

David was taken aback. He'd never asked her what she did for a living. He assumed she was early retired or something. How did he completely miss stuff like that?

Angela continued. 'And this is our new friend, Ruf, whom we met today when his dog sadly drowned in the lake in the lower fields. So we've brought him to dinner to cheer him up.'

Ruf just nodded.

David reflected that that wasn't exactly true. But it was kind in its paring and sparing of the truth.

That only left one more couple David didn't recognise, quite young-looking, and Anna Lovren.

'Hi, I'm Anna. I'm fifty-four and a confirmed spinster. I lived with my mum till she died, in 1998, and she left me Rose Cottage which you all know and wish you could live in. And a pot of money to keep me in style all my days. So I travel and write travelogues that don't get published, which makes me intensely jealous of Jan C. But it's a nice life. I've been a member of St Mary's for too long to recall – my mum and dad took me from birth. I remember Reverend Samson. I run the programmes for the elderly and shut-ins including the lunch club and the visiting scheme. So I do justify my existence a bit.'

Everyone gave a polite laugh.

The final man spoke. 'Last but not – well, hopefully not – well, maybe we should be least, because didn't Jesus say something about the least being the first? Or something like that. Anyway, we're the Picketts. Ella, my wife, and me, I'm Aaron. We live in Drake Cottage, not all that far from Anna. I'm a retired store manager and she's a – '

'Let me say it!' she cut in, nudging his arm.

'Oh, yes, sorry, dear, you tell it. So, I ran an electronics store for thirty years. We don't go much to St Mary's but Ella knows Mary Granger from – well, I'd better let her tell you that!'

'He's my husband,' she said. 'Usually he's quite well behaved. I am indeed Ella Pickett and I managed a flower shop and then ascended the ladder to district manager. I oversee the flower arrangers in church even though we don't come often, and that's how I became friends with Mary.'

'Well, that's everyone,' Mary Granger said. 'Except, Anna, I think you do yourself down. Tell everyone what you do as a steady job.'

'Oh, all right,' she said, 'as long as I don't get the predictable reply. I'm a psychotherapist, I work in the NHS.'

'What's the predictable reply?' David asked.

'You don't really expect me to tell you?' she asked, looking right into him.

Holly provided the answer. 'The predictable reply is, "I suppose you're psychoanalysing me, then."'

'It was worse at uni when I did my psychology degree. You can imagine, at parties people were always asking each other, "What are you studying?" and if you said "psychology", you would so often get, "Are you psychoanalysing me, then?" It became a real pain. Only one time, this older woman reacted by saying, "You can't see inside my head. Don't think you can see who I am. You can't see inside my mind unless I let you." Which made me think, "Wow! That was more revealing than you realise!" But it does still happen. I have a better answer these days.'

'Which is?' David asked, genuinely interested.

'No, I'm not psychoanalysing you, you'd have to pay me a lot of money to do that.'

Everyone laughed and tittered.

'Let's go in,' Mary said, trying to get off the beanbag. 'I'll – oops – little help here – thank you, Greg, that's kind – I'll tell you where you're sitting when we get in the dining room.'

They all trekked through. 'Now,' she said, 'Bill is at the head of the table and I'm the good and compliant wifey to his right as we look at it. Next to me is Ruf, then Angela, David, Holly and Greg, meaning that at this end of the table is the lovely Anna. To her left is Aaron and then Ella, then Brian, then Jan, finally

Ian followed by Sue which brings us back to Bill. And you see we're all alternating, male and female. Do sit, where I've put you.'

There was a little hesitation and reminding, and everyone sat. David was opposite Brian Carstairs, which made him glad it was a wide table. To his left was Holly Ruben.

The other side of her was Greg, then at the end of the table, certainly within reach for expecting conversation, was 'the lovely Anna', the head-doctor. Doubtless she was already weighing him up.

'You OK?' Angela said, just to be kind.

'Yes, thanks. It's nice to be here with you.'

She leaned over and pressed her shoulder against his, affectionately.

'People will talk,' Brian said from across the table.

'People will always talk,' she answered. 'How are you, Brian?'

But before he could answer, Bill said, 'I'm going to give thanks. You can join me or not according to the colour of your allegiances. Let us pray.'

David looked around and saw every head bowed but no eyes closed among the four non-St Mary's members across the table, all in a row. He closed his own eyes.

'Dear Father, thank You for so much. Thank You for these festive days of remembering together the birth of Your Son, and the way the seasonal bonhomie draws people together in an agreed atmosphere of celebration and goodwill. Thank you for sending Him, Your only Son, born at Bethlehem for us. Thank You for so many good gifts, most of all for friends and friendship, as we gather round this table. Thank You for all the food and drink we're about to enjoy, and – '

Mary gave a little but well-directed cough.

He hurried to a conclusion, 'Oh, and yes, show mercy upon all those who have so much less than us. Amen.'

'Amen,' went round the table.

Brian seemed to have forgotten the question, or even that it had been asked, so Angela left it.

Mary and Bill left the table. Mary came back with a tray of bowls of soup, with baskets of bread rolls. She served them, offering tomato or butternut squash and lentil, and went out for more. Bill started going round attending to people's drinks, and brought Ruf another cold Fosters. Angela had Mary's punch, while David went on to red wine.

Once everyone was served, they all began, and Ruf was finished in a matter of seconds. Taking advantage of the initiative, he said, 'So, David. You taught at my school for a while. You never taught me, but I was there. Do you know what the kids used to call you?'

'Mr Sourbook or "sir" most of the time,' he said, a little wary.

'Yes, but you had nicknames. Every teacher has nicknames. Boys often called you "Berserk". That came from turning "Sour Book" into "Bour Sook" and then "Ber Serk". Especially when everyone knew you hated Bubble Bairstow and there was that fight in the staff room and everyone said you'd knocked him down and kicked …'

'How is the soup?' asked Mary, loudly, cutting Ruf off.

Lots of comments of, 'Ooh, lovely,' and 'Did you make this yourself?' and 'Did you grow these tomatoes, Bill?' ensured that Ruf wasn't able to retake the floor.

Angela gave David a concerned look.

Ian Staines said, 'Well, what about this weather? It's been lethal, hasn't it?' and the conversation went round for a while about incidents of dented cars and slipping pedestrians.

But David was beginning to feel really vulnerable. He'd decided, wisely he felt, not to answer the blatant untruth of the accusation. But what more was yet to come?

CHAPTER EIGHTEEN

The soup was finished without incident, except for Brian demanding to know why all these people were in his garden or study or house, all of which was handled with gentle respect by his wife, Jan, and by others.

Bill and Mary Granger cleared away, and in the pause before the main course, in a moment's hush, Ruf said, 'So, Mr Sourbook, David, was trying to explain to me before about being kind because God is kind.'

'That sounds interesting,' Greg Davis said, encouragingly. 'Tell us more.'

'Well,' Ruf began. 'Where I come from what they're doing isn't called kindness. We call it something else.'

There was a hanging silence. David went red – he could feel it, right down his collar. He dared not engage Angela's face.

Anna spoke and broke the thick air. 'I think they're just becoming new friends, that's all.'

'There is no soul without kindness,' Ella Pickett said. 'My mother used to say that.'

'Really? What does it mean?' Holly asked, continuing to distract attention from Ruf. 'Does it mean that everyone has some amount of kindness in them, or they wouldn't have a soul?'

'No. Not that. At least, that wasn't the intention of it. She meant that without kindness, no soul can exist – anyone who has no kindness has no soul. Wasn't that what Dickens meant – that Scrooge was essentially soulless – a chained ghost? And soulless people are ghosts even before they die?'

Aaron Pickett answered his wife, 'I don't think that's quite what Dickens was suggesting, though not far from it, perhaps.'

David went cold, like ice had formed in his very heart. He remembered how he'd told Angela he neither had kindness to give nor wanted any to be given to him. Did he have no soul? Was he, all these cold years, a walking, chained ghost?

Ruf had only been waiting for a gap in the talk, and said, 'Oh, I reckoned more than that.'

'Well, I'm sure they're old enough and wise enough to work that out for themselves!' Sue Staines put in.

'OK, well,' Ruf continued, 'David let me change out of some wet clothes in a spare bedroom. Do you know what he's got in his other spare bedroom? A huge teddy bear, nearly as big as him! Makes you wonder what he gets up to in that house all on his own.'

'I think we're probably ready for the next course!' Mary Granger said, standing. There was general agreement. She and Bill went off and brought in a trolley with heated compartments containing plates, dishes of vegetables and potatoes, gravy, and so on. Mary started to hand these out as Bill went back to the kitchen and returned with a huge roast turkey and a roast ham on another trolley, and knives to carve them.

Angela was trying to talk nicely to Ruf, who seemed agreeable enough. Anna Lovren spoke quietly to David while the food was being served. In-between them, Holly and Greg were heads-together having their own intimate moment.

'Are you OK?' Anna said. 'He seems to have it in for you.'

'Yes, I'm OK. Maybe he's trying to assert a bit of independence – make it clear he's not some charity case.'

'Mmm, maybe. Tell me, do you have family?' she asked.

Alarm bells went off inside him somewhere. She wanted to know about his childhood. 'No, not really. Some distant relations I'm not really sure about, and not in touch with. Both my parents are dead.'

'No brothers or sisters?'

'There was a sister but she died before I was born. Of meningitis. I never knew her.'

'What was her name?' Anna asked.

'Michaela.'

'That's a nice name. So you were her replacement.'

'Was I? I don't think so. I was just me. Though the fact they'd lost her made them very protective of me. I was glass.'

'What were your parents like?'

'What were they like? I don't know. Who knows what their parents were like? They were just my parents.'

'OK,' Anna said. 'Did they argue in front of you, or fight?'

'No, not that I can recall.'

'Were they very calm people?'

'Calm? Quiet, I suppose. So, yes, I suppose calm. Not noisy, anyway.'

'What effect did Michaela's death have on them, do you think?'

'I suppose they had a terrible sense of loss. An emptiness. And they feared losing me.'

'Why did they fear losing you?'

'Because I guess they knew you can lose a child.' He thought that was a bit obvious, and wondered where she was going with this.

'So they smothered you with affection – always kissing you and cuddling you and asking you if you were all right and getting you anything you wanted?'

'No, well, not particularly. They kept a very careful eye on me and wouldn't let me do anything dangerous or be out of their sight much. But they didn't smother me. They did buy me loads of stuff.'

'How long ago did they die?'

'Dad in 1992, Mum in 2008.'

'I bet that left a big gap in your life.'

'No. I didn't still live with them or anything. For some reason I resented my mum for most of my life. I liked my dad, and he died young, but that's cancer for you, isn't it?'

'Did your mum really miss him after he was gone?'

'I suppose so. She had friends, though.'

'Did you go to see her frequently – try to look after her a bit?'

'No, she was fine. She was healthy right up to when she got the chest infection that killed her.'

'Do you think they intended to have just one more child after Michaela died?'

'I'm not sure they intended to have any more. Or maybe they did intend to have me, but then had to be so careful to protect me that they couldn't have any more. I don't really know.'

'And you never asked them about that?'

'*Ask them?* No. I couldn't have discussed that with them.'

'Do you miss them?'

'Not specially. You know, people get old, and they die. It's the way of things.'

'Do you have any special or particular friends? People you see a lot of and you're close to?'

'I tend to be very happy with my own company. I'm self-contained. I don't need other people all the time. Oh, look, turkey and stuffing!'

The arrival of his plate was his signal to break off from the conversation and attend to potatoes, vegetables, and helping himself to more wine on the table. He looked across and saw that Ruf's lager bottle was empty, but there was red wine in his glass. That didn't make him happy.

'You OK?' Angela asked him.

'Yes, you?'

'Yes. Let's hope our guest is!'

'It would be a lie if I said I'm not feeling a bit wary,' David admitted.

'So, David,' Aaron Pickett said. 'You were a physics teacher. Can you explain relativity in words of not more than three syllables?'

His heart sank. He hated these requests, particularly about relativity or quantum mechanics. Why didn't anyone ever want to know about fluid mechanics or the first or second law of thermodynamics?

Everyone was watching him. Even Ruf was leaning round Angela to listen.

'Are you sure you wouldn't rather know about entropy?' he said.

'What's entropy?' said Jan Carstairs. 'I mean, no, forget entropy, tell us about relativity and Einstein.'

'Well, if you're sure you really want to know …'

He hoped for dissent, but there was none. With a sigh, he launched in.

At the end there was a puzzled silence. 'Can we talk about something else now?' he asked.

Mary Granger said, 'Let's eat!' and everyone started eating.

Smaller conversations broke out again and David was happy to talk to Angela for a while.

'What did Anna want?' she asked.

'To find out about my family and relationships. I thought she said we'd have to pay for that kind of psychoanalysis.'

'Yes, she did. You lucky fellow!'

'I can hardly believe my good fortune. Protect me from any more.'

'Oh, I don't know. I think she's to be trusted.'

'Great. This is delicious.'

'They're both great cooks and fantastic entertainers. They do this every year, and other occasions, for all sorts of other groups and charities. They have a real gift of hospitality. They do loads of stuff in the garden in summer months as well.'

And so the meal continued, with conversations flowing between small-group chatting and whole-table debating, with much mirth and no little drinking of wine by those who weren't driving. David was dismayed to see Ruf had been quietly refilling his wine glass repeatedly. He wanted to move the wine bottle away but feared the reaction.

The main course was cleared away. Desserts appeared – Christmas puddings, mince pies, cheesecakes, cream and brandy butter. And it was well into this course that Ruf, now slurring his words slightly, said loudly, and without pausing for breath, 'You,

David, you had a reputation as being hard-faced and unfair. You gave my brother two detentions he never deserved. You kept a whole class in for making noise and you got a friend of my brother's expelled for breaking physics equipment when it wasn't even him who did it. You were hated. You could never take a joke and everyone cheered when you left. Nobody liked you.'

'Such is the lot of the teacher,' Greg said. 'To which I can testify.'

Bill Granger added, 'You seem to rather have it in for poor David this evening, despite how kind he and Angela have been to you.'

'It's not him, it's her that's being kind. He's a teacher. He's the enemy as far as I'm concerned.'

'What?' asked Bill. 'Even after you've left, even when you've grown up a bit, even when he tries to help you personally, he's still the enemy? Isn't that a bit unfair?'

'Look at you!' Ruf said, red-faced now. 'You and your posh houses and your nice clothes and your holidays and your expensive riches. You have no idea about me and people like me and real life. Your religion is a load of rubbish and you're hypocrites, all of you.'

'Oh,' Bill responded. 'I see. And what is it, I wonder, that we're being criticised for? Is it how hard and long we had to work to get to these positions, and how much we've had to give up to work as we do? We do this to serve, as well as we possibly can, to help people when they really need help, and not at all for self-aggrandisement. Is it the money we're paid, of which we give generously to others? Is it how little spare time our jobs leave us, yet which we still use to volunteer and serve? Is it our houses that we try to use to bless others, not just ourselves? What is it you so object to?'

Ruf started to stand, and said, 'What I ...' then put his hand to his mouth and went a funny colour.

'Oh dear!' Mary said.

He managed to half-turn before the torrent began, so it went down Mary and the floor rather than the table. But the smell was instant. And Mary's dress was covered down one side.

'Oh dear!' she said again.

The table deconstructed into various levels of shock and horror, variously handled with grace or annoyance. Angela stood and took hold of Mary's arm. 'Come on,' she said. 'I'll help you get changed.'

Bill took hold of Ruf's arm, similarly, and it was clear that he had managed not to get anything on himself. But he was in no condition to stay. Bill said, 'Ian and Sue, please take everyone through to the sitting room where we will serve coffee in a little while. Take your drinks with you. Leave everything else to us.' Then, to Ruf, he said, quite kindly, 'Young man, you need to come with me.'

They left the room, and Ian and Sue did a good job of shepherding everyone through to the sitting room, where the fire still crackled heartily. David sat on the white settee, and Anna plonked herself down next to him.

'Hello again,' she said, quite jauntily. 'I have a feeling we've only just started.'

This time he didn't mind so much. 'OK,' he said. 'Ask away.'

She took a sip of her white wine, looked him straight in the eye and said, 'OK, I'm going to rough you up a bit. I bet when you sit down and someone starts talking to you, you wish they'd go away.'

'Yes, but that's a man thing.'

'Is it? Most men have plenty of friends, often mainly other men, and are comfortable in their company, and in mixed company with them. I bet you also have difficulty sometimes, when you see a person, deciding whether that's someone you know or have just seen often.'

'Maybe. So?'

'That's because, like an ASD sufferer, I think you have some people-blindness. You don't mark out as special in any way the people you know. Relationship doesn't "light them up". It doesn't put them on a different "register". And that's why you tend not to make friends. Every time you see a person again or engage with them another time, *they* will be expecting an increase in the level of relationship, but your "engagement level" just slips back to zero each time. You treat them like the last conversation or times together never happened. Not because you've actually forgotten them, but because it never marked them out in any way as significant individuals. People you cared about. People either think you're very "cold" or have a very bad memory, or you've just decided you don't like them very much. That isn't actually true, mostly. You just don't register them as in any way special, so you'd pass them in the street and not even differentiate between them and someone you've passed often but never actually engaged with.'

'Well, that's not entirely true. There are people I pass and say hello to.'

'In general, I think what I've just told you is true. Tell me it isn't.'

'I guess it may be.'

She looked intently at him, seemingly taking him all in, and said, 'I'm going to fly a kite here, if you'll let me. Tell me about the earliest, really sad dream you can remember.'

He was puzzled. But also intrigued. What *was* she getting at? 'A sad dream?'

'A dream that was so sad it made you sad even after you woke up. Really sad. The first you can identify.'

He thought. That was a challenge. He was impressed by how she waited and said nothing. Then it struck him. 'Oh, yes. This is strange. I was with my sister, in a tunnel. Dark, like a London Underground tunnel. She was much younger than me, maybe only two or three or so. And she slips and falls on the live rail and is electrocuted. I look at her dead body, and the sense of loss is overwhelming. I feel so utterly sorry for her, lying there, all dead. There's this terrible feeling of regret, like a horrible, sick nostalgia. Like a yearning for something I never had. Like I knew I hadn't loved her and now I couldn't ever make up for it and love her like I should. Truly, truly awful. Such heart-tearing, self-reproaching regret and remorse. And when I woke up from it I did still feel terribly sad and full of loss and like I could never put it right. And that has stayed with me, my whole life, whenever I remember that dream again.'

'How old were you?'

'Maybe nine?'

'What did she look like?' Anna asked.

'What do you mean?'

'Apparently you never saw her, so what did she look like in the dream?'

'Well,' David hesitated, 'like the pictures we had of her at home.'

'Look, David, my friend, let me be totally honest with you. This is not just psychotherapy. I'm going with a strong gut feeling here, so bear with me. I've learned to listen to God as well as use my training. I believe I have a gift of a certain sort of insight. So, let's see where this leads. If you're willing. No charge! Would you describe her to me, please?'

He drew in a deep breath, and searched his memory for a 'real' image. It came. 'She had a round face, she was about two, she had blonde hair, blue eyes, a sweet little nose.'

'That's a lovely image. In fact, it's quite an emotional image, I feel. So, bear with me. Do you ever get a terrible yearning? Do you sometimes feel like something "out there" or "deep inside" is calling to you, pulling some sort of unknown need or loss from you, or drawing you to itself to find something that gives you the answers to yourself?'

He was surprised. 'Yes! At dusk, I often sit outside and look at the sky and something pulls at me, like a great yearning. I've sometimes wondered if maybe it's God. Or that which makes us imagine God. Something "out there" that seems to have the frequency of my soul, and is transmitting, calling.'

'Right,' she said. 'Well, hold on to your seat. I'm going to have to do this quick and dirty, though I'm very happy to see you again as a friend, privately, after this. You might be surprised at a Christian telling you this, but I don't think it's God. Or, anyway, not just God, or maybe God is using it to call you but it's not initially about Him. I think that yearning is for your sister, Michaela. And it's a yearning for all the relationships you could have had in your life if you hadn't felt like that about losing her. That single loss has made you unable to face loss and so unable to "see" other people so you can't form real relationships with them. It protects you from further loss. It wasn't your parents who reacted that way to losing her, it was you. It's made you a bit like someone with ASD. You don't fully "see" other people. It's not that you're unkind, you just don't see in people what it is that draws kindness out of us. That needy, inviting, reaching-out, human soul. Can you see what I'm getting at?'

'I suppose so. Yes.'

'Well, here's the real kicker. I'm really sticking my neck out here. I'm putting some pieces together, which if I'm wrong will just lead to nothing but if I'm right could open all sorts of things up for you. You need to check Michaela's birth certificate. I don't think she was older than you and died before you were born. I suspect she was younger than you and that memory of her face is a real one, and you knew her as your little sister, maybe doted on her, and you were there when she died. You lost her, and you've never been able to face it or recover from it.'

It was head-doctor madness. 'Oh,' was all he could manage.

She continued, verbal scalpel shining in the subtle lights. 'Are there no pictures at home? A family album? Something with all of you on?'

'My parents kept the pictures. I only have one or two, of me, or me with them.'

'What about when they died?'

'Cleared out, I suppose.'

'By whom?'

'By me.'

She just looked at him. Was that contempt? Pity? Confusion?

'David, look again. There must be something, somewhere.'

215

'OK,' he mumbled, not really intending to. He needed to escape. 'I'm going to go to the loo.'

'Sure. Thank you, David. Think over what I've said. Come back to me if it starts to make any sense.'

When he got back he joined Angela, and they drank a coffee together, and he was once again among the throng. Soon coats were going on, and fond farewells were being exchanged with festive friends.

As Angela drove them home, he said to her, 'What an evening! What a bunch of crazy people! They are the cracked club.'

'Really? You mean Anna. I'm not going to pry, but she's certainly not crazy.'

'Hmm.'

He mulled and mused. Her birth certificate? He had no idea where to even begin looking for it. Maybe she meant online? And pictures? They were gone.

This, surely, was the worst kind of raking up, and he was sure he could sue her for it. Though clearly she meant well. And she was a good friend of Angela's. But a cynic would call it manipulation, even hypnotism. Hmm.

And did that only serve to confirm his concern and suspicion about Angela, and about the whole group from the start, that there was some sort of shared not-quite-saneness about them?

PART THREE

CHAPTER NINETEEN

It was Wednesday, 23rd December.

She drove. He looked about.

There beside the road was a very bedraggled and ill-looking dog. He stared at it as they went past.

He said, 'That dog looked really sick. I bet it's going to throw up. I once saw a dog licking at its own vomit.'

'Oh, no, don't tell me,' she pleaded.

'Yes, it was all yellow with chunks, and it was licking at the chunks, and then this other dog came along.'

'No, surely not ...'

'Yes, it started licking as well. Doesn't the Bible say something about a dog returning to its own vomit?'

'Yes, it's from Proverbs, repeated in Second Peter, but that doesn't make it a pleasant subject for conversation in the car!'

'I was only saying.'

'You're a strange, strange man.'

'It's why you love me.'

'Because you talk about dogs licking vomit – no, I don't think so.'

He looked across at her, driving so warily, like a woman, and saw the little smile on her sweet face.

'And if you think *that* story is going to ever make me more inclined to kiss you ...' she added.

'It passes the time,' he said, referring to the journey.

'There are nicer ways.'

It wasn't even white any more. A dramatic thaw overnight had melted all the snow and ice apart from the occasional pile which was thick enough to have resisted. The roads were completely clear. But water in puddles and little trickles was everywhere. Dampness pervaded.

The drive was boring, but fairly free-moving. It was the day before Christmas Eve. And this certainly didn't look or feel festive.

He felt tired. He'd slept well enough, but not long enough, due to this early start. He felt a bit like dozing, but didn't know how Angela might take that, so he stayed awake.

Still, he was looking forward to meeting Andrew, at the end of this dull journey. It started to drizzle. Like the air had suddenly become tiny droplets of cloudy water. She set the wipers going and they streaked and smeared across the screen. 'What a dreary day,' he said.

'OK,' she replied. 'Let me tell you a bit about Andrew, so you know what to expect and how to handle him. He's lovely, he really is, but some advance briefing will help you and him. Are you ready?'

'Yes, I am ready.'

'So, my sister Thelia is eight years younger than me, so she's forty-four. She had Andrew when she was thirty-four. OK, for a teacher of maths and physics that's not too hard – he's ten. But he's quite slight in build so you'll think he looks about eight. He is the kind of ASD sufferer who has difficulty feeling things. He needs to rock sometimes to feel himself and distinguish himself from his surroundings. And he may be quite ferocious in his hugs. He needs to chew really hard things from time to time, but like many of his needs they have to be controlled, so he's allowed three boiled sweets out of the fridge to crunch on every day. And we don't worry about what it might do to his teeth, because he has to do it, and he seems to manage OK. He has to ask for his three sweets, as one of many means to get him to vocalise, and he has to look the person in the eye when he speaks to them. If he uses repetitive speech patterns we try to get him to rephrase what he's said properly.

'He loves numbers. He's quite a mathematician. It's his main obsession. Along with Lego and Star Wars, so he has lots of

Lego, lots of Star Wars stuff, and lots of Star Wars Lego! And he can talk about numbers and Star Wars and Lego till your ears drop off, so he's limited to half an hour a day on each. Which I think is a bit generous, but Thelia sets the limits, not me.

'He finds surprises hard, and changes in routine, and sometimes new people. Routine and predictability are his mainstay, his safe ground. He needs them. But, again, we have to work round them sometimes. Change is inevitable and he has to be able to adapt to it, and has to learn to, with support.

'Er, let's see. He gets tired so he has an afternoon nap. Never push him away, however hard he squeezes you. Always look him in the eye when you speak to him, even though he probably won't be looking in your eye. Be gentle with him, and we don't punish him because punishments just don't work. Any questions?'

'Does he bite?'

She held up her left hand, showing a wide scar on her wedding-ring finger. 'Nearly took it right down to the bone. But he doesn't any more. Hardly.'

'I'll cover that with a ring one day.'

'Promises!' she said.

They drove in silence for a while, then David said, 'I wonder what happened to Ruf.'

'He won't be up yet, I don't think, judging by the state of him last night.'

'What will Bill and Mary do?'

'Have a stern but kindly word with him, I'd imagine, both of them together, about what's appropriate and what isn't. And maybe about showing gratitude to you rather than bashing you.'

'Hmm.'

'How did that feel?'

'Surprisingly embarrassing, especially in front of all your friends.'

'All of whom were on your side.'

'Really?'

'Absolutely!' she affirmed.

'Even you?'

'Especially me!'

'But now I've blown it with the sick dog thing.'

'Yeah, that was a shame.'

After a pause she added, 'Oh, yes, by the way, leave yourself free for Christmas Day dinner.'

'But I've got stuff in.'

'You've got stuffing?'

'Yes, stuffing, ha ha. And everything else for a sumptuous, festive feast for one.'

'Well, keep that for our New Year's Day dinner. Be free Christmas Day.'

'Am I coming to you?'

'Just keep it free.'

'Not the crazy club again?'

'What if it was? But no.'

They arrived in time for the handover before Thelia went to work, but David had to have his coffee in the kitchen while Angela went in with Thelia to see Andrew.

Thelia was a little shorter than Angela, with similar hair, a longer face, and glasses. Her eyes had a darting brightness to them, like a bird. She welcomed him with genuine warmth before taking Angela in to say hi to the boy. Thelia was wearing a nurse's uniform.

David sat in the kitchen/diner and looked around him. On the wall was a picture of a Star Wars electronic voice mask in its box, and a picture beside it of what seemed to be the same box, but wrapped in gold and red paper. Next to that was a large-faced clock, and a list of events for today, with careful timings. He saw that Andrew's lunch was to be beef chunks in gravy, with raw carrots, raw onions and lightly boiled potatoes, followed by a crisp apple. Then there was a planner to count down to Christmas Day. Then a reminder of some rules – things Angela had mentioned to him.

He sat on a stool at a breakfast bar. There was no tree and no decorations. Only some Christmas cards stuck on the fridge door. Out through French windows the garden looked dull and soggy – battered by the recent weather. A bit like he felt. Dashed upon the rocks of outrageous misfortune. No, maybe that was a bit strong. And dramatic. Just a bit jaded from the unpredictable and rather strenuous nature of life with Angela. 'Life with Angela'? Really?

He was woken from his reverie of letting thoughts from the last few days flow across his awareness by Thelia insisting, 'David? Goodbye!'

'Oh, sorry, I was far away. Goodbye. Have a good day.'

'See you later,' she said. 'Help yourself to whatever you fancy.'

'OK, fine, thanks, bye,' he managed.

Angela stood behind her. 'Come and meet Andrew,' she said.

He got off the stool and followed. He always seemed to be following her. Life with Angela?

Andrew was, as Angela had told him, slight in build and small enough to have been more like eight. He was sitting on the floor next to a huge tub of Lego, some pieces of which he had out already on the bright, red and cream carpet. He didn't look up, but David saw the face of an angel. Red hair, pale complexion, pleasant features, a band of freckles across his nose.

'This is David who I just told you about,' Angela said, going and sitting in a brown armchair over to David's right.

Andrew stood, looking at the floor. Angela nodded David towards him. He went over, stood a yard away and said, 'Hello, Andrew, it's nice to meet you.'

Angela gave a little cough, and Andrew, still looking down, said, 'Meet you, meet you, meet you.'

Angela responded. 'That's very nice, Andrew, but can we try it just once and complete, please.'

'It's nice to meet you,' Andrew said, then promptly sat down again.

'Maybe David will play with you for a while,' Angela said.

Andrew peered into his box at his precious pieces. David seated himself on the carpet near to him and looked around. There on the mantelpiece over the fireplace, which had a portable electric fire in it, were the same pictures of presents and schedules as in the kitchen/diner. Again, there was no tree and no decorations. The room had a settee, with some bits of paper and a laptop on it, and to the left, towards the front windows, there was a large, maybe black, armchair that looked particularly battered.

Angela saw him looking and said, 'It's his bouncing chair. He's allowed time on it each day.'

Andrew had a row of small towers of pieces. There was one of only two pieces in yellow, then next to it, three in red, then larger again in blue, and so they continued in ever-larger numbers in a perfectly straight line. There was a couple of inches between each stack. David noticed, though, that they were built with two bricks in one direction held by the next two bricks, above, in the other direction, giving them strength and stability. It was all very carefully put together and seemed to rise and then level off, like a bridge, as each succeeding tower got thicker rather than taller so they wouldn't fall over.

'Is it a bridge?' David asked, but got no reply, nor any flicker of recognition.

Andrew was working on the eleventh tower, in red, then sat back to look at it, so David took a red brick and added it to that one. He pressed it on. Andrew looked at it, his face screwed into a ball of thunder, and he swept the whole tower onto the carpet with his arm. Then he pounded it with his fist.

David said, 'I'm sorry, Andrew! What did I do wrong?'

Andrew just sat and stared at the remaining towers. David looked at them. What was he missing? Then he said, 'Primes! Andrew, primes! I'm sorry, I ruined – let's see, I ruined thirty-one. You have two, three, five, seven, eleven, thirteen, seventeen, nineteen, twenty-three, twenty-nine and then thirty-one. I'm sorry.'

Andrew started scooping up the pieces, breaking them carefully into singles, and dropping them back into the box. David didn't dare help. He felt terrible. He'd ruined Andrew's mathematical design, which probably meant more to him than David could imagine, and he'd most likely just ruined any chance of getting on with him.

He looked at Angela. She just raised her eyebrows.

'You're a clever lad to know prime numbers,' David said, but got no reaction. Andrew just sat beside the refilled box, cross-legged on the floor, no longer sprawled and having mathematical fun.

After a very uncomfortable moment, he put his arm in the box again. Maybe …

He fished out some red tiles onto the carpet. This looked hopeful. He started again, building rather as before. David kept quiet, and watched, and counted. He noticed Andrew started by pressing his hand flat on the carpet, as if to mark out a place. But he didn't build there, he started next with one brick. Then one brick in the next place, then two. Three, five, eight, thirteen followed. Then a painstaking twenty-one, by which time David was certain.

'Fibonacci numbers!' He cried. 'You're building towers of the Fibonacci numbers.'

'What's that?' Angela asked.

'It's an important mathematical progression where every number is the last two numbers added together. Brilliant! So that pressing of his hand on the carpet designated a space – zero. OK, then I'll set you a test, young Andrew. Can I get some bricks from the box, please?'

Andrew gave the tiniest nod, and David began. He made small towers, each of the same colour, just as Andrew was doing. He built parallel to Andrew, so he was looking at him as he worked. He started with one, then four, then twelve other numbers, and stopped. Andrew had been peering over at him as he worked on his own rising towers. David's didn't look so impressive in height, but he reckoned height wasn't the point for Andrew. Not at all.

He said, 'So, Andrew, do you want to put in the next number?'

Andrew stopped what he was doing and went very still. The look on his face was unreadable, but it was something. Wonder? Annoyance? Happiness? Anticipation? Frustration?

He started to stand up, very slowly, and came round to stand beside David, then he sat down, and took bricks from the box. He placed them as the next tower – a blue 'three'.

'Wow!' David said, ruffling his hair. 'Do just one more so I know it's not a fluke.'

He made a yellow 'two'.

'Amazing!' David cried, and Andrew beamed.

David was so excited he knelt up, and Andrew threw himself at him and hugged him so tightly David's face was being crushed by Andrew's. He allowed this for as long as he felt he could, then said, 'OK, sit down, Andrew, and let me ask you some questions about it.'

Andrew let go and sat, still bright with joy.

'Firstly, what is this?'

'Decimal places of pi.'

'So it is. So it is. Now to sixteen places.'

'Is this something extraordinary I'm not getting?' Angela asked.

'Not so much extraordinary in itself as in that he knows them. So let's find out how much he knows.' David took out his phone and called up some numbers. 'Andrew, taking the first 100 decimal places of pi, what number is in 100th place?'

'Nine.'

'How many times does six occur in those 100 places?'

'Nine.'

'What is the mode?'

'Nine.'

'He's just saying "nine",' Angela said.

'No, he isn't. And the median?'

'Five.'

'And the mean?'

'Four point seven seven.'

'What number is at pi to 1,000 places?'

'Nine.'

David rocked back in total amazement. 'That's not just "good with numbers". That's incredible.'

Andrew looked up, almost into Angela's face, and smiled, his face lit up like a light bulb.

'I think he's found a new best friend,' she said.

The first part of lunch was fine. They all sat at the table in the kitchen/diner looking out of the French windows on to the dreary garden. Angela and David had sandwiches while Andrew had his beef chunks in gravy and crunchy vegetables. But over his apple, he became increasingly agitated. David noticed he kept looking towards the clock.

Angela said, 'Andrew, we are going out after our lunch. But we'll take the usual route and be back in forty-five minutes, into the nice, safe, warm house, and have a cup of tea. You don't need to get worried about it. It's the same as every day.'

Andrew showed no reaction. Angela explained to David, 'He doesn't really like going out, because the world out there is full of uncertainties, whereas in here it's so much more predictable. But that makes it so important we take him out. He just cannot miss out on the wider world and all it has to offer. So the going out is itself part of the daily pattern. Which helps because doing it is part of the regularity on which he so relies. To make it easier, if he's at all anxious, we take the default route, which is as predictable as possible. If he's in a good way on a particular day, we'll take a slightly different route. Clearly today it's the default route. Out and back in the expected time, and a predictable routine once we get in. You'd think he wasn't even listening, wouldn't you? But he is.'

'What are the rules once he's out?' David asked.

Andrew took such a bite of his apple that the sound covered over the first words of her reply, so she gave the noisy boy a sideways glance and started again. 'He isn't allowed to engage in mathematics or talk about mathematics, Lego or Star Wars. He isn't allowed to sit down unless we give him permission. That's it, really.'

'Not wander off?'

'He wouldn't.'

Andrew finished the core of the apple, seeds and all, and went to the sink to wash his hands. Then he stood, staring into the sink, immobile.

'Andrew, outdoor boots on, coat on, then we'll go.'

Andrew didn't move.

'Now, Andrew, please,' she said, firmly, and he shuffled off into the hallway. David and Angela followed and watched him as they put their coats and shoes on.

'Here we go,' Angela announced, and opened the door. Andrew shrunk back from it, but then proceeded outside with them.

It was mild in the air. But grey were the clouds and strangely threatening the yellowish light in the sky. Andrew seemed unaware of them, but fixated instead on the ground. He gave the impression of being fascinated by everything near his feet. They walked along a paving slab footpath to a park entrance where gravel paths circled the grass. They crunched along. They heard Andrew counting his steps, and Angela gave him a nudge and said, 'No, Andrew.'

After a few more paces, she said, 'Sometimes, if there's two of us, like Thelia and Martin, or me and Thelia, we give him a swing between us.'

'Andrew, do you want a swing?' David said, feeling quite bold and also affectionate towards him.

He stopped and held out a hand either side.

'Oh, you are privileged!' Angela said.

David and Angela each took a hand, lifted him and swung him forwards. He was surprisingly light. He swung up and back, and his feet hit the ground again.

He made a noise.

'Ask,' Angela said.

'More, please.'

They did it again. They repeated it some six more times before it got a bit strenuous, and stopped. They continued walking, Andrew head down. He picked up a leaf, and held it up to David.

'Five parts,' he said.

'What colour is it?' David replied.

'Brown.'

'Is it heavy or light?'

'Light.'

'Is it new or old?'

'New,' Andrew answered. That puzzled David, but he let it go. A matter of definition, no doubt.

'Can you see an old one?' he asked.

'Old ones are all gone.'

'Ah,' David said, enlightened. 'Would you like to sit on my shoulders?' He looked across at Angela, who nodded and smiled.

Andrew put himself right in front of David and just stopped, facing forwards still, waiting.

David went right up behind him, put his hands fairly heavily on his shoulders, and asked, 'What do you say, Andrew?'

The little shoulders shrugged.

'What do you say if you want a ride?'

'Ride, please,' he said.

David picked him up under the arms and lifted him over his head and onto his shoulders. He really was very light. Immediately, he started playing with David's hair.

Angela said, 'Is that all right, David?'

'It's fine. It isn't a wig.'

And so he carried him, like one person travelling along, and it gave David great comfort. Something he hadn't expected. 'Is he OK up there?' he asked Angela.

'Yes, he looks happy,' she said.

'Then that's two of us,' and he was sure he felt Andrew's legs give his neck a small squeeze.

David was unaccountably pleased.

As soon as they were back inside the house, Andrew said, '153 leaves. That's nine times seventeen. And it's fifty-one times three.'

'What is the prime factorisation of 153, then?' David asked.

'Three squared and seventeen. Primes,' Andrew answered.

Before David could congratulate him, Andrew grabbed him round the middle and squeezed. David placed his hands on Andrew's back and squeezed also, knowing that the sense of that pressure was what the boy needed to feel. And so they stood, for long seconds, and it was as if the relief and joy of Andrew had gone right inside him, and he felt it too.

It was good.

They started off in the car and David was looking ahead as if at the road, while the world around them darkened, but in reality he was looking at her. He looked at the shape of her. She was quite nicely shaped. Not fat and not thin. Not twisted or bent! And her face was very sweet, and he liked her somewhat straggly hair. He couldn't help notice how she drove. At first, she took her hand off the wheel whenever she needed to operate the indicators. She looked altogether stiff and uncomfortable. Her face was a little intent. She kept shifting herself in the seat by pushing against the floor. Then, after about five minutes, she relaxed. She kept her hand on the wheel and just used her fingers to operate the indicators. She settled and her face relaxed.

He said, 'Do you know, it is said by those in ergonomics that when a man drives a car, it becomes a sort of extension of himself. The driving of it is somehow "natural". When a woman drives a car, it's a machine she must master and control, and not at all a part of herself. Not "natural". So, a man drives the road, while a woman drives the car. Do you know you just settled into it after five minutes as if it took you that long to regain your confidence?'

'I suppose I'm vaguely aware. Perhaps I'd describe it as being extra cautious to make sure I'm attending to what I'm doing and driving safely, rather than lacking confidence.'

She sounded just a tad tetchy. 'Sorry,' he said. 'I didn't mean to criticise.'

'That's OK. Let's play a game. What are the two letters in the English language that don't appear at the end of words?'

'Ooh,' David mused, 'that's hard. Let's see.' He went through the alphabet in order, out loud, putting likely letters aside. 'The answer must be j and q.'

'Brilliant!' she said, nudging his arm. 'I love the logical and so ordered way your mind works. So neat and methodical. No shooting off in the dark, just lay it out in order and look at it calmly. I love that about you. Your turn to ask me something.'

'OK,' he said, feeling very pleased about himself. And her as well. He asked her what was the most commonly used letter in the English language.

'Let me think,' she said.

She mused quietly for a while and he looked out at the darkening horizons and the colours of the earth-liberated sky, the blues and silvers and the streaks of cloud like distant mountain ranges, calling to him.

And so it continued, as she drove and he became more and more weary.

CHAPTER TWENTY

They sat at his kitchen table eating pizza and sharing a bottle of cola. It was delicious, but moderately guilt-laden. David was surprised with what gusto Angela tucked in, a large piece of the multi-meat pizza hanging over the edges of her hand as she forced it into her mouth, tomato stains surrounding.

When she managed to swallow, she said, 'He really took to you.'

'And I to him. Like you said before, he is lovely.'

'That connection is a big deal. Thelia was more pleased than you know. That mathematical game, and I guess the way you did it, really made a connection with Andrew, and that's a rare and precious thing. So, thank you.'

'Do you think that wipes out the licking sick thing?'

'A distant memory. Except that you just reminded me.'

'I really enjoyed meeting him, and I hope very much to do it again.'

'I suspect you may well. You might get fed up with it.'

'Are you? Fed up with seeing him?'

'No.'

'Well, then.'

'But he's my sister's child. My only nephew.'

'Granted,' he said, round a fresh piece of the pizza.

'I bet you never took to any of your students like that,' she said.

When he got his mouth working again for speech, he said, 'While slightly insulted by the assumption, I'd have to admit it's true.'

'I think that's not just testimony to Andrew, but to the fact that something in you is changing.'

'I wouldn't disagree,' he agreed.

They ate and wiped and slurped.

'Can you stay the evening and maybe watch telly with me?' he asked, surprised at his new-found boldness.

'Yes, OK, but I can't stay late as I have to be up in the morning. And anyway I've had less sleep than you!'

'Oh?'

'You slept in the car.'

'Did I?'

'Yes, Little Noddy, you did.'

'I'm so sorry! I didn't know.'

'It's OK.'

'What do you have to do in the morning?'

'Christmas stuff. Have you bought me a present yet?'

That came at him out of some blind side. His brain froze. A present for her? He hadn't even bought her a card. Evasion was called for. 'Well, now, next you'll want to know what it is. Wait and see.'

'OK.'

So, that meant she'd bought him something. What could it be? Tomorrow, he would buy her a card and give it to her tomorrow as well. He would also buy her a present and some wrapping paper and give it to her on Christmas Day. Finding the right present would be a lot more difficult.

They cleared away the detritus and went into the front room where the Christmas tree blazed its jolly colours. Yet he felt he'd become somehow detached from Christmas altogether. Maybe that was just the lack of any decorations at Thelia's house and the very different environment he'd been in today. He hoped so.

She sat on the settee and he picked up the remote and stood, finding the guide and flicking though.

'Oh, my goodness!' he exclaimed. '*It's a Wonderful Life* is on in fifteen minutes.'

'That's that old film with what's-his-name Stewart that's supposed to be the most festively heartening Christmas film ever made, but it's in black and white.'

'That's part of its charm!'

She looked a little disappointed. 'Can't we watch something else?'

'Trust me.'

'Would you buy a used television from this man?' she said.

'Well, you should. He is to be trusted on all matters relating to the festive season. I'll get us some coffees and the chocs tin and if after half an hour you hate it, we'll watch something else.'

'Deal,' she said. 'Give me the remote so I can choose what it will be while you go and get coffees and chocs.'

He gave it to her and left the room.

Bearing two coffees and the tin he returned, and it was nearly time to begin. She had it on the right channel. He gave her her mug and was faced with an uneasy choice. He could go and sit on his armchair, or sit with her on the settee. He wanted to sit with her. Time to be bold. He put the tin on her lap and settled himself down beside her, not touching.

She didn't react. After all, they were friends now, surely, and today had been a very 'bonding' experience. And she owed him. Sort of.

The film began. 'It's a wonderful life,' David said, holding up his mug.

'Here's hoping,' she replied, and chinked hers against his.

He got comfortable.

After half an hour of pure nostalgic and festive joy, he said, 'So, to continue or not to continue, that is the question.'

'Continue,' she said.

'And now I'm going to be very bold, and put my arm round you, as long as you don't worry that that will lead to passionate embraces and the loss of your honour. And brash behaviour.'

'I think putting your arm round me would be entirely appropriate,' she said, and leaned herself over towards him. He put his right arm round her shoulders, and she settled herself against him so that her head was on his shoulder.

'Ooh, you have bony shoulders!' she said, and he feared she was about to change her mind. But instead, she sank down a couple of inches so her face was against his chest, and said, 'That's better. But keep still or I'll pinch you.'

Gosh, this was nice. She made him feel really good. It was warm, and comforting, and intimate, and trusting, and made him remember about getting a cat. Or, maybe, forget about getting one.

They watched in silence apart from one or two questions she asked about plot and characters, and when it got to the point where all the money goes missing, he realised she'd fallen asleep. She was resting easily against him, and that made him feel even more special. He moved his left hand across and stroked her cheek, ever so softly, with his thumb. She moved slightly, but didn't wake, so he kept the side of his hand against her face. It was smooth, and lovely to his touch. If he'd been in any doubt about his feelings for her before, he was no longer.

The film ended and as the music played, she woke up. She took a moment then said, 'What time is it?'

'Half-past nine, just gone.'

'Ooh, I've slept through half of it, haven't I?'

'Yes, but it was very nice just watching over you as you slept and stroking your cheek with my thumb. And you can always catch the second half another time.'

'You stroked my cheek?' She sat upright. 'You see how one thing leads to another? I'm a ruined woman. Despoiled. Stripped of my honour. I'll be shunned from one end of the town to the other.'

'Yes,' he agreed, 'but it was worth it!'

She thumped him playfully and smiled an angelic, sleepy smile. 'You're a brash fellow! I'd better get going. Much to do. If I don't see you tomorrow I'll see you in church Christmas morning, 11am. And don't forget about Christmas dinner.'

'No, I won't. Are you OK to drive?'

'Yes, I'm fine. Thanks for today, you've been a revelation. I think Thelia is going to be begging for you to come again.'

'That's nice. It really pleases me how I got on with Andrew. He's a great kid.'

'That he is, and I'm really chuffed you were so careful and affectionate towards him. That's from the heart. That's heartening.'

He recognised some unusual feelings churning in his chest. Love for Andrew – so it seemed. And love for her. Love for two people in one day. And yesterday he saved Mrs James.

'Oh, no! Mrs James!'

'What?' she said, shocked by the sudden outburst.

'What if she's come home and she's wondering where Harpie is?'

'No. Surely she won't be home yet. Not an old lady like that who very nearly died. Even these days they'll have to keep her in for a while, and there's no one at home to look after her, is there?'

'No, she lives alone. At least, that's how it's always seemed. I'll put a note through her door. "Dear Mrs James. I've got your dog" – no – that's a bit blunt.'

'Sounds like you've kidnapped it.'

'"Dear Mrs James, I'm sorry but Harpie passed away and I've looked after his body for you." And sign it and tell her where to come. Something like that.'

By now she was putting on her coat, and she reached up and kissed him on the cheek.

'You're a good man,' she said.

She hadn't pulled back very far when he turned his face and they were eye to eye, lips to lips, only inches apart. He went for it. He brushed her lips lightly with his, engaged her eyes close, and said, 'Goodnight.'

'Ooh!' she said. 'Goodnight.'

She opened the door and stepped out.

'Was that – all right?' he said, worried.

'It was very all right. And my honour is intact. All good. Thank you again, Little Noddy.'

'Goodnight, Angela.'

And with a final smile, she was gone.

He watched her as far as the car, where she turned and waved, and he waved back. Then he closed the door, and shook with excitement. He returned to the living room and hardly felt able to sit down. Good grief! Was this it? Was this the real thing? The Christmas tree blazed with promises of festivity and everlasting happiness. He collected up the mugs and chocs tin and took them to the kitchen, putting the mugs in the sink (a thing he never did) and set the tin on the worktop. He was singing – well, mangling very badly an old favourite that was hard to sing – 'The First Time Ever I Saw Your Face'. Squeaking and croaking, he carried on. It sounded fine to him, in the circumstances. He actually burst out laughing, and he knew his face was alight with beams of joy.

Returning to the front room, he made himself sit, first on his armchair, then where he'd sat with her. Where he'd cuddled her. He threw himself back against the cushions and stared at the glorious tree. The fabulous tree. The Christmassy Christmas tree.

'Time for wine,' he said, and ejected himself upright, and skipped into the kitchen again. He got a large glass of the mulled wine and warmed it in the microwave, then took it back into the living room, where he got the TV remote and decided to do some channel hopping. Oh, what a glorious day! What an amazing Christmas. Hardly noticing the listings scrolling before his eyes, his thoughts went to Andrew, that lovely boy. He surprised himself with how very fond he felt towards him. Was that just some sort of overflow from his feelings for Angela? No, he genuinely loved the boy. And that was a revelation. My goodness, life was changing fast. Who would have thought? He would buy Andrew a present as well. Lego? Star Wars? Numbers? He'd noticed that Andrew's tablet was far from the latest version. Hmm. Would such a large gift be appreciated?

Hmm. He'd love to make such a gift to him. He could ask Angela what she thought.

If he was 'Little Noddy', what was she? Not 'Big Ears', to be sure!

He took a large swig of the mulled wine. Delicious, he congratulated himself. Such joy. Such solitary joy. Such hopeful joy.

He selected a compilation of Christmas *Morecambe & Wise* and laughed so hard his ribs began to ache. He had two more large glasses of the mulled wine, not least because he was going to be too excited to sleep much tonight. Oh, there was the one with all the news reporters doing songs from *South Pacific*! Such hilarity! Such good days they were. Or were they? Such good Christmases, perhaps.

As with all good things, it ended, but he was nowhere near ready for bed, so he put on his DVD of *Scrooged* with Bill Murray. What a film! He laughed and he nearly wept, as well. Such good, festive fiction.

He woke at half-past one, the TV screen with a notice on it warning about copyright theft, and the wine glass cracked on the carpet beside his chair. No wine on the carpet, though.

Ha! He threw the glass in the kitchen bin and headed upstairs, feeling very groggy but no less festively inflated. 'Angela and Andrew,' he said. 'The lady and the lad. The babe and the boy.' He brushed his teeth, plugged in his phone, threw his clothes on the floor (a thing he never did) and climbed into his bed. He pulled the covers up around his neck and a tremble of sheer exhilaration went right through him. Was there ever such a day?

Wine-befogged, he did sleep, and dreamed of Lego bridges, leaves and being crushed. Also of warm embraces and soft faces, touching tenderly.

He was standing outside the door of an old house, set alone in some wooded place, in a still and preternaturally silent night. The door was in a small porch set into the corner of the house, and he was underneath its roof. Behind him and to his left was just emptiness, and on the walls to his right and ahead, creepers seemed to be hanging down rather than growing up, and continued even right around the door. Something was giving wan light, and all he was seeing was the old, wooden door of apparently thick, gnarled planks and the porch wall it was set in.

Without warning something started to bang heavily on the door from the 'other side'. Banging and shaking and bursting like it must break out, any second. Petrified terror fixed him, and he just stood and stared at this appalling door, alive with the bending and pressing of what was after him, behind it. For untold seconds he was rooted, awaiting that awful fate as any second it was bound to burst upon him, full of dreadful malice and arcane intent. So sick of fear was he that he couldn't even cry out, but just simmered in his own terror.

Sweat stuck his legs to his sheets, and as he writhed he became the more entangled. He reached for the bedside light and switched it on. Relief flooded him to be in his bedroom. He shoved back the sheets and duvet to break free, and levered himself up to go for a pee.

Back, he straightened the bed and got back in. He lay down. Doors, he recognised, and things trying to get out, were deeply Freudian. The return of the repressed. And Anna was one of those Hallowe'en Head-Hounds, who had now made thin the screen between the worlds of his mind.

Now something was trying to get back out.

He began to worry as he lay there. When he saw Andrew again, what if Andrew wasn't so affectionate towards him? What if his expectations were too great? Would greeting Andrew with too much enthusiasm upset him and make him withdraw inwards? So maybe he should greet him with less outward affection himself. Ah, but what if that made Andrew feel less assured of his fondness and left him feeling uncertain and betrayed? So difficult, these emotional relationships.

Then, what of Angela? No wonder nothing this wonderful had ever happened to him before. It was obvious, in the small, dark and nakedly sane hours of the night, why that would be.

Because nothing ever was that wonderful. She would draw him in with hidden promises of ecstasy and warmth, then when it all went wrong, no doubt at his fault, leave him more battered and unhappy than ever before. It was all a fool's paradise. It held only sadness and a loneliness more intractable and painful than any he'd known.

Night's terrors were mere shadows compared to the light of the day. Or so they seemed, gladly. David woke to bright light through his curtains. And was there ever such a morning? Why, it was Christmas Eve! The most magical eve of the year! And here he lay, warm and safe and cosy, with a woman out there who loved him and her nephew who delighted him. Why, if they married, Andrew would be *his* nephew!

He didn't want to stir, but then again he was far too excited to just lie there. Presents to buy. On Christmas Eve! Was there ever such a festive thing as that?

Suddenly, he was raised from his bed as if by a divine touch, and stood, stretching and embracing the day. 'God of all kindness, God who *is* kindness, I thank You!' he said, partially because he felt like it. Partially because it just seemed to happen. 'If You're really there. If not, then take no notice, it's just me being silly.'

Would she arrive with croissants? No, she said she had things to do. But that wouldn't stop him driving up to get two of them to have with a cup of tea for his breakfast. Such a day. He attended to his discarded clothes from the previous night – discarded as if they represented his old life. He dressed in one of his smartest shirts, a fresh pair of trousers, even though the others weren't really in need of washing, and a nice, patterned, V-neck jumper. He admired himself in the full-length mirror inside the wardrobe door. He smoothed silver-grey hairs to the right side. 'Quite a catch!' he said. 'The silver locks of the silver fox!'

Assuming that the thaw had continued, he selected a nice, wool jacket to wear in place of the heavier coat. Downstairs, he put the kettle on to boil and headed out of the door. The world was mild, bright and full of Christmas charm. He got the car out and drove straight to the bakery, leaving it on the yellow lines outside because it was, after all, Christmas Eve. Inside the shop he bounced up to the counter and ordered three croissants. He noticed a box on the counter collecting for NewLink, and remembering (to his amazement) that it was Mary Granger who volunteered for them, he neatly folded a fiver and slipped it in.

Croissants in hand, he departed, wishing the staff 'A very Merry Christmas!' and imagined they must have thought some vision of Christmas itself had just visited them. Christmas Yet-To-Come.

Back at home, he reboiled the kettle and made tea, switched on Radio 4, and settled down to a delicious breakfast, picturing Angela sitting opposite him. And Andrew.

As he washed up, he visualised the day. Shopping for presents for the two of them. And a card for Angela. What about a card for the church? Hadn't he heard an announcement that there was a board at the back for just that purpose? Yes, he was sure he had. He would pin it there with pride.

Then the most extraordinary thought struck him. So out-of-somewhere it was, that he had to replay it through his echoic memory. Which was strange in itself because echoic memory only worked for sounds you'd actually heard. He would go to visit Rufus and take him out for a coffee, or whatever he preferred, at a proper coffee place, not the bakers'. A posh coffee. Fear grabbed at his innards but the impression that this was what he should do was so strong it allowed no rival. This was what he would do. And jolly good it would be. And Ruf would be so amazed and touched it would stick in his mind and illuminate his Christmas. Even his Christmases Yet-To-Come.

My, my! Who was this fellow standing at his sink? This festive fellow?

'David!'

It was Bill Granger, holding a newspaper in his left hand, and smiling broadly. 'Come in, my dear fellow. Come in.'

David went in.

'Can I get you a coffee or something?'

'Who is it?' Mary's voice sang from somewhere.

'It's David Sourbook, come to see us.'

'Oh, lovely!' she called, and he heard her starting down the stairs.

'Actually, I've rather come to see Rufus.'

'Really? That's jolly decent of you. He's around somewhere.'

'Hello, David,' Mary said, greeting him with a slight hug and a warm kiss on the cheek. 'Would you like a coffee or something?'

'He's come to see Ruf,' Bill explained. Then he called, 'Ruf! Someone to see you!'

'Come and sit down. How are you?' Mary said, and David accompanied them into the sitting room. Ruf was sitting in there watching the TV, which was back where Mary had told David it normally lived, in front of the French windows.

'Ruf, feet!' Mary said.

He muttered, 'Feet!' and pulled his leg off the side of the armchair and sat up.

'Hello, Ruf,' David said.

He didn't look pleased. 'Oh, hi. Have you come to have a go at me?'

'My goodness me, no!'

David went and stood between him and the TV, which continued to drone on behind him. 'Not at all. I'm sure Bill and Mary have done that quite effectively. No harm, no foul, as far as I'm concerned. I've come to take you for a coffee, or whatever you prefer. How about it? Christmas treat. My shout.'

'Well, that's jolly generous!' Bill said.

'Oh!' Ruf said. 'Ah, are you sure? I mean, sh – shine on! I don't really know.'

'I bet that was what you used to say at school all the time. Come on, it's Christmas!'

He looked less suspicious. He looked at Mary and Bill and then back to David. 'OK.'

'Well, come on then! Do you need a coat? We're in the car. It's not cold.'

'No, I'm good. OK.'

'How are they treating you?' David asked as he drove.

'OK. They're OK. They did grill me about the meal. I don't actually remember it. I was drunk.'

'Oh, really?'

'Yeah, more than I remember. Anyway, whatever.'

'Well, never mind. I bet it's awkward living with the likes of the Grangers.'

'No, they're OK. Though they won't let me do weed anywhere in the whole place and they warned me they'd throw me out if I did. And they said I can't have my mates round because they said they couldn't be sure to keep order. But they said I can go out to see them. They let me get up late and watch the telly. They fed me really nice food. They even let me drink yesterday evening – a bit. They talked to me and didn't put me down. They actually listened to me. I'm better off. It's good you arranged that, you and Angela. She's hot, by the way. Seems a lot younger than you, though.'

'Hot? Isn't that a rather old-fashioned word for you?'

'It means she's fit, you know. Cool, I guess you'd say.'

'Well, thank you.'

'Can we go for a burger? You taking me to a coffee house? I'd rather get a burger.'

'If you like, OK. That's not far.'

They drove in silence for a while, Ruf seemingly happy just looking out of the window. David knew a shortcut route to the burger place on the main road out of town.

'Here we are, I said it wasn't far.'

'Right,' Ruf said. 'Safe.'

'Sure, yeah,' David agreed.

Inside, he asked Ruf what he wanted.

'Take a seat,' David said. 'I'll bring it over.'

The place had no particular decorations, or even acknowledgements of the season, other than offering some festive menu items. David was unaffected. Still inspired by the day and his mission, he got himself a large latte and a cookie along with the stuff for Ruf and brought everything to the table by the window Ruf had selected. Ruf grunted when he set the tray down, and made a grab for the huge burger.

'Always ready to escape?' David said as he sat down.

'What?'

'Sitting by the window – looking out for trouble? Ready to run?'

'Why would you think that?' Ruf said through a mouthful of meat and bread.

'Two reasons. One, you're sitting by the window, and two, the company you keep.'

'You don't get to talk about the company I keep. They're my mates, not yours. And you know what I think of yours.'

'Really? Still? OK, I'm sorry, you're right, I have no right to comment on your friends. But maybe if you could get away from them, you could get away from the sort of trouble you get into.'

'Apology accepted. What would be the point of that?'

'Clean up your life.'

'Be like you?'

'I'm no shining example.'

'Shut up, then. Why are we even having this conversation?'

'Because I'm an idiot and very bad at saying what I want to. I should leave it to Bill and Mary. And the hot Angela.'

'OK, David, I'll cut you some slack, seeing as it's Christmas. Say what you want to say.'

'I think you have real potential. But not here. Not with this crowd.'

'Oh,' Ruf said. 'You and me, we see life differently. You think you could cut loose from all your friends, find a different life and then make new friends to go with it. I think that's totally bogus. My friends are my life. They are who I am and where I belong. I think the very idea of getting rid of them to improve my own life is seriously twisted. Not good.'

David was taken aback. 'My goodness!' he said. 'Here's me trying to help you sort out your life, and rather, you're sorting out mine!'

'Now that's the kind of person I can respect,' Ruf said.

David was even more impressed. 'I have to apologise to you. I see my easy assumptions about people falling to dust before my eyes.'

'Makes you wonder. Who's sent to who?' Ruf said.

CHAPTER TWENTY-ONE

Reverberating from his outing with Ruf, and feeling very good about the fact that it was an act of kindness, though also aware that he had perhaps received more than he had given, and yet also aware that that was perhaps the very nature of kindness – it provokes blessing all round – David went on to shop. And to be shopping for presents for two such beloved people on Christmas Eve was beyond his ken, wonderful. A revelation. But what to get?

He'd start with Andrew. The shops in the centre of town were not bad. They, and the streets, were full of smiling and harassed people. A sort of slightly strained merriment seemed to fill the air. Everywhere Christmas songs leaked from shopfronts and swirled among the myriad displays of festive items and seasonal offers. Santas collected for disadvantaged children. Lights twinkled, streamers fell, trees were festooned and tills jungled.

He tried a particularly well-stocked and friendly toy emporium. But he saw nothing that dented his desire to buy him a new tablet. He looked in the toy section of a big department store, but nothing suited. Yet he stopped and laughed till he cried when he saw that a vertical sign that in full said 'Stuff You Need' had had a pile of cases put in front of it and just read, 'Stuff You'. He pointed this out to an assistant, who rather than changing it went off to get his friend to show him. He heard them laughing as he left the shop.

All right then. The computer superstore. It was full to busting and every member of staff was already engaged in quizzes about Wi-Fi and gigabytes and handsets and compatibility. He found the tablets and looked over them. There was a nice one at just over £150. Andrew already had one of the same make. That would suit. He looked at the specs. It seemed excellent. But was it too much to spend and so cause embarrassment? He imagined the look of surprise in Andrew's eyes as he saw it, just in its box, maybe with a tiny festive bow in one corner. This, surely, was kindness. He would do it. He picked one up in its box and carried it to the till, queued and paid by card. Done. Now, Angela. Oh, so much more difficult!

He went into the covered mall and sat on one of the wooden benches to think, and look around him. Perhaps he'd be inspired. What did she like? She liked church. She liked religion. Was there a religious shop of some sort in the town? Yes, but then he might be getting her some book she already had or some picture that was of the wrong flavour. No, that was a minefield he'd do well to avoid. A trap for the unwary. Nothing religious.

OK, something general. A nice picture. An ornament. A vase. Not a new vacuum cleaner. He remembered when his dad did that and it wasn't forgotten in a long time.

Nothing too expensive, but not cheap tat either, which was a careful balance to keep. Goodness, this was a trial! But a joyous trial! He looked at his watch. He had plenty of time. He would just wander, and see what he saw. Good plan, old man.

He was far too happy to maintain his usual dislike of the centre of town this close to Christmas, and just embraced it all. The full, festive furore. He saw a card shop and went in. He found some religious cards, and selected one that was a painting of the holy family, central and close-up, with what seemed a carefully realistic setting in darkness behind them, and the Christ-child radiating a subtle glow that didn't so much illuminate as change the nature of Mary and Joseph's faces, so that an unearthly wonder held them. He knew she'd like it.

Then he went back into the big department store, wondering about an amaryllis. He passed a display that had a Rudolph nicely fashioned out of twisted branches, and on the forest floor beneath him, pine cones were scattered. But a small cluster of them had found their way right underneath his tail. It looked for all the world like he'd disgraced himself, and David was once again lost in merry mirth. He really must visit this shop more often. But no amaryllis.

He carried on. Aha! The art shop! In the window there were various works, modestly adorned with the odd coloured bow, in red and green and gold. Nothing garish or cheap. He went in. On the walls were many more scenes of country life, still life, and city life, but he was more interested in the vases and ceramics. And there it was. A glass vase, exquisitely drawn into beautifully strained convolutions, with valleys and curves writhing together as it climbed to a swirled and fluted lip. It had flecks of the most brilliant red glass set in it, and inside the vase, a single red glass rose on a brilliant green glass stem. The rose spoke of his love for her, the whole thing was a quality piece which would adorn any stately place, as doubtless her home was. And it had been knocked down from over £200 to a mere £75!

He examined the ticket. It was by noted local glass artist, Emily Thrape. Noted by whom? Many things were 'noted' but that was far from a recommendation in some cases.

'Good afternoon,' said a voice like flowing silk from behind and beside him. He straightened, to see a tall lady in a swathe of pink and black, her face made up as if for a royal dinner, her hair pulled back into a sculpted bun. 'Are you interested in the Thrape?'

'The what?'

'The Thrape,' she said, extending a manicured and slim-fingered hand towards it, showing no sign of recognition of the friendly game he was playing with her.

'I was wondering who noted her.'

'I'm sorry?'

'It says she's "noted". I was wondering by whom.'

'In various arts journals over the last two years or so since she achieved prominence. This is remarkably cheap for one of hers. I'm tempted by it myself.'

'So I should definitely buy it today.'

'Definitely,' she said, with no hint of a smile.

His cheek was unbearable and unstoppable. If it was such a bargain, why should she be so keen to sell it to him, seeing as it would be snapped up at any moment?

'Do you have any other Thrapes?'

'Not at the present moment. She doesn't create to order.'

Like God, then.

'Is it for a gift?' she asked.

'Yes.'

'I can gift-wrap it very carefully for you so you can add wrapping paper without needing to open the box it will be in, surrounded by bubble wrap.'

'Bubble wrap?' he said, surprised that it wouldn't be something much more exotic, like shredded Egyptian linen.

'Yes, it's the safest thing,' she affirmed.

'Then I'll take it. Cocoon it in bubble wrap for me.'

'Certainly,' she said, bending as if she'd been trained how to bend, and lifting it with admirable care.

As she walked away he was sure there would be some sign of a raised eyebrow or a small sigh, but there was nothing.

She took an age to wrap it, so he looked around the shop. When she finally appeared with it, in a box inside a paper carrier bag, he paid with his card and she said, 'Now, I suggest you don't hold the carrier bag by the handles, they're strong enough but it will likely swing and bump into things. Put your arm around the box and hold it that way.'

'Thank you,' he said, smiling at her nicely, 'you've been most helpful. Merry Christmas.'

'Yes, Merry Christmas,' she said, with no hint of festive gladness.

He left. Next, wrapping paper, and get this thing home as soon and as safely as possible.

He went back to the card shop and bought some nice gold paper and some small bows, and headed for the car park. Brilliant. In the High Street, carollers were singing with the Salvation Army band and it was all so jolly it could have been an

American film. But no, it wasn't like an American film because it was genuine, and wonderful, and actually Christmas Eve. The most wonderful evening of the year. For reasons he was only just coming to appreciate.

He cleared the kitchen table and laid newspaper on it. He unrolled the gold paper and sized it all up, snipped, stuck with intense care, and was greatly impressed. He signed her card with, 'Love from David', and stuck a small bow on Andrew's tablet box. All good. Time for a cup of tea. Dusk was descending, and he would certainly go and sit outside and enjoy it on such a day. A day on which he still glowed with an inner festive flare, much to his amazement.

Some half-heard, faltering echo from an unnamed, distant place warned him that that might not be such a good idea, today. But he didn't want to heed it.

Tea in hand, Eeyore-contained, he sat on his bench and looked at the dusk forming across the road, and across the fields and across the world and across the universe. Without hesitation it took him. As the trees and fields lost all light and colour, the sky behind and above them became pure silver-blue with suggestions of streaks, held aloft by forces unknown. The sun was gone already, but it lit from below a dome of distant indigo, an arc of hoary mist. Like mountains on a distant planet, vast valleys on some other world, it called to him. Tears welled in his eyes. The Yearning burned, and his heart leapt in his chest.

'Who are You?' he said, and the semblance of the features of a face assembled in the vision. The face of God? It resolved, becoming the face of a child. A young girl. It was a round face, with bright blue eyes, and straggly blonde hair. Skin that was brown and smooth, and such a smile, looking right into him. She was gazing up at him, holding his hand, and the scene moved, as in life, not still, as from a photograph.

Eeyore fell from his hands and the weight of the tea smashed him into pieces on the paving slabs. Such bitterness of loss and such sweetness of love flooded him all in a moment, like a great nostalgia, but with the depth of a long reality. He yearned, he stared, he reached, he could not have. The Yearning spoke to him, had his frequency, called from beyond. Because it was Michaela. Just like Anna said. This was his dear sister. Torn from him at her most sweet and precious. When she was three and he was eight.

The image solidified, until he was there. He saw her eyes looking up at him, so intense and engaged, her face intent on him, her smile that warmed him in a place that nothing else did. He saw himself holding her little hand, and how they went around together, him looking out for her, she looking up to him for company and safety, affection and guidance. More, indeed, than she looked to their rather angular and indifferent parents. He saw the loss of her, and it nearly split him in two. Of course, they'd never been down an underground tunnel together. She never fell on a live rail. She died of a disease. But that dream was an expression of the loss – a dark and secret route into what had been denied him on the surface. The tearing away of his little sister at her sweetest and most devoted. That tunnel was his deeper mind giving him a route out. And a route in. Even their ages were suddenly clear to him now.

There were no tears. They had retreated. Just a dry gasping and sobbing at a reality so disembowelling, so utterly full of regret and irredeemable loss, that he felt like he was stunned into a static shock. There she was. His and gone. Real and lost. Dear and dead. Michaela. Micky. He'd called her 'Micky'! Then the flood broke and the dammed tears flowed. 'Micky. Micky. Micky. Come back. Don't be gone. Don't be lost forever. Come back to me! My Micky!'

She continued to smile, and to hang on to him. He wondered if he would see an image of her, sick, dying, in her little bed. Perhaps it was protective kindness, but none came.

As he sat there, music drifted in as from a place infinitely removed, beginning as an undetectable melody, and gradually settling into an old and vaguely familiar tune. He couldn't exactly place it, but it was about love being unreal, and then seeing her face, and becoming convinced.

He was singing along, very badly, and her face had become almost the only thing he could see, right up to him at the age of three, as it had so often been as they had lived as each other's companions and more than friends. For those musical moments it was beautiful. He was back there. She was with him. All was right. Her face meant everything to him.

Then she was gone again, and it was grinding loss and stomach-twisting regret. Never to see her sweet face again. He'd failed her. She had died. She who depended on him so much, was lost. Gone. Failed by his protection of her. He should have died, not she. Not dear Micky.

And it wasn't angels that took her, despite the words of his mum, nor angels who now protected her as she lived with them. Nor, indeed, had she become an angel, as some had said. No. She belonged here, not there. It was nothing at all to do with angels. That made him angry at his mum, for such softening deception. Resentful.

What? That was the face of Andrew. Just for a moment, his face replaced Michaela's, smiling, happy, looking at him, then he was gone. And all that was left was an empty yearning for nothing, because there was nothing. Stultified, bored-out, empty, nothing. And tears. And a broken mug.

By the time he went in, he still felt that something awful had happened which had separated him from the world. A gnawing grief in his guts, her face in his mind, missed beats in his heart, an empty disassociation from his house, all warned him that something had changed. The broken mug was left outside. It seemed symbolic, but he knew not how.

Christmas had gone but even the sight of the tree didn't alert him to the fact. A festive freeze had come, so deep it allowed no sense or recognition of itself. He was numb, in some slightly disembodied and worrying way. It wasn't a nice feeling. Anxiety crept round the edges of it, like gnarled fingers round a door ajar.

He slumped into his armchair. Life had ended. What had promised life had brought him death. The Yearning had tracked him down and found him. And it hadn't been any of the things he'd imagined. It certainly wasn't God. It was guilt and grief. Gut-grinding, grim, grey, grief.

He stared. He waited. But nothing came and nothing changed. Had he even, actually, died? Had a heart attack happened when his heart missed those chest-hollowing beats? Was he now seeing this as an empty ghost, about to be whisked away like a shade of mist to some lesser place to wait and repent? It chilled him. Like a chill of the grave. He feared it, like Scrooge at his engraved stone in the presence of the Ghost of Christmas Yet-To-Come.

This was horrible. This was truly unsettling. He really needed to do something before he fell into a pit of psychotic catatonia. He should make food and eat. Ghosts didn't eat. He would eat.

A glimmer of hope returned and he had wisdom enough to warm it and make it grow. He stood, shook himself, and went into the kitchen. Ah, cooker. Ah, radio. Ah, kettle. Yes, all good things. This was a night for scrambled eggs and tinned tomatoes on toast. Quick, cheap, easy and nutritious. With a cup of tea and some Christmas biscuits, watch some mindless festive fare on the telly. All that would see him right, or so he hoped, still feeling weak and wonky from his brush with nonexistence.

He whistled 'O Holy Night' as he scrambled, toasted, boiled, spread and carried. Minute by minute he was feeling progressively stronger and less alienated from his life. It had been an awful experience. Why should he be so unfortunate as to suffer so on Christmas Eve?

He could have put on a DVD but they didn't connect him to the world in the way he felt he needed. He should watch something that would engage him, and which he would have to follow, on the telly, so he rejected Carols from King's College and found instead a documentary about children's knowledge of the Christmas story in the Gospels. It was well-presented, without unnecessary bias, and he ate as he watched. Normality descended with a sense of great relief. But sadness and a new revelation of loss and how it had affected his whole life hung in the wings, because that part was simply true. Tears immediately blurred the settled world as he thought of how he *had* known and *had* lost Michaela, and how that had ripped from him not just her but something of himself as well. Something that had been missing ever since. The Michaela part of him, a part which had been huge and huggy. Bart the huggy bear was Michaela, too, he saw. Andrew represented the same thing. How he had loved holding Andrew's hand and swinging him with Angela. And Angela? No, that was entirely different.

Kindness had been torn from his heart, ripped from his living flesh, and with that, God as well. Relationships had been juiced from him like squeezing an orange. Dry, he'd been left people-blind. It all came together in this. Now, at least, he knew. But that didn't for a moment soften a pain that had entered his life like a gut-punching bullet and laid his entrails out on the floor.

He was unable to finish his meal for very sadness, and just bowed his head as salty drops plopped onto his eggs and tomatoes.

Now he knew her. And now he'd lost her. Joy and pain mixed like a deadly cocktail, and too late, he'd swallowed it down.

Had he ever felt so alone? Alone, yes. Constantly, in a way. But *so* alone as now, this moment? No. His whole life he'd not known it, but he'd been half a person since he was eight. The thought rushed at him that it would be better to be dead. He didn't particularly want to be dead, but now he knew why he'd never particularly wanted to be alive. And what had been calling to him; it really wasn't life. Anna, so perceptive the other day. What had his number was grief, and loss, and sadness, and regret. Unfixable, irremediable, truly lost and truly gone. Micky. Her sweet face and trusting eyes, her swinging hand and whispered jokes, her shared laughter and doting, depending affection. All, all, all, gone. Long ago.

He scooped up a forkful of scrambled eggs and put it in his mouth. He chewed. It had no flavour. And it was cold. And salty.

He swallowed. He took tomatoes and continued to eat, because that was what he was doing, not because it had any pleasure or meaning.

Was this his life, now?

CHAPTER TWENTY-TWO

Time is a wonderful healer! By half-past eight he was feeling much better.

Oh, to be sure, he knew that a door had been opened. An ancient, dark, creeper-framed door, and a journey begun, and it would not be travelled in so short a time. The dark railway tunnel was indeed a long-buried way in, and way out, to what had held him and dogged him all his days. But his days were not over, and therefore the tunnel before him had light at the end of it, if that wasn't too much of a mixing of images and insights. And there was a definite relief in knowing the truth about Michaela, and how he'd loved her, and she him. He would, in time to come, set himself to truly rediscover her and honour her memory, whatever that would mean. Even a bitter darkness was a doorway into light. Or could be, surely.

He wasn't exactly happy, and definitely not feeling festive, but a certain hopefulness had replaced despair. In a way, what he'd lost had long been lost. It was his past that had been blighted, and darkened by it. His future would be lit by it. Philosophical or not, a settled calmness had come to him, and he was glad of it.

He'd had some mulled wine which had perhaps helped, but he hadn't had much, and it wasn't strong in alcohol, so it had merely fuzzed the edges. He was, in fact, thankful for the revelation. It wasn't just 'a truth', it was his past, and his problem, and his Micky. It was a door to a new way forward, and better times. He knew that. Anna had been right to point him there. Painful though the pointing had proved.

Scrooge came to mind, about keeping Christmas in his heart all the time. Now, he would see people. And love them. And find kindness in his very being. And maybe even the kindness of God. For therein lies the soul.

When passing the kitchen table to fetch some nibbles and mulled wine a little later, he saw Angela's card there. He'd forgotten all about getting it to her. He'd just have to give it to her tomorrow. What a day he'd had! How surprised she would be when he told her about it. What else could happen?

He settled down to continue watching a festive show when his mobile phone rang. How annoying! Who on earth would ring on Christmas Eve at such a time? He fetched it from the table. No caller ID.

Disguising his irritation, he said, 'Hello?'

'David, this is Thelia. We met yesterday.' Was he an idiot? Yet she sounded upset.

'Yes, we did. What is it?'

'David, are you sitting down?'

'No.'

'Well, I think you should.'

He sat.

'David, I have some bad news for you. I don't know if Angela told you about her heart condition.'

He went cold and something inside him froze solid. 'No.'

'David, the vast majority of the time it doesn't affect her at all. She even forgets about it. It's a rare condition to do with her heart's beat and rhythm regularity. But when she has an attack it can be life-threatening. David, I'm so sorry to tell you but she had an attack this evening, and she's in ICU right now as they try to get her heart to beat properly again. We can't visit so I'm not even coming at the moment. But obviously we're distraught and I know she'd want me to tell you. I don't know if there's someone who can be with you?'

'Will she pull through?'

'She has every time so far, but a number of times it's been touch and go. All I can do, and I'm really sorry about this, is phone you if there's any news. Do you want me to do that whatever time it is, or do you need a cut-off point?'

'Any time. Any time, please. On this number. It's always charged and on. Oh, this is so awful! When will we know if she's going to be OK?'

'By the morning. If they manage to get it stabilised she'll be out again, right as rain. If not, well ...' and her voice went all wavery.

'I'm so sorry!' David said. 'This is awful. Is there anything I can do?'

'Not really, but thank you for asking.'

'How is Andrew?'

'He's asleep. He doesn't know.'

'Well, if I can come and pick you up, even in the night, or stay with Andrew while you come here, or anything, I will. Gladly. And thank you for phoning me.'

'Angela is fortunate to have you. Thank you. And Andrew was so thrilled to meet you and play with you. He isn't thrilled by many people – it's part of his condition.'

'Angela told me. I thought he was great. Oh, goodness, I hope she comes through this.'

'She always has so far. Just pray. I must go. Goodbye, David.'

'Goodbye.' Too late, he added, 'Thelia.'

This could not be real. He stared at the phone. He was stunned. He was emptied. Guts on the floor. Again. Not Angela. He'd just lost Michaela. Not Angela as well. How could this be? Why hadn't she told him? Why was this happening?

And pray? How could he pray? Actually, he could pray. He could go to the midnight communion service at church and pray. That's what he would do. Prayers there would be heard, surely. In the House of God. Among the People of God. He would go.

He stared, and saw nothing. He resisted feelings of anger and blame. He'd had enough bitterness and regret for a year. For ten years. For a lifetime. This is when you either turn *to* God or you turn *on* God. The latter was somehow tempting, but the former at least held out some kind of hope. Some kind. Any kind would do.

He threw the phone quite hard onto the settee, then immediately regretted it because he needed it to hear from Thelia. He went and picked it up and opened it. Of course it was fine. But he was angry. Resentful. Someone, somewhere, or something, had fouled up, surely. Why hadn't they fixed this thing properly before? Why wasn't she on some effective drugs to prevent it? Funding cutbacks? GP not willing to prescribe them?

He imagined her, lying in some ICU bed, tubed-up and on a respirator, medics working to revive her, life hanging by a thread. Poor Angela. Why? Those defibrillators, did they leave bruising? Days of aching? Muscle damage?

The telly was still blaring so he turned it off. Now what? It was over two hours till the service. What could he do?

And poor Thelia! How must she be feeling? With Martin away and no one to comfort her. He wished he could pray for them, but that would have to wait.

And all those friends! How must they be feeling? Their images slide-showed in his imagination – Bill and Mary Granger, Greg and Holly, Anna, Ian and Sue Staines, Aaron and Ella Pickett, Jan and Brian Carstairs. They must be distraught. He felt the pained anxiety of each one, even Brian.

Oh, my goodness! He'd just remembered each one of them by name, could picture their faces, and felt inside him a genuine concern for their angst. Good grief! Where did that come from? That was new!

He felt utterly helpless. Helpless and hopeless. Utterly useless. This was no good. Wallowing in his sadness and theirs … This was negative, and he needed to be positive. If there was really nothing he could do, then he'd better do something else. Write a poem. Yes.

He got out all his poetry stuff – pad, notepad, pencils, pens, erasers – from the drawer and laid them out on and around his lap tray. He put some Fauré Pavane on the CD player at a low volume, and sat. He stared past the tree at the dark curtains, put the end of a pencil between his front teeth, and went into a mull and a muse.

He scribbled on the notepad, 'Anaesthetise my pain, Let me not feel again,' and looked at the two lines. He had the ghost of an idea to write something about how seeing and feeling his loss of Micky had seemingly and suddenly opened him up to seeing the pain of others. Remembering their names and faces! Overcoming his people-blindness. It was a revelation. Nothing less. Like the proverbial cartoon light bulb flashing on above his head. Mind you, it had started before the revelation of dear Micky. Since meeting Angela and her mad mates.

But those two lines should be separated by a different rhyme. He wrote in-between them, 'I cannot stand the knife', keeping the surgical theme of what his loss had done to him – cutting something out. So he needed a last line to rhyme with knife. 'Life'. 'The blade that drained my life'.

He wrote out in full on the A4 pad:

> Anaesthetise my pain,
> I cannot stand the knife,
> Let me not feel again,
> The blade that drained my life.

Satisfied with that, he carried on. Now to tell that it was a loss that did this. 'The loss that cut me deep', and to rhyme with it, 'The wound that made me seep'. Good. And in-between, something about the effect of it on him. 'The pain that made me blind'. And as a last line, 'But left no scar behind'. Because he was unaware of what had happened to him. No, if line two is about being blind, then make the hurt relate to the eyes – 'and crying'. Good. Better. He wrote it out in full on the big pad.

> The loss that cut me deep,
> And crying, made me blind,
> The wound that made me seep,
> But left no scar behind.

Now, to make clear this effect of making him blind to people, and blind as well to what had happened to him. 'Of loss or pain was none, And seeing folk was done'. He didn't like 'folk' for people, but it would do for now. How this past event was left behind, covered over, hidden from him. 'As left was all the past'. Should it have a comma after 'left'? Yes. And as a last line, something about how this brought him peace but at the cost of relationships. 'A lonely peace at last'. Good.

He wrote it out carefully.

> Of loss or pain was none,
> As left, was all the past,
> And seeing folk was done,
> A lonely peace at last.

Now, time to reveal what happened. He felt like doing this verse all in one go. He toyed with phrases.

> Then came the crash and burn!
> The pain of that past loss!
> And so at last I learn,
> The day that made this cross.

A cross that referred to the fact that it was among these Christians that this had developed in these last days. And what has this revelation done to him? He thought and scribbled.

> In seeing then that scar,
> In feeling new that grief,
> It dawns that people are,
> Now seen in new relief.

Good. He liked the sense of something 'dawning' in particular. A new beginning. Hopeful. Straight on to the big pad. Going well. What next? How he has seen Michaela, and what that's done to him.

> I sense the sister ripped,
> I grasp the pretty face,
> And realise I'm gripped,
> By new sight in this place.

New sight. Yes. New awareness of people. New sensitivity to them. And to finish, important to say that this has done good, for all its pain. He worked on it.

> It's good I've felt this pain,
> And how at last I saw,
> That this is what I gain:
> The people I'll adore.

A last verse occurred to him, fully formed, so he added it on.

> Was it God, made this be?
> Opened eyes, that were blind?
> Made a new man of me,
> Because He, is just kind?

He read it out loud, all through. Still unhappy with 'folk', and also with 'adore' in the second to last verse, he set to address them when his doorbell rang. He was very tempted to leave it, as it was late, but thought he shouldn't. Especially as whoever it was had actually found the bell.

There stood Greg and Holly, looking concerned. Their faces brightened as he said, 'Greg and Holly! Come in, please.'

They took off their shoes, even though he said there was no need, and followed him into the living room.

'Can I get you a coffee or something?'

'That would be nice,' they agreed, and he set off to make three instant ones. And get the tin of biscuits.

He brought them all in on a tray, and as he put it down on the table he said, to his surprise, 'How are you both doing?'

'Us?' Holly said. 'We came to find out about you!'

'I guessed that much. But you've known her longer than me. How are you?'

'We're worried and upset. But we've been here before. And you seem a lot closer to Angela than we are. How are you, all on your own here?'

'Were you sent? By the others?'

'No, we just all agreed someone should come and we're free and we volunteered. Come on, how are you doing with this?'

'I'm shocked. Stunned. Disembowelled. Drained out. Unable to function. So I decided to write a poem.'

'Really?' Holly said. 'Can we hear it?'

'No. Far too early in the creative process for any of that. Sorry. Also a bit too personal. Biscuit?'

'Thanks,' Greg said, but Holly declined.

'I'll bet you lot are really upset,' David said.

'Of course,' Holly replied, putting her mug down on the coffee table. 'It's been the best part of a year since Angela had one of these. You tend to forget about it, and then wham! It happens again. And it's terrible. All upsetting and worrying and everyone phoning each other and people going to the hospital and messages about how bad she is, and then she recovers. Thank God! Which we do.' She started to cry a little, and dabbed a small handkerchief at her nose and eyes.

Greg put an arm around her, and she gave a little lean into him to thank him. David was amazed at how he was observing such subtle stuff, to which he had been pretty much blind up till now.

'I suppose you pray about all this,' David said.

'Yes, a lot,' Holly told him. 'Do you?'

'No. I can't. But I'm planning to go to the service tonight and pray there.'

'That's brilliant!' Greg said.

'You can pray anywhere,' Holly put in. 'At home, in the garden, in the street, in the police station if you get arrested with Angela. Anywhere.'

'That's easy for you to say,' David countered.

'No, you can,' Holly insisted.

'Yes, but,' Greg said, 'David feels the need of being in church or being with Christians to pray, and that's perfectly understandable.'

'But you need to know you can pray here. God will listen,' Holly insisted again.

'*You* think that,' David explained, 'but *I* know that I don't belong to Him like you do, and I'm not even sure who He is, or *if* He is, so I need help if He's going to hear me, and that means praying where He listens and hears – in church or among His people. That's how it feels to me.'

'I see,' she said. 'Fair enough. And anyway, it's brilliant that you're coming. We'll see you there.'

'You might not. I think I'll be sitting with my head down the whole time just calling out to God and I might slope off once I feel I'm finished.'

'Quite right,' Greg said. 'But it'll be good that you're there, anyway.'

'I wish more people just bowed their heads in church and called out to God,' Holly commented, with a little passion. 'It'd be a good thing. Real progress.'

'That's not aimed at me, is it?' Greg asked.

'No, silly!' she said, laying a hand on his arm. 'Forget I said it.'

'Well, it made me feel better,' David said, to encourage her, and because it was true. 'Could she really be dead by the morning?'

A dark shade fell over Holly's face. 'Yes,' she said, simply but gravely. 'We're all aware that one day it could well happen.'

She looked down at the carpet. 'The older she gets, and the more times it happens, the greater the probability of that being the outcome, every time. And we're very aware that this could be the day. Sorry.'

CHAPTER TWENTY-THREE

So utterly different were the circumstances that it all felt like he'd never been in this place before in his life. He hadn't noticed so clearly before the distinct old-wood smell, sweetened slightly by something spicy. All the pews and beams now seemed dark, as if the very wood had been made sombre by the centuries of faithful prayers in times of war and of peace, new life and sad death, bells and silences. The thick, stone pillars were objects to be avoided unless you intended to skulk, which he did.

Two men were at the back sorting out service leaflets and carol sheets, and were taken by surprise by this early arrival. They gave him one of each, and a red communion service book. He saw the rector at the front of the church but immediately bowed his head and went for the pew just in front of the back pillar on the right-hand side. There he knelt on a patterned kneeling-cushion, and laid his forehead on his folded arms along the top of the pew in front. And settled himself.

The organ started up and he realised he hadn't been praying but dreaming, half-asleep. That simply would not do. So he started to mutter, very quietly.

'Lord, God of kindness, please be kind, because You are kind. I'm not bargaining with You, God, I'm just pleading with You what You've shown me. Please be kind now to Angela, who is lying in the ICU in the hospital gravely ill and in danger of dying. Look, Lord, let me be frank. Here's how I feel about this. I've lost Micky, Michaela, and I can't lose Angela. Please don't let that happen. I've come here to plead with You, Lord God, so please be the kind God You are and overlook all the wrongs I've done and all the ways I've ignored You, and answer this prayer for me.

'Look, Lord, I know that's too much to ask. Why should You forgive me years of ignoring You and sinning against You? Why should I expect it? Only because You're God, so Your resources of kindness must be vast, enormous, literally infinite. So, look, that's what I'm bringing here, to You, God, not any goodness I might think I have, but Your kindness, which I believe You've shown me is Your essential nature, so please, make Angela well. Make her heart beat again, like it should, properly.'

He paused, and listened to the organ, and tried to evaluate his prayer. 'Lord, I believe. I think I do. I believe You are God and You've been calling to me. Through The Yearning, even though, it turns out, mostly it was about Micky. And that snapped my eyes open when I saw it, like a searchlight. Surely You were behind that, because of how it seemed to come from so far away, and somehow so deep inside as well. It was a revelation. You revealed Yourself and Micky. Michaela. Oh, You're not bothered. Micky. You reveal things, don't You, God? I remember that. You give epiphanies. The last book in Your Bible is called Revelation. Or Revelations. Anyway, You shone that insight right into me, and it's changed me. Suddenly I saw those people. Suddenly I'll be able to relate so much better to Angela, whom *You* put in my way, didn't You? Like an angel?

'So, Lord, and again I'm not bargaining because I know that's wrong. But, God, if You did all that then You can't intend to take Angela away from me now. Unless she is really an angel and she has no place here and this is Your way of getting her home again. But I don't think that's right. You want us to be together. That's presumptuous. Sorry. But I think You do. So, Lord, please make her well. Please listen to all the prayers of all these good people, and heal her. Tonight. Not because of me, but because of them. And for the sake of this place, where people have cried out to You for generations and ages.'

He stopped again, and listened, and thought. People were starting to come in for the service. He kept his head down. Some people came into the pew right next to him. He didn't look up, but he could tell from their voices that it was a young family – father next to him, two children, then the mum. He stopped speaking out loud. He was in the zone enough to pray in his head.

And so he continued. The place filled. The choir came in. The rector stood up to welcome everyone. David intended to ignore it all, but then the rector said, 'Now, we have some sad news tonight, about our good friend Angela Adams. She is a regular member here and has been for some years. Sadly she has a heart condition which can flare up out of the blue and put her, quite literally, at death's door. Which is where she is right now, as she had an attack this evening. Most of our regular members know already, and they will feel that we should pray for Angela before we go any further. We've been here a number of times before, and the Lord has always pulled her through. By tomorrow morning she will either be home again, quite well, or she won't have survived the night. And she will be in that other, greater, better home. But we want her here, and well. So we'll pray together and then we'll carry on with the service as usual. Let's pray.'

He paused, and was heard to draw in a long breath. 'Dear Lord and loving Heavenly Father, look with mercy now on our dear sister, Angela. We thank You for her. We thank You for healing her in the past. Let her know that we are thinking of her. Heal her completely and restore her to us. Guide the hands and decisions of all those who are caring for her. And grant peace to her family and many friends. In Jesus' Name. Amen.'

The 'amen' was echoed round the church, then the first carol was announced and the congregation stood to sing. But David stayed where he was and got back to praying. He knew the little boy and girl the other side of the father were peering round at him, but he ignored it.

'Dear Lord and loving heavenly Father,' he said. 'I'm sure you won't mind me learning from the rector how to pray. That's what You pay him for, I should think. Thank You for Angela.

She's been a revelation in my life, and in less than a week I feel like I'm a changed man. You've healed her before, many times, so please just do it again. Heal her completely and restore her to us. Guide the hands of the nurses and the decisions of the doctors. Give her the right and very best treatment. In Jesus' Name, answer us, O Lord.'

And so he continued, quietly, fervently, as faithfully as he knew how, and as humbly and trustingly as he could muster. Until the rector stood up to preach, and the thought impressed itself upon him that perhaps he should listen. So he sat up properly, and listened, wiping some stains from his cheeks. He sat very still, so as not to attract any attention.

The rector began, from the pulpit, high on the left side at the front of the church. Six feet above contradiction. No, don't be like that. 'As is my custom at this traditional time of year, I have sought out a humorous story to begin our thinking together this Christmas Eve. It concerns a retired vicar. As you know, old vicars don't die, they just have to move far enough away that they can't do any more damage. So this vicar had retired to the country, where, as a widower he lived alone, but on Christmas Eve his three sons always came to stay for a couple of days to share Christmas with him.

'Now, two of these boys had followed in their father's footsteps and become vicars, but the third was the black sheep of the family.

'So, it was Christmas Eve, and the three boys arrived for their Christmas, and after a while of all chatting together, everyone went off to bed. In the morning the father got up first, went downstairs, got the log fire going and stood in front of it, warming himself. The first son came down – one of the vicars. "Good morning, Father," he said. "Good morning, son, how did you sleep?" "Very well, thank you. And I had the most amazing dream. I dreamed I died and went to heaven." "Really, son, and what was that like?" "It was just like being at home. Lovely." "That's wonderful. Come and stand beside me in front of the fire," the father said.

'Next, the second son came down, the other vicar. "Good morning, Father," he said. "Good morning, son, how did you sleep?" "Very well, thank you. And I had the most amazing dream. I dreamed I died and went to heaven." "Really, son, and what was that like?" "It was just like being at home. Lovely." "That's wonderful. Come and stand beside me in front of the fire," the father said.

'Lastly, the third son came down, the black sheep. "Good morning, Father," he said. "Good morning, son, how did you sleep?" "Terrible. And I had the most awful dream. I dreamed I died and went to hell." "Really, son, and what was that like?" "It was just like being at home. You couldn't see the fire for vicars."

'So, Christmas Eve once again. And the time-stamped story of a donkey, Mary and Joseph, angels, wise men, an inn, and an innkeeper. And the birth of the Saviour, Jesus Christ, for us. And I'd like, this year, to think about someone who doesn't actually appear in the story, but does appear as a major character in many nativity plays, and whose part is implied in Luke's telling of it. The innkeeper. All we know from Luke is that they put the baby Jesus in a manger, a feeding trough, because there was no room in the inn. That has been taken to mean that only the stable of the inn was available. In recent years there's been a bit of controversy over whether the word Luke uses for "inn" actually means "upper room", implying we're talking about a family home, but we're going to stick to the traditional interpretation, that it means "inn".

'So, here's our innkeeper. Rushed off his feet with every room filled for the great registration, ordered by Caesar himself. He's just settling down to watch *EastEnders*, thinking he's at last got everyone settled and fed, when there's another knock at the door. "Good grief, what now?"

'And he's presented with a young couple, the wife explosively pregnant, desperate for somewhere to lodge for the night. In letting them in, please note, he is letting *Him* in, Jesus, the Saviour. In finding room for them, he is finding room for *Him*, the One God sent, the Messiah, the Lord.

'And I need you to notice, and we will look at, three things. First, without knowing quite where he could put Him, this innkeeper let Him in. Secondly, without knowing the glories that would follow, he let Him in. And thirdly, without knowing the disaster that would follow, he let Him in.

'Three points. Without knowing where he could put Him, the glories to come, or the disaster to follow, he let Him in.

'Point one. There was no space, yet the innkeeper let Jesus in. Did he see the importance of who the child was? We don't know. Did he just have compassion on the young couple? We don't know. Did he have some forewarning, by some angel? We don't know. Given that I know so little, why am I a vicar? We don't know.

'Yet the point is, this man didn't know where he was going to put the Christ, but he let Him in. He made space. He rearranged his priorities. He unsettled himself. He got his tired butt out of his armchair and made way for the King of kings. So I have to ask. Are you willing to do that? Inviting Jesus in to the home of your life and family is not some easy thing. He unsettles stuff. He makes Himself at home, actually. He starts throwing your furniture out of the window and buying new stuff. He changes your dining room into His study and your spare bedroom into a storage room for His gear. He re-landscapes your garden! He sells your car! He signs Himself into your bank account! He unplugs the telly!

'The innkeeper let him in. Will you?

'Second point. Glories followed. Quite swiftly, really. Those shepherds! Not normally bringers of glory. But they'd seen angels. Been spoken to by angels, heavenly visitors. Told, indeed, to come here, to this inn, to see the Son of David, the Saviour of the world. They brought heavenly messages, and a sense of the touch and presence of God on this amazing night. The innkeeper didn't know when he let Mary and Joseph in that this would follow. And many who let Jesus in don't have any idea of the glories that will follow. The love that He brings. The forgiveness and sense of being truly forgiven in God's presence that He brings. The beautiful, sweet, holy joy that seeps into you sometimes like a crack into heaven has opened in your life. The presence of God that settles on your life and begins to change everything because it's just so good.

'I've known of many churchgoers who were attending services "religiously" for decades, but no one ever told them about asking Jesus to actually come into your life. You know, Revelation 3 verse 21, "Here I am! I'm standing at the door and knocking," the heavenly Jesus says. "If anyone hears My voice, and opens up that door, then I will come in to them, and have a meal with them, and they with Me." And I've seen a light in the faces of old ladies who never knew such a thing could be. A life they never imagined they could experience, especially as the next thing they were expecting was death. A gentle joy bursts open within them like some heavenly flower, and they no longer "come to services" – they worship the Lord! They no longer "say prayers" – they chatter away to God! They no longer "read the Bible" – they devour it for more of Him! This is Jesus, and the effect He has when He comes in.

'But, thirdly, and you're maybe wondering what this might be, the innkeeper let them in, not knowing what disaster would follow. Maybe as much as two years later, wise men, Magi, appeared. Bearing gifts but tipping off King Herod that an upstart King was in Bethlehem. So he sent his soldiers, and can you imagine the effect on everyone as they went from house to house, slaughtering infants in front of their parents, leaving ripped and bloodied little bodies in the streets. Maybe the innkeeper had no small children. But he knew that harbouring Jesus led to this cruel carnage, this day of dark despair. Wailing and woe filled the air. A town in turmoil.

'Be in no doubt about this. Harbouring Jesus causes trouble. Those who really stand with Him will face persecution. Those who speak for Him will earn a reputation as a religious nut, as arrogant, as a Bible-basher, as a gay-hater; as a holier-than-thou, God-squad, science-ignorant, closed-minded fool. In many countries Christians are still viciously persecuted for standing by the Name of Jesus. Especially, but not only, Muslim countries. They get arrested. They get fired. They get beaten up. They get killed. And even for saying that, I may be branded a stirrer of hatred and a Muslim-beating, prejudiced, colonialist swine.

'I have a friend who works with the Church in Uzbekistan. Church leaders there, despite keeping their heads down, are regularly raided by the police, their laptops and phones confiscated, and they are thrown into jail. For being faithful to Jesus, nothing more.

'Jesus comes in and causes trouble. He demands absolute allegiance. No compromise. No half-decided faithfulness. Total loyalty. He said, "If anyone would come after me, they must deny themselves, take up their cross, and follow Me. For whoever would save their life, will lose it; but whoever loses their life for My sake, will find it. What does it profit a person if they gain the whole world, and end up losing their very soul?"

'You see, we have to be very clear who He is. He is the Son of God. He is the creator, the redeemer, the only means of salvation, the only route to God and the Supreme One before whom all will finally bow the knee and whom everyone will finally confess as Lord – most to their shame and disgrace, but the few, as He Himself said, to their everlasting glory and joy. It is only in knowing and being sure of that, that we open our hearts and lives and give Him this troubling sovereignty over us. If He doesn't come in as Lord, He doesn't come in, despite any amount of being religious, good, nice, generous, truthful, hardworking or anything else.

'Is this some new teaching, some new-fangled religion? No, it is the ancient gospel as He Himself spoke it. When the innkeeper invited them in, he invited Jesus in, and that spells trouble. Because the world at large will not accept the authority of God. I saw an interview once with a man who said, "When I die and stand before God I'm going to tell Him all the stuff He got wrong and I'm going to let Him know He made a right mess of things down here." Well, actually, no. You're going to turn to water as God reveals all the sin and wickedness and arrogance and smug indifference of your life. And the God-hating you've harboured all these years. And you're going to repent with cries and wailing for forgiveness, but it will be too late.

'What am I telling you? Don't invite Jesus in? Hardly. Invite Him in, but know what the consequences might be. Count the cost, as Jesus Himself said to do, in Luke 14.

'So, there. The innkeeper. He isn't in the story, but then again he is. He invited them in, despite not knowing how he'd fit Jesus in, despite not knowing the glories that would follow, despite not knowing the disaster that would follow. But he did the right thing, and we remember him for it, on this night above all nights, 2,000 years later.

'Invite Jesus in to your life. Not sure where you'll put Him? Don't worry, He'll rearrange everything that's needed! Glories will follow. And troubles. But if He is who He is, how can you not invite Him in?

'In the Name of the Father, and of the Son, and of the Holy Spirit. Amen.'

And David said, 'OK, God, if you're speaking, I'm listening.'

CHAPTER TWENTY-FOUR

He didn't think he'd sleep, but the traumas of the day had wrung him out like an old, grey, stinky sink-rag. His phone was on charge and nearby. He sank into the bed as if it was marshmallow and dreamed of tunnels and faces and hospital beds. Somehow it concerned him repeatedly in the pit of his dreams that Eeyore was still lying outside, broken.

Oh! It was so loud! That tune! He woke and realised instantly his phone was ringing, on full volume, just as he'd left it to do. He crawled across the room and fumbled with it in his sleep-inebriation, but managed to get it opened and alive.

'Hello? Hello?' he said.

It was Thelia. 'Oh, David, I'm at the hospital. I had to phone, my mobile is losing battery. It's Angela. She's died …'

There was the sound of a soft 'th', then it was totally silent. Dead. Gone. A sort of hanging, squealing emptiness on the other end.

He stared at the phone, dropped it, reached forward and threw up heavily on both the mobile and his nice carpet. Acrid, foul waves came up into his face, but he didn't even care. He slid sideways into the floor and lay there, wiping vomit from his mouth.

He stared at the skirting board, and its white paint. And the carpet touching it. And he was blank. He retched a couple of times, but he was empty. Emptied out. Hollow.

She was gone. Angela. Micky. Both gone. Loved and lost, in the space of hours or days. It was like a deliberate act of cruelty. Make him see them, love them, need them, then strip them away, like ripping him in half.

'Oh God, oh God, oh God,' he muttered, to the painted wood. 'Where are You now? And being kind? Being kind? Come on!'

He thought, 'I'm never going to church ever again. I'm never going to talk to any of her friends or see Andrew, ever. I will never pray and I will be just who I was, a week ago, before this sick joke.'

But then a strange warmth came over him, and he thought, 'Actually, no. Because of Angela, and Andrew, I won't go back to that. I'll grieve with them all. Now I have something to offer as well as to accept. I'll honour her memory by being what she was teaching me to be. I won't go back, I'll live with her in my heart, and in my memory, and honour her. I will honour Angela in my heart. I will.'

That heartened him, and the smell of the vomit broke through again. 'Blast, yugh,' he said.

Clearing it off the phone and the carpet distracted him for a while, as he did it in a sort of daze. Once the phone no longer smelled of vomit and the patch of disinfected, watery damp on the carpet was covered in newspaper, he made tea. Always tea. It's what we do. Maybe something about the ritual of it provides a focus. Maybe it's almost religious, like for the Japanese.

He sat at the kitchen table, with Radio 4 telling all, but hearing nothing. He stared at the mug – a big 'Thank You' mug that he'd bought, not been given. That kind of said it all. Tears welled and fell, streaking down his cheeks in hot rivulets. Angela. How could this be? He'd only known her five or six days, yet she was in his heart. She held out such hope to him. Yet not just she. Micky also. But Angela was alive now, and with him, then suddenly taken. That's how it felt. Taken. Ripped away, ripping him open in the process.

How long had he been in the numb cradling of the mug? The tea had gone lukewarm and the ceramic button on the design had made an imprint on his hand. He took a long drink of it and tried to concentrate. But on what? On her death? No, on what to do now.

This was desolation. The buildings destroyed, rubble everywhere, smoke lazily rising from piles of useless debris, death lurking under every mound, and a stillness in the pungent air because all was done. Finished. Laid waste. That's how he felt. Desolation.

Why should this happen to him like an unseen, dark finger pointing at him out of some hooded and unnatural shroud? As in the 'no clothes on in public' dreams, he saw himself at her open graveside, stripped naked of any festive future. Inwardly, he stared, blankly, horrified.

Oh. Yes. What to do? Go to see her. Thelia would be there. Perhaps some of the others. They wouldn't refuse them to see her now. He would go.

He poured the remaining tea down the sink, left his mug in there (a thing he never did), put on his coat and walked out of the door. There was Eeyore, half his sad face looking up at the sky. Irritated, he kicked it against the house, and he broke into shards and lumps, strewn across the paving flags. Then David regretted it, but it was done and Eeyore was gone. It was strangely symbolic. It was like that mug accompanied his life. *Had* accompanied his life. No more.

He got the car out and drove to the hospital, careful to watch what he was doing, aware that his mind was elsewhere. Resenting the ridiculous standard fee up to three hours, he parked in the hospital rip-off car park and made his way in and to the reception desk. A sleepy woman asked him if she could help.

'Is Angela Adams still on ICU?'

She consulted her screen. 'Yes. The lifts are round to the left. Sixth floor, follow the signs.'

'Thank you.'

He went up, and his anxiety seemed to rise with the lift. By the time he stepped out, his heart was chafing in his chest. He followed the signs, left, and arrived at the ICU door, where he had to press the intercom button and wait. He put alcohol cleanser on his hands while he waited.

'Yes?'

'I'm here to see Angela Adams.'

'Come in.'

The door clicked and he walked in to a tear-streaked Thelia running up the corridor, hair flowing out like a mad woman, and throwing her arms round him. 'I'm so sorry!' she said. 'Angela is alive. My phone died in mid-sentence, and I don't have your number anywhere else to ring you on another phone. We woke Holly and sent her round but she must have just missed you. Come and see Angela.'

'But – '

'Yes, I know, what I said was, "She's died three times" and I was going to say that each time they've managed to restart her heart, which is a real miracle, and the third time the rhythm resettled and now she's awake!'

He stopped, slowly bent forward, and something that held him up broke, collapsed inside. He sank to his knees in the middle of the corridor.

'David! David!' Thelia said. 'Get up. Come on. She's waiting.'

'I can't!' he managed. 'I don't think I can move. This is too terrible and too wonderful. I'm done.'

A tremor shook him from knees to shoulders. Suddenly the rector was by his side and he helped Thelia get him to his feet.

'Come on, David,' the rector said. 'Angela is asking for you.'

He let them support and lead him into the part of the ward with the beds, and to the side of the bed where Angela sat upright, looking a bit washed out but nowhere near as dead as he'd been led to believe. She was on a heart monitor, and had a tube from a suspended bag going into her left arm, and there were puffy, dark rings under her eyes, but, all things considered, she looked rather well. She held out her arms towards him and said, 'I'm so sorry.'

He fell into her embrace, pressed the side of his face against hers, and wept. And wept and wept. And she held him. He didn't need a chair because he was half on the bed. Everyone else went away. Even a nurse came up but went away again, muttering, 'I'll come back in a while.'

Who can say how many tears a man may cry? But this was a revelation. A torrent of hurt the like of which might be compared to Niagara Falls. He couldn't stop. He didn't want to stop. She didn't ask him to stop, but gently stroked his hair and his left cheek with the fingers of her spare hand. The other arm never stopped cuddling him. His right hand was on the flimsy sleeve of her hospital gown. He was helpless. Humbled. Hollowed. Healed.

Twenty minutes passed. Half an hour. The nurse came back three times, but each time made some comment about it being all right, and only needing to take some blood and do a test. The rector came and said goodbye, and prayed a blessing over her. Thelia came and went a couple of times, and the nurse eventually took the blood with David still being comforted at her side.

He didn't stop until he stopped, which was a good thing. He knew his eyes must be puffy and red, and his face forever streaked with hot tears, but he actually felt a little better.

'Goodness!' she said, holding him by the shoulders and looking at him. 'If I'd known you'd be this upset I wouldn't have died!'

He gave a little chuckle, and searched for his handkerchief. Fortunately his nose hadn't emptied as well, which would have been a right mess. 'I threw up on my phone at home,' he said.

'Where is it now?' she asked.

'In my pocket. Would you like a little lick?'

She laughed so loud she had to be shushed by a nearby nurse, and said, 'Sorry.'

'I am undone,' he said, 'as Helena declared in *All's Well That Ends Well*.'

'You wouldn't say that if you could see this gown,' she replied. 'It is I who am undone.'

'I love you,' he said.

'Hmm. Great declarations ought not to be made in the presence of great stress. Though that said, I love you too.'

He sat in the chair by the bed. 'When do they let you out?'

'In the morning. As soon as I check out OK. Which I will. Panic over. Again.'

'You should have told me.'

'I was dying.'

'No, before then. Durr.'

'I would have, but I forget. It's not like I think about it all the time.'

'Will you need a lift home?'

'No, I'm to stay here the rest of the night, then Anna's going to come in the morning and bring me to church for the special service. But I'll need a lift after that. Goodness! It's Christmas Day already, isn't it?'

'Are you sure you're up for all that?'

'I'll be a bit bruised and battered, but do you think I'm going to miss Christmas Day with my church and with you? No way!'

Now, in what remained of the early hours of the big day, he couldn't sleep. 'What was all that?' he had cried out in a never-ending stream from the very depths of his being? Would Angela think him some idiot? She didn't seem to. She seemed to know what was going on. But then that was her – or she gave that impression.

Did angels have dodgy hearts and end up in hospital? Of course, if that was part of the mission!

At least he didn't have to be up at all early. The service wasn't until eleven, so he could get up at ten and still make it OK. He tried to comfort himself with that thought as he was so tired, but couldn't drift off.

There was certainly a lot inside him that needed to come out. My goodness, he'd been living in a dream. All these years! Half a person ... And a thought struck him. Less than half. The loss of Micky, which led to the failure to engage with so many others who would willingly have been his friends. And the really big missing piece, the piece that *was* behind The Yearning, in a way – God. Because nothing that strong, nothing that directed and 'pulling', nothing that unified a force so distantly 'outside' with a feeling so deeply 'inside', could be other than God Himself. It was both objective and subjective. It was real and it was felt. He now knew who that was, and that He wanted to come in. He, David, was the innkeeper.

He turned on his side. What were the three things? Without knowing where he'd put Him, without knowing the glories that would follow, and without knowing the disaster to come, he let the Christ in. Yes, well, he probably ended up regretting that bitterly. I'm very far from ready for that.

A touch of heartburn dug at his chest, so he threw back the duvet and went downstairs to get a glass of water, hoping to avoid needing the yucky aniseed-tasting, gloopy medicine in the kitchen cupboard. And there, held by magnets on his fridge door, were the three cards. He'd never noticed, but the one from the church had a stable scene and the innkeeper, standing at one side, beaming, caught in the holy glow of it all. Ha! Had the rector designed that with his sermon in mind? Even so, the innkeeper looked a happy chappy. And that was the point. What he was witnessing far outweighed the rearranging, and even the looming disaster. And the glories foretold far greater joys.

Chastened, but not yet christened, he took his glass of water back upstairs, and got warm again in his lovely bed.

'OK, then, I think I know You're there,' he muttered, as the downy duvet of blessed sleep crept over him at last.

What?

The phone? So loud! That tune again!

What time was it? Five to ten. OK, no problem. He stood, and walked over to the mobile.

'Hello?'

'Hello, Little Noddy. Time to get up.'

'Angela! How are you?'

'I'm fine. Now, you haven't forgotten, have you? Eleven, at church. I'll get mobbed, no doubt, but I want to sit next to you. So be there by five to at the latest. Did you manage to sleep?'

'Yes. You?'

'Like the dead!'

'That's not funny.'

'No, OK, sorry. Anyway, see you soon, and Merry Christmas!'

'Merry Christmas!' he replied.

'And David, whatever you've got for me, bring it with you, wrapped or not.'

'Oh, it's wrapped!'

'Love you.'

'Love you. Bye,' he responded.

Festive fantastic or what!

Two boiled eggs, toast, tea and a couple of Christmas chocolates later, he walked in the main door of St Mark's along with a steady stream of town folk joining Her Majesty at an Anglican church on Christmas Day. He hardly noticed the red service book and carol sheet thrust into his hand as he came inside.

And there she was. Not the Queen. Far better. Being treated like a queen, Angela, surrounded by well-wishers and relieved friends, including the rector, and his wife, Ruby, who had a smile on her face like it was truly Christmas.

David was hesitant to intrude. But the rector noticed him and came over. 'You made it!' he said, and embraced David in a friendly but not intrusive hug. 'Did you get any sleep?'

'Yes, thanks. Eventually.'

The rector stepped away and looked at his face. Then his expression brightened and he said, 'You look quite well, considering!'

'I think I'm full of relief. And thankfulness.'

The rector clapped him on the shoulder and said, 'Good for you!' and walked off to get robed.

David approached the gaggle, beginning to break up for the start of the service. Angela saw him, and her face lit up, despite being still a little puffy. There was a great smile, but also a wistfulness around her eyes, and an intensity, as she took him in. It occurred to him that coming so close to dying might do that to a person. She hastened over and swept him up in an embrace bigger than Bart's, and whispered in his ear, 'You are my Christmas.'

She was wearing a dark green jumper over a white blouse, and brown boots up to just below her knee, and light-coloured tights under a fawn skirt down to just above her knee. She looked fresh and huggable and lovely.

Around him suddenly was a gathering of the friends, but Bill and Mary didn't have Ruf with them. No surprise there.

He was greeted warmly by Anna, Ian and Sue, Bill and Mary, Holly and Greg, Aaron and Ella, Jan Carstairs and Brian, who clapped him on the back and said, 'Hello, Edward. Merry Christmas!'

Lucy, Luke, Amber, Darren, Josh, Katy and Kai also came over and shared their unbounded and youthful joy at seeing Angela well again. And greeted him with fondness. Festive fondness, or something more profound?

Angela grabbed his arm and sat him down next to her. They were halfway forwards, on the left of the church, with him sitting to her left, and she next to the aisle. She found his hand, held it, and pulled it across onto her leg. That was very nice. He could feel her firm thigh through her skirt. Her hand was warm and soft and firm.

He looked around. The tree seemed bigger and brighter than before. He noticed that its lights looked evenly spread, but the baubles and tinsel gave a more randomly scattered impression, as if they'd been put on by children. Then it occurred to him that that was probably exactly the case, and it seemed even more festive.

The rector and reader arrived. No choir. The rector was resplendent in a white and gold chasuble over a long white alb, and the reader had cassock and surplus with a blue scarf hanging in two drapes down his front. The organ stopped playing 'Silent Night' and the rector welcomed everyone, giving especial thanks that Angela was once again delivered from a hospital bed and well enough to be among them all. A round of spontaneous applause followed, and Angela looked embarrassed, but when it died down she stood up and said, 'Thank you all so much for your prayers.'

The service then got underway with 'The Holly and the Ivy', and readings, and the rector finding out who got up earliest, and what presents had been given or received, and there was another carol, 'Hark the Herald Angels Sing', which almost raised the ancient roof. Then the reader stepped up to give a talk. The sadness of his wiggling jowls was entirely denied by the glint in his shining eyes, as he got the children to help him to tell how Jesus was received by some and not by others. Then he thanked the children, gave each a chocolate gold coin, and sent them back to their places.

The rector stood up, and said, 'Thank you, Barnabas. Let's take a minute. There won't be much peace and stillness on Christmas Day. So be still for a moment or two. And if you want to invite Jesus into your life, do it now.'

Angela squeezed his hand, but bowed her head and prayed. David had heard well enough what had been said, but he just stayed as still as he could inside, allowing no pressure to respond to this frightening challenge.

And yet, something came over him. Very gently, like some sort of floating chiffon. It felt like the precursor to all festivity, to all of Christmas, and every light and carol and gift and family gathering, squeezed together in one encounter. Related to The Yearning, but not precisely the same. It came before that. He thought he vaguely recognised it as original Kindness and unfathomable Joy.

'And now,' the rector announced, 'we're going to sing the next carol.'

There was no coffee after the service because people wanted to get off to family festivities, but more people gathered round Angela to wish her well, and David found himself beside the rector at the door.

'Merry Christmas,' the rector said.

'And a very Merry Christmas to you,' David replied, shaking the offered hand warmly.

The rector shook his hand with a greater firmness and said, 'Have you found what you were looking for?'

'Err, I'm not sure. But something has certainly started to happen, to change, in me.'

'That's not a bad place to start!'

CHAPTER TWENTY-FIVE

He'd probably never had so many people wish him 'Merry Christmas'. It was as if they all knew he was 'with' Angela. What that 'with' was, he was not much more clear than they were. But, anyway, he was cheered and buoyed and felt part of them all. He really looked forward to seeing them again soon – to his great surprise, even accounting for his sense of festive frivolity. It was Christmas Day, after all.

Sitting in the car, he handed her first the card. She opened it and loved it, kissing him on the cheek. She gave him his card, which he opened. It had a picture of Noddy, his blue hat with a bell turned into a red Santa hat with a white pom-pom. He was standing beside his little yellow car, waving cheerily, with snow all around, and Big Ears sitting in the car looking cold and annoyed. It said, 'Merry Christmas, Little Noddy', and inside, 'Lots of love from Angela'. He leaned over and kissed her quickly and demurely on the lips.

Then she pulled out a parcel and handed it to him, shyly. He opened the red paper with care, and inside was a boxed set of DVDs entitled, *Quanta, Quasars and Queries: a Spiritual Search for the Theory of Everything*. It looked very good.

'Thank you,' he said. 'I'll enjoy that. That's really kind.'

'Kindness is all,' she said.

He reached into the back seat and presented her with the boxy parcel. 'Careful how you undo the box,' he said.

She made a start, peeling away layers, until the bubble wrap unrolled and she had the vase and the rose in her hands. She put the rose in the vase and stared at it. He wondered what she was going to say, or if she liked it.

'That is exquisite!' she said. 'I don't think I own anything so beautiful. I'm impressed! Thank you so much!' and she kissed him on the lips, briefly.

'You can put water in it, or not, depending how you feel.'

'I'll experiment. I see you have another box back there. Is that for Andrew, by any chance?'

'Yes, will you see him?'

'You can give it to him yourself. That's where you're taking me for lunch.'

He was so pleased. 'I've really taken to him.'

'I know. I'm quite jealous,' she said.

'You needn't be. Kiss me.'

'In the car?' she said, feigning shock and violated horror.

'In Little Noddy's little car,' he said, and she kissed him lightly but at greater length on the lips.

'Kissing in the car isn't normally very demure, but it is Christmas Day, and I am feeling fully festive!' she said, with the smile of an angel from under some straggly hair.

The world flew by as if the speeding car was, in fact, the still centre of all things. Which, in a way, being with her had become.

He told her all about the revelation of the previous dusk.

He said, 'I'm in a whirlwind in a whirlpool on a spinning planet in a spiralling galaxy.'

'That must be dizzying.'

'It is; it has been, except there is a still centre to it all. I've suddenly found my long-forgotten sister, Micky, and I've found you.'

'I think you've found yourself,' she added.

'That's even more clichéd, and in a bad way. I shouldn't be seeking to find me. Finding me isn't the answer. Finding the coordinates of the universe and the heavens, that's the answer. Maybe even finding God in The Yearning and in my life, that's the truth of it all. That's where hope lies because, in truth, we *are* in a whirlwind in a whirlpool on a spinning planet in a spiralling galaxy. All of us are.'

'OK, you're right,' she conceded, 'but in that place, set in the right setting and coordinates, there you are. You've found you, as well. I agree, not as the goal or fixation it is for so many people, because then we're just onions. But as a by-product of finding the true coordinates, there's you. Mostly, of course, far outweighing all else, finding God means finding yourself, in relation to He who made you, nurtures you, died for you and wants you. And in finding me, there's you. And in finding friendships, there's you. And even in finding Andrew, I suspect, there's you. So how many more findings of yourself might there be?'

'Yes, all true. But that's not the question I want to be asking. I want to be asking what's objective and real, not focusing on the subjective I feel. Can't you see it's a real danger in our self-obsessed "buy yourself a new you", "you're worth it" society, that we too easily just try to find the real "me"? The Yearning was God reaching out to me from afar and from within to find Him, and find you, and find Micky, and find friends and church, and find Andrew. It must be focused on the outward and the objective, surely, to be real.'

'I think you're just being too analytical.'

'Are we arguing on Christmas Day?' he said.

'Yes. You can pull over and let me get out of the car.' There was a moment's silence. 'You do know that was a joke, right?'

'Do you see me pulling over?'

They both laughed. 'I suppose,' she said, 'I'm just really concerned for how you haven't found you, in all these years, and how it was stripped away from you at the age of eight. And now you have found you, and I want you to be heartened and upheld and strengthened by that. That's all.'

'That'll do me,' he said.

'I'll drink to that,' Angela confirmed. 'What a Christmas!'

David felt so happy and relieved he said, 'He gave you back to me. He was kind.'

'He *is* kind,' she added.

'He is Kindness.'

287

'That's what I tried to tell you, days ago.'

'I know you did. But I discovered it, too.' After a pause, he said, most profoundly, 'In the presence of Kindness, you can cry.'

'That's profound!'

'I know.'

'I think you have a lot more crying yet to do,' she said, kindly.

'I know. Anna will help me, and so will you. Release me. The dam has cracked. My eyes have been washed already, so that I see differently.'

'Flipping heck! That's profound as well.'

'Yeah. I rather liked it.'

His mind flew to an image of the battered-looking Mr Edmonds from the fish and chip shop, and he realised he would invite him round for dinner, sometime soon.

'Has it occurred to you how quickly you've changed over the last couple of days?'

'It was kind of instantaneous. Like a light going on. Suddenly I really *see* people, like Anna said. Amazing.'

'Yes, but has it occurred to you what that means?'

'No. I mean, other than that it's been a revelation.'

'Hmm. Yes, but for it to have that effect on your view of other people, doesn't it occur to you that that's rather unusual – special?'

'Yes. What are you getting at?'

'Well, come on, David, what am I getting at? O profound one!'

'Hmm?'

'Don't be silly, Little Noddy!'

'Perhaps you've heard something I haven't, Big Ears.'

'Such an epiphany – where did it come from?'

'You really want me to say it, don't you?'

'Yes, why not. Say it.'

'God did it. It must have been a revelation from Him to have such an instantaneous and profound effect. There, happy?'

'Ecstatic. Why was that so hard?'

'Because it's what you wanted me to say.'

'So you were just being difficult.'

'Something like that. And the fact that I'm not much past just accepting that there is probably a God and His nature is kindness. So I wasn't just being difficult.'

'Speaking of being difficult,' she said, 'you do know, don't you, that Andrew will probably treat you at first like he never met you before?'

'Yes, it's the ASD. He reverts to zero as a sort of default setting in relationships.'

'Don't be too disappointed.'

'He'll warm to me. He does have a memory.'

'Good.'

Thelia threw the door open with arms outstretched and a tear-laden, 'Merry Christmas!'

The little holly wreath on the knocker fell off in surprise. David picked it up and hooked it back on. The sisters were embracing and stayed that way. When they parted, Thelia said, 'Hello, David. It's great to see you again. Merry Christmas!' and they embraced as well. It was surprisingly comfortable.

'Andrew!' she called. 'Come and see who's here!' Then more quietly she added, 'We can but try.'

He didn't come. David could hear a rhythmic squeaking and he put two and two together. Sure enough, in the front room Andrew was bouncing on his battered armchair.

'He gets extra bouncing rights at Christmas,' Thelia said.

He was wearing his Star Wars Storm Trooper mask and he said in an electronic voice, with each bounce, 'Lift off! Lift off! Lift off!'

David went and stood right in front of the chair, took a step back and said, 'Andrew. Hi, it's David. Come in to land. Jump to me on the fifth prime number. Ready? Two, three, five, seven – '

At 'eleven,' Andrew launched himself, arms out, and David caught him in a big hug. The squeeze from Andrew was enormous, and he just didn't let go. And David really didn't mind. He was giving needed contact and affection to a child necessarily starved of such things.

There was a great warmth between them, and it wasn't just the heat of their bodies.

'Do you want us to prise him off you?' Thelia asked.

'I think my need is as great as his,' David answered. The mask wasn't pressing against his face, which would have been painful, but into his shoulder, which was OK. Bony shoulders that he had.

At length it was Andrew's arms that gave out, and he slid off down to the floor, and actually laughed.

'Touchdown!' David said.

Andrew rolled onto his back and said, 'Touchdown. Touchdown. Touchdown!' and everyone joined him laughing on Christmas Day.

Andrew looked up into David's face, and nearly directly into his eyes. David smiled down, a great beam of happiness and affection.

'David, are you OK with Andrew?' Thelia asked.

'More than OK.'

'All right, Angela and I will go into the kitchen. I'll send you in a coffee. Keep it out of Andrew's reach.'

'OK.'

They settled down onto the floor and Andrew tipped up the whole box of Lego. It made quite a mound.

'What are we making?' David asked.

'Millennium Falcon,' he replied. 'Millennium. Falcon.'

David decided to just watch, for now. The coffee arrived and he sat cross-legged on the floor, near to Andrew, clutching the hot mug for safety, and watching what the boy was doing. It didn't look much like the famous spaceship, but then it was early days.

Thelia and Angela were in the kitchen a long time, with, he imagined, lots of hugging and weeping and thanking God. Eventually, with the *Millennium Falcon* taking shape, the call came for Andrew (he assumed it was for Andrew) to wash his hands for dinner. David went as well for a 'comfort break' and to keep an eye on Andrew, just in case. Then they went into the kitchen/dining room at the back.

It had been transformed. There was a colourfully lit tree, there were paper streamers, there were lights hanging from the ceiling, there were drops of cards down the walls. The table had an unlit candle decoration at its centre, and it was festively laid with crackers and red and white placemats and jolly paper napkins.

Andrew just stared, and Thelia said, 'He's been prepared. He knows he'll be going back in the front room after. He can cope with this for a while.'

'So this is the "Christmas room",' David offered.

'Time for the present would be after lunch, I think,' Thelia said. 'In fact, after "The Queen", I'd say. And thank you very much, David, that's really kind. He might or might not show much reaction today, but he will really enjoy it. OK, let's sit.'

The plates were at the four places, one on each side of the table. Andrew was on David's left, Angela on his right. Andrew's sprouts were deliberately undercooked, and his roast potatoes overcooked to 'extra crispy', and he had some poppadums as an extra treat. David's plate was loaded with turkey, stuffing, pigs-in-blankets, sprouts, carrots and roast potatoes. On the table were cranberry sauce and gravy. He had a small glass of Merlot.

'Grace first!' Thelia said, and she led them in a prayer of thanksgiving for the day and the feast, and for poor Martin, stuck sorting out a software glitch on the company's computers in Dubai until next Wednesday at least, and not forgetting those for whom this was not a day of celebration. Then crackers were pulled, hats affixed by all, terrible jokes read, a toast made, and the eating began.

After a while, Andrew held up a sprout on his fork like a lollipop and stared at it. David copied him and said, glaring intently at the sprout, 'I once tried to carry a huge vegetable onto an aeroplane, but they wouldn't let me. They said it wasn't cabbage lug-in.'

Thelia and Angela just looked at him, but Andrew erupted in laughter and said, 'Cabin luggage. Cabin luggage. Cabin luggage!'

Then the two women joined in the hilarity. David felt they'd perhaps had a Cinzano or two before lunch.

'You do seem to be on his wavelength,' Thelia said, with a big smile.

'And yes,' Angela added, 'that's a good thing.'

'I'm enormously grateful,' Thelia added. 'It's so good for him.'

'I think maybe it's good for me,' David confessed. 'I think he's helping me to play out a long-lost and deeply missed relationship from my own childhood.'

'Really?'

So, Angela hadn't said a word about Micky. Rightly.

'Yes, I lost a little sister when I was eight. I think it left me scarred ever since. But I'm just beginning to accept that. Somehow, Andrew reminds me of her. I'm not sure how or why.'

'Oh, the depths of our subconscious minds!' Thelia said.

'Yes, until they come to the surface,' he added.

'Cabin luggage! Ha ha!' Andrew said.

'We can't light the pudding, I'm afraid, because Andrew doesn't like flames,' Thelia said, holding the famously dark and glistening dessert aloft on a fancy plate.

She set it among them on the table, and began to spoon it out. There was a jug of cream, and David took some and passed it on to Andrew. He tipped some on and passed it back to his mum.

'I hope you like lots of large pieces of nuts in it,' Thelia said, 'they're for Andrew in particular, but I do love almonds and walnuts myself.'

'Oh, yes!' David agreed. 'My favourite! You can't have too many nuts in a Christmas pudding.'

'Nuts. Nuts. Nuts!' Andrew said.

'OK, Mr Repetitive,' Angela said to him. 'Let's hear a sentence instead. Say something to David, who is our special guest this Christmas Day.'

Andrew raised his gaze and, again, nearly looked David right in the eye. 'Where's my present?' he said.

From sheer shock everyone reacted with merry mirth, then Angela said, 'I'm not sure that's quite what I was thinking of. Anyway, Andrew, dear boy, what have you got David?'

'Secret,' he said, looking down at his pudding.

'So there *is* something?'

'Secret,' he repeated.

'I still haven't heard a nice sentence for David,' Angela insisted.

'Thank you for coming, please come again,' he said.

'Now you're just being cheeky,' Thelia put in. And Andrew smiled, grabbed David's hand, and squeezed it till their fingers turned white.

David reached over, patted Andrew's hand with his spare one, and said, 'Release me, you Wookie!'

'Ha!' Andrew said. 'Chewbacca!' and let go.

There was an armchair and a sofa and a TV in the dining room part of the kitchen, and David watched 'The Queen' with Angela pressed against him on one side and Andrew the other, and sensed that he'd never felt so 'held' and loved any time he could remember. Nothing, in fact, had ever been so deeply and truly and fully 'festive'. Her Majesty's message seemed to be lost in a haze of warm delight. And it wasn't the Merlot, of which he'd only had that one, small glass.

Afterwards, David fetched Andrew's tablet from the hallway table and presented him with it.

'Andrew, this is for you from me, with love. It's like the one you've got, and will take all your stuff just the same, but it has newer and better features as well and will be faster online.'

Andrew hugged it in its box, then put it down on the dining room table and went into the front room. He came back with a small package, and handed it to David.

'From me,' he said.

David opened the red paper and found inside a book, entitled *God and the Reality of Everything*.

'That is so kind,' David said. 'Thank you, Andrew.' Then, taking his life in his hands, he stood and said, 'Can I have a hug?'

Andrew hesitated, then tackled him with a full body press and clung on until his arms gave way again.

'Thank you, you do me good,' David said.

The rest of the afternoon was spent with David and Angela watching the TV in the dining room, and Thelia coming and going, keeping an eye on Andrew in the front room. She was also trying to watch the post-Queen Bond film along with them.

At half-past four, Andrew came in, looking like he wasn't sure why, then he climbed up on David's lap and sat there. He rested his head back against David's chest and put his thumb in his mouth. Violent sucking noises followed, but nobody minded. And thus they all sat for the next forty-five minutes. David was, once again, in a kind of heaven. A Kind Heaven.

Then Thelia said, 'Andrew, time for your proper nap. Say goodbye to David and Auntie Angela.'

He shifted as instructed and hugged Angela without mercy, then David.

'Thank you for coming, please come again,' he said, finding now the prearranged spot for the sentence.

Thelia took him upstairs.

Sitting side by side on the settee, alone at last, David said, 'You know, I still haven't been to your house.'

'So?'

'Well, I do love you, I really do. But I can't help but remember something you said to me long ago. Huh! Long ago! It was only days ago that we met. Anyway, back then, you said that the difference between someone human and an angel is that the human person goes home when it's all done, but the angel has no home and just goes back to heaven. So, it worries me that now you've reformed me and all, you'll just not be here one day soon. Gone. Back to heaven.'

'When you see my house, you'll see more than my house. And we're going there later, for the evening of Christmas Day.'

'What?' he said. 'No! It's Friday night. I have to go for fish and chips. I always go for fish and chips on a Friday.'

She looked really concerned, like he'd hit her round the head with the back end of an uncooked cod.

'Oh, OK,' he said, 'seeing as it's Christmas!' and he nudged her arm. She pinched him.

Thelia came back down and made them all a cup of tea, and they talked together about what had happened to Angela, and what was happening to David. It was good to try to give some words to it all. David recognised Thelia as a very insightful and careful person. Her words made David feel stronger.

Before they left, she laid a hand on the shoulder of each of them and prayed for them. She included that God guide them in their relationship for the future. Now, that was quite a thought.

Angela brought the vase and rose into her house and put them in pride of place on the table in the front room, with some water in the vase.

The house was bare. Bare boards underfoot, in some favoured places covered by a simple mat. The walls were magnolia, and David saw only two or three rather generic pictures. The furniture was acceptable but basic – in the front room, a settee and an armchair jostled for the comfort of an edge of the brown mat, on which the slight coffee table had taken up pride of residence. A small TV stood forlornly in the corner, near to a front window with plain, cream curtains. It all screamed, 'Nobody cares about me!'

They sat cuddled up on the settee. The house wasn't even warm. But she'd turned the heating on, and put the fire on in here.

He said, looking at her with concentrated concern, 'Are you sure you're all right now, I mean, your heart? You're not going to have a sudden relapse or something?'

'Why, are you afraid you'll have to take out my false teeth?'

'You don't have false teeth. Be serious. Are you OK now?'

'Yes, I'm fine. But, you know, David, in some ways I think you've been more battered than I have.'

He gave a small laugh. 'You're not wrong! I feel like my life's been cracked open. My heart, I suppose you'd say. So that its hard outer shell could fall away and the soul of kindness begin to flow in there. If that makes any sense at all.'

'Oh, it makes sense!' she said, smiling at him. And so she stayed, for a little while, just holding his hand. Then she said, 'Look around. This place has no heart. I don't live here, I stay here. Oh, it's my house. But it's soulless, isn't it?'

She looked left and right, indicating the room, or the whole downstairs, then upwards, indicating the upstairs.

'Like I said, I don't live here, I stay here. And no, we're not going upstairs. It's a mess. But for this evening, this evening of Christmas Day, here we are, together, and there's really nowhere else I'd rather be. We can watch telly, have some supper, drink a little wine, laze about together, make a jigsaw, play a board game, or just talk.'

The house came to life. This was, in fact, David realised, the only place he wanted to be as well. He caught an image, here, of that amazing dream that had so affected him, of Michael, Sarah, Emily and their parents, playing and sharing together, but here, in this place, as if kindness was the true coordinate and overlap-point of the universe – the kindness there and the kindness here made them one. What need did he have of fine pictures and riotous colours, fabulously bedecked trees and twinkling lights?

He had Angela and he had new friends and he had Andrew. The very walls seemed to swell, and warm, and glow.

'You know, don't you, that I haven't responded, religiously, yet,' he said.

'I should hope not! I should think you've just about put your foot to the path. It's a journey.'

'OK, then, as long as we're clear on that.'

She grabbed and squeezed his other hand and held both together in hers. Then she shifted herself slightly away from him and turned more face-on. She looked at him very seriously, still holding his hands between hers. 'OK, then, let's be clear on this. Let's talk. We've been kind of thrown together, haven't we? All in a great sudden. And I have a sense that God's been behind that, stunningly swift as it's been. And my faith means I have to be careful, and not lead you on, and keep things right. Even being here together on our own has dangers, and so we need to be sensible, old and crabby though we are. But my love of you, whatever exactly that is yet, doesn't depend on you responding in a certain way to God. I'm not using it to pressurise you into anything. That's very important. I love you because I love you, because I find you fascinating and funny and I like spending time with you. We fit. There would be a question of whether I could ever actually marry someone who didn't share my faith in Jesus, but we're not anywhere near that territory, so having said it, put it out of your head. You've started on a journey towards God, I do believe. And I'm to be part of that journey.'

She smiled right into him and it lit him up inside. 'David Sourbook, I love you for you. Like kindness has to be kindness just in order to be kindness, so love has to be love just in order to be love, and I love you.'

Then she kissed him, full on the lips. It was all so reassuring. It encouraged him.

He said, 'I'm relieved I don't have to explain what exactly this love for you that I feel *is*, and that I won't get a verbal slap again for saying it, even so soon, because it does seem like I've known you half my life. But I do, in some imperfect and not-yet-fully formed sense, love you.'

She smiled like 1,000 angelic suns and kissed him again. That smile was just for him.

Yet, even so, there was a nagging niggle at the back of his head.

He said, 'You know, seeing this house hasn't really convinced me it's your home and you aren't an angel, about to disappear back to the realms beyond.'

'Really?' she said. She dropped his hands into his lap and placed her hands either side of his face, warm and soft on his cheeks. 'I don't think you need to worry,' she said. 'Angels aren't allowed to do this. If they even *can* do this.'

She placed her lips against his, and brushed them lightly from side to side. Then she took in a breath, and said, 'I need you. In my life.'

He smelled her, enveloping and musty-sweet. Then she pressed her lips against his, and kissed him, soft and deep, long and moist.

After time, they parted, happy, relieved even, and she stared at him, such affection in those lovely eyes. The look, so intent, seemed to be inviting him into her very soul.

Maybe he really didn't need a cat, after all.

She stayed so very near, and put her hands on his shoulders. 'I want to have lots of Christmases with you. I want us to deliver church newsletters, sweep old people's snow, do a Christmas clean wherever's necessary, make Andrew happy, join our friends in celebration, organise shoeboxes for poor Romanian kids, sort out dead dogs, shelter the outcast, and be together.'

'You mean, *be* together?'

She said 'Of course! Look at my house. Where I stay. Which feels so unloved and so unlived-in. Where I've never got round to making it a real home. Don't you get it yet?'

'No. Get what?'

'I suspect you're *my* angel.'

'But show me unfailing *kindness*
like the LORD's *kindness*
as long as I live'

1 Samuel 20 verse 14
From the Old Testament
of the Bible
(NIV UK 2011 version, author italics)